Praise for Carole Maso and *Defiance*

"Bernadette is a fine monster in the prison-doll tradition, dishing out delightful contempt for the vicious society she believes she mimics, even the young men she so clinically seduces . . . and in feverish, incantatory prose she shifts the shards of her past, trying to grasp the precise mechanics of class and sex that sealed her fate. So relentless is her honesty that this hard-boiled book turns unexpectedly tender as Bernadette drops her mask—her defiance—to show the human face beneath."   —*New York Times Book Review*

"The last testament of a brilliant unrepentant murderer taking on her century is ferocious and uncompromising. A plunge into utter despair and horror while keeping her tough chin up. Like all of Carole Maso's writing, *Defiance* is a work of great craft, intelligence, and passion."   —Robert Coover

"Shockingly original. Ms. Maso's novel is a convincing study of a brilliant yet damaged mind, and a sharp exploration of new extremes of cynicism and darkness. Powerful and mercilessly disturbing."   —*Wall Street Journal*

CAROLE MASO, the director of the creative writing department at Brown University, is the author of four acclaimed novels and a book-length erotic prose poem. She is the recipient of the 1993 Lannan Literary Fellowship for Fiction, as well as numerous other awards, grants, fellowships, and residencies. Maso has been profiled in the *Washington Post*, the *New York Times*, *Poets & Writers* magazine, the *Village Voice*, *Elle*, and *Vogue*, among others. Her novel *The American Woman in the Chinese Hat* was a *New York Times* Notable Book.

"*Defiance* is a passionate performance, stylistically brilliant, authentic, and daring. The novel reads as a fable written from a dark place, yet it is an illumination for the reader."   —Maureen Howard

"The startling power of Maso's fiction resides in her ability to locate, distill, and rejoice in the erotics of language. [Her] vision is uncompromising . . . psychologically astute and emotionally devastating."   —*Out* magazine

"Maso takes great narrative risks in this provocative meditation—as much an indictment of class and gender inequalities as a character study—and again proves herself a writer of daring originality and moral consequence."   —*Publishers Weekly* (starred review)

"A vivid rendering of the psyche of an unregenerate murderess. Maso's most convincingly textured and technically accomplished novel."   —*Kirkus Reviews*

Defiance

a novel by

Carole Maso

A PLUME BOOK

PLUME
Published by the Penguin Group
Penguin Putnam Inc., 375 Hudson Street, New York, New York 10014, U.S.A.
Penguin Books Ltd, 27 Wrights Lane, London W8 5TZ, England
Penguin Books Australia Ltd, Ringwood, Victoria, Australia
Penguin Books Canada Ltd, 10 Alcorn Avenue, Toronto, Ontario, Canada M4V 3B2
Penguin Books (N.Z.) Ltd, 182–190 Wairau Road, Auckland 10, New Zealand

Penguin Books Ltd, Registered Offices: Harmondsworth, Middlesex, England

Published by Plume, a member of Penguin Putnam Inc.
Previously published in a Dutton edition.

First Plume Printing, June, 1999
10 9 8 7 6 5 4 3 2 1

Grateful acknowledgment is made for permission to use materials from the following copyrighted
works:
Excerpts from *Femininity and Domination*, by Sandra Lee Bartky. By permission of Routledge.
Excerpts from *The Courage to Heal Workbook*, by Laura Davis. Copyright © 1990 by Laura Davis.
  Reprinted by permission of HarperCollins Publishers, Inc.
Excerpts from *The Art of Mathematics*, by Jerry King. By permission of Plenum Publishing
  Corporation.
Three figures and excerpts from *Structures and Categories for the Representation of Meaning*, by
  Timothy C. Potts. By permission of Cambridge University Press.
Excerpts from *The Physics of Immortality: Modern Cosmology, God, and the Resurrection of the Dead*,
  by Frank J. Tipler (Doubleday, 1995). By permission of the author.

Ⓟ REGISTERED TRADEMARK—MARCA REGISTRADA

The Library of Congress has catalogued the Dutton edition as follows:
Maso, Carole.
  Defiance : a novel / by Carole Maso.
    p.   cm.
  ISBN 0-525-94307-2
       0-452-27829-5 (pbk.)
  I. Title.
PS3563.A786D44   1998
813'.54—dc21   97-42996
                                                         CIP

Printed in the United States of America
Original hardcover design by Arturo Sevangelo Facilisi

For
Christine and Cathleen,
my sisters

Gratitude to:

Carole DeSanti, for the length of the leash.
Helen Lang, for locking me in the dungeon.
Louis Asekoff for his third eye, sixth sense.
Laura Mullen, blood intelligence.
Barbara Ras, lucidity, grace.
Elliott Moreton, scholar, mathematician, linguist.
Christine Brown and Cathleen Giannelli, sisters.
Brown University, stage set.
Dante and Shakespeare, guardian angels.

There's a hole that pierces right through me.
—EURIPIDES, *Medea*

Act One

It's a memory, so you can change it—prolong the moment before rain, turn down the thunder, black out the lightning, change the emphasis, rearrange. It's a memory, Bernadette, so you can perfect the scene, straighten the crooked man, and the little girl—her splayed walk home. It's a memory so you could allow it to collapse, implode, or you could close it down altogether. Crush the hero seed in your palm.

You could count, Bernadette. Count every vein in every leaf, count every leaf on every tree. Out the window of the tree house now—is that thunder? You might divide the vast night into quadrants. Or paint the world by number. All the threes will be indigo blue—and the twos that sort of blowsy green of summer. Is that lightning? Paint it white, fluorescent white. Not to forget purple tinged with rust in the bruised morning. Pink.

Look to the sky. Straighten, no matter how painful, the bow-legged Cassiopeia in the star-filled night. It's gorgeous up there, you've got to admit. Objectify your fear. Put all that longing and sadness and trust into an oblong box—no wait, that's not a box—that's a tree house. And they are just about to climb into it again. There. There now.

Vulnerability of three a.m. when the voices—those sentimental hobgoblins haunt my few hours of so-called sleep with their quaint visitations—the child once more in a torn and flowered frock, and the brave, bewildered one: brother. Antic, animated once more, climbing into a tree house, performing strange, ceremonious rituals in the laughable, fatuous black.

That it should come to this finally! A chorus of late night myopic angels limping through this their appropriated narrative. A little nightmare choir of crowing know-it-alls. What do they know? A fractured grim lot cooing in the dark.

She could count. Count every leaf . . .

Yes, but she can't count. Not anymore. The numbers have left in my hour of need. And numbers once were everything. I sit here and wait—but no numbers come.

Most cruel, final joke.

That it should finally come to this. Season of convergences. At last. Three more months left to live now, or so they promise, and I cradling in the crook of my arms, this infamous death book—the journal of demise I have agreed to write for my colleague Elizabeth Benedict. And what else is there to do for amusement I ask you? She's asked me to write, because no numbers come.

For what it's worth I will write what comes to mind. For what it's worth. Not much.

I move forward without desire or hope of salvation. No indeed, quite the opposite. I imagine words will only tighten this tightening noose. It won't be a noose, of course. That was for my Pappy O'Brien, the noose. No Houdini, I do not expect to extricate myself, exonerate, or in any way escape this box plunged into water, secured by chains. I do not hope to turn. I do not hope to save myself—least of all that. No, I do not hope. One does not kill two young bucks from Harvard University and live. No, one does not in their most adorable post-coital bliss *kill them* and get away with it. And certainly not in the overheated state of *Georgia*, where I've been rotting these last six years, waiting, waiting. Tomorrow and tomorrow and tomorrow. This creeping petty pace indeed! Will the end ever come?

Give sorrow words, Elizabeth whispers. And I agree if she will only, *please, please . . .*

Ensure nothing this time interrupts or goes wrong. I have suffered long enough now.

She has assured me. She will take care of it this time. She promises. *I promise.*

And so why not? I place myself in this tight narrative, just one more prison, in a world of prisons, knowing full well the ending in advance, the beginning, the sordid middle. A story like a vice, future reader, innocent reader. You with your bleak, internal demands. You who feign suspense or harbor closet wishes for redemption, salvation—or at the very least a little flourish of transcendence—don't look for it here. When you reach into this toothed, confining box, know what you're getting into. Is that lightning? All right then, take my hand. *There, there now.* Let the rhetorical celebration begin!

There will be sideshows, a house or two of horrors, some jolly fire-works, hoots and hollers, something for everyone along the way. Gorgeous young men, a smattering of porn, a thousand cheap tricks. Enough to satiate all of us. Last cynicisms, last gasps. So welcome to the fun house. The Backwater Correctional Facility. A rather nice corrective to Harvard, don't you think? Already I make a slapstick of these pages. And I have scarcely begun. Mocking your sentimentality, your hopes, all cherished forms of discourse. Dear diary. Dear novel. Dear trumped-up narrative. Garish last stands.

I am the cult figure, leader of the pack: *all my pretty ones.* Cult of the Disarmed, Cult of the Lonely, Cult of the Female Genius, Cult of the Elective Mute, Cult of the Enraged. And I have grown, with some dismay, gracefully into this last role—keeping a veiled eye over my ruined flock. I have grown nicely into the glare and flare of it. I am popular. Who would have ever imagined?

Cult of the Clear Eyed: I have killed with great deliberation, in the full surge of my sanity, two lovely young men: Alexander Ash-meade, my first and most scrumptious occasion of sin—and having tasted it once—irresistible, irresistible—a second time, what a waste. One Payson Wynn. Cult of the Most Unholy Trinity.

I having strangled these babes in their sexual slumber—and I was their *teacher* no less. No, one would have to pay dearly for such treachery. Disobedient, ungrateful, devouring wretch that I am. I am not blind to the norms. They trusted me as men carelessly, always, trust women—as if this trust, this confidence was their birthright. A mistake—in this case, at any rate.

Rage of media and lights. They have come today hoping I might sign a release so that I might with any luck, be executed on TV! The media—a different sort of executioner altogether, with their electronic, blunt purpose. Their commercial purpose. Cult of the

Anything in America. Cult of the All-American. Today in appropriate righteous indignation I tell them to get the hell out. Still, still—on another day, lights, lights my friend! How at this point can one imagine dying without them?

They never stood a chance, horrified jurors, most horrified judge. Alexander, like any addict, asking at the very end for his share of oblivion. His mouth spewing blood like some black numeral. Beautiful, beautiful . . .

What is the blizzard he asks for still? Alex, Alex, is that you? What is this blizzard, my pole dog, my dark star, my last coordinate. Can you feel the pull?

Bernadette! Bernadette! He calls across the abyss. And when he appears, it is by surprise—coming like love, or sudden summer lightning. *Bernadette!*

Look, you can be reckless if you like. You can call the black volts right up to this house in the trees—it's only a memory, for Christ's sake. You'll be okay, safe. Their meager positive, negative, positive, flickering in the night, is nothing to you. You might shout to the lightning, call it boldly to your side. Cassiopeia weeping in the night without gods. Take out your small box of paints.

Is that lightning? Don't worry. He'll keep you sheltered from the storm.

Oh, those awful italicized voices. Couldn't they just pipe down now? This miscreant troupe of omniscients spewing their wisdoms and visions. This lapsed, treacherous chorus, with their dour instructions. Those grotesque cheerleaders I have lived with my whole life. Weird late night solicitations. It's the nightmares that make this life untenable. Is that lightning? I look to the guards making their checks. Is that you? My mother among the rubble still standing with her rosary over my bed. *What are you doing here?* Mouthing her Hail Marys. She doesn't seem to recall that she's lost her faith. It all comes streaming back. Just a child all of a sudden, skipping down a Ballyogan road.

Skipping?

No hope, Mother. No hope of rehabilitation. These numbered days. No hope. Once more I am set apart. No. Moved again. These ever-diminishing rooms. Three months and counting.

The tabloids come more and more frequently now. The first woman to be condemned to death in the history of the state. Yes. One hesitates ordinarily with the fairer sex. But I have killed two young men, and can never be forgiven. What monstrous, remorseless creature lives in me? Oh yes, there are indeed things never dreamt of in their philosophies. Pickle my brain if you like after I'm gone. Most vile, most pernicious woman. *Something,* of course, *must be done. Something*— as they all keep saying—judges all, powdered wigs all—*must be done:* two blooming young men—cut down—and the ancient fears, prejudices, hatreds, rise up.

So skip the group therapy and the arts and crafts—the whistle making, the basket weaving—the little jobs one gets to foster humility, patience, camaraderie, commitment. Too late. I have been moved into the next to last cell of waiting. So that we may *detach* now, *disengage.* And I have, it is true, I have become genuinely fond of some of these girls. Besides Elizabeth, I would have to say they have been among my only friends in the world. It has meant something.

In my rather cozy grave, where I sit now, receiving visitors, students of crime and the like, reading magazines and the mail, accepting party favors, *why thank you*—all the latest mood-altering drugs and writing, writing. This countdown notebook. Soon to become dissertation fodder. Soon enough. How easily I take on the role. Diary keeper, a silly ordinary life at this stage—my small pink book, my lock and key. To be normal at this late date. Reading magazines, gossiping. The girls giggle, polish my nails! But I am a monster. They were nearly asleep.

Asleep, yes and so certainly not, I will not be left to rot here *indefinitely.* I am to be made *an example of.* I am after all a famous woman now, extravagantly wounding and wounded—with my gorgeous, defiant stigmata—newly minted saint of all women's causes. I shall be put in my place. No inauspicious and thrifty end for me: *I shall be history.* With an elaborately choreographed method of exit. Still haggling for the right to televise my dying—a life perfected, completed finally by the eye of the camera.

I am a beast I am told (they were helpless). Nearly asleep. The most vulnerable a man can ever be. Yes indeed. I do remember that. I do.

That twice I killed, with my so-called free will, knowing clearly, knowing absolutely the difference between right and wrong. My little lambs, lamblings. My little boys playing at grown-up things. To me they gave their last full measure of devotion—my eggy patriots. They trusted me. Yes, of course they did. My eagle scouts. My soldiers.

And so I have been condemned with some real enthusiasm and flair to death in the electric chair for the murder of Alexander Ashmeade, *a human being,* as they said at the sentencing, a student of mine, wholly exceptional in thought, word, and deed. Wholly admirable. And for the murder of his little friend, Payson Wynn, *a human being* as well. A bookish, imperfect intelligence. Yet nonetheless *quite dead.*

It's a memory, so you can change it stupid—warp it along the lines of infinity if you like, stretch it into submission so that the hand abstracts across the sky in veins of light and the pain is only thunder. Turn the ring into a star, the star into a code pulsing in a lost language. What does it say? Harbinger of love. Safe. Something senseless. It's a memory so you can free yourself of it Bernadette. Believe us. Trust us.

Might there not have been a way to have gotten free? As the numbers always suggested? As the numbers implied? A small defiance?

I write. Because no numbers come.

Language, my inadequate ally now. Language with its ambivalence, incoherencies, lies. Bear with me. Though I *seriously doubt after extensive consideration of the text that I shall be in anyone's eyes even the slightest bit redeemed.* Is that what I am hoping for here? Some last martyred status? Something salvaged from the wreckage? No.

Let it go quickly. These last hundred days. I want no intercessions, no beseechments, no nonviolent actions, no, no. Let me go, one of their failures. Let me go, unsaved.

Here I am at this late date, thanks to you and your *bright ideas,* Elizabeth, smack up against the so-called *language problem.* Oh the irony is not wasted on me—the silent one, the one who shunned speech for so long, the little mute girl now in the last business of making language. Right up against the fucking brick wall of the so-called *representation problem.* If there might only be a way to understand those incessant voices in my head. A way to manage them, decode them. After all am I not still that genius girl? Might it not be possible to grasp? Since no numbers come.

It's the solitude that's unbearable . . .

The hiss of the trees in the strange sky. In the distance—why does this story linger there—after a lifetime? A lifetime of calling it up. You can try to make it come closer. Make it surrender its heavy-handed revelations. Who's that on the glib horizon? Almost within sight now—Janie, is that you? Harbinger of love.

Barbarous nights. The hot seat warming up. As I move toward that dark luminous number that has always existed in me, just out of reach. God knows I've tried, I've tried to get there some have said I have succeeded more than anyone else alive right now. My omega point. My asymptote. Not much consolation. Insoluble equation right there outside my grasp. Others maintain that fierce number does not exist. One reaches continually for ghost solutions. For ghosts.

Janie is that you?

How to decode? How to know? If I could only crack the thing. This impossible search

Janie is that you?

Let you = Janie.

That x: is (x, you)?

Paint it red and up close and hard and blunt inside. It's like you're drawing and dreaming and remembering and wishing all at the same time. It's a memory and you'd like the last words to be certainly, or of course, or without doubt, or doubtless.

Again, there is no place for the child to go. It is summer and the father is at work, and the brother, dropped out of summer school, is at work and there's no question of affording a babysitter, and the mother worries about vague and random things: a man in a mask with a knife, or another man, someone who seems nice, lifting the child's dress with bribes of candy or books. No, there will be no leaving the child alone.

She'll have to go to work with the mother, that's all there is to it. She'll have to go to the phone company—there's no other way. But she's going to have to stay silent and she can't—she's got to be invisible. In other words she can't be seen. In other words, she's got to stay hidden all day under her mother's desk because no children are allowed there. It's not a kindergarten for Christ's sake, it's not a nursery or a petting zoo or a playground—it's a job, and the daily wage must be earned honestly.

So the child will have to be smuggled in before everyone else arrives. She's about five, I'd say, and she's already quite adept at practicing silence. Bright light filters through the dusty venetian blinds, striping the room. She gets under the desk and it seems her mother is always wearing the same striped dress and she is dizzied by it, the child, jailed once more. Sometimes she can make the stripes move and swirl like a zebra walking or a barbershop pole—but sometimes she can't. They just sit there on her mother's dress. Imprisoned in the nowhere to go; at least she'll be safe there, the mother reasons, in the incredibly cramped area near her feet. During the day she'll pass her bits to eat, drinks. And the child, armed with a flashlight, will read and sometimes sleep, lulled by the drone of numbers her mother repeats all afternoon long—and by the heat. She falls into her mother's exhausted voice as it repeats TRafalgar 2-5863. She will forever after this summer associate tenderness with numbers, love with numbers—salvation—the numbers that came first from her mother's mouth. They were the code she spoke with the child under the desk. A way to stay safe.

She falls into the abyss of her mother's long sorrow. She feels dizzy, and it's so hot. Under the desk close up she sees the runs in her mother's hosiery, stopped right before the hem by small dabs of nail polish. She rests her hands on her mother's worn shoes—over the shoes that have been repaired too many times now.

Zebras . . . Swirls . . . She's sleepy. Hour after hour the child drifts in a blur of numbers. Finding patterns for a while, which dissolve then regroup forming new configurations. Let t equal all the trees in the world she thinks. Let x, let x . . .

And PRescott 3-2908 and, and—

Until day is done and her mother puts down the black microphone finally and the numbers stop and she slouches toward zero. She makes the sign of the cross and she pats the child's head, and motions for her to come and slowly and they make their way toward home through a haze of numerals: the mind's dark emblems. Sanctuary. But on some days, and she can make out no discernible difference in the days—her mother will pull away after the endless litany of numbers, away from the desk—summoned by the shiny new shoes of the boss and walk down the hall to his office. The child can see his feet, as he comes to take away her mother, and his feet seem to be making strange little dance steps, which she tries to connect on the floor after they've left, trying to understand. It seems like an awfully long time that she's sequestered there down the hall, the better part of an hour as best as the child can calculate. She waits, as always, patiently. Always such a good little girl. So obedient, so quiet, so smart.

But on one day the shoes dance into the room and they do not dance away. They stay. And the child, of course, is still hiding—so she can see, but only a little. And the mother begs, *no, anywhere but here,* and the mother pleads, *no, not in here,* and the man laughs and says, *why not?* And he instructs the woman, the mother, her mother, to sit back down in her chair. She swivels away from the child and toward the black shoes of the man. *Yes, like that,* he says, her legs still covered by the striped dress, poor creature, zebra caged prisoner.

He begins, of all things, to sing. And the little girl lowers her head to the floor so that she can see him. He has taken his penis from his pants and he is twisting it in his hands, the big, bald man and he—and this part seems so unlikely—and yet, it is what she hears, he sings, red-faced, sweetly. God, this is awful. Quietly at first, *Baa-baa Black Sheep, have you any wool?* And her mother, in the most petrified and childlike voice sings back while patting her lap, *Yes sir, yes sir, three bags full.*

And he sings, *One for my—*

And she sings, *my master. And one for my—*

And he fills in the blank. And they sing together, *And one for the little boy who lives down the lane.*

And then again, *Baa-baa Black Sheep, have you any wool?*

Yes sir, yes sir, three bags full.

And three times she pats her lap.

And his penis is getting bigger and redder as she whispers, *isn't that enough for now?* and he laughs and reaches for her hand.

Oh no, Mrs. O'Brien. Now you know what comes next. And in her weekly humiliation she takes off her shoes and stands up. And now the child will witness, and this in a way is the worst of all; she sees her mother in stocking feet, move to the middle of the room. His penis is still out, and her mother in stocking feet, places her hand on her hip and with the other arm makes a sort of S shape. It's funny, it looks funny for a minute, amusing, like maybe she'll be happy or something, but then it becomes all too clear: her cracked, exhausted voice—this sad, necessary task.

She begins to sing, in a meek and mortified voice, and he yells, *I can't hear you, honey, a little louder,* until the mother and the daughter are just children together, cowering. I can't hear you. And she starts again, this time like a child in a pageant, she sings:

> *I'm a little teapot, short and stout*
> *Here is my handle, here is my spout.*

The man in the shoes has taken a seat on the mother's desk; the man in the shoes is moaning.

> *When I get all steamed up, then I shout*
> *Just tip me over, pour me out.*

And he is humming along as she repeats, *just tip me over, pour me out.* Again he groans. And the woman is on one foot, tipped over, off balance, emptied of everything, shaky on this one leg, and the man breathes heavily, only feet away from the girl under the desk. He motions the woman over to sit on his lap.

And the little girl under the desk wishes hard—*if only the numbers could start again.* Surely everything would be back to normal then.

And he motions for the woman who is weeping now to come and sit in his lap, *Here BaaBaa Sheep,* he mutters, *just one bag, just one bag full.* And he lifts her dress slightly and fingers her garter belt and reaches up for her woolly stash.

And see now how mysteriously the child has turned into a girl all of a sudden and then she's even older and bigger, and she can scarcely fit under the desk anymore, and then older, aging in the room, a little bit older—until she and her mother, they are just two women weeping together.

And the man goes faceless and empties himself this time into her scallop-edged handkerchief.

But it's not over yet.

Her eyes brim again and he is saying, *shh, shh, BaaBaa Sheep* and she is already gagging as he puts the soiled handkerchief into her mouth and sings sweetly to her, *Baa-baa Black Sheep, have you any wool?* And she, it is the routine, that much is plain to see, sings in a muffled voice, choking back, *yes sir, yes sir, three bags full.*

That a girl, that a girl, he says, and he reaches his hand deep into her mouth, saying, *Suck on it a little.* And then he takes the gag out and opens his wallet, and she is on her knees thanking him. *Thank you, sir.* Kissing his ring. To make ends meet—in those days, just to make ends meet.

Someone, something, deliver them, we pray, from this sing-song, from this ludicrous, this demented tea party, this sadness, this night without day. Grant them peace. Not this. Look how they seem to be conscious and unconscious, alive and dead at the same time. Poor cats.

In the night that never ends the mother feverishly recites numbers in the sanctuary of her sleep.

And in the night, the child, small again, keeps her cold vigil over the mother's bed and takes careful, bloodless notes, instructions, reminders to herself, love letters to the person she vows one day to become.

Class: we have sealed a cat inside a steel chamber, together with a "diabolical device": in a Geiger counter there is a tiny bit of radioactive substance, so small that the probability is only one half that an atom decays and one half that no atom decays. The Geiger counter is connected to a relay so that if it detects an atomic decay, a hammer smashes a flask of deadly cyanide gas. If it does not detect a decay, the flask is not smashed. Thus, if an atom decays, the poor cat dies. If it does not, the cat lives. We all know perfectly well what we would see at the end of an hour if we were cruel enough to carry out this hellish experiment: the cat would be either alive or dead.

According to the mathematics of quantum mechanics, however, the cat is neither. At the end of the hour, the wave function of the cat is not the wave function of a dead cat, nor is it the wave function of a live cat. Rather, it is the wave function of *both* a dead cat *and* a live cat. The true wave function is the *sum* of the dead cat and live cat wave functions. Quantum mechanics says unequivocally that the cat is simultaneously dead and alive, in gross contradiction to common sense and to what we would actually see. There is universal agreement among physicists that this sum is what standard quantum mechanics predicts.

Oh bliss! Alive *and* dead.

See how he waves through the green still. Bernadette! he cries, I'm up here! I'm up here!

Shall we talk for a moment about the satisfactions of premeditation? The planning, the budgeting, the preparation, the primping! The way girls once, in some other world, must have readied themselves for dates. A slow seduction. Nothing pushy. Nothing vulgar. A smart and careful seduction. The beauty of the plan was half the pleasure of it. And it is the reason I shall burn. For having committed a thoughtful crime. Not a crime of passion. As if thought were not our most passionate, our most ardent aspect. Never mind. I had waited patiently for the full flush of my power. My one moment of beauty. Thirty years in the making—unmistakable—that face in the mirror. Indulge me, would you? I am just trying to amuse myself. That face in the mirror . . . Though it was only Alexander's death I planned, ladies and gentlemen of the jury. OK, I speak nearly ten years too late—but Payson came later. In a moment of misbegotten spontaneity. Payson came quickly, deliriously; I having acquired a taste for it. Have I mentioned that? The sloppy, botched thing. I was found blithering at the scene up in a tree. Dear God! *What a sight for sore eyes you are, Bernadette O'Brien!*

* * *

Yes, I admit, I violated their basic trust. They had entered my monastery to pray, the chosen ones, and had met, oh, with something quite other than what they anticipated. An ordeal, we could call it, of punishment and reward. This all too perverse set-up that is private education: quasi-familial, quasi-erotic rivalries of all sorts among themselves and of course *avec moi*, their mistress of ceremonies. The public humiliation, the deceptions, the subversions, the groveling— well, you can see how things might very well get out of hand.

Elizabeth, is that you perchance, back at last from your Fulbright sabbatical?

Elizabeth, my only friend at that friendless place, hard at work on her book, even then to be entitled *Against a Feminine Masochism*, of which my little death journal shall now be the centerpiece. It's nice to be doing something a little useful here at the end. Were Elizabeth here now—but with any luck she will not return until after my execution—should it come off this time.

Elizabeth, alas, the first and with the exception of Connie, the last friend I ever had. Some days the very *word* friend can make me weep. Dear friend. Her friendship had frightened me, as I knew not the least thing about a friend. Had there been friendship videotapes, like the pornography ones, I might at least have feigned, have emulated those postures. *Friend.*

We had met at the picnic to welcome new faculty. I just a child sucking on a soda, she a woman laughing in the grass. We were the two female hires, or so it appeared, for that year. From the beginning it was a happiness to be around her.

Elizabeth with her lover Fann from the biology department, her cat *Chantage,* blackmail in French, a black male, yes, her love of murder mysteries, her fascination with my Fall River. Her obsession with Lizzie Borden. Her taste for the lurid, the garish, the gothic. The gruesome details we spoon-fed to one another. She treated me as an equal, she invited me into her intricate, eccentric universe, where lute players arrived at her door as a gift, where praying mantis eggs came in the mail—*they are friends of the garden,* she explained, *dining as they do on beetles and flies.* The altogether wacky range of her interests. I, the

pale, naive attendant at her side. Observer of her astute, almost surgical feminism. The vanity of her intellect, her hypertrophied morality.
I listened riveted as she'd flit from subject to subject—*a raft of plagiarism* had been brought to her attention, and she was to head the *sorry
tribunal.* At a conference she had met the most extraordinary pair of
albino transsexuals! Her collections of things: dolls, paperweights,
lovers. The ongoing mess, which she relished. The bright parade of
mistresses—her sexual ease—her gossip, her indiscretion—*oh that one
would make an excellent gynecologist!!* There had been something ongoing with a fashion model and she'd share the travails. I'd get the
breast reports regularly. How in the early years they had to be taped,
flattened, leveled. Then the push-up bras for that hourglass look, and
when that did not quite do the trick, silicon implants had been necessary. *Breast augmentation, breast enhancement.* And then finally some
years later, the breasts lopped off, the silicone having broken and in-
fected the surrounding tissue. Breasts, at any rate, having gone way
out of fashion again. *All for fashion, all for the whims of men: straight
men, gay men.* She was altogether appalled *how ghastly!* But she could
not keep her hands off that one. *The raised flesh, sexy . . . those scars.*
And how she worshiped. *Oh, bring on another false idol,* she'd bel-
low. Her idolatry. Her willingness to be idolized. Her love of being
idle. Her fierce, shining, intractable beliefs. Her little girl delight at
the first snow—her thrill at a sudden storm which when it came arrived *like love or grace.* Her grace. Her priorities. Her quotable quotes.
Her Angela Carter, her Simone de Beauvoir, her Simone Weil. Radcliffe professor of Women's Studies. Mostly I listened. Her passions.
Her priorities. *Violent women are such because they have been acted on violently. . . . The stronger prey on the weaker, alas. . . .* Her judgments.

Teena, Connie, Cherie, Tawana, Faye, Latasha. Were they so mis-
named? Was there a terrible code in the arrangement of the letters
that offered these women up, in specific, to the world? Was there no
way they might have been spared?

They were babies once. The women of this prison.

They were girls. They were just girls. Writing in their diaries.
Jumping rope. Playing in sunlight.

And in rain light, what went wrong for them? Dragging their
feet, holding hands.

The failure of the world to work right. Nothing is equal here.

What is this odd, momentary feeling of tenderness I harbor for this cussing and vulgar and wounded lot? Connie at my side now, winking, looking over my shoulder. *What are you writing?* And then, *Tell me a story. Please!* she, the child; I, her forsaken mother. And I tell her about the house in the trees once more.

One hears suddenly the thousand blooming mouths of that leafy chorus in the air, as I weave for her a sort of garment, as if to hide for a moment the blue of our prison shrouds. For one moment, our lives ordinary, equal, unexceptional. Our dooms the usual ones, like other people's.

Anyone, even you, is entitled to wish.

Hopeful Connie, waiting for a story. Hopeful Teena, eyeing Faye, who has laid her heart bare. They move me today beyond reason. They astonish me—that they wake up at all—go about their day. They impress me. That they will make love in the unforgiving, impossible night. Such bravery. *One is making the other ring like a bell right now,* Connie says. She smirks. Through the burden of darkness, their sounds—alive with hope and future—after all they've been through. Caught in the warden's light, but ignored, forgiven, granted this small reprieve. Judgment held, judgment spared—for once. The warden's quiet solidarity. Matriarchs.

Her quotable quotes. Her Angela Carter: *all wives, of necessity, fuck by contract.*

Fann, her beloved, doting, long-suffering better half, immersed in her biology and her beloved research and her Liz. Elizabeth. A *raft of plagiarism.* Her rage always intellectually qualified. Oh, she might have been an example to me, had examples been what I sought. Had examples been of use. *Well, they've got no notion of intellectual property these students. News to them that they don't own everything! Their little white necks on the chopping block, squirming! Well, what happened? They were sent to hear the dean's rousing sermon on the issue and nothing else came of it.*

Her pronouncements: *women accept less pay because it is sexually exciting to earn sixty-two cents for every dollar a man makes.*

Elizabeth, weird, wired, holding court—what does she know?

Your favorite student, murdered, how dreadful!!! And she winks. *How monstrous!* And she gasps. *You must be crushed,* and her wink. *Ah, la petite morte, indeed!*

The masters of patriarchal society make sure that the models set before us incorporate their needs and preferences. You can be sure of that!

Every faculty member I made the acquaintance of over my years there seemed, I must say, quite mad or daft in some way. It was an odd and motley crew and I felt for the first time in my life not quite so strange—dare I say it, even slightly at ease. Who would have thought the triumph of the mind, the refinement of the intellect, would look like this?

I came to observe rather more closely some of the great men, some of the *pillars of the university* from a new vantage point: colleague. The dispositions of these indignant, superior men, the gaudiness of their obsessions, their mini-lectures and pontificating, their dismissals, their peculiar brand of condescension, their attempts at seduction—oh you can imagine the tedium—while at home their chirpy or broody or witty wives sat, utterly bored. And of course their melancholia, their regrets. They were appalled that their stellar, geniusy lives had led them here finally to this. They were all falling short—and making the rest of us pay for it. I must say I remained unmoved by them. The alcoholic, the pedophile, the actor, the fraud— now found out. These performing fools. The classroom, with its great adoring audience.

And the students, my little foul-mouthed patriarchs with their *problems.* Trying to retrieve that which will never again be theirs. Tiresome. Tiresome. And how they balk! Not a graceful bone in their bodies. Complain if you like, go ahead, if it makes you feel better. No more special admission considerations, then? No support services or designated scholarships, no special departments, *no African Studies for you? Nothing for you?* Except a curriculum stressing all your eggy achievements, not to mention as a bonus, *just for being you*—a great job and a lushy pay check. Simply for being you. Take solace in that, my wounded, my lost, my poor little rich boys.

* * *

They do not doubt that there will be room for them. That each has had a place reserved with his name all along.

The dream, and it keeps coming back, even now: to walk into any room unafraid.

Look, out there—in the distance a figure. Poor Child. Couldn't there be a nice, a reassuring voice of some kind coming from off-stage right somewhere—at the scalloped border, some comforting, gorgeous, lilting song drifting across the field from the trees; or rescue—bleeding into the scene? Warm. Tinted rose. Flowing. A curtain of soft blood.

It's a memory, so you might make it pretty, Bernadette. The world will be glowing and lit. The trees will caress. Will bow down and protect them. Anyone, even you, is entitled to wish.

If only there were a way to calculate or otherwise tame—to parse, to control these messages. Voices in my head. Come on, Bernadette.

$$(\, (\text{Any person } x: \text{may (wish } (x) \,) \,) \text{ AND person (you) }) \Rightarrow \text{may (wish (you))}.$$

The rest of the world at bay. The rest of the known world far away. My brother, he's forgotten to punch out his time card. Or he's fumbled the ball again, he's drunk too much, or alienated the girls with his glares, that barely veiled contempt, he's failed his final exam again—but not here.

Not here. In the leafy afternoon and evenings that were ours then. He is busy hauling wood or electrical wiring—moving a speaker or attending to a leak in the newly built skylight. This house in the trees: it was a place in the world one might actually live. This eccentric structure in the air. Our suspended existence. The terrible teasing by those girls in homeroom or the other hundred daily dismissals, gone. The factory floor.

He smokes cigarettes, drinks, plays music as loud as he likes. What was on the radio back then? I remember only the manic tapping of his foot—leg up, leg down. And I, motionless, holding my mind just so in hopes of solving a particularly tricky problem of geometry. The place inspired such thought. I, sitting for hours there, free of guilt, free of worry, residing blissfully in the luminous grandeur of the mind. Remembering now might make the numbers return, no?

He is never still. He is always in motion: lifting weights or rigging up a new surveillance system of some sort—wielding a hammer, a screwdriver, a saw, in this, his supreme invention, his only notion of paradise.

And it was a paradise. This matrimony of trees and sky, freedom and light, cool breeze. A kind of defiance. From time to time he would come over to examine my notebook—symbols from an awesome and inaccessible world, his hairy hand like a gentle monster from some ancient place. And I, bifocaled, rarefied, with my one horn, my fragile pterodactyl wing, some monstrous hybrid no longer capable of flight—my brain bloated on a stick-figure body—enormous, insupportable.

Vaguely and only in glimpses in those early days do we sense we are doomed. Mostly I am too involved in these fragile, precious, coveted, long after-school afternoons. I shed for those few hours my grave adult self and simply relax, playing earnest, childish games with him. *Lucky duck,* I'd say. *Silly goose,* he'd reply. *Partridge in a pear tree,* I'd sing in my croaky voice. *Little sparrow. Birdie in a tree house. Birdbones Jones.* In those few precious hours of enforced silliness, where I was as carefree as I would ever be.

Where did such unlikely ease, such affection originate? I must admit that I have always admired the stamina of children, their capacity, despite almost everything, to insist on some small claim of happiness.

A paradise. Angles of the mind: in our leafy kingdom, where he presides princelike over his small principality: music, light, the roasting of hot dogs, of marshmallows over a small flame. Kingdom of Bounty, of Freedom, of Fire. And in that kingdom in the trees during those few years, the leaves seem to absorb our mother's sadnesses and prayers, her wracked hosannas, her well of hopelessness, her tortured sleep of numbers, twelve novenas, and fifteen Baa-baa Black Sheeps. The leaves absorb and muffle the bleak parental order, those endless concerns, and we are a little free. Silly. I am in pink satin slippers up there and he has built me a petite throne. One day he promises, he'll get me a princess telephone. *Oh yes,* I say and I enter the charade.

Starry kingdom. Bride white. Leafy quiet. No mad kingdom of the blind, kingdom of the mute. No night visitations, no incestuous idiot offspring whispering—paralyzed, paranoid, degraded, unnatural couplings, disgrace. No blood—no, that is far off tonight. All hate. All pain. All that is crazy or brutal or mean or incomplete. That Fall River falling away. Just my brother Fergus playing Eric Clapton songs on his guitar and singing. High up, far, far off, away.

Afternoons of utter exuberance. Flecked, dappled grasses. We wore laurels in our hair. I wove him crowns of leaves, berries, sea grasses, starling feathers. A teenage Jesus. Leafy kingdom. Small empire of bliss. Notice how artfully I have constructed this! Trundling along on my little feet carrying nails and timber, singing.

Singing? Good God!

Who has brought us here? Who positions us this close to happiness, to peace, and then snatches it away? Who allows us only a glimpse—but a glimpse nonetheless—before blindfolding us? A taste of sweetness in the dark. *Honey, honey, honey moon, lucky duck, silly goose,* and we are gluttons for it. *God it's beautiful up here!* But then just as suddenly darkness comes and our bodies are draped in irrevocable night. Or so it seems. It certainly feels that way.

My brother wielding a blunt ax, looks up from his labor. Out of nowhere the awful friends, in beards, with swill.

All harshness—all that is vulgar, random, impossible, returns. And like a cartoon, garish, bloated—I am foiled again. Beating my breast. All Fall River streaming back. A chorus of fishbones and weariness.

Pale droning of factory and trash fish. Paint the little girl in the corner pink. It's memory so there aren't the same rules. She could choose to alter the central fact—that he is going to die—but she doesn't choose.

the central fact f: {

    f = will (die (he)) AND

    could (choose (she, alters (she, f))) AND

not (choose (she, alters (she, f)))

}

He took me to the river. He took me to the dark and beautiful river. We fished with chicken backs and string. With worms. We watched the damned take our bait. Not squeamish with worm and hook not squeamish I would take the fish by the tail and whack it unconscious at the river's rocky edge. Stunned in an instant. To me it seemed like kindness. To me it resembled mercy.

What is this dream, bleakly repeated until it becomes a torture of sorts? Those hours at the river. *Stay. Stay.* No cans floating downstream today, no fish floating on the surface. No horse fly. No Shoofly. Assume a form congenial brother then—*let us go.* Let us drop our nets. Today no urge to go out wading, no urge on my part for once to die. No swamp Ophelia this time. Today we even swim—and I am not mortified in my bathing suit, and I am not stuttering and apologizing for my size, my bony elbows and knees. No today all is right. He waves to the fishmonger and the fishmonger's friend. *Fergus stay.* He walks down the lane, in odd relief, suddenly diminished, like Mother, Father all the people of this world—*stay.*

In the mute years. In the mute and furious years. In the mute years I made her acquaintance. In the years when I was still a girl, I discovered her harbored in my girlish body, an altogether darker resident, tougher, more resilient, a shadow figure who mouthed *patience, faith.* When the time presented itself she promised we would become one. *I promise.* This interior voice, this figure of wild, rarefied beauty, in love with the night—and this odd promise. *Better days.* This sometimes brutal, always replenishing dream. To relieve a little the suffering of childhood—my diabolical sister. She's singing inside me. Unravished. Unvanquished. Resolute. Whole.

I am the bemused recipient of dozens of letters each day written in the persistent other tongue of those who are going to survive, those who are going to live. Rife with advice, with consolation, I've received countless proposals of marriage, potions from the witches, vials from the healers, advice from the Sisters of the Sacred Heart, propositions by the score from the perverts. All mine now. *Here's your mail Medea.* Jody the mail girl smiles. And I wonder for a moment how

Jody knows about Medea. But I am delighted she has acquired some knowledge along the way—a myth, a metaphor and I think *why yes, maybe there might be some small smidgen of hope, oh, why not?* And it's a nice little thought, while it lasts. But then I remember, of course, it's one of the names the tabloids liked to call me. Oh how clever, that Jody! And why do I think that knowledge is still power? Has it ever liberated me? Gloomy genius. Like these letter writers—prisoners of ideology or sex or neglect or the thousand other things—nothing has set me free.

The mail today begins with female brine shrimp. Everything starts out female, this writer writes, and she includes elaborate, detailed scientific instructions on how to turn men into women again. One's head fairly reels. Oh the separatists are having a field day with me! There are the usual clitorectomy letters, all sorts of other angers and injustices spewed my way. An exhausting business really. Some are petitioning that I may be allowed to die by lethal injection instead of the electric chair. A kinder, gentler death, they argue, in this kinder and gentler fin de siècle. But they forget I am premeditated, unrepentant. No, I shall get the full brunt of the state's rage in sparks and flashes and fireworks and flames.

Dear Bernadette, Dear Monster, Dear Heroine—

Elizabeth and her dinner parties, her soirées, her effortless entertaining of friends and students and Bunting fellows, and lovers and former lovers to be, in the endless semesters which were ours together.

So welcome to the Fun House! As if we have not had *quite enough fun already* now they have schemed in a last flourish to get me on national TV where we can all confront our various griefs and other *feelings* in front of the legions.

And the tabloids just won't quit. Still asking about my boys, my fancy pants, my pets—how dare they? The TV news shows come and go inquiring about my little perfections, my delicacies, my whiffen-poofs. As if they could be summed up. As if they could be forced to mean something. My beauties. My prizes. The ones I loved best.

They seem most interested that I did *not* kill in self-defense. That they were planned in some detail. No comment.

Oh they are so transparent. How hard they try to put us in a made for TV movie or some schmaltzy novel. Assignable, comprehensible, antiseptic as one of their fictions. No audible comment.

My silence makes me appear all the more heinous. The television audience, having reached their verdict, breathes a sigh of relief. One hundred days and counting. It's going to be a cinch to electrocute me.

Though on the flip side, oh yes, I've got my supporters right outside my window—that is if I *had* a window. They are now, as my death day approaches, chanting, chanting little slogans with my name—repeated approximately at twenty-second intervals. Who has dragged that little girl along in this ghastly heat? She fingers the hem of her dress.

I do not particularly care for these fans. Have no desire to be made into something I am not. At the trial my little lady lawyer *doing her best*. What a joke. Didn't she know that for killing two of their own in one of their finest institutions, one of their most hallowed, most holy, most coveted places—that there would be no mercy shown, oh, the penalties will be the maximum all right, for crimes against their kind.

The tabloids, pure products of Great Britain, and then taken to their logical, excessive extreme by America, go wild each step of the way. I am Medusa. I am Medea. I am not Archimedes. I am Lizzie 2, I am the Hatchet Woman of Harvard. *What hatchet?* I am the Hysteric. In the end mine is the PMS Defense. I am icon, scapegoat, hero, monster. I am to be made *an example of*. Payson Wynn, with that ridiculous name, is called the Wynn Kid. And the headlines: *The Wynn Kid Loses*. Alexander Ashmeade is turned into every kind of ash, as you can imagine. That they have tried to reduce my exquisite act to some perverse, cheap trick. Of course they try. I know what I'm dealing with. I am the cult figure. I am raving genius.

Oh, I suppose soon enough you would like me to *prove* to you my genius. *Convince* you. This is not a free show. No such luck.

The strange burlesque of these pages. Oh to be commodified, usurped, trivialized, not only by the tabloids, but by myself. This ludicrous presentation, this packaged, sanitized, absurd character, I create for you: Bernadette.

And who can forget that last day in court? All of them, all of them there for the verdict, and then later for the sentencing—though you could hardly say it was exactly suspenseful—not by any means. At any rate there they stood, recording, taping, documenting in every conceivable way my every move. I am popular, have I mentioned? God I am claustrophobic in there! Guilty of murder in the first degree of Alexander Ashmeade, *a human being*. And they are hanging on my every word. Guilty. I was just a girl then. The secret bloom of youth and blood. Torn red dress.

Bernadette Joan O'Brien, do you have anything to say before sentencing?

Oh, what was Mother's expression? You could hear a *pin drop*, that's it—you could hear a pin drop. All of them with their held breath. *Do you have anything to say on your behalf before sentencing?*

Just—

And I look to the judge and though I whisper I'm amplified for all the world to hear. *Just tip me over. Pour me out.*

Peculiar trial. Most peculiar. *Peculiar indeed!*

A lot of talk at the trial about waste. Pain. She's trying to make some kind of case for me—I don't envy her—the little lady lawyer—her job. A back row of feminists lending their support. I must say I view their enthusiasm with some suspicion. They assume damage, abuse. Waste. Pain. They assume some monstrous, patriarchal betrayal of one sort or another is responsible for all this. Waste not. I too find waste, especially the waste of food, an atrocious thing. I pick the chicken carcass frighteningly clean. I nibble even on the ornamental cabbage. Weird, starving woman. At the trial . . . *Oh why must I play back the trial in my head again? After all this time?* They were two of my best, my most sublime students—utterly engaged, flexible, intelligent, charming. Did you feel contempt for them? *No.* Did you ever feel threatened by them in any way? *No.* No—one hesitates to say it—yet it must be said—I did not feel much. Though perhaps I did once feel—I remember missing. Missing Alex, yes, I believe so, quite poignantly, quite keenly. Alexander. He could have stood here with me in defense and Payson then our victim. Maybe even our child might have survived. Maybe I too might have survived. Might have survived. Revise, revise. Perhaps it is the most cruel, the saddest part of this preposterous narrative. They are all dead. I would rather be telling other stories, doing other kinds of work right now. And yet . . . How the numbers vanish. A punishment no doubt. Tonight I wish Alex were back, *my pole dog, my coordinate.* I might have told other stories, stories of delirious love pacts, new levels of mind, achievement past my wildest dreams. But none of that could ever have been mine.

Reiterated at the trial: I was scrupulous with all of my students—utterly fair, genial, nonpartisan. Ask any one of them. I look on them fondly. They did their best.

The mail gets stranger and stranger in here—or perhaps I am the one who gets stranger. Months to go or so they promise. Months to endure now, only months. Yes but *how many months?* Would you mind being *a little more specific* this time? I'm exhausted. It's this damn self-scrutiny, day after day—these endless hours of picking and poking. Probing. Damn you, Elizabeth, for this book. You hand it to me and promptly leave for Australia—to be with your gender aborigines or whoever the fuck they are. Your barrel of monkeys.

In the mail today an old headline: HOW THE GENIUS GOT HER JOLLIES. Appalling, really.

A double set of impassive parents, staring. Worn, but well-mannered: contained, grim, glints of intelligence, but only glints, now and then passing over their faces, no resemblance in the end to their sons. A grief there veiled, a grief deferred, an embarrassed grief, not unalloyed with shame. Like the parents of those dead by AIDS. But this was worse—horrifying.

Their strapping, beautiful boys, having given in to shall we say the darker pleasures—and stopped in that position—forever.

Impossible to detect that their most beloved, most chosen children had been butchered—murdered while studying in those most hallowed halls, in that clear, safe place. Look how they stare, how they scrutinize me—their strange prurient interest in the underclass now met. These strange fish—sterile, pale WASPs in the first degree. Stone. Payson and I watched them that night from the grassy knoll, through the glass. They were dining—actually not really eating, not much. A stiff drink, a limp lettuce leaf or two, some cold cuts, a cold platter of condiments, another drink—their precious, overbred canines by their sides. Every cliché in the book. These poor, privileged, sheltered people, with their secret handshakes and clubs and codes— trying to keep their dynasties for Christ's sake, intact. These were people whose tragedies were ordinarily of an entirely different sort— boating accidents in Nantucket, private plane crashes, drunken driving. Not this. Falls from polo ponies, that's a good one. Skiing or hang gliding or skydiving mishaps. So sorry. Not this.

Cruel, insoluble equation of rich and poor, splintered dilemma of day and night, peace and war. The black man in the broad-rimmed hat whispers, run. See, there's help if you concentrate hard enough. Run, he says, getting smaller and smaller as he runs toward the impossible night-scalloped border—

Where there are always guards and guard dogs waiting of course.

In the interval between dark and light and dark again in the light-ninged night—she might change from child to adult—in a lightning flash back to child again in the dream-ridden, eternal night.

She can turn down the sound so that no thunder is heard. No barking or darkness or dogs. For a while. So that the girl and the darkness tinged with blood . . . Paint it five if you like.

In the interval he changes from brother to man, then to soldier boy, bye-bye. The child cries.

To be scrutinized by baboons. My precious work, on a final theory, the final laws of nature, dragged out at the trial and studied by their dull, dim, nitwit minds. Its unearthly integrity lost on them. They call me imperialist, reductionist, they ridicule my assumptions, they gape in amazement. Even I am surprised with some of what I have come up with. It was me and not me. It was solace, it was every-thing for a while. Clever, clever girl. My most precious blood—used to indict me further—my work, my masterpieces. Such seamless, brave work—why was it never enough? The only place I felt calm, at ease, completely challenged, utterly engrossed. Where I ran once and did not tire. Why? Why? Why could I not stand aside, as I do now, and simply admire? What was the restlessness, what was the bitterness? Never happy with what I'd done. Malcontent. Disconsolate. Have I mellowed so much in here? The search for the starting point to which all explanations may be traced. Such hopeful, audacious work. What went wrong?

That they used my work, the one sacred thing, to try to prove I was a wacko is the inexcusable trespass. My so-called big science debased. My pleas for a superconducting super collider mocked. Oh the cheap shots! That they sat there misinterpreting, misconstruing, and using it to point to my excessiveness, my mania, and therefore my guilt—not acceptable.

My investment in beauty—a kind of ruse or refuge. The beauty of present theories of particle physics just a shadow of the beauty that awaits us in the final theory. Such was my conviction. A home in all the ugliness, all the horror. My particular brand of religiosity. Poor, silly shrike.

I am guilty—but my work is innocent. I pray you to leave it be.

Treating my immodest rush of numbers as an obscenity, these pornographers—proof of a tormented, deranged psyche.

The numbers are innocent.

On the witness stand my competitive colleagues, betrayed, testify: *Often we find these to be the sporadic articulations of a morbid mind— impressive, yet curious assertions of a person not in control of her reasoning powers—as peculiar, as going too far . . .*

Peculiar indeed! Most peculiar trial! With the little lady lawyer trying to keep me quiet and I in a rage rising in defiance, blurting out, *Peculiar indeed!*

Miss O'Brien!

The little lady lawyer takes me aside and says, *Anger is out, Bernadette. Contrition is in. Repentance is in.*

Passivity, guess what, is in again!

My little lady lawyer, one Amanda Hudgins, from the ranks of privilege; she would fight *fire with fire*, as she said, this time. Spanking, sassy, smart. *I was at Smith when you were at Harvard*, she confides.

She smiles in some elusive solidarity. I had the whole new girls' network behind me—I had every advantage. But what defense was there? What were they trying to win? *I have never seen such cynicism,* she said to me, *such resignation.* Child of privilege, a silver spoon, a diamond ring, golden ringlets, *And where, little Amanda, would you have seen such a thing?*

The little lady lawyer trying to shush me and trying in vain to drum up *a little sympathy* on my behalf.

Not to mention my work on the Omega Point. They scoff. My nifty physics of resurrection. Downloading the brain and hoisting it off into space. Eternal life: A way out of here. Did it not promise a way? A refuting once more of the heat death. A promise that all did not just go on and on, again and again, forever into eternity. Most unprofitable loop. Did they not understand what was at stake?

Bernadette! Bernadette! he cries. He's holding the ring.

Hopeless household. Fergus is enraged again. More keenly somehow than the rest of us he feels the tedium of our days, the misery—and dreams—still dares to dream himself free. *You are the most pathetic people I have ever met,* he spits. Lighting matches. He is determined to escape. And he'll come back once he is free for the adored, peculiar, bookish girl. *I promise, Birdbones.* Oh, he won't forget her. He'll buy her a piano and a calculator and a fishing pole. He *promises.*

And she'll buy him a baseball mitt one day and a good fishing pole and some stereo speakers like he wants and a camera so that he may go photographing fire. Today she waits. She's waiting for the money tree to grow.

Don't leave me here alone.

The adored brother, killed quickly in one of their fancy foreign wars—

Question: *Did you love Alexander Ashmeade?*

Yes, I believe I did. He was my pole dog.

What was that blizzard you asked for, Alexander?

Let us go then into our storm of numbers. He had a mind of extreme subtlety. It was without rival. *Were you jealous of him then?*

He was nothing but an inspiration.

Let us go then there—and I will describe to you sexual shapes—triangle, rhombus, trapezoid—trapezoid, my sweet. Torus, Klein bottle, the curve of normal error. The witch of Agness; the cardioid. Oh yes. To whet, to edge, to egg you on.

Listen to him, Bernadette. I'll keep you sheltered, he sang sweetly. But now he is crying, standing by the beaded curtain. Please don't cry, Fergus. And the little girl. The little girl holds his hand and the dogs howl. And he combats the black forces of his psyche and the lightning night for her. She's just a child. The sky cracking open. The lit gagged grass. She's just a child. Patience, Bernadette. Bide your time.

My lawyers with their hodgepodge defense. First I am merely misguided, misunderstood, their "Gee, Officer Krupkee" defense. By the end I am raving, genius, lunatic. But I resist, dismiss all such claims on my behalf.

My little lady lawyer's desperate, dire attempts at renovation, recuperation.

We are gathered here today. We are gathered here today to try one Bernadette O'Brien. See how callow, showy, scoffing, hubristic still. Without satiety—still. False teacher, true teacher, who is she? Who freely murdered one Payson Wynn in cold blood. Self-canceling, self-disabling from the start. *Speak, we beg thee,* the little lady lawyer pleads. *Say something.* Say something in your defense, before it's too late.

Don't go.

Is that thunder?

Don't cry.

If you could have protected someone, you'd have picked him in the night-tinted sepia like a memory, so safe. But not here, not here, and no one suddenly we know or recognize.

It's a memory so when the child cries out in the dark in the trees with the dogs, someone certainly will be within the reach of her voice.

The university students change out of their polo clothes, shower, and prepare for the evening meal. Put down their racquets. Powdered. Cologned.

Shouldn't we go now?

*   *   *

In a gruesome turn the families want—oh *the families. What do the families want now?*

Ridiculous black comedy and I the crippled vaudevillian thumping, thumping out a useless code. If there had been one shred along the way of hope. But no, only more jokes.

There is enough melodrama, there are enough histrionics in the world to go around without any more high-pitched, false crescendos. Your cherished, well-guarded notions of conflict, denouement—forget about them. Retribution and redemption. Artifice. I do not fancy making an already sensational business any more so. One could withhold details, build suspense, every hack novelist knows how to do it. But I loathe those trumped-up narratives. Look, at the time I was apprehended, I was newly pregnant.

You, my wiggy jury, wielding your electrodes and your cracked jurisprudence, your Law of the Land! After much speculation, after much discussion as to whether or not I would take the stand—*here I am!* My little lady lawyer reasoning that *any pregnant woman* draws sympathy—that surely you would not put one with child to death. Harboring the baby defense. Yes, the whole truth then. See my belly, my swollen breasts, my dumb, bovine face, beatific. The father of the child: sadly, alas, deceased. The widow on trial for her life. The skull breaks in predictable ways. There were only a few moments of pain. Or was it strangulation? Hard to keep straight for you who stand in judgment of me. Yes, they had confided in me, yes, they had given me their trust. At their most vulnerable moment. Must we go through this again? God, there was an extraordinary beauty about them like that. And about me admittedly in those months I was with child, alas.

They call me names. The prosecution acting like mischievous children who had caught something more terrible than they had hoped for certainly, in their brainy, ingenious, homemade traps—and now they would begin their experimentation.

The adrenaline that enters an animal's body, the anxiety at the moment of death is detectable in the meat on your dinner plate. It leaves a certain taste.

Wings pinned back. Electrodes to the brain. Shaven . . . Last rites . . . Dear God, what are we doing? What have we done?

The God is not just—we hold these truths to be self-evident—and you his wiggy representatives on earth. All too willing to carry out his will, his whims, as you see fit.

Do you then not, fair judge, appreciate the beauty of my design, the beauty of the repetition, the delicate patterning, the double helix? Do you not see what preparation, what elaborate planning, what care and attention went into every step? Does it count for nothing in your eyes? That one, extended, heightened moment in this otherwise humiliating life—when I was beautiful and strong and free, ladies and gentlemen of the jury—I recognized it that day in the mirror and I knew I would have to act fast. Those precious few weeks when I was capable of anything. Not homely. Not afraid.

The dream: to walk into any room . . .

You can, you can be reckless if you like, Bernadette, you know you can. You can call the black volts right up to this house in the trees—it's only a memory, for God's sake. You'll be okay, safe; their meager positive, negative, positive, flickering in the night, is nothing to you. You might shout to the lightning, call it boldly to your side. Cassiopeia weeping in the night without gods. Take out your small box of paints. You can color this numbered shape, the one that has lingered for a lifetime on the periphery, like some wretched sadness or crimson—illegible banner from the static inner life—useless, stupid equation.

Is that lightning? Don't worry. He'll keep you sheltered from the storm. Sure he will and doubtless and no doubt.

Look Bernadette, he's back again. He's back. And he holds the ring. Take his hand.

Scarred night. And I am woken again from the terrible lightning night, and get up and press against the bars, nearer to that bluish and bruised angel. She's got a swollen lip. She's got a cracked and crooked hip. She's limping toward home, torn.

Assemble the night. Arrange the necessary, inevitable players on the greeny downs, cradling tennis racket, polo mallet, red pony,

T. S. Eliot, chemistry book. Arrange once more their shocked faces. The grisly news. My disheveled psyche—is that you? Saying *reckless*, saying *you can paint*, and *patience*, and *hero*—won't they just be quiet for a while?

When the time came, after much preparation and anticipation— when I reached this strange zenith—hour of our first meeting oh!— how weirdly silenced I felt once more staring into the abyss of him—as if a brother had died. *Come here, young man.* A church burning in my head. And *tardiness shall not be tolerated*, and other platitudes escaping my mouth, and I am appalled as anyone that this is how I sound, when I finally speak, so priggish, and he is nodding his head.

Assemble the night, with its sole star: Alexander, Alexander, named for kings, how lovely you were! And with a mind just a notch below my own. Altogether astonishing. Utterly, utterly— flexible, inventive, fluid, elegant—willing to follow me anywhere, willing in the end to do everything I asked. To sacrifice everything. To give up everything. I pray he never guessed. It was not adoration I felt for him in the end; it was not revulsion, no, it was something far worse—it was something close to neutrality. Why? How like specters everyone in this cold narrative. Alexander. Name of kings. I anoint you in almond oil and myrrh. I set this stage more carefully, more deliberately than you can know. At the height of my power, during the brief moment when the world was mine. His amazing brain. Mead. Ash. Alex . . . Sh—Sh—Glowing in the loamy evening dusk—what? Placed on his pedestal out there, gently, careful, that turn of leg, that span of wings, chest. Oh you are beautiful like that. But he's tired, tired of posing, of being so admired, up there, so dead, he steps down and sits near me on this prison bed now. Tired of funeral garb he begins to disrobe. He lays down on the stone slab of floor.

Alexander, how have you been?

He is beautiful, beautiful and his head which houses the brain turning a pale violet in the last light. *Where are you going?*

One can scarcely bear it—this book of solitudes, of dirges. He turns away from me, like everyone. How all the characters in this flat

narrative seem like ghosts before my eyes. Poor, pale apparitions.
Sorry.

Many years ago now, my admittance into this prison—like the
first day of school—this sepulcher. My arrival greeted with a fanfare
of a sort. I am escorted down the wing slowly for all to gawk and
point and curse. But I just stare and they are silent, or become silent,
I can't remember anymore, and instead of jeering and spitting, they
turn away from me, like everyone, as if they'd been slapped by the
stinging ferocity of my intelligence, or my hatred, or my dread.

If they feared me they did not let on. If they loathed me. Strolling
across the green in their whites. The asylum, in the days right after
the murders, and the doctors in their bright whites and the nurses—
I'm feeling a little nauseous—I've got to say. I feigned madness then:
a hand through glass, a bit of gibberish, dizziness, so as to stay near
those trees, that green for a little while. Hoping for some solace.
Comfort. Succor. But there is no comfort. A little *Milk of Magnesia*
please.
    What I have become is this:
    Or rather . . .
    The results of my physical revealed I was approximately six weeks
pregnant at the time of my arrest in the trees outside the burning
Piggly Wiggly. Hound dogs barking around the truck. And the
sirens, no sound coming out. Fire. The lit gagged grass. Choking on
the smoke and sadness. Up there the wretched, singed Bird. *Bernadette
you are a sight for sore eyes!*

Days after I am apprehended we all learn of the blessed event together. I am newly pregnant. Miracle of miracles. The families want,
oh what do the families want now? in a last desperate act of resurrection
to honor their dead sons, they want to keep the child. Really it is
Alex's family who would like the little prince most. They file the
blood papers. *Run!* Even if the little darling is harbored in a murderer's body. He shall be theirs. The tabloids having a field day! In an
eerie turn they want to take the murderess to court to force her to
bear the child. They arrive in black ermine and black pearls and top hat
to collect the sad dauphin in advance. Sign on the dotted line. Oh

no—there shall be no killing the little god inside me they all insist. I shall not murder thrice.

There are thus two "worlds": in one the cat is dead, and in the other the cat is alive. If a human being is added to the system—to look and see if the cat is alive or dead—then the interaction of the human with the cat system would force the human to split as well. Other humans looking at the first human and also the cat would also split into two worlds: in one they would all see the cat alive and would all agree the cat is alive, and in the other they would all see the cat dead and would all agree the cat is dead.

Ah, but not to worry. I am monstrous, remember? Nothing will grow here. I refuse the child. A late, dangerous miscarriage at the end of the sixth month. Blood and veins and bones. Nothing can grow here. The doctor revealed it was a girl. Of course.
Elizabeth smiles. Are you back then, Elizabeth?

Despite what everyone says: sex addict, sex goddess, professor of desire, temptress, *maîtresse;* I know nothing in this regard. I never lost myself—not even once. Dispassionate, I killed them in their post-coital bliss. Clear-eyed. It makes me worse, somehow.

And the blood test proved the child to be Alexander's. Alexander— *a human being.* Darling halted product of our tender marriage. *Do you take this man? I do.* Brief nuptials. The red-soaked veil.

We are gathered here today. Alexander, is that you? Calling *Bernadette, Bernadette!* Calling *marry me, marry me.* Holding equations, rubber gloves, straps, ruined child? A high-intensity desk lamp. Ah yes, I recall, his aptitude, his appetite—*Bernadette!*
Rest, my sweet.
I put a pansy in his gluttonous mouth. With dirge in marriage. A pansy on his tender chest. Rest now, my love. Alas, goodnight, sweet prince.

When the child is born I'll say, *Your father was a rocket scientist lost in the stratosphere. A dreamy math man juggling infinity.* When the child is born I'll say, *Your father was a bonnie lad, gone back to wretched Limerick, I fear.* When the child is born I'll say, *Your father was a boy gone off to a fancy foreign war. Dead and gone. Your father was a firebug. Your father was a swindler, lady's man, hooligan. A tinker, a knacker, a good for nothing. Your father was an eggy Harvard man. Nose in a book. Gag in his mouth. Out in the bayous somewhere. Your father was a Piggly out in the fucking mire. A Fibber McGee. A foppish mophead. Your father was a Piggly Wiggly who went wee, wee, wee, all the way home.*

How pleased this little book makes me from time to time! Oh yes, Elizabeth. Wee, wee, wee!

Early on I had severed myself as best I could from circumstances that might lead to heartbreak. To experience heartbreak once and only once, and then never again. Look, out the window, here they come.

No one is home but me when the men dressed as soldiers come looking for adults at our address. No one is home but me. Just once. To have one's heart broken. Once and never again.

Father appears as they lug stars and stripes down the lane. *Mr. O'Brien, sir?* the soldiers say.

They're whispering. Whispering. All right—she can turn it up, but not without risk. Let's listen for a minute.

Don't go.

And her mother reciting, as if in her sleep, the terrible numbers of the phone company.

Isn't that thunder? Shouldn't we go now? She loves him so much. It's only a memory locked in the prison of a woman's head.

Is that thunder?

That x: is (x, thunder)?

He's standing with his friends, this pathetic fraternity. In the riotous, raw night. The boys slapping each other on the back, passing out beers, what the fuck—Hey, where's Jane?

In the bannered, meaningless, jingo-jargon of the poor, who always go. Why must it always come to this? The lower-class, defeated, Irish, and the solution that is always alcohol and the war.

* * *

Shall we gather at the river? Sweet Lord, shall—Someone is singing. Plush voice, calm and saying *hey girl*, down the hall.

Maybe things could have worked out differently if there had been but one friend back then. Secrets shared in the afternoons after school. *Friend.*
I watched Mother and Minnie Grace practice at it.
And the women in here—their easy camaraderie. Shall we gather? The whole male world recedes, leaving them a little free. Like children who have made a momentous discovery. They are giddy, delirious—despite everything. A turning point, a salvation, who would have thought? in the 99th hour.

If there were a goddess—if there were someone up there just for her, who might understand . . .

What fresh hell is this? Sashaying down the hall. Singing. Enter Beatrice.
Hello, my name is Beatrice Trueblood and I've come to speak with you. Well-meaning, isn't she? Bright-eyed, bushy-tailed. Oh the wholly inappropriate attempts of my newly appointed social worker, Beatrice Trueblood. Taking notes, calling for assistance, telephoning lawyers, *not more lawyers*, what does she hope to prove? *Spare me this,* I hiss into her perky ear. Not another stereotype at this late date. Please no.

She sits across the table from me. I discourage her. She assures me she has the patience of a saint. I discourage her. I try to palm her off on Connie. I tell her not to waste her energy. I tell her it is hopeless. I tell her it is over. Other days I refuse to speak to her. She wearies me, she bores me. I just wish she'd leave me alone. Take her book of small miracles and be gone.
A last punishment. That they should send me *a cheerful negress.* Ghastly, that they should at this late hour bring out most cruelly, their kindnesses. I trust none of it. A last torture. They have sent her here for such a purpose. To lure me, to bring me out—*oh why now?* She comes absurdly with her workbooks and notes, her twelve Bibles, her self-help, her book of appeals, her stays of execution, her slave nar-

ratives, good God, her happy papers. What can she possibly hope to
achieve? A murderous, condescending subject, quite a challenge for
the young black woman, a baptism by fire, and yet she seems quite
calm—faced with the monster—reveals no nervousness, no fear.
Strange one.

God, they are diabolical, these people who hold the keys. Most
cruel and unusual. This, then, is what I am asked to contend with.
After a career of reason and precision and exactitude, antiseptic perhaps, but never reductive, never—This, this is what it has come to.
This last bit of mumbo jumbo. Oh the language she speaks: *abandonment issues, empowerment . . . Empowerment, indeed!* Shall I tell you about
empowerment? I have already informed her, nicely of course, that
should she choose to talk in that absurd vocabulary, I shall not talk
back. The weak, vaguely articulated intercessions of a sweet young
Georgia peach. *Beatrice.* Here for a little *stress management*, are you? Is
that it? This feel-good generation. This *exorcise your demons*, then proceed. This harness your rage, this drop your chains. But tell me that
they, spouting their inanities, believing in reasons and causes as they
do, are not enslaved. The trendy, sentimental legions. *Abuse,* their flavor of the month. Oh I will tell you about *abuse!* And *abandonment!*
Why should I with my delicate, my calibrated sensibility, and at this
late hour, be forced to endure this? The predictable course she sets out
on here. What does she hope to salvage? What can she hope to save?
Terrible last remnants. Pieces. I her egghead Humpty Dumpty. Much
too late to put together again.

She comes writing on small pieces of bright orange paper, well
one can scarcely help but notice—it being the only color left in a
world drained it seems of all color—for quite some time. On these
tiny notes, in her neat handwriting, the world as one knew it once—
heightened, animated, bright. My ever-diminishing . . . *And what on
earth can she be writing down?*
  Last glimpses. And I remember how the square of terrible night
once gave way to day. The windows of that house. Yes, to the turmoil
of another day. I am kidding myself—that there might have been a
way through this. A different outcome. To have lived happily. *Why*

have you come? Speak, Beatrice. She smiles and shrugs. Says she is attracted to lost causes.

But I shall not, no I shall not be her flavor of the month. What is she selling this time? *Dysfunctional what?* She's turned us indiscriminately into the same shattered child. Again and again. Her one note. No I will not be one of her enthusiasms, one of her textbook cases, her poster child, her *raison d'être.* Go somewhere else, my friend.

Speak to me, she whispers.

And where is her anger? Little Black Missy from the Gorgeous State of Newt Gingrich and the Ku Ku Ku *yes they cooed in sleep* Klux Klan, all manner of cruelty and racism and misery and greed? The goddamned Piggly Wiggly State. She has come far and she is grateful for it. She has *risen above her circumstances.* Oh let us hope it is not so—some phony, uplifting scenario, poverty and endless discrimination turned in the nick of time, transcendent.

They file into the house of failure one by one. These teachers—the priests and nuns—the ones who loathe and fear and worship me. They bow their heads in reverence and disgust. I watch the grim procession from the dingy window.

I don't have any desire to see them out of context. I wish they'd stay where they belong—against a cloudy blackboard, ringing a broken bell or scolding Jimmy Dolan, who is evil. I just wish they'd go away. I don't want any more trouble or excitement. If I could just be excused from school that would be enough.

They look around and I feel the shabbiness of our existence and I am embarrassed. Why do I care about what they think?

Father Donnelly, who teaches math, who hates me most, speaks first. Of course he's the one to speak first. *Your daughter . . . Can't teach her . . .* He is so miserable that this be so. Why her? *Genius.*

And they all chime in, revealing the numbers of the IQ test. The so-called *Intelligence Quotient.* The number placed on little Birdy. On these birdbones. If they would just go away now and leave me alone. And they start in talking about options, alternatives, different schools, babbling, mocking, chiding us, insisting—speaking in the language of separation. *With already one child halfway around the world and in a war. Can't you just leave us be?* And I feel my brain beginning to separate, break into different planes. And their language separates into strands, *a shambles,* and the house is falling suddenly into the evening's darkening ash. It is winter. Mother is boiling vegetables amidst the amber bottles. My father pours them until they go out. And lit up he says, he yells, *Enough now and out!* And my mother is trembling in the stinking room of cabbage and overachievement. *Everything a shambles.* They treat this genius bit as just more bad news. And it is, of course.

And I am exiled again. Cast off.

Mother begins to cry, and she hugs me to her breast and she whispers in a kind of hiss, *Don't leave me here alone, Bernadette. Don't leave me here.*

I am mute.

And numbed and shocked by such a sentiment.

Please, Birdie, promise you'll stay, stay . . .

She holds me tightly by the scruff of my neck. *Don't leave me here alone . . .*

And she is orphaned now, poor child, once more by her intelligence. *Mother,* I think in defiance, *but Mother, I am not like you.*

When I first got here they tried to work with me, to get me to somehow love that inner child, but I can't help it. I despise her.

At age seven I choose to be the drowned Ophelia for Halloween, ghastly child, whom you ask me to love—blue lipped, flowered and drenched, accompanied by Fergus, cradling a skull, my lanky Hamlet—lighting fires, shooting BB's at small birds, choosing already: *not to be.*

Would that my grave be water and not this hard chair at the end of the long hallway. In my hair I wear seaweed Fergus has collected. Sweet Ophelia. And I, in flagrant disregard, against the blueness of my dressy pallor, decided even then (this is for you, Elizabeth), not to be the victim here, not to give in. The two of us in the dissipated endless black. *Confusion now has made his masterpiece. Trick or treat.*

And for a while, in spite of everything, the child finds a companion there. Through all the misery and sadness and rage. She is safe in the bard's arms. My beloved Shakespeare. He gives chaos form. And she recites, *Be bloody, bold and resolute.*

* * *

It was, like most I suppose, a household arranged entirely around the needs and whims of men. Those better halves. But now they all know it officially. I am superior to all of them and I let them know it—officious, insufferable child that I am. Who were these people I lived with? They embarrassed me. Sins of vanity, sins of pride. Hate me then.

But that is not it—they did not exactly embarrass me. What? What was it then? Words cannot conjure up a coherent image, but disintegrate like dust.

And in school they call me Jew girl and Little Jew. She's got to be a little Jew girl—with that monstrous intellect and face and nose in a book. The pathetic philistines of that diocese. That threatened and static community of ignoramuses. And when I injured myself on purpose in gym class they called me Jew foot.

Others, the few Jews in town, whispered to my parents—*She is adopted, no?* How, they wondered, did such a mind, sublime and perfect, rise from such unpromising soil, from such ashes.

Such poverty of imagination and means! Who stood a chance there? Look at them. Mother in her shroud and father in his cap . . . their long winter's nap. They are the walking, long-suffering, living dead, lost without candle or map in the year of our weariness, 1967. Exhausted, insomniac—poor wretches. Without knowledge or marrow for the stone soup—without resources of any sort—how will they prepare a place for her? Starving girl. Deprived one. Urchin. She's dying in the local Catholic school. Our Lady of Sorrows aptly named. Place of no fish—place of relentless boredom and insult. Misery.

Those girls hide her glasses. Call her names. They mock her: the locket she wears, her crooked teeth, her frizzy hair. Throw stones, those girls. Rip pages from her books. Oh why that? Anything but that.

The stale crusts of their unkindness. She is resolute. She believes she deflects their greatest cruelties—does not incorporate them. Is somehow above it all, goes unscathed. She is wrong of course. Jesus Christ, it's easy to see that now, *after the fact.*

And almost always, without fail, Fergus is there to protect her

from the little uniform-wearing, pigtailed monsters in that schoolyard. Brother hero—much feared by those little snot-nosed Bible tot-
ers, who called me Jew girl all those years, as if it were the highest of
all insults. Jacob Perlman turns and turns again. *Who said that about
my sister?* Fergus, always there, when I needed him most, *without fail.*
Such a phrase, without fail. In that house of utter failure.

*Behold a child suffused with light—the small genius of her being. She's
tearing her hair out at the grave.*

*If she could make Janie appear. It's a memory after all, and she'd like to,
she's a magician after all, but she can't and he's getting drunker and drunker
and it looks like she's not going to come and I shout Janie, I shout Janie across
the decades. Crazy Janie. He's waiting for his sweetheart to come and say
good-bye. And she'll come, sure. Doubtless. No doubt.*

*To bid him adieu. If she could only change the tone. Throw in some
French to escape the dismal and wretched and small—transform the scene for
a while. It is, as you know, a memory. Janie will come. The thunder can't
hurt you anymore.*

$$P \, (\text{will} \, (\text{come} \, (\text{Janie}) \,) \,) = 1.$$

$$P \, (\, \text{will} \, (\text{come} \, (\text{Janie}) \,) \,) \mid \text{wait-for} \, (\text{I, her}) \,) = 1.$$

Just when I thought I had derailed those sentimental hobgoblins
with their ordinary balms, their salves and treacle, trying to disturb
what I hoped would be some semipeaceful sleep, unsullied, to ease us
into the end. Why me? Why do I get a black woman, intoning
through the absurd complicated filigree of my death-row grating:
live, live.

In order to make the commitment to heal, you have to believe that
healing is possible. You need to believe that there is "a light at the
end of the tunnel," that others have made it before you, and that you
too can succeed. You need to have hope. Hope is a powerful motiva-
tor and a great antidote to fear. Unfortunately, most survivors find it
difficult to hope.

When you were growing up, your hopes were smashed again
and again . . . As a child daring to hope, you were crushed when

things didn't change. Hope seemed like a cruel sham. Out of a need for sheer survival, you set hope aside.

Think about the times your hopes were crushed while you were growing up.

MY HOPES TODAY

Even though you may have set aside hope when you were young, consider feeling hopeful today. You are an adult now. Things are not the same as they were when you were growing up. What would happen if you allowed yourself to hope again? What's the best thing that could happen? The worst? How might hope be different today?

Even though you may have set hope aside when you were young, consider feeling hopeful today. But I am exuberant in my doom and find no hopefulness in the recurring image of her. Whispering in my damaged and mournful ear. See me, I beg you, Beatrice, as I really am for once: an inconsequent figure on the landscape, aimlessly roaming now in a minor light toward darkness.

I try to capture a little for her the tedium of my days here. There's no sanctuary here. No chicken and chitlins here, dear one. Look, I'm so tired. But she just says, *Let your rage run out now.*

The hair shorn, at the grave.

That's me all right, there in the corner fooling with the stereo, trying to find the music. Sucking on a hard candy my brother has given me. Helping him separate the seeds from his marijuana—that's me, little stooge, little dope, packing for him a pipe of hashish. He cannot imagine the lengths, the distances I will go for him. That's me, still a child, putting on his Janis Joplin now. *Little Girl Blue.* With arms and legs now securely attached. *You are a doll.* Securely attached. Nothing crooked. And he is whole in the evening light too. Nothing flying apart or shattered yet.

Imagine she says *let your rage run out.* She has in good faith handed me a book of women's slave narratives which she thinks I might find edifying. One of her cherished books. And I have promised her that before my departure I shall indeed read it, if it would make her happy. It's the least I can do—and I am not disinterested in the topic. No on the contrary. Meanwhile she is working with Connie and the rest of the gals on *separation issues. Abandonment issues.* We have begun to practice separation. *Yeah right,* Connie says. Connie is one of the ones marked to live and so she must practice such things. Must imagine *window* and *door.* I would have had a far different job had I been forced to live. Connection would have been my task. Connie sits on the bed and like a child lifts her shirt and shows me her belly with giddy glee. She has *Lyla-Jean,* her daughter's name, tattooed around her C-section scar. She is going to live. *Come on, Bernadette, don't you want to too?*

How is one to concentrate in here? With the pep talks and advice and now Connie. I think it's Connie, three a.m., shouting out, *Leave your lips there like that!* How am I supposed to think? Still I carry around this pale noctuary, this death book, pressed to a cold heart— this last flourish.

July dwindles, dear God. How much longer?

The desire for winter light. Never again to be mine. Except inside. Where it has always resided.

Connie cries that she wants to see the sky. She knows if she gets on cooking detail she might get to see a small piece of it. *Look, Connie, there will be plenty of time for the sky when you're out of here.*

Wouldn't you like to see it too? Say yes, Connie begs.

That's Beatrice, I suppose, getting to you. Connie listen, I say, *there will be no changes of heart or mind, no petitions, no stays of execution, you got that, Connie? You're my friend is that right, Connie? I'm counting on you.*

Gray mare at midnight. She comes in exhausted. Mother. Removes her shoes. Glimpses me cradling an enormous book. Startled, bewildered, *Isn't she too young to read?* It is something I think I should hide, something indecent, this reading. She catches me off guard. I am lost in Pascal's *Pensées,* in the icy ferocity of the intelligence. Infinite chaos separates us.

*　*　*

The strap was a foreign language in our house. That lifted motion an obscure syntax. My father was not a violent man. He lacked the conviction, the interest. But something Fergus has said has utterly enraged him. He removes his belt. *Why must he do this in front of us?* My mother averts her eyes, but I just watch. Fergus comes to us after it is over and asks us to examine the welts. *Go ahead, touch them, Bernadette.* Then he goes out and signs up for the war.

Maybe I'll be killed. Maybe I'll be killed there, he says, a way of punishing my father without lifting a hand, of beating my father back.

This still life: the leather strap like a tail now on the table. Beside it a package of gauze bandages. *Why are we forced to watch?* My father, a ruined man, is in control, if only for fifty lashes. Then he dissolves and it is his face in the end that is soaked in tears and my brother who is resolved, steely-eyed. *Maybe I'll die.*

Look how they pass things to each other in the steel-blue light. Callused hands, stained hands. Exhausted in their prison of manhood. And the machines. The canning factory, the printing press, or wherever else work presented itself. Passing now a beer, another, sad stories, no rest. Father's been fired and everyone knows it again and he can't get any work. *And there's talk of your Ma being replaced with someone younger.* And he comes in drunken, swearing, hollering at the top of his lungs. *A pox on your houses!*

And Fergus raises himself, rising from the bog for a moment and they shout together weeping, defeated, *a pox on your houses.*

Together we go to the burial ground. He carries today his latest report card. The record of his failure. He wants it gone. I look at him quizzically. *Why do you want to bury it?*

Oh Stringbean, you wouldn't understand. How could you possibly ever understand?

I want to say *empathy*, or *empathetic*, but this is a word he may not know and I do not want to estrange him further. My vocabulary, my diction, condemned everything my family was—or so they believed. *Where'd you learn to talk like that, Bernadette? Think you're better than us?* I wanted desperately to be legible, if only to him. We went to bury things often there, after that. The most despised parts of the world, all that made us miserable or afraid or ashamed we'd put into the earth's dark vault. Forever more. I think now of all the things we buried that would not stay down. Digging and digging, he swears and speaks to me in mangled fragments. We are nailed to this clandestine, shameful spot; the report card says he will not graduate. Only after his death will he receive an honorary diploma.

Once we tried to grow a money tree, but it never bloomed. Inauspicious, inconsequent. We had planted five Kennedy half dollars and we watered and waited for signs of life. *It is crucial,* he explains, *to water after burying or replanting. Crucial.* Open-armed, full of minute possibility for a second—*it will grow this big—you'll see. You'll see.* My brother's arms outstretched. Crucified against the sky. What in the world were we thinking? Those five suffering heads burning, turning the world to ash.

What is hardest perhaps is the discrepancy between his intelligence and the performance of his intelligence. And so they assume him stupid—a grave error, in this case. His teachers just can't seem to make him learn. Something keeps him restless, circling back, unable to alight. The words are a hash, I'm afraid. The cruel reversal of letters. He can't sit still. *Don't worry, son, I'll see there's a job for you.* How will he ever bear what his father has had to bear?

No.

He's still young and left to play his small manic games of war in the tall grass. Defending his life. *Fergus, suppertime! Fergus, would you come in for supper now?* A boy far off. What is this fury? Who calls? He sets small fires. Rigs booby traps. Sneaks up behind enemy lines. *Fergus!*

And by the time I arrive on the scene he is already ten. And it is as if I have *sprung from the womb like that*: studious, ridiculous little prig. How awful. How could he not have hated me? As I would have hated him. For he was never resigned to the dunce's hats that the schools conferred on him, and he never stopped fighting—proving his intelligence over and over to anyone else who bothered to pay attention. And when the accolades came, the prizes, the scholarships for me—all for me—this *preposterous little girl*—well—how cruel, how unfair. How could he not have despised me?

I'll keep you sheltered . . .

But he is always kind. And the tortures are always directed somewhere else. To me he offers shiny things or candy or berries. We go to the river. He takes me to the aquarium on Cape Cod. We spend precious hours in his tree house. We review his scrapbook from long ago—a thousand times in those years—Our Lady of Sorrows burned to the ground. His beautiful book of fire. His book of char. He tries to keep his anguish and rage far from me. His demented friends away from me. He loves me, protects me, even from himself. Offers me flowers and shiny things. A locket with our pictures.

He gives her a hand up into the tree house. He'll keep her sheltered.

How many times was I granted entry into that private kingdom in the sky? Higher and higher in the trees. Light—Savor the radiance for it lasts only a moment: sweet air, the smell of the sea, no care— Fergus, we were high up—I, your faithful mockingbird. Brief respite. He had built me a small bookshelf in the corner.

(anyone$_1$ wh-$_2$ that t_2 hurts$_3$ t_3 (anyone$_4$ wh-$_4$ that t_4 hurts$_5$ t_5 him$_1$)$_{N''}$)$_{N''}$ (t_1 hurts$_6$ t_6 himself$_1$) $_{I'}$

And through the lens of the telescope, the periscope, the microscope—our minute observations, our terrible omniscient vision. *Look! Oh look!* In utter silence, in the quiet, as if we were watching a silent film, only in vivid color. There's Mr. O'Rourke beating his wife. Through the binoculars. She's screaming, her mouth is wide open, but no sound comes out. A child comes to her defense, smashing tiny fists into the brute's back but he seems utterly unaware. We watch without human feeling. We shrug.

Bridgette Kellman prepares for bed. Cathy O'Malley talks on the telephone. Her endless jabberwocky.

Crying children. What are they to us? From this lofty vantage point? All the helpless ones.

Bottles breaking in the street. On a sea of troubles—tumored fish, floating on their sides. All the casualties of our sordid, small lives: broken condoms, breaking glass, muffled sighs. The wreckage of an average night. Mr. Adams on crutches at the vacant window staring out in his underwear.

* * *

That corpse you planted last year in your garden. Has it begun to sprout? Will it bloom this year?

This then became his real home. Having built it, having installed his music. With love. Lovingly. The mattress. The beaded curtains. Three mannequins, sexless and bald, stolen from a downtown store window served as ornament.

He peers through the lens. In search of last virgins. *There.*

How to get it even a little right? How to strike the right pose?

Enormous head, small, shriveled heart. Sophisticated mind with the emotions of a child. Always ill at ease, I try to strike a remote and casual pose for him. *Say cheese.* I do it for him though I am mortified. Standing there, precocious and awkward, trying to mimic a life. What a joke. How to even remotely strike the right pose?

In an abandoned building Fergus has found a water closet where he has set up a dark room. I was only rarely allowed to accompany him there—to this secret place, where he went so many of the days he cut school. Hour after hour behind the black curtain. My brother, photographer of fire.

Here demons are given free rein. A magic act, with all its absurd and pathetic and cruel aspects. The power here to bring up images, and just as quickly blacken them. I saw him mutter and laugh as he too came into better focus for a moment, behind the curtain, in red light, a person alive, vibrant with desire—before he darkened and fell back into the gloom again. A place where he was lifted from his usual brooding—at a slight remove from himself—or so it seemed. I watched his pictures rise from the water. A world on fire. Or a dog with jagged collar, or the spongy hands of priests, their polished shoes, their neatly oiled hair. An altar. As quickly as they came into being, he could simply by refusing to release them from their chemical suspensions, make them die under his hands and be gone. In that nihilistic laboratory. The demigod laughing maniacally.

* * *

Patience, Bernadette, not yet. Hold your rage a little longer. Keep your head.

It was as if their undergraduate education had come to be an immense transfiguring voyage. *Patience, Bernadette.* A ride filled with desire and hope, a journey filled with longing. Even love. It was an intimate time and with the very best of them, I remembered; understood their early passions, proclivities, ideals, talents. Those of us who did the teaching animated those malleable figures, fueled by our own longing and regret. Oh it is somewhat pitiful all of it. We rendered these students heightened, alive with all possibility, all hope, all future, the best of us, and yet—something made me capable of killing them—these great transfigured creatures—of killing all that. Not the killer who renders his victims inhuman—and so makes it possible to do the most unspeakable things to the objectified beings. No, they were all too human, I'm afraid. I knew them exactly, exactly. Look, there is no pointing to what went wrong here. There is no reason that has always existed in me—a place, if we could just reach it (Beatrice and the legions that have come before her have tried all right) that would make this thing come clear. Killing my potential—was that it? *Oh please.* Spare me the burden of your need. There is no key myth, I'm afraid. Close this book now if you are waiting for that. You may puzzle to your heart's content—no motive is forthcoming, but only—oh look on the horizon now, back from Roma:

Minnie Grace O'Malley, eternal pilgrim, brought rosaries blessed by the Pope home to my mother. Delighted, my mother dropped at last the dingy sock she seemed always to be knitting back then and relaxed into the few years of fervent prayer she still had left.

Hail Minnie full of Grace, she would always say when her friend appeared. And indeed the only times Mother seemed truly vibrant and alive were around the sparkling, sensational Minnie Grace—a preposterous, irresistible figure. And even I, I must admit, even I, skeptical, retiring, disengaged, judgmental, was quite fond of her, even charmed.

She had entered the sisterhood, as she liked to say because she was called, only to find out that she had misheard. *Jesus is a love all right,* she'd say, *but he's not much of a bridegroom, I'm afraid.*

Not man enough, huh? my mother would retort with uncharacteristic bawdiness and they'd laugh.

Her most spectral bridegroom, her ghostly lover. Slipping the ring onto her finger.

Minnie Grace was a curious, rare creature from a scarcely believable world where love, where fun, where story, where all that was foreign to us, flourished.

My mother forever *tsk, tsk*ing her friend, rolling her eyes, begging for mercy from the hilarity of Minnie Grace's stories, laughing out loud. For the love of God.

Out loud.

What were you two cackling about, my father undressing, washing in the dim bulb light of the bathroom. *What was so funny?* As if it were a personal insult, a defiance, the laughter of women. Women suffered, people suffered, women suffered. That my mother laughed—even as infrequently as she did and against incredible odds—laughed boldly, promiscuously, without discretion and loudly, was unforgivable to my loutish father. He was offended by it, he was jealous of it, something smarted in him. The brute. He felt excluded I suppose. The bastard. My mother by then having already put up with a lifetime of his moody isolationism. She stood for it all, always. This laughter, being one of her only defections. But he succeeded in making her self-conscious about it, guilty, dirty, even. Soiled. Before too long she and Minnie Grace would meet outside of the house, and often during the hours he worked—continuing against the solemn and absurd occasion of his petty, petulant anger.

My father, outraged as always, mutters at my birth—talking about the wiliness of women, of wives—*Stupid woman*—and my mother praying to Mary or Minnie Grace or someone to help her. *It was your responsibility to prevent this. Yours.* And she believes it, of course. Stupid woman.

Still, I am born. There is not, to either of them, ever any question of my extermination. Even if the means had been readily available, even if it had been free. Talk behind a closed door ten years after my birth reveals other children—the product of my father's various unholy alliances—that conversation littered with every kind of hurt and scourge, but never once is the word even uttered. *Abortion.*

The unwanted child outside, privy to it all. Grave adult, caught in a child's body, I pity you.

Quit acting like a Magoo now, Fergus, and get on with it. Go ahead now, my son, and my father watched him disappear into the building that had taken the last life he himself had had in him. Fergus, his shoulders slumped, his head hanging. *Go on—and we'll hear no more of it!* Fergus smoldering, walks miserable into the factory. *Go on!* Dragging fury.

She walks through the airless halls, across the drab gray floor of the world trailing a flurry of bright orange notes—in that place all but drained of color. She walks vibrant through the horrendous gloom. Foolish one. She won't last long.

And she is at my beck and call. Obedient one. What makes her tick? She sits and listens as I talk gibberish. What does she know? *She'd like me to trust her,* she says. She'd like me to try to give her a shot. *What do you hope to save, dear Beatrice?* She takes my hand. She might make my life less excruciating. She might—*It's too late,* I tell her, *too late.* I lay stillborn in her loamy palm. She shakes her head, *Never too late Bernadette, never too late, you hear?*

(I see where this is going and I do not like it one bit.)

Only afterwards, I tell her, my mathematics are described as debased—the utterances of a madwoman, a juggler of mystical concepts, the sporadic articulations of a morbid mind. The curious assertions of a person not in full control of her reasoning powers. A peculiar mathematics.

How does that make you feel? she asks.

How do you think that makes me feel?

Bernadette! he cries, *take my hand. There. There now.*

The Eternal Return says that all events in nature repeat themselves in exact detail again and again. In particular, in the future an exact copy of you, dear reader, will read an exact copy of this death book again. And this will be repeated again and again and again without limit. There are only a finite number of possibilities. These will be eternally repeated. It was thought until recently that the Eternal Return was a consequence of physics. Both classical Newtonian mechanics and nonrelativistic quantum mechanics, indeed, love "recurrence theorems" as consequence.

I have spent much of my career refuting the Eternal Return and you may locate the notes among my things taken away that prove rigorously that the laws of general relativity and quantum mechanics will not permit the universe to be "permanently finite."

Mother sits on my bed. Ice floes pass—the black gaps between us. I am so young and already so isolated. My prodigy as they call it, keeps me away from the one person I most want to be near. Her gray hair escapes the orderly coif she began the day with and I just stare. She puts her exhausted hand on my miraculous forehead with fear, some fear; we are able to touch but never to connect. She would, for odd comfort, after the late shift hold me in her arms. After a time she would fall asleep on the second single mattress in my room, singing a little Irish song to sleep. She sings herself to sleep walking down a green road in Dalkey, modulating as she always did to a minor key, her voice a tremulous, imperfect thing, trapped now in my last ears. *Mother.*

She sleeps. Stay in your Ireland now. Stay. Close up I study the movement of her eyeball under the swollen lid, watch her lower lip tremble. Her lips dry and cracked. All through the night she jabbers her numbers. The remainders of her day. All night I record them in a book. No rest poor thing, no respite.

She gets up several times in the night. Something has utterly fatigued her. In her night shroud. Her pale rosary, lighting the way. Poor gibbering thing.

Isn't she too young to read? It comes back to her in baffled half sleep. *Isn't Bernadette too young? Isn't she?* She doesn't know the half of it. The things I'm too young for. Years later, on the witness stand, my mother, testifying on my behalf will display the same baffled look she did then. *What can she say to save me?* she wonders. She talks across the abyss. *My daughter,* she sputters. *They said genius child and took her away from us,* as if the naming had caused the problem. Now, it was as if these crimes were one last emblematic, permanent act of intelligence she was forbidden to enter. The mind gone awry. I, her only daughter gone terribly wrong. Yes, terribly, terribly. An unspeakable sadness.

She smiled and praised. She stroked my hair when I delivered my straight A's. They were like slashes across the page—those A's. She knew to respect them, and yet they frightened her. She never understood what it might have meant to me. Of course she did not; I scarcely did myself. Unspeakable sadness.

And she is nervous, fearful always at my next, my next, always another, then another intellectual triumph—her smile was a kind of absence. *Mother, come back.* Crueler than ordinary absences, *come back*— her smile seemed disembodied, disingenuous, and I could feel my own despondency set in at her response—a kind of frenzied misery. I should have preferred the grades, the accolades to have gone unmentioned, unnoticed. I should have preferred to have covered it all up as the small hand moves to cover the sex in shame—or the mouth that should not speak. *Never tell anyone.*

Cover up, she says. My intelligence—it's too personal, it's too radiant. It comes steaming off me—something indecent. I cast an eerie glow.

Cover it as one might cover the budding breasts so as not to attract attention. The blushing moist star. The shoulders folding inward. *Apologize.* The opening. The extraordinary passion of the blooming brain.

You look at them tiny from the edge of the scalloped, sepia-tinted frame. Integers on an infinite plane. As if by design. How lonely you are out there, where you've always stood.

The optimum moment. Having reached the height of my powers, in my thirtieth year. To avenge, to perfect, to rectify—was that it? So as to continue unmarked. Was that it, so as to continue unscathed? Or was it the plan itself I derived satisfaction from, definition from? The plan over the years becoming the most essential part of who I was. A reason to live. Without it I would have scarcely survived those years. And the plan was beautiful was it not? A kind of perfection—my finest hour. It was the second death—thoughtless, sloppy, unpremeditated—where I stumbled—for consolation, for company— where I fell.

On Fridays I'd ask Father Donnelly for extra math problems so that I might have something to divert me from those interminable

Saturday afternoons with my father. Though they became more and more difficult, apparently impossibly difficult, they remained soluble. Father Donnelly and the rest of those poor buffoons incredulous each Monday. *Why you, sniveling, skinny ingrate? Why?*

She nears my cell each night. Beatrice. I turn on the light. *And what are you doing here?*

She scribbles little notes. I look over her shoulder at the dull prognosis. *A profound lack of affect. Patient killed to feel connected, alive, aroused.*

Oh, is that what I do then?

Unseduceable. Poor wretch. She will never feel one moment's gratification in any of her numerous, diverse, and involuntary erotic encounters. Pity her those years in front of the pornographic screen taking notes. Mouth on cock, just so. Bovine stare. Little yelp.

My perverse and ever darkening theater.

It's great to note successes, but it's also important to actually stop and celebrate. In doing so, you inspire yourself and you inspire others, and you give yourself a well-deserved breather.

Take a few moments to think about various ways you might celebrate your accomplishments. You could throw a party. Go out to dinner. Brag to a friend. Get a massage. Try skywriting. (Be creative.)

In one workshop, survivors got together in groups of four and made lists of ways to celebrate. One group came back and proudly read their list: "Dance naked on the beach. Fly a kite. Go shopping. Eat dessert. Spend time with kids. Don't call Mom." Everyone in the room cracked up.

And each of us in here day in and day out hauling our catches, our long dead ones. *Our accomplishments.* Connie, dragging Lyle, her father, *I swear it was an accident,* parading Lyle out on a meat hook, gutting him one more time, for all to admire. And I with my beautiful boys. The girls never tire of them. With their triple stars: head, heart, and pubis—my demigods. All intelligence, perfection, skill. I do not exaggerate this. Their great cocks—*more!* the girls yell—these leviathans.

I don't know if I want a man more or a window, Connie says. *I want to see the sky.*

No window, only winter light, where it has always resided, inside.

Hey, look, I know the feeling, Connie says to Latasha, as they walk down the hall away from me. *Even though it was self-defense with me and Lyle. Really, I swear it was. I could have been out of here by now, back with Lyla-Jean, but no fuck, what a mess.*

Chaos in motion and not in motion. Connie eyes the room suspiciously. Violence in the cup, the brush, the pillow. Everything dangerous. What else might break or shatter or hurt? Is there never anything even remotely like protection? One feels constantly braced. The unactivated violence in all things, dormant in the shoes, the sink, in still things. It preyed on you even then. All that potential. One had to remain en garde always, always, even around the silent things. In the corner the sink turns to some woman scribbling in a notebook. As of late. Awful. An awful business. In a society that privileges action over inaction, being over nonbeing, one has to beware. This prison—and the prison of the psyche—where the numbers no longer come to set me free, but hover, static, nearly static. I am desolate. It is laughable that they ever held me, ever meant anything—Last positions of mind. Once they had meant something.

Why did I think the numbers might sustain? Where have they gone, dear God?

It's the isolation that makes this life unendurable finally.

Couldn't there be a nice, a reassuring voice of some kind coming from offstage right somewhere—at the scalloped border, some comforting, gorgeous, lilting song drifting across the field from the trees; or rescue—bleeding into the scene? Warm. Tinted rose. Flowing. A curtain of soft blood.

You could count your heartbeats. And the trees—god the trees are beautiful aren't they, this way, back-lit? You could count every leaf. Let t = all the trees in the world.

It's a memory, so why don't you try to? You might make it pretty? The world will be glowing and lit. The trees will caress. Will bow down, protect them. Anyone, even you, is entitled to wish.

Beatrice. Picking through her slave narratives, boxes of bones, small escape hatches, psalms, and spirituals, I look up from my evening's ration tar and feathers. *Well, Beatrice, what fatuous bit of optimism have you to convey today?*

Shall we gather . . . she hums.

The women in a semicircle, smoking cigarettes, trading gossip, intimacies. There's someone who cares about them. There's finally someone who listens. I hear them with their *bitch* and *girl* and *you go girl*. Their distant cackles. Their jive talk. Their cruelties and affections. *Well isn't she acting just like Miss America?* Their humor. Their yelps in the night. Could anyone be as lonely as I am now? *No.* It seems scarcely possible to reach new heights of estrangement and solitude, but four a.m., Connie and the rest of them, far, far off—in pleasure—and I am scared. We may as well be millions of miles away. I stare over the fields and fields of my solitude. The voices now, one by one, dying away; they come up close for a moment and then trail off, fading. Failing. If one could rewrite. Where would one begin? She might take my hand. *Bernadette, hey.*

Anyone, even you, is entitled to wish.

Veins of light illuminate the sky, there's an enormous hand hanging in the sky, palm side up—lighting up one, then another line. Life line. Heart line. This will happen. And this. All this. A sky of fearful possibility. You'll be—
    Lucky in love. He's waiting for his Jane, his true love now. He's got the ring in his heart pocket. He'll marry her when he returns; it's a promise. And he's waiting in the night, in the trees with the little girl, after his friends have gone, for Janie to come.
    In the memory, this locket, anchor, the woman wears around her neck—this small killing bottle, glass world, she dangles like a charm and looks into occasionally—in the memory in the bottle—place of dog hair and tooth and

velvet, lightning, cries—he opens another beer and waits: in the cruel, stupid, baffled punishment of his life.

In the small killing bottle where there's not much time left is there?

No more factory at five a.m. No more dirt and darkness and dogs. There's a war.

He fingers the hem of her dress like a wound or a code.

Was that thunder, and closer now? Nothing to be afraid of. But she is afraid. She's just a little girl, seven, maybe eight, yes, on the verge of her eighth birthday. Take my hand. And she does because she loves him and they climb up, up into the tree house in the sky in the thunder, in the lightning into the trees, and she knows better, but she does not care if she dies—she would give up her life—silly, melodramatic, inappropriate, late last overtures in the sky in the night. Give up your little life, Bernadette—soldier, pilgrim, stone. And hurry, he says, and careful, take my hand, little saint—before the rain.

If there were a goddess, if there were someone up there—just for her—who might understand.

That's lightning—now count—1, 2, 3, 4—then thunder.

The sky with its dumb green glare. Take my hand. Paralyzed like an animal in the headlights of a truck.

Bewildered. And his friends. Fists at his back. A kind of pummeling. Nuggies, they say. Neck vises, and other displays of affection. You dumb fuck. A term of endearment, apparently, holding him tightly. Tears. Yes, perhaps tears, marijuana and bloodshot eyes. What's up with Jane?

Rain now. I'll keep you sheltered.

Safety is the experience of being protected from danger and hurt. Within a safe environment, we can relax and be ourselves because we know that our well-being is secure. We feel free to take manageable risks toward growth and change. When you begin to talk honestly about your life in a safe environment, healing naturally begins to happen.

Safety is the basic right of every child, yet many of us were deprived of this right. Parents and trusted adults are supposed to protect their children from harm, yet when we were abused, these trusted adults, in many cases, *were* the harm.

Feeling safe is at the core of the healing process. You can experience moments of safety with a trusted therapist, a close friend or partner, or through sharing with another survivor. If you haven't had the benefit of safety in these circumstances yet, you can begin to explore the possibility of feeling safe with yourself.

Thinking about safety when you've known only danger, hurt, and betrayal can be terrifying. The very concept of safety may contradict all the experiences you've had thus far in life.

He licks the hem of her dress like a wound.

I'll keep you sheltered, he sings, sweetly. Isn't it pathetic? But now he is crying, standing by the beaded curtain. Please don't cry, Fergus. And the little girl. The little girl trembling holds his hand and the dogs howl. She's afraid. And he combats the black forces of his psyche and the lightning night for her. She's just a child. The sky cracking open.

Fingering, like a hollow rosary, the child.

Clinging to his jacket, behold, shouting something—love or don't—but no sound coming out.

Thumping with one foot on the rim of the bloodied door: a telegram.

How can they find the right address with everything covered over like someone's already died? The draped path home.

It's a memory. She ties herself to him. Sets fire to the tree they are perched in. Feels them both go up in flames. Watch them burn. Before the telegram and the terrible purple bunting. Flames—because she doesn't want to live without him. Dead together in the electric night. Because she knows he will never come back alive.

Eenie, meenie, minie, moe.

Electrocuted, drowned in light, bound.

It's a memory so she can warp it, open it along the lines of oblivion. Now coming into the foreground, licking the edge of the frame: fire. The disintegrating frame.

Behold: a child suffused with light. The small genius of her being.

The short-circuited sky alive. Cruel and violent. Indifferent executioner. Maybe we'll be struck, he says laughing. And somewhere someone is already weeping.

It's Beatrice, deserted. In the distance, dogs. It's their mother being passed the telegram from the government.

All this held in the prison of a woman's head.

* * *

Appalling ruin of another afternoon. My father and I walking back with our furies in the failing light. What mythic, doomed path is this, my increasingly troubled mind has placed us on this time?

Why are we on foot, I wonder? What's gone wrong again? The car's broken down no doubt—left for the mechanic to collect and re-suscitate. We have done this to our sorrow: My father swearing, *God-damn motherfucker* and the mechanic shaking his head, *piece of junk.* Fergus already somewhere taunting him—*piece of crap, piece of shit—seeing your girlfriend again, Loverboy? And using Bernadette as your cover?* Yes, I have accompanied him as usual. *How dare you? How dare you, you piece of shit. I'll tell Mom!* And Fergus is pressed against the wall again: *the fuck you will.* And he never does. He never tells.

My father and I walking down the crooked street finger our fury beads. Another year, someone new. Saturdays, my day with him, his one day free—no one else to watch me, I guess. Mother at the phone company, Fergus standing on the gray factory floor.

Each Saturday both before and after the death of my brother, both before and after the ring was buried, when I was a child before speech and then at the time of language and then after that, when I became what would be called an elective mute for some years, speechless, I would spend Saturdays with my father.

My father and I lumber larger than life, through the streets. Loverboy and his weird sidekick. Objectively, he is handsome, no one can take that from him: black hair, green eyes. And such bravado—his drinking mouth, his two bits of charm, his jaunty full-of-shit, crank, crackpot schemes in those early years when there were still schemes, in the years before Fergus's death. Get-rich-quick horse and dog racing tricks, idiotic lotteries and fast exchanges, petty crimes and payoffs and extortion. He is confident, having been buoyed up once more, shored up by the absurd parade of women who lavish everything they have on him. He is handsome, in a decadent, ruined way, grant him that. It is his one inheritance. His one free ticket in a world that exacted a great price from him. For Christ's sake even I grant him that—that free fall, that free ride. Soon even it will pass, masked by despair.

How is it possible that such a handsome man can ever have produced such a homely daughter? And I am. I am homely—tall, so tall, I must certainly appear older than my age, and so skinny. Fergus calls me Stringbean and Bean Pole and Olive Oyl and Bean Stalk and Little Beanie and Birdie—with that kind of metallic red hair that curls in all the wrong directions. A tuft of tortured hair and glasses and birdbones.

We walk toward home in the excruciating afternoon. From afar he is patriarch, protector, keeper of the keys. Great, and as of yet unrecognized, unheralded, antihero. Charismatic and walking in shadow. And I am composed along similar lines in tattered Grecian garb, a mourning angel wringing silent fists, captive, with no language for any of it. Grief, as hidden now as it was then, despite these paltry attempts at penning it for Elizabeth. Elizabeth who will explain all this after my death. As if there were explanations. Alas, to be a mystery even to myself. I have committed heinous crimes. I have killed two men, two young men who did not hear the war call, or the drone of the factory floor. Two men on the threshold, as they say, of their whole lives. Students of mine. Dead. Pity them. And so I shall pay with my own life. Foolish Birdbones. Birdie. Tuft of tortured hair.

How silent the chamber of afternoon. We are on our way back to the only thing that is ours, the small, dark rent-controlled house. We don't own anything. Not even our rage yet, or our fear. He's still swashbuckling, full of himself. We are on our way home to Mother, returned from the phone company and her litany of numbers, already preparing the gray meal of meat and potatoes. Mother, ever helpful, all day reciting numbers into the black microphone. Where is she when I need her? Exhausted and boiling the grim dinner for Father and making every excuse. Mother—his cycloped, myopic accomplice. *Husbands,* she'll tatter. *And boys will be boys will be boys.* Her hundred messages of clemency and forgiveness. They are not like us. Her grotesque fear of abandonment; and the price she paid not to be left. Men must be given *license, freedom.* She stands at the dark pot with her usual evasions and clichés and excuses. And later in the next room at night, I can hear her, her endless, useless bargaining with Jesus, whom she loved—until he deserted her too.

How to make this stop?

Fergus comes in with his burden of factory floor and drone, trying to shift its terrible weight away. I am inadequate; I cannot lift this thing, a failure. To love someone so much and be able to do so little—

nothing. He enters the room fighting, and smiles at me with some small hope—and I am ecstatic—until he too settles into the Saturday supper's gloom. Nothing can dispel the exhaustion of this small huddle. Father asking Mother to get him another beer, and another, and Fergus sneering, *Get it yourself.* As I silently replay the tawdry events of day.

Absurd decorum of the desperate, heterosexual afternoon. Stupid rituals of water biscuits and tea. Of sherry and flimsy nightgowns and fuzzy slippers; whiskey doled out in thimblefuls. Groaning of the bed, the small predictable torments, my father's howl and what I have come to realize were the feigned orgasmic cries of his women. Here in the correctional facility, the prisoner village, I hear the real thing, all night, every night. They coat, they soften, they tear down the night. Only I am outside of it all—silent.

I locate now those long afternoons with my father as my first acquaintance with terror. I was mortally afraid of those women and their power over him. Fearful of their casual, coy, closely guarded secrets, their lady fingers, their lady slippers, their perfumed bodies. I recall those afternoons as all chaos, and darkness, and squalor. Still, I am riveted to the spot—to the slurred voices, to the songs, to the demented laughs. The intimate conversations—they may as well be speaking in another language—the wavering and murmuring dialog I'd imitate later mimicking their despised honey voices and idiocies, so as to punish my father, and in some way keep him indebted to me, along with all the others he owed things to. He never knew in those years when I might speak, or what I might say. I, his small, perverse jailer. Prisoner of this mute genius child, with her silly, irredeemable chip. Through these amorous routines, she works out complex algebraic equations, or reads Shakespeare and Eliot and Descartes, or composes haiku on her arm, trying to force the world into seventeen syllables. Weird genius girl. Deserted. Marooned.

Entombed in another Saturday afternoon. I am more trapped than you know in this pathetic deception. So many years his melancholy front, his steady, sober accompanist. Silent, dwarfed by the simple acceptance of my position: daughter. Why, in all those years, do I never rebel? Am I so sorry for him? Maybe so. It is clear he is damned. We both know it: something in him is so broken. Nothing will ever, despite his gaudy charm, go right for him. He is perpetually running bare-assed, falling on his fallen pants—being chased down a long alley, mortified. And I am retrieving his wallet, his keys. What is wrong with me that I am sorry for him still? He with his small pitiable disgraces. He is not stupid, never stupid, but he is, even back then, defeated. Son of a coward, as he always said. Shaming and ashamed. He is the child still descending the dark cellar stairs. His father's body hanging in the corner. Dangling, still warm. My father is only nine years old. And I am sorry. Truly. For this.

Stumbling, running with his pants down—in the humiliating and punishing afternoon that never ends. We're at Solita's again, the sweet Portuguese woman in sexy housewife garb: apron and mules, a large headband, a feather duster, even. Now and then she'll pick up a wooden spoon to stir the chorizo and kale for her husband's dinner, making her slow stew. My father is impatient, ready to devour, but she is in no hurry. It's their ritual, of course. Each time, with real skill she takes him to that explosive moment—while doing a chore of some sort, he urging her into a back room, she waiting and whispering and teasing and swatting him away, swearing. And he says, as he always does, *Watch your mouth there's a child here* and she says, *What the fuck kind of man can you be,* as if she has forgotten, *bringing a child with you!* And she begins her elaborate sex talk with him, sometimes in Portuguese, sometimes in English. *Watch your mouth, she's not deaf you know, she's just mute.* And she says, *Fuck me right here if you are in such a hurry, on the floor* and he delirious, grabs my math book, and says, *Birdie, could you go into the other room for a while,* in the afternoon that will not go away or end. And now it is he who swears, *whore, mulatta bitch,* I can hear them through the flimsy door and she just laughs and laughs. I imagine that she derives not only pleasure but power from his every dismissive remark. She has the laugh, the attitude of someone who cannot be hurt or simplified or disgraced anymore. I try to draw pictures of her laughing, in the margins of my notebook. Solita, gulping and sighing and screaming and laughing at him. And she continues to laugh when her brother comes in and finds them wedged in some corner. And he chases him down the ludicrous alley home. I follow him, forced into a sympathy I do not want to give. She chasing after me, singing my name, saying, *Bernadette, catch!* and she throws me the keys.

* * *

Let's see. It's Pretty Mother this Saturday. She's lovely really, isn't she? When I get glimpses of who my mother might have been, what she might have had for herself after all, under different circumstances. This pretty mother is my mother, raven haired, relaxed—without the phone company or the burden of husband or children yet. She's enrolled in some local Catholic college. She thinks she'd like to teach. *Catholics are the best in bed,* she whispers, and I imagine her green eyes are shining, her pale, pale skin, her lilting, barely audible voice. Her bare breasts slung with medals of the Virgin. And I too am prettier, sweeter than usual. I watch myself wandering the hallway of our happy home in this sanitized rendition—Father, beaming, and Mother, pretty, free of worry. We have done this to our sorrow. Someone is singing. Someone is painting the walls. Someone has called offering jobs. We are imagining new lives, rehearsing them, practicing optimism. Saccharine, unforgivable child, that I am. I watch Pretty Mother prepare for my father. He has dropped me off early for some reason and I am left alone with her. Sitting in front of the mirror with her she asks, *Do you like to watch your mother put on her face?* I nod yes, though I am lying; it frightens me, like almost everything does. She smiles. She smells so nice. She combs my hair gently, the tortured, electrocuted tufts. Woe is me. Woe is my mother. There is something here almost unbearable to see.

Pretty Mother makes my real mother seem all the more drab when we arrive home, flushed for the evening meal. I, too, have been unfaithful to her, and I am ashamed. Father is slightly gentler with her than usual. *What's wrong Colleen,* he whispers to her, but she just weeps.

You're a Fibber McGee, Patrick O'Brien!

In the hierarchical, impoverished afternoon where we are always trudging on foot, shoeless, my father and I approach the mansion. He in his lover's attire; I ragged and torn, already orphaned. She is regal in *bustier* and satin gown and father and I must mind our manners, drink tea from the silver tea set and eat the French cookies nicely, one at a time. A little boy in hat and knickers embossed in the chocolate. What world, I wonder, has he come from, as I nibble on his toes. What world has produced this smiling, privileged long-haired youth?

What would a wealthy woman want with my father? She is purring and cooing and gurgling. I have no inkling—I am a misfit. Incapable of telling this. Freakish. I don't get it. For I have never understood the rules of attraction, or the secrets of sex. I remain unqualified. What is an orgasm? I have no idea. It has eluded me. All of it. Always. She will lead him into the bed chamber after the appropriate protocol, this I know. I will be led into her husband's *chamber* as she always refers to it. She is older. She is exquisitely bored. Surely she hopes this ruffian will provide some amusement, some diversion. What insupportable story of salvation, I wonder, does she tell herself? Had he a brain in his head, my father at this moment might have become a blackmailer or an extortionist or at the very least a gigolo—she was willing—perhaps too willing to pay for services rendered, with her husband's money, maybe the ultimate aphrodisiac. To pay, if for no other reason than to ensure my father's return. But he is an irritating, pompous man, interested only in his dime a dozen, crackpot schemes. Such is his tiresome, his uninspired, self-righteous pride! Accepting money for sexual favors would have been a dishonor, a disgrace, a sign of weakness. My father paid off my brother increasing rates to keep him quiet about these Saturday trysts. It was the currency our family traded. Money with its cruel and shameful power. Money configured the lot of us. Kept us in our proper relationships. Paying Fergus, in the end was the way my father maintained power over him, kept him despised and powerless. And it was the way from Fergus's point of view, he controlled my father, caught as they were in their paralyzed, unyielding death grips, their stunned, warped orbits.

And so it is the child in the wealthy man's chambers who is left to take full advantage of the bleak predicament of their lives. There is money everywhere—in the man's drawers and jackets, in the man's cigar box, left casually, and always the same amount. It is as if the woman in *bustier* and the child are in some silent collaboration, some elegant co-conspiratorial arrangement. Money left on the rich man's desk, where the child suffers—see how she suffers all afternoon sequestered in the gilded chamber.

Lady fingers. Lady slipper. All in all a lady. Look to the lady: removing her *bustier* now.

One way or another one must pay for one's perversions, one's tastes. But why the child in this airless, moneyed parlor?

On the lavish desk: writing plumes, fancy inks, paperweights, a million useless things. There's a wing chair and a reading light in one corner. And at the end of every session, the father unlocks the door and gawks at her, wrapped in silk and jewels, expensive indelible inks on her hands. Tourists in the death palace they can't enter, and, now, can't ever really leave. He smiles. He believes they are, for an afternoon, possessing these rich people—owning them. What a joke.

Who put the overalls in Mrs. Murphy's chowder?

No bribery of soda or candy can dispel the gloom on the way home. No ceremony of ice cream or sing-song. And he spits, *if you were a normal child,* but I have never been normal, and now on top of it all I am mute—by election. *I suppose you want those fancy cookies. I suppose you want party dresses and girly socks and all the things I can't afford.* Did I say he was never stupid? Of course he was. In the stupid, bitter, claustrophobic afternoon.

We are prisoners in this aristocracy of desire, this dull bureaucracy of want. I am locked inside with the golden key. Poor Fluke. Poor Birdie. Trapped in this unlivable jeweled cage. I sit in the plushness of couches and press a letter opener to my throat while a background of overripe, histrionic sounds comes from another part of the vast house. If Fergus were still alive he'd have found us by now.

In the room, I am large next to hundreds of tiny ornate picture frames, framing I suppose, what is most precious to them: mother and father, son and daughter, captured at every age. The parade of inheritance. Family: the sanctified, official version, the heirs apparent, all holding enormous keys. Brilliant futures. Did they know I was the poor child, standing in their houses, in the wretched afternoons, alone?

"Let's prove *without leaving the room*, that there are at least two trees in the world having the same number of leaves . . ."

Even though we've parked the car some ways away, Fergus would surely have found us by now. Pounding with the absurd door knocker. Rescuing me from this terrible tower room, where the flowers, there are so many of them, steal my breath. He would help me collect the money. And we would leave.

And the money? What did I do with it? Every week, I placed it like roses, at the feet of my mother's statue of the Virgin. Each Saturday evening I would slip into her blue-lit sepulcher, while Mother performed her ablutions. Strange intermediary, I passed the riches, from one woman to another, under the auspices of the Blessed Mother herself. How could my mother question or refuse such a thing? No, alas, Mother never questioned anything. God moved in terrible and miraculous ways. In mysterious ways. I could hear her: *Holy Mary, Mother of God, pray for us sinners, now and at the hour of our death, amen.* For what else could I offer this wretched woman but the reiteration of her faith and some cash? Each week I brought home one hundred dollars. Perverse little wage earner. I have no idea what she did with it. Perhaps she has said some extra novenas for me. Christ knows, I could use them. I am going to rot in hell. I have to date, refused the intercessions of the monsignor on my behalf. And every intervention. No special petitions, please.

Ludicrous, agreeing child being dragged through the agonies of another Saturday, cradling her genius and books, her pencil box and protractor, her ruler. If genius could only protect this tableau. Can you see it? Little bookworm with her philosophies and math in the awful afternoon. She moving miserably though the stations of the day. And her father, the peacock—shiny, dapper, smiling, accepting a gift at the door of cheap cologne. And for the child? A doll. Shirley giving him a big smack on the lips. That's what she called it. A smack on the lips. A doll in a pink vinyl raincoat and a purple plastic poodle. *She has children my age,* she says. *Off to their grandmother's today.*

And I am a misfit again. Freak. Laughing stock. My father ridiculing both Shirley and me, over the doll and the plastic poodle. He hates everyone today. Another house to adjust to. This one replete with Home Sweet Home above the door, and photographs, of course, in dusty, smudged Plexiglas—the dull-eyed offspring. The house decorated for Halloween. Demented jack-o'-lanterns, skeletons, stunned cats. Soon there will be turkeys, pilgrims, and Indians for Thanksgiving. Then the candy cane tree will be dragged out, the mute useless angels, the bells. I sit in the kitchen amidst a sea of candied apples, or Easter eggs or some such thing and wait. Those cowering, embarrassed afternoons. I open my notebook. Just scribbles—nothing really, from which occasionally significant numbers will rise or odd patterns. All of this contoured, punctuated by the incomprehensible language coming from the nether world of Shirley's bedroom. Phrases like *the rubber broke,* and my father storming out into the kitchen in a rage, to collect me and shout, *this is a young woman,* and he was referring to me, *who will never allow the rubber to break. Mark my words,* he says, dismissive, superior, and then slams the door. Endless histrionics of the pathetic afternoon. Oh Loverboy, oh Feverhead. The wasted afternoons.

Misery of the defeated afternoon. Look to the lady. She's slow moving, perfumed, tremulous. But he's too tired or something. It's easy to hear. *Impotent.* She's had it with him and his failures today. And he slinks away, feeling oddly virtuous and cheerful, and devours one ice cream after another. *Who put the overalls in Mrs. Murphy's chowder?*

Where are the husbands? All these women with their brutal, insistent need acted like my father was the only man in the world. His thick, ink-dyed hands, his blue veins, his condescension, his mild expertise drove them wild. I am making this up. A brute. Out of work, or working nights, or Sundays, and vulnerable, as a result, down on his luck—I have no idea what they saw. And I am ever-patient, scribbling and scribbling and waiting forever for Fergus to come. Brother-hero pulling up in his shining armor. I cower. Get down on all fours. What I would see then was more obscene than anything else I was forced to witness: the violence between father and son. Trespasses and insults and recriminations and threats and *why Bernadette* and *not Bernadette* and she's *just a child* and *your own daughter.* And he lifts a hand to the half-dressed woman, whoever she is, and I oddly enough, run to protect her, *Look to the lady!* And Father says, *For the love of God, Fergus, how have I raised you?* And Fergus releases his clenched fist of blood, his pinched fist, and demands money in his open palm, *Now.* And he takes me away in the tortured, incredibly sad, and grievous afternoon. This quaint ceremony of male instruction and bonding done, once more at my expense. For today.

Fergus takes me to the river. He removes his work boots, his bandanna, and he puts his head in my lap. I hold his rough skull and cradle it in the evening that comes all of a sudden. *I'll protect you, Stringbean. I'll protect you. I'll keep you safe.*

Some time after Fergus's death, my father stopped taking me on his appointed rounds. It is possible that he himself around this time discontinued these forays. Though I can't really say. But one thing I know for sure. Something ended for good with Fergus. For all of us.

Shall I confess here that I missed them in a bizarre way, when those visits were finally terminated? Saturdays were suddenly empty, and I was left to my own devices. It was the only secret, the only intimacy we ever shared, and must I say it—I felt eerily closer to him as a result. Related for once. There was no other ground on which we would ever meet again. I heard his come cries. I smelled his women on him. And do you really believe this? Think about it. I despised him. Get used to it.

Connie comes in, having just made her trip to the visitor's room and today she is beaming; she's hit it rich, she's struck gold. *We're getting out of here, Sweetheart. We're going to heaven tonight.* She calls the guard, the handsome Italian woman with the baritone voice, the one I have heard Connie whisper to in the middle of the night on the floor of the Correctional Facility, *Correct me.* Connie calls her into the hall to witness the ceremonial opening of the salvation package. The guard smiles. Only I am clueless as to what Connie holds, now raising it into the air. *It's the newest thing,* she says. *A double dildo. It's called a Boomerang! For simultaneous penetration, it goes like this,* and she tries to tempt me with it. *Let's give it a whirl.* And I would love to give it a whirl—just once.

How have I forgotten Donna, until now? Bella Donna. Polish siren. Giving instructions. Smoking as she lowers herself onto his mouth. Her thighs like a vise. Not satisfied to be satisfied once. Gluttonous and indifferent to his desires. I watch because I am fond of her, from the outside window, where she will from time to time wink at me, or give me the thumbs up. I watch as he passes out, leaves us all behind with the most extraordinary bellowing and swearing and I am fatherless again. And grateful to her for it. She puts on her housedress and says, *I'm not finished yet. I'm not letting you off so easy, Loverboy, Feverhead,* and she comes out to the garden by me for a while in her fragrant, blooming housedress, her breasts half-exposed—not giving a damn—not giving two hoots, as my mother would always say, about anything or anyone, but her own pleasure. We lie outstretched in the sun and she brings me out a parasol to protect what she calls my perfect skin, and she brings me a glass of lemonade with a cherry in it, and she peeks in the window at my father and says, *guess we got him pretty good this time?* She lays down next to me and we bathe in the sun. I tell her the one about the farmer, the goat, the wolf and the cabbage. He's got to get them all across the river safely. If he takes the wolf with him the goat will eat the cabbage, I explain. If he takes the cabbage the wolf will eat the goat. She makes the most extraordinary face. Only when the man is present, I tell her, are the cabbage and goat safe. So how will he get her across? She looks at me speechless for a second, shrugs her shoulders and says, *I need to get my batteries recharged now, Darlin',* and she goes back in. And she's got a million demands and ideas and positions until she is finally rendered senseless, but rises, and it is shocking the way she rises, quickly and in monstrous perfection from the ashes, larger than anything I have ever seen. And when Fergus pulls up she says, *Get the fuck out of here and never come back.* Donna in her perfect, uneducated intelligence and confidence. She in her sexual blur—at the height of a kind of power women get at these times. This woman who only moments before seemed so incapacitated, tortured, weeping even—now resurrected, intoxicated and intoxicating.

And I am two-minded. And I am two-hearted. I feared and loathed these women who disrupted everything, who turned us all into stooges in the ghastly afternoon But I am also irresistibly touched by them. Their willingness to imagine a way free, on an unlikely afternoon once in May, with a bragging, silly peacock, crackpot.

My heart hurts. The bloody, fibrous stubborn organ feels turned inside out. The tip hurts. I can't even describe or imagine what the tip might be—but the pain—strange, insistent, blunt. My brother whispering, *Little Beanie, I'll keep you safe.*

Connie ambles in again still holding her Boomerang. She knows better than most that what goes around comes around. Yet there is hope, one day if her *behavior improves*, she might get out of here. Only I have been given a death sentence. I am the one in ripped prison garb, Connie the one with sewing kit, dreaming. *I'd think you'd seen a lot of action,* she says, *if I didn't know better. What a waste.* In the wasted afternoon. My compromised clothes.

Connie asks me what I am writing in the Death Book today. Because they are trying to rehabilitate her, correct her, because they somehow must try to imagine her out in the world again, she is forced to attend group therapy. She has just come from a session of *sharing and caring*, as she calls it, and she is practicing now on me. She must go five times a week because she does not, as she explains, *engage well*. For practice, she is to ask what is on one's mind, what I am writing in my infamous Death Book, for instance, and then through *an act of empathy* she is to try to identify with the situation and to think of *a comparable experience in her own life*.

Because I am fond of Connie and would like to help if I can, even in a fatuous recovery, I tell her in brief, about accompanying my father on his Saturday afternoon escapades. Connie brightens, pleased to so easily be able to relate, to call up a story of her own. She laughs with crazy glee, and remembers Lyle, her own father on the farm in upstate New York. Already one can feel the peril of this caring and sharing routine. *She too accompanied her father on dates!* she exclaims.

You've got to picture it: they're in the wilds, somewhere up near the Canadian border and they're driving and driving—Lyle, the semi-retarded father and our Connie, the child, say eight or nine years old. They're in a truck and he's carrying in the back huge cylinders, huge vats of what Connie calls *cow giz*. It's his job to inseminate every cow from here to kingdom come with this enormous plunge gun. And Connie, she's not allowed in the barn, but sometimes she'll sneak in anyway to see the cows raised up on these amazing contraptions, splayed and humiliated, legs dangling, bellowing and afraid. But at the same time, bovine, mysterious, wielding extraordinary power, even grace, in that position. The child sits with the farmers' wives in the bright farm kitchens. Connie pulls the skin from her face to show what they looked like with their hair pulled back into tight little buns, in the ghastly heat of the afternoon. And she is offered milk and cookies every time and they sit in silence, little Connie and the grim wives. The husbands away, of course, out birthing or something at nearby farms. Cookies and milk and little chitchat against the mewling and braying of cows, against the heaving pulse of the barn. Lyle drooling in his drenched overalls, wielding his blunt and clumsy, his extraordinary elixir. Oh the throbbing churn of it all! *Now ladies!* His passionate, deranged face. Connie waiting with the demure wives. And when its finally over, Lyle with his slurred stare knocks on the kitchen door to collect Connie, nudging her to the next farm, far off.

* * *

She has left the door ajar and I wander into the room where my father sleeps under a cashmere blanket. He is a bauble, an ornament on this highly decorated stage. He is an acquisition, a pride. He is breathing evenly and lightly, his mouth slightly open in the great chamber. Vulnerable beyond belief, free of worry for once. He is barely recognizable separated from his malarkey for a while. How strange, how silent. He seems to be smiling a little, in this gilded cage. Pathetic, trapped bird, whom I love. Helpless, but mercifully unaware, surrounded by the extraordinarily bright and glittering framed photographs of strangers. Babies with already so much more than we'll ever have.

Who will love us? Who will love us, unposed, out of focus, roaming outside the picture plane, unframed, toward home? Who will love us? Blurry, torn, overexposed?

I pierce my pinkie nail into his hand. Nothing wakens him. I try others—my forefinger, my thumbnail. He sleeps. And we float above our own poverty for a moment, and are given a brief intimation of escape somehow; a glimpse, in that vast room. There in the precious, the lost time of the madrigals, where we dangle, poor, strung-up marionettes. Who has pulled us into these knotted, contorted postures? Who has broken us? Our wings beating against this vaulted, ornate ceiling until we are bloodied and we drop. It is me on the floor. In a bleak confetti of self: scribbling, wishing. Birdbones. Beanstalk. Two hoots. Oh Loverboy. Oh Fever Head. Demented, lady fingers. The car's broken down again. One hundred dollars. In the Godless, fatherless, impoverished afternoon. Little Beanie. Hour of death. Who will help us now?

Act Two

Act two? Who is the godhead who numbers the acts of my life, ordering them, though this was to be *my notebook*. The omniscient hand insists, forcing its way in. If you thought by writing you had control—think again.

Who is that child forced to dance through streamers and confetti and alcohol on a table for Kennedy half dollars? A jig, a reel, her brother before her, ten at her birth—in a kilt or some such thing, like a little Mickey Rooney, like a teeny dancing Fred Astaire. Dance, dance, little man, little chip off the old block, little lady-killer, don't disappoint. What am I thinking? No, of course, he is never asked to perform.

By the time I was born my mother was already a bitter and worn woman. My inauspicious arrival when she was forty, a mistake, of course, conceived one New Year's Eve on the boozy floor. I am conceived cynically on a desperate New Year's Eve and greeted, darling zygote, in my one molecule of being by the dying salutations of 1960. A screaming awful baby, a punishment for my mother's carelessness, a tether—and at this late date. To ensure my mother will not sing again, will not dance—and only the minimum of laughter. While my father and brother go out roaming. My father slamming the boy on the back saying, *one day you'll be a lady-killer all right.*

Little chip off the old fucking block.

As midnight approaches I can hear them all cheering me into dubious existence from inside the walls of her body. Waiting already with arms lifted, waiting to pelt me with Kennedy half dollars. The president's not even dead yet and his head hasn't been splattered onto a dress or emblazoned on a coin yet, but they're waiting. I, in my forced and mortified girlishness—dressed in frills and patent leather. And it hurts. Didn't that occur to anyone? That it hurts. Didn't anyone ever know that? What was wrong with them anyway? In my bows and petticoats, wrapped up tight like a ludicrous present, to be given for the pleasure, the gratification of the other party guests. *Dance. Keep dancing.*

And so I am forced to perform, spindly, miserable, humiliated creature—awkward girl. I know they are making fun. *Bernadette!* they shout, clapping, patting me, teasing, their throwing arms poised. Six years old, the targeted one. *Bernadette, dance on the table!* And it is awful, *Dance, Bernadette, dance.* It is ghastly, barbaric, unforgivable really—as the year turns. And my mother too, clapping, tipsy, determined—bent on joviality and new starts.

Still waiting are you for me to put on *yet another* little show? Don't hold your breath for the genius card. I have danced enough for my fucking supper.

Small yachts dot the harbor. Can you see them? A thousand points of light. *How pretty!* Percival leads his polo pony into its stall. Charles lobs a tennis ball. Indeed, yes, they are an altogether exalted lot, my students. My young men. Jaunty, bouncing, brilliant with privilege, and its attendant attributes: confidence, optimism. Summering in Newport or Martha's Vineyard, still children only several years away from little boyhood, digging on a beach, constructing great towers in the sand. Mother is not far away. *Come now, Preston, Theodore, Sterling, to lunch, to lunch.* The winds blow gently on them, in the distance a boat's mast bisects the horizon *on Donner on Blitzen.* The extraordinary blue where they've detected already great mathematical properties, harmonies, proportions. With their natural aptitude for living, their love of assonance and pleasure. Lobsters, crabs, *Wellfleet oysters please,* on their plates. Danger is still some ways away. It is part of their ease, their largesse to believe it is elsewhere, and always shall be so. Even in these times, they are protected, or so they think. A modern-day plague, then, or so they say. A ravaging death, but not for them, only a latex sheath away.

They are altogether too cozy, too gentle, too slack for my purposes, alas. Too protected. Not in love with the right things. Not much flexibility there. They are all safety, these baby birds. Having never ventured far from their downy nests. They must be pushed, must rise to the challenge, or remain forever in a minor light. In order to make the kind of progress I have in mind they must be broken. I don't think they understand. How essential it is to their creative thinking and to their growth. I expect a great deal from the handful of boys I decide to shepherd, to guide. I don't think they quite get it. They should at least know that; they should enter knowingly. I plucked them like jewels; I offered them sanctuary, respite; I handed them the way into their potential. I took time away from my most precious research. And I, so accommodating, so accessible, so modest, given the enormity of my own talent, so reasonable, given the absurdity of the set-up. My level of commitment, of sacrifice, of interest in them strains credulity, at times? I agree. Two of them I even granted the privilege of touch. Consorting on that most intimate and crucial of levels. Bad luck. Two of them, alas, are dead. Oh it is hard to feel sorry for any of them. My nursery of pampered weaklings, my bald baby birds, little dreamy, downy things. Birdbones presiding. I am well acquainted with the harm just outside their nests, the edge of the precipice, the glittering electric night. Without me they will not even come close. Oh they know this; they are no dopes. And yet they have no idea what it will take to get near the thing they now have only intimations of. The most fleeting of intimations. What it will take to make the very least progress. Having been sheltered so nicely to this point. How to harness their intensities (mostly sexual, they are eighteen or so after all) and from that cultivate the passion and discipline and hunger and rage so necessary. Yes, of course I remember—their testosterone highs, their *desire* all over the place. They must learn to focus, to channel, to maintain it, to control. Control—to know when to release and when to keep it. Oh any one of these boys might have the capability of going to that most coveted, most sacred place—but obedience would be required—and disobedience; reverence—and irreverence. Look, otherwise it is a waste of my time. Oh this wretched present tense. At any rate, if they are not willing to entertain what it will take, then they are in the wrong place. And a few did drop out but most of them stayed around to take it. I had the most distinguished Peter Piper Percival Preston Chair, after all. No time to waste on those who are not serious. May I remind them that they are no longer young—enter this now, or don't. I've got much work to do. Oh the highly guarded, the most extraordinary project that I have been forced all these years to keep under my lid. A much hushed project. They would have thought me lunatic, impolitic, and worse, if they knew. And so I led that double life. Keeping up a respectable and excelling front, throwing the community a bone now and then, while all the while harboring the secret, the true, the blindingly brilliant secret work to myself. The Distinguished Peter Piper Picked a Peck Professor and her handful of bleary, tender, budding Petergeniuses. Traipsing behind her with their desultory, their yet-unfocused talent. They've got far to go.

Don't you think my boys come fresh-faced and rather luscious on the first day of class? Earnest, worried, proud, virginal. Having left their anxious check-scribbling parents at the door. Their preciouses now in my care. Their sweet overachievers. On, on then to further glory, our sons. On Payson, on Preston. They come with all the earmarks of privilege, entitlement, some of which I quite admire: their stubbornness, their unwillingness to give up, collapse, or fade. Their health, their good teeth, their perverse Presbyterianism—even the Chinese students are Presbyterians these days—their good looks. The breezy, ordinary, easy way of them, their carefree jauntiness, their endless tact, the drinks at five, their gentle careerism, their assumptions. Assume, assume. Their bird books and binoculars, their love of music. The altogether humane and civil stature of the haves. I walk down the aisles and gaze at the venerated, anointed, chosen ones. My delectable innocents. In shiny shoes, in jeweled crowns, in fig leaves and cod pieces and cocoa butter, in cloaks of mad ambition. I had waited a long time for this class.

And weren't you always in one way or another singing for your goddamned supper?
Never sang.
No, never sang. That much is true.
Danced.

This is the light of the mind: surgical, perfect. These are the saving, perfect chilly directives of the mind, my youngsters. And so, for another year, class commences. Not the lesser wish for immortality, but rather a nostalgia for the eternal will fill you, my friends. So wel-

come to the Hotel Infinity with its infinite possibilities, permutations, perversions. Pleasure, if you'll allow it, off the fucking Richter
scale. Do I scare you? This class is not for the meek. Nor for the
mediocre or otherwise inconsequent. I ask you in good faith, each and
every one of you—*What are you prepared to do? What are you willing to
give up? Where are you willing to go? And most importantly of all. Who are
you prepared to be?*

What do you know? You have no notion of beauty. No notion of
sex—what you call sex—*what is that?* The grinding of bone against
bone, hip to hip, for release. My poor, pathetic undergraduates, you
would deplete your passion, your precious small energy on such an inauspicious and transitory activity, lamentable really, *Mr. Jacobson, Mr.
Wells, isn't that correct then?* My lamentable, my silly, my priapic, my
hormone machines, my well scrubbed, my perfect scores—you are
everything but innocent. No, never innocent: one does not get to
Harvard University these days on innocence. *Who are you willing to be?
Mr. Newington?*

Don't you love the arrogance of the gifted male child? *Yes, Mr.
Pratt, I am speaking of you.* The take-for-granted attitude of your
money—so ingrained you do not even realize what it means—oh all
right, in that way I suppose they were innocent. *You're here on scholar-
ship you say, Mr. Price?* Save your stories for someone else. *Let us begin,
shall we, my little godheads?*

My sweet phallocentrics. You lead with your penises. Your in-
choate desire is everywhere. I ask that you focus. My one genuine demand of you. My one gift. My austere aesthetic. Just for one moment
try, try to approach the brilliance that is mine (they lift their head to
the glare): woman.

Fall River is not far from Cambridge. One imagines being able to
throw a fucking stone at it. We're that close, but we're worlds apart.
They are your age, the last time I saw you. Night follows night.
There's no day in sight.

But we were worlds away, weren't we, Fergus? I think of all the
humiliations. I think of all the goddamned places we tried to escape.
Tried to get lost. While over here they are fucking *found*, sitting on

their beefy thrones. I swear to you, brother, it's a stone's throw—that close.

How about a glass of milk, Stringbean?

These were my young men—a mélange as it were of contemporary social mores and manners, quiet rebelliousness, guilt and self-aggrandizement yoked with a healthy dose of self-loathing, of sentimentality, of baby talk, of urgency. Not to mention nerdiness. Geeks their whole lives.

Oh see how quickly my Adonises turn gawky, pimply, miserable. In a turn of my head toward the prison wall. In a change of light. Fickle, aren't I? The light of the mind indeed. Tonight they are a pitiful lot. Poor little rich boys.

They had had altogether too much pressure from the checkscribblers. But more important it was the demands of their talent that had exhausted them—there had been too many intellectual burdens and responsibilities too early on. As a result they displayed a kind of guarded restlessness, a newly surfacing desire to throw the self away, surrender—to become only the passionate receiver of attention. Many of them having been deprived the attention they most longed for. Despite their brilliance with computers, their aptitude at science fairs, and whatever else young men had to do these days to get into Harvard. The dude ranch, the spelunking, all great on the resume. The rich I presume are as the rich have always been—absent, off making investments, or traveling the world. The offspring having everything of course and nothing at all, simultaneously, grew up into some of the most extraordinary fallen fruit. Every year a select few were always completely ready for the descent by the time they got to me. Oh the thrill of it! And I, veiled missionary, dared them, urged them to allow whatever it was that had, in fact, already begun to happen. The dizzying freedom of the intellect! Let us look then you and I for what Yeats described as the click of the well-made box. The fit, the bliss, in the mind. And I was privileged, and I do not use the word lightly, to work with these men. In concert with all else I have described, many of them had *considerable intellectual gifts*. And so I dared them. Dared them to be better than their little simpering, hurt selves, neglected, poor dears, misunderstood *yes*. It was a dare they were scarcely aware

of. They didn't know what hit them and were genuinely surprised to
find themselves day after gloomy day in my small office, asking for it:
more talk, more theorems, more stimulation. And the ones shut out
would appear at my steps as well, murmuring, caught off guard in
some strangeness, some unrequited love. Caught in complicated, sur-
prising need. I was immensely popular by then—the combination of
my particular brand of chic sadomasochism, and my simple, straight-
forward *brilliance* proved, I suppose, irresistible. I do not mean to
sound self-congratulatory here. Much credit must go, must always go,
to my passionate subject. It was the extraordinary, mind-altering ma-
terial of the class itself that so floored us—face to face with the great
thinking, the great uncertainties, the beautiful, heart-stopping configurations, the gorgeous patterns, the deep design. The rings of integers. The set of points which a function approaches arbitrarily close
to but never attains. Alas, what chance did we have? They gave in, all
of them.

And they look at me with the utmost gratitude. They are like
those who had all along presumed themselves free only to realize
slowly, yet violently their true predicament. And I give them a
taste. Where the mind moves toward embrace, toward thorough
engagement—the only bliss for some of us this stay provides. But oh
what a bliss! And I too, despite everything am not without gratitude.

*Chromaticity today my little lambs. Who can explain the Four-Color
Map Theorem?*

*Admit it, Bernadette, you've never seen such beautiful shapes. She bisects
the night, places the stars into their quadrants. Dispels from the earth the
anvils and weevils and fish and the weeping floor of the world. The dogs—
banished. Divide right, bisect, left, forward march, so they are only barking
heads. Nothing to fear. Remote, elongated parallelograms. The world, the
known world, predicted, color-keyed: friendly maps, smiling guides, nothing to
fear now.*

In that house like a crypt, strange epiphanies, grace notes, from
time to time. The paper keyboard I made to maniacally play Bach
night and day. Bach is defiance: pure joy. Reverie. Still it is a macabre
scene, mute player on a deaf piano. A madsong, a thumping, a call for

help, under the electric light bulb. My mother listening to my silent concert. As she secretly puts away money in hopes of buying me *a real piano one day*. She thought if the piano sang, then I might too. In that house like a crypt.

In that house the mistress insists that the slave keep her child confined to a box. Too much trouble otherwise. All that crawling and what not. When he is two years old he has never walked. He dies in that cardboard box. The little paralyzed limbs.

Some came exuberantly to crack the code. To nail the sucker down. To master the mysteries. To discover the New World, as if it awaited them, theirs for the asking. Others, came with trepidation, with a nearly religious, devotional sense of the unknown. With trepidation and fear. The fear is what I found most delicious, most irresistible, when they were at their most vulnerable, blurry. There now, steady, steady. Hold on to it now. See it through now. Try this. Consider this then. Like hoops of steel. Oh that five hours a week with those dreaming boys. A classroom of precision and discipline. A classroom of outrageous desire. A classroom of awe. They came to stare at the great opaque indifference of the numeral. And there they began to see the face of God.

Each year I'd scrutinize the new crop, looking for candidates and biding my time. Observing the feverish, swollen lower lips, itching to be kissed—these dreamy children—their naïveté, their perfect surrender. That explosive, barely tapped sexual energy that might be capable of almost anything, and when the right candidate appeared— then *anything, anything*. Give him then a little taste of it. Just a little. Once the candidate was isolated. A small, but distinct, a piquant taste. Slip him a glimmering, translucent number—off in the distance. Taken out of ordinary time and space, I would whisper sweetly, *Feel, how you are not among us anymore*. It would take one touch, one nudge. But when would our candidate show his face? When would that day come? I had waited already so long.

And while I was waiting, it is absurd, the whole thing, while I was waiting, I trained. I made myself strong. It is preposterous really

to think of it. Birdbones lifted weights. Used machines. Worked hard
to acquire a body that might—hands that might—thighs. Our elective mute learned to *enunciate*—took *elocution lessons*—recited poetry,
out loud—why? Because silence would no longer do, because mildness
had to be banished, because modesty and humiliation—it exhausts
me now even to think back on. There was more than enough to do in
those years, oh yes; God knows, no one was in more need of rehabilitation than I. And such grim toil! Always more work. The hair was
the first thing to go. The red tufts cropped close. I studied hundreds
of pornographic films. For what did I know of any of this? They were
hilarious. For the execution of my plans, I would need to simulate
lust, emulate *engagement*. For hours I practiced the various looks of interest, of pleasure, of abandon in the mirror. What a sad scene this is.
Opening my mouth just so. Whispering. Practicing breathlessness.
Learning to shudder. Thus began my period of monstrous obedience.

Only connect. As Beatrice likes to say.

I am struck still when I think of it, by the lovely innocence of
those sexual revelers. The unabashed inhibition of those who are
lucky enough to simply enter freely the luxury of its full glory. I am
struck by the wholesomeness of it. The giddiness. The girl in cowboy
hat and holster. The man in the maid's outfit. The light bondage and
blindfolds—the tickling. The soft, luscious, gooey journey the self
sets out on. The cuddling, the coddling. All the breathing and shrieking of that sweet annihilation. That small taste of oblivion as they
imagine being pleasured by the minions, or suspended from the ceiling, a kind of heaven. Always sure they'd return unscathed from their
explorations, their glitzy dangers. They weren't playing for keeps.
Certainly not. Just a moment of relief.

The novitiate shall possess a somewhat cold and glittering acceptance of all the events to come—though he can scarcely know what
they might be. A fearlessness at the cliff. The novitiate shall be simultaneously young and old, innocent and wise. He shall arrive carrying
an abacus, a beaker of pure clear water, a roll of plastic wrap, this passionate child-man. It will take one look, one touch for the descent to
be acknowledged. He will be a child of privilege and resignation.
Flamboyant, reckless, but not outwardly so. Luxurious, lush, a sensualist, but not outwardly so. Exacting, creative, decadent. Placing the

family jewels in his condom for texture. Someone who at some point has been estranged from his truer self, his less acceptable self—and who longs to be reunited with that darker, more authentic aspect—though he does not have a clue about that. It will need to be reawakened in him. The mother of the novitiate had seen it early, and redirected it, and the child grew up simultaneously cheerful and bereft.

As a result the novitiate, having been purposefully disassociated from this other self, will feel a strange inexplicable sadness and rage, as he is never entirely *at home*, as they say. Yet he has, because of his gentle breeding and advantage, tempered these dark feelings, always exercising a modicum of care and tact. Nevertheless, they creep up on him—and sometimes he thinks he can remember or recognize something there. But what? He is like someone who cannot decipher his own handwriting any longer.

And as I visualized more and more precisely my novitiate, my desire as well, heightened, became more and more specific. A new confidence was moving in born of resolve, a kind of sexual bravada. *Imagine!* Another dimension to my intelligence. A new ferocity, a clarity never experienced before and never to be experienced again. But it existed here for one moment once. No one could dispute that. No one could take that away. It became a hovering thing—nearby, just outside of my reach. I was a cat in the austere stillness right before the calculated and perfectly executed pounce.

She ambles in and I freeze her in my dilated eye. What's that? She carries a dead child in a box. Enough already.

For an extended moment they wanted me to curtail for them the anguish of their freedom. Wanted me to put them in some exquisite, torturous box. They who had every hope, every possibility, every talent, almost every talent, every everything, wanted a little less of it for a while, the burden was too great; and it is to my mind how I got away with as much as I did. They had the luxury, the most interesting ones at any rate, to be comfortable, grateful even, some would even say excited by my strictures. A dark relaxed laughter and a puerile cynicism played out against a dramatic, impressive backdrop that was their future of extraordinary brightness and safety. They could well afford to endanger themselves a little, put themselves in some small jeopardy for a while. My bleary, wayward patriarchs with their blood-less formulations. *Your meditations on zero leave me cold. Your cute musings on the empty set. Your graceless, humorless approaches. Self-loathing becomes you. Prove to me if you can that you belong in this class.*

Mr. Starr. A star indeed! You insult us all with your simple-minded ni-hilism. Mr. Starr stay tethered to the desk until you come up with a plausible scenario for this problem. Oh and he did, oh and they did. Often enough. When pressed. My pretty empty-headed ones. When pressed.

And Mr. Wynn. What about you Mr. Wynn? A rather unremarkable performance I must say. Your bland mathematics. Show some flair would you my boy? Remember, Mr. Wynn, it don't mean a thing if it ain't got that swing.

I observed my chicks ever so closely over the years; they were re-markably alike, and after a while I understood what actually might be possible. In the years of teaching I honed my skills. Hatched all sorts of plans. Was anything ever so premeditated? I think not. For a while I was their age and in the beginning for a brief time I was even younger than they. But while I got older, they never aged, each year, a fresh crop. A bizarre and static parade. I think of Fergus—eternally my boys remain his last, his permanent age.

In the interval he changes from brother to man, then to soldier boy, bye-bye. The child cries. The mother tinted sepia like a real memory waves a pretty scalloped handkerchief as if this were another war. It's the old movie version of herself and in it she waves the perfect square of grief and cries.

Don't go.

Is that thunder?

Don't cry.

If you could have protected someone, you'd have picked him okay, in the night-tinted sepia like a memory, so safe. But not here, not here, and no one suddenly we know or recognize.

It's a memory so when the child cries out in the dark in the trees, someone certainly will be within the reach of her voice won't they?

Oblivious the university students change out of their polo clothes, shower and prepare for the evening meal. Put down their racquets. Powdered. Cologned.

                              * * *

My buffed, my smooth-tailed, my hand-picked, my ever-eager
A#1 over-achievers in your haughty high hats. You impress an easily
impressed non-mathematical academy, easily. You confuse minor success with genuine achievement and are satisfied with it. You enjoy
rewards you do not merit. You seldom acknowledge failure. The per-
petuation of the mystery and difficulty of your pursuit, shrouded in
secrets and misperceptions have made you vain, arrogant, out of control. The indifference of the community at large has made you bitter
and catty and desperate. Tedious. You possess a bookish, imperfect intelligence. I am here to help you see what a woefully small distance
you have gone, what an unimaginably far distance there is to go. I
come here like an Olympian holding an excellent torch, and in the
other hand a fist of black streamers to signify this demanding, relentless blood sport. All that is required—the grave, the playful—all that
is necessary. License and discipline. Rigor and recklessness. Accompany me there.

   Or not.

To expose the trendiness of your thought patterns, your reliance
on gimmick, your sloth, yes, your sloth, my little Protestants. No
honest work ethic left as far as I can tell. You with your breeding and
hymns, your family fortunes, your Buffys and Binkys and Bims. So
that you might look like this: ragged sweater, canvas shoes, glasses.
Your sandy hair, your kindnesses. You are not without your kindnesses. I remember. My baby patriarchs.

   My shooting and losing stars.

Let us say that I am in a room full of books that collectively code
a computer program capable of the Turing Test—in the Chinese language. We know that the running of any program is equivalent to
opening a book, reading what is written, remembering some of what
is written, and going from one book to another. Suppose that someone passes under the door a piece of paper with Chinese writing on it.
Now I know no Chinese, so to me the writing is just meaningless
scratch marks on paper. However, if we believe the strong A1 propo-
nents, then simply by following the instructions in the books I can

make marks on another piece of paper—meaningless marks to me—
which will be correctly realized as coherent Chinese by the Chinese-
speaking humans outside the door. In fact a conversation in Chinese
can be conducted by this method, and the Chinese-speaking people
will believe that there is a Chinese speaker inside the room. Therefore, have I not passed the Chinese-speaking Turing Test? If the Turing Test were a valid test of intelligence, we would have to conclude
that I understand Chinese—which as I have told you I do not. Without taking the pencil from the paper please articulate in full the flaws
in my argument.

My warmth, my attention, my generosity in the days I allowed
them a glimpse of it, my soft, fuzzy side, only suggested to them
what else I might provide. It was crucial to keeping them in line,
tethered to me, humble, exquisitely desperate. My subliminal vocabulary pressed this issue into being. The text that existed just under
the surface. Their progress relied on it. The places one had to go in order to thrive. The places I pushed them, at first gently. *Good. Steady
now. Keep going.* They were losing the memory of how easily once they
had been satisfied.

Oh to turn my elaborate, delicate, well-considered and highly intelligent acts into a series of pornographic gestures. Subtle, complex
expression reduced to industrial sexual terms. Behavior patterns all
archetypal. A bagful of psychobabble. My exalted purpose debased.
They do not know. To have changed my monstrous pain into something comprehensible for themselves. The suffering of *the victims. The
victims,* as you like to call them. If you insist on calling it suffering.
But they suffered only a moment. There are only several ways to take
the breath away. These boys had come willingly to my wormy mausoleum, fascinated with my night. Were they not in love with my
blood culture? My surges. My elaborately charged universe? And had
they not courted disaster?

I look up from his extraordinary paper. *What is this blizzard you
ask for, young man?* A veil of white.
Alexander Ashmeade, born guilty, like all of us, alas.

* * *

They are there in the trees in the early evening turning dark and the brother is saying good-bye to his friends. He is about to leave, about to go at the height of the action, to the stupid unpopular war. A volunteer of all things, in perverse, reverse fashion. As if to spite them. But how can you stop him? What can you do to make him stay? Stay. Don't go. You're only eight years old and it's already far too late. Don't—the only one she ever loved . . .

If there were a way to keep him. Please him.

Beloved . . . go, don't go, don't. But no sound comes out.

He felt it was the one thing he had somehow gotten right. In a single decision he was finally making some sense to himself. Indisputable gauge of valor and courage. Manhood and maturity. Flaunt it: the poor, dumb pride. Ostentatious show of virility and purpose. Like Father, spending money he did not have to impress women he did not love, my brother dreaming of some permanent, irrefutable glory, some firmament he might finally walk on, honored and deserving, some starry acceptance.

Helicopter, terrible wind, impossible swamp and grass. Fast camaraderies in the mud of those who risk everything. The possibility of a sudden obliterating death giving everything its delirious spin. How sorely they are in need of repair. But they are men and poor, contingent, without the ordinary dignities or respect, and hurt by it.

And so I watched, helpless, as I always was back then, watched my beloved brother in those long weeks of preparation move toward that other place. I never pleaded, never begged him not to go. I feared insulting him. I feared being the one to snatch away, or at the very least, to belittle his one remaining shred of dream. Coward, that I am, and have always been.

He's standing with his friends, this pathetic fraternity. In the riotous, raw night. The boys slapping each other on the back, passing out beers, what the fuck—Hey where's Jane?

In the clubhouse in the trees high up, Jimi Hendrix. Are you experienced? The hero-brother asking—his rhetorical, drugged numb rage.

In the bannered, meaningless, jingo-jargon of the poor, who always go. Why must it always come to this? The lower-class, defeated, Irish, and the solution that is always alcohol and the war.

In the star-spangled night. O voluptuous dark. Seedy on black velvet. Doomed flaring horses carefully painted by number, above the couch, and the Virgin, and Elvis.

All this is played out in a woman's head, yep, that's you, Bernadette, who has time on her hands. Time to burn.

In your pretty cerebellum. You're pretty on the inside.

It's a memory so you can keep it as something in a locket if you like: little and perfect and finished and carry it around, glittery fetish, press it up to her fiendish and bitter breast.

But what could I have said to him? What can one ever say to another? Advise another? What do we presume in such a role? The gap between those, even between those who love each other, who consider themselves to be close, is unimaginably wide. We are separate, alone, outside each other's grasp.

If she could have protected someone.

could (some person x: have − protected (she, x)) $\Rightarrow$

In the lightning flash-look: a bitter, young man, a joint in his mouth on the way to the war. Don't go. You'll die. If you could only stop this. Console him about Janie or any of it. The factory, the sadness. Stop this. You'll die, you say to him, but no sound comes out. If you could let him know what you know—but you can't stop it—you can't do anything to stop it—and you know that it is—it must be—it's your fault. You can't make him stay. He is going to die. Because there is nothing you can do.

But boys will be boys will be boys will be boys will be boys will be boys. No one is listening.

Paint the planes of his face green and gray and brown and beige. Camouflage him. Keep him safe.

But you can't keep him. Help him now out of his gray factory dressing gown. And you in a tangled flowered dress. Take it off.

I'd like to tell you about a small, silent auction, Beatrice. A minor prostitution ring. Dreadful, dreadful. No maybe not yet. *Hey,* she whispers, *it's okay.*

* * *

Through the skylight the heaven's fraud. *If you lie on your back.*
You can see . . . Is that Betelgeuse? Paint the heavens black and red and blue
lit up. You can divide the night into fractions, divisible light, while he weeps
and sighs. There the archer, the bow-legged Cassiopeia, yes, that's Betelgeuse.

A woman weeping—that's their mother.

From where has my mother summoned the strength and focus for
the speech she is about to make? It rises in her with such clarity and
force that even she is surprised—she's hard to recognize—even to
herself. She comes center stage for once. *Listen:*

It was because of me that you lived at all, she hisses. She had saved
him in the treacherous, pneumatic night. She had nursed him back
month after month. *Your father had left you for dead.* The scarred lungs.
The fear. The endless night and Saint Jude. *I did not save you, did not*
save your life for this. Not for this. And she is crying and pleading with
him, and then she takes him by the scruff of the neck and whispers
into his ear, *Do you understand what I am saying? Not for this.*

And Father entering the room swats her away. *Colleen!* He is thick
already with bravado and bravery and hero music. Jesus. Soldier son.
He puts his enormous arm on the arm of my brother, remembering
Korea—the best years of his life.

The war's on and he hears the dark hero music. Isn't that just night
breaking apart again? Nope. It's music of friend and brotherhood and doomed
music of country. Hup, two, three, four. Hup, two, three, four.

A woman weeping. Yeah—that's their mother all right.

The Annunciades arrive (dear God, not again) dragging their Jesus and Mary, their piety, their holy of holies, cupping their hell
word: *genius.* Rage of the silent child.

And my father bewildered, and my mother ashamed, and Fergus
sitting silent in the corner staring.

These late solicitations. Reminders to me that even then I was
condemned. Grim child—most often at the action's periphery in this
house; why am I forced center stage?

Father Donnelly leads the procession this time. They have stolen
someone else's armor—numbers—her numbers—and are reciting out
loud the unlikely sums to my parents. Father Donnelly most bitterly.

The intelligence quotient. He's incredulous again. *Why her?* When it was all he had ever loved?

And with the next recitation he is on his knees, nearly weeping in adoration. *Why the child?*

Thou shall not worship false gods, idiot. His stupid, ludicrous life. He's saying, *She's way beyond us,* he's whispering, spitting, *I can't instruct her any longer,* and Fergus is laughing maniacally and looking like he might kick the father down there on the floor. *Genius.*

And my mother looks away as if my genitals were exposed, as if I were performing some throaty sex act before them all. She is afraid and ashamed.

And the sisters nod, *Immodest waif, who flaunts God's gifts, who refuses the ordinary life. She's in need of humility. The devil's in her.* Next they'll say *exorcism.*

And my mother leaves the room as if this is just one more bit of bad news. *Taking a perfectly ordinary child and turning her into a freak.* She's heard enough.

He sings, "In-A-Gadda-Da-Vida," something senseless, made more so by repetition and his slurred—

In-A-Gadda-Da-Vida, Baby—Don't you know that I love you?

Behold a child suffused with light—the small genius of her being.

If she could make Janie appear. P (Jane) *It's a memory after all, and she'd like to, she's a magician after all, but she can't and he's getting drunker and drunker and it looks like she's not going to come and I shout, Janie across the decades. Crazy Janie. He's waiting for his sweetheart to come and say good-bye. And she'll come, sure. Doubtless. No doubt.*

P (will (come (Janie)) = 1

Attention. Then, forward, march. Discipline of the ages. Attention! P (will (come (Janie)) | wait − for (I) her) = 1

A woman weeping.

My mother prays to the white ceramic Virgin imploring, *For we implore thee, speak to me,* and the little mute girl watches from an unlit corner.

Speak back to me, beautiful mother of consolation, she prays into the light. The serenity.

Silent, shadowy daughter, in the door jamb, in the sad backyard, or kneeling next to the leaky sink.

Speak to me, my mother implores. Still staring at the Virgin. *Bernadette, please speak to me.*

And the little girl writes $dy/dk = ky$ and hands the glowing slip of paper to her mother—

Who crumples it. *Speak to me.*

While my brother pretended to despise my father, it was in part my father's love he was trying to gain when he enlisted for the war. And I am appalled by it still: what one man will do to win another. The transparency of the love of men for each other is something that was readily obvious to me, even back then. Their perverse pacts, their obscenities, their competitiveness, their sparring, the protection of their property, their borders, their sniffing and snorting and chortling at each other. They were in the end, the only ones that really mattered to one another. Women were inconsequential. Elizabeth, I wish you were here.

Low bellowing would issue from the back of the house while mother was at work. Fergus berating my father about the other women, I suppose. Setting himself up as the watchdog, small morality squad, judge. It did not, to my mind, seem to come out of any real concern or allegiance to my mother. I believe Fergus wanted to keep Father in line so that he might have someone—he so desperately wanted someone to look up to.

Mind your own business. Do as I say, not as I do. Better yourself. Tired clichés of the afternoon. And Fergus decides to go to the war. Who could top that? The proud, dissolute father. And they are somehow reconciled over it. So much stupidity and recklessness and bravery.

He had bathed him in gin to get his fever down. A sweltering Labor Day weekend. Every doctor away. My father pouring bottle after bottle into a tin basin. *Live!*

Three pounds. He had fit in his palm. *Live, Goddamnit, live.*

The men in stars and stripes come. Bad news then?

* * *

Who shall love the bones of the dead? Who shall care for the bones of the hanged slaves? The women tend them. Bringing them out in sunshine and indoors in the rain. And when they disappear one day the children say the bones of the hanged are castor oil.

The clothes of the dead, wrongly accused, hang in every tree. The colored people won't touch them—*run!*

Land of the free. Home of the brave. Give me a break.

But he is focused for the first time on something far off. He draws a figure on a piece of paper and attaches it to the refrigerator—an emblem—I know not of what, a goal or a target, only he and my father seem to comprehend the significance of. Their co-conspiratorial laugh. The rage of the father flowering, mushrooming in the life of the son. The son carrying the drugged, black bloom of the tyrant to war. The failed men and the price they paid. They hear the hero music.

And the mother is shouting now *don't go* but it's as if no sound is coming out. They are laughing and slapping each other on the back over her voiceless objections. But I hear her; it is only they who are deaf. Where does she gather the courage suddenly to stand up to them? My mother who never said anything to anyone. Never had she spoken out of turn, or disagreed with my father. *Stay.* From what hat does she pull this strange magic?

Fergus, I beg thee, Fergus, I implore thee. Look to the mother! And she is calling up all the nice things she can remember: the turtles, the Fourth of July in Boston, the jugglers on the pier, fishing. As one about to be assaulted by a rapist, with little time left, she tries to appear human, with real feelings, real memories, so as to divert him from his monstrous deed.

And now she recounts his infancy once again. Damaged, skinny, injured creature, she made him well. Night after night after night—intensive care, fear, debt, sacrifice. Hole in his heart. I gave you everything. I saved your life.

Pity them: this fractured, laughable pietà. Mother and son. Fissured, breaking, broken.

But the men are chattering. *A patriot!* they say. And *honor* they say, and *homeland.*

*I don't give two hoots about this country, not two hoots, and neither do
you! You know perfectly well it's true.*

Colleen, they mock. *Colleen,* they say. *Why, we're surprised to hear you
say such a thing!*

The brutal cutting off of her.

Honor thy mother, Fergus. Have you forgotten?

What did women know of war or what might send a man there?
What could she possibly know of those shining, studded moments—
buddies arm in arm, the testosterone high, and the thrill of the end?

Woman, you are to be seen and not heard.

(She was a looker once. I'm not kidding you. With incredible
hooters. And she loved getting it in the ass.)

Yeah, right, Torpedo Man.

She is a work horse now. She has no voice. She has no say. Her
breasts sag. Gray mare of morning, you rise at five. Bear your burdens
in silence. She feeds them. Loves them. Guards their lives. Why?

*I'll protect you. I'll keep you safe, Little Beanie. From the sharks and
the dark. The snakes. All spiders. Don't be silly now, my goose. And not to
worry about me, my Birdie, nothing will happen to this lucky duck. I promise,
promise.*

Promise me.

I promise.

There will be a name for it finally. It will be called dyslexia, but
there is no name for it yet. He is smart, he is almost too smart, but he
fails almost everything in school, and he's a *behavior problem* too.

Something is reversed in his brain. His is a genuine intelligence—
but it can't find paper and that's all anyone seems to care about, it's
got no way out. He'll find no solace in the alphabet or numbers.
Everything's a jumble. A cacophony of symbols and signals.

There's a priest, oh yes, Father Peter, who has agreed to do reme-
dial work with him if he'd like. And hour after hour they sit at the
Formica table sounding out the world phonetically. Like a prayer.
And the angry little boy furiously tries to carve his initials or SOS or
something—slamming the books to the floor—He'll never get it
right. He's never going to get it right.

* * *

He sings "In-A-Gadda-Da-Vida," something senseless, made more so by repetition and his slurred—

Anyone who hurts anyone hurts himself—something senseless made more so, made more so . . .

In the clubhouse in the trees up high. Psychedelic posters on the wall. Jimi Hendrix and his swirling sunglasses—the purple and orange and acid green sky, paint it nine. And the music. Are you experienced? the hero brother asking— rhetorical, drugged, numb rage.

In the lightning flash, look: a bitter young man, a joint in his mouth on his way to the war.

Don't go.

He licks the hem of her dress like a wound.

Bernadette! he cries over the years, *Bernadette! I never meant to hurt you. I never meant—*

Fergus, rest.

After my brother's untimely, violent demise in an absurd cause, Mother entered the ancient fathomless grief one reads about but rarely sees. Nothing could console her and it gave our small, claustrophobic world a stunningly black aspect. Mother, a creature now of monstrous stature, utterly perfected. She rips her garments, she pulls out her hair, she shrieks and rages, but she never weeps. Our lives were ice, stone, bitter wine, bread we could not eat. I am mute. I am frightened of her—and of everything.

She wails. Tears her hair. Beats her breast. God had turned his back on her. She had given him nothing but devotion and he had forsaken her. She had loved him selflessly since she was a child in Ireland.

We have been faithful to you O Lord and you have broken us in the place of jackals.

It is into this place, this fanged, forsaken cave that Minnie Grace, intrepid and on tiptoe walks in with coffee cake. She massages my mother's shoulders and tells us a story, distracting us for a moment from the dead Fergus who is everywhere. We sit in our mortal misery, listening. My father in the shadows drinking beer after beer, singing the sad songs to his son. In this place of skulls and extinguished things.

Love is forbidden. Happiness from now on is forever forbidden here. Kindness. Still Minnie Grace enters shining her love light, opening windows, cutting cake into perfect pieces. *How about a fresh pot of coffee?* My father, constricted, diminished, trudges out of the room hauling his wretched universe. I can hear him still shouting at giants, cursing them, throwing things so small and insignificant that they remain completely unaware of his presence. Poor fool. Later on he'll write letters to the editor. To the mayor. To the president.

How the room regroups around the father's leave-taking. The two women knit in closer and I too, and we are gathered in a kind of half circle and Minnie Grace whispers: *Come with me, dear Colleen, dear Bernadette, to Elizabeth.* And for a moment I lose the story in the simple feminine naming of things. Minnie Grace smiles and stares far off. Look how she is inventing our salvation:

It is in Elizabeth, New Jersey, of all places, where the statue of the Virgin in an enclave of roses has been seen of late to be weeping. *Glistening tears,* Minnie Grace whispers, *run down her alabaster cheek. And they say her robe is glowing* casting the grotto into a blue perfection. Miracle of miracles. *We must go!* She takes my mother's hand.

Minnie Grace squeezes my mother's hand, this hopeful, loyal little woman, but my mother just smirks and shakes her head. She is steely, unequivocal as she was once and only once before—the day she begged, implored Fergus not to go—no sound coming out. *No.*

My mother is shaking her head and mouthing her unbearable no. She is battered by this last defection. Destroyed by her lack of belief—the one thing she ever possessed—and the void that remains is larger even than the space Fergus has made. *Why have you forsaken me?*

She renounces everything in blasphemy. I sit in silence in the corner moving away. I despise her for giving up now. She looks up at her friend as if she's been bludgeoned. *But Minnie Grace I can no longer believe.* She stands in the wreckage of roses and creeds and makes her way down the dark hall. Even Minnie Grace this time cannot change the room's tenor. I sit with her speechless among the ruins until she finally asks for a few things she might bring along to the blessed site. She will in all the years still left, carry the sacred torch for our family, with its double flame of sacrifice and forgiveness. She will even come to visit me here. Says even I shall be forgiven. She contacts the monsignor on my behalf.

Back then, I collect the things she asks for. I even find a work shirt of Fergus's for Minnie Grace to bring to the Blessed Virgin, with her glistening, possibly glycerin tears. *We will shut our eyes tight and we will open our eyes and she will be weeping her most precious tears and she shall purify our lives. And the night will be lit from within as if the earth is glowing.*

This is our best hope then. Minnie Grace and a suburban ceramic virgin. Minnie Grace, alone, kneeling at its petite feet. Forgive me. I do not mean to mock her. She was the closest any of us ever got to a genuine friend.

She takes our things to the sacred site to be blessed. She sets out alone. Pray for her. She sets out alone without Colleen, feeling her friend moving in exactly the opposite direction away. Pray.

And I am left again in the dark parlor to bang out fugues on the cardboard keyboard I have fashioned—the only beauty left in this world. Mute, shunned. If there is a God he is in these notes.

And I am left again in the kitchen to make Father his dinner of potatoes and trash fish—of frogs and snails and puppy dog tails. Mother having called a moratorium on all the things of this world. She lies sequestered now in the back room. She'll miss three months of work. And inexplicable stomach pains will keep me home from school. Everything separates us, and to try to compensate, Father for this brief time works several jobs and I out of boredom or sadness or something begin preparing the evening meal each night for him. I watch my father devour his catch. *Eat up now, Birdbones, Olive Oyl. Come on, honey.* I purse my lips. I shake my head. No.

So much darkness has collected. I wonder how we will ever survive. A silent film in which our sorrows are always multiplying—a river blackened by more and more fish. I invent a melancholy soundtrack to play.

There is an enormous jigsaw puzzle begun on the cardtable that has sat in the months since Fergus's death, unfinished. Where are the clues here? The interlocking edges in this sadistic jigsaw? Key pieces deliberately discarded by some practical joker, so that the picture whole is always outside our grasp? My father sighing picks a fish bone from his teeth. I walk the narrow halls dead but unascended, starving, anorexic, lugging my original sin . . . through this useless purgatorio. I carry my mother a loaf, a fish, a jug of wine, the special kind she likes with a basket around it, and leave it at the mouth of her grotto, her blue enclave each night, where I hear her quietly weeping.

I am placed for a small fee which my father will collect, wherever we go, at county fairs, at local radio shows, at libraries—*don't tell your mother*—while my brother looks on thinking, thinking what? I am placed on soap boxes to solve problems of mathematics in my head, recite Latin, spew off world capitals. He's thinking I must enjoy the attention. Strangers gawk, amazed by the depth and breadth of my knowledge—*just a child!* My brother regards me sadly. Dunce's hat. Can't sit still. Dunce's stool. And I am placed on some garish, unwanted throne. I am cheered by the goons who have come to cluck and drool, and he looks on from his dark classroom corner, still, where he stands, even now, failing.

I feel you. I feel you falling, Fergus. From the trees. From our Fall River. I feel you. From our parent's defeated mausoleum. You say you can't breathe, surrounded by gray like this. You say you can't live like this anymore. How can we live? How can we live like this? Dear brother, pass quickly through this station of resignation and pain. Wronged, hurt, miserable on your factory floor—let's rush the rest of these wretched events.

Fingering the child like a hollow rosary or code—help! Lamb of God, who takes away the sins of the world. Have mercy on us. Lamb of God who takes away the sins of the world—look to the mother: A milky lass. Swinging on a blue swing toward paradise. Chestnut brown hair, green sparkly eyes, white, white skin. Playful, voluptuous—

Singing.

*Just tip, just tip me—*And what I'd like to know, Lamb of God, is why whenever you had the choice, you chose against us?

She pumped with her legs high, high up to the sky, singing little made-up songs. She ran there through a field of tangled grass and wildflowers. Moss. Lambs. Running down the cobblestones, fetching her father in the pub. Carrying with him a pail of water, home. Singing together a little drinking song. A weeping song.

Who's there? Who dares disturb this torpor? This oddly comfortable misery? Midnight or later. The inmates earnest at their play. Beatrice, dear optimist, is that you? Come to rescue? No. Then who? Who interrupts this inhuman sleep banished of everything recognizable: rest, peace—bereft of dreams. And now who comes with small nagging voices, with requests, with troubling news once more? I can't take this.

It is the three kings as I like to call them, bearing as they do their dubious gifts: *the child is a genius, the child, the child*—with their unwanted, uncalled-for epiphanies. Oh Jesus, not again.

Having *tested way off the charts. Intelligence quotients.* This schooling *woefully inadequate.* And I am banging on my paper keyboard and thinking *just shut up.* They look around. That such a mind could have sprung up in such, well, modest circumstances, they are taking notes, unpromising—underprivileged even surroundings, *oh my.* And my parents incredulous, just stare. *We always knew she was smart.*

You don't seem to understand, Mr. and Mrs. O'Brien. No you don't seem to understand.

And I am caught. Identified. Separated forever from them. And everyone. It's official. Forever.

Genius. Prodigy. The savior in this shabby manger. Long awaited. The kings stare at me jealously, *Why you? Why you?*

Yes, my father says, *there must be some mistake. She doesn't even speak.*

I am a thorn in everyone's side. Will not speak. And now genius. Full of spite. Speechless. What next?

She is only nine, my mother pipes up. *She's only nine.*

Not spoken since her brother left for the service. This time we are still waiting for him to die.

The following day, the day after the visitation, Sister Perpetua with her holy of holies summons me to her antechamber. The wooden Jesus seems to splinter and bleed in my presence. I offend him.

We are equal in the eyes of the Lord, she says. *Practice humility, my child. Now go back to your classroom and we'll talk no more of it.*

* * *

She wanders into my room late at night. While I am sitting with a French book. She brushes the hair from my face, takes my papers away. *You have chosen to be alone. Don't choose that, honey.*

And what have you chosen? I think.

I didn't know I was choosing it. I thought marriage would be something different. I thought children would be something else. Her voice veers off— *Company . . .*

We are exiles in this sinking boat. Drowning. Then drowned. Exiles—church on fire. Burning. Then burned.

We had been one once. Long ago. In the waters of her body. We were happy there. Were we not? I insist we must have been. One in the same. Where we could still be our dreamings selves—the selves that loved metaphor, dreamt, imagined each other into blissful existence. Peace. Perfection. No harm. United in hope. Only to be orphaned at birth. And orphaned again by speech. And then when the teachers came in their ghastly single file . . .

The girls? Where were the girls? I rarely saw a girl amble into my department. That exclusive, condescending, superior Mickey Mouse Club. It was as it always has been. The girls, ridiculed, maimed, chewed up and discarded went to gentler majors: psychology or literature. And who could blame them?

I listen to Elizabeth, my one friend, on her one subject. It is my entertainment in the years I am at Harvard.

She is working on a book called *Against a Feminine Masochism.*

Whatever pertains to sexuality including sexual desire and fantasy will have to be understood in relation to the larger situation of subordination.

It was men, according to Elizabeth, men all along who had a way of keeping women unsatisfied, wanting all the time. Her hypothesis being women had deep intimations of ecstasy and that was what kept them lapping after men. Those women panting and preening for just a little taste of it. *The fools.* To have been content all that time with only moments. To continually buy into the possibility, the promise but not the delivery. It took prison to expose the truth: women satisfied other women. In every way. Men's best-kept secret. Of course it was. I introduced this theory of Elizabeth's to Connie, and she was only too happy to test it out on every new young thing to come in the door.

A woman's passion is supposed to serve male privilege, not challenge it. As Sandra Lee Bartky has noted, "Those who claim that any woman can reprogram her consciousness if only she is sufficiently determined hold a shallow view of the nature of patriarchal oppression. Anything done can be undone, it is implied; nothing has been permanently damaged, nothing irretrievably lost . . ."

It is always the case with power and the stronger over the weaker, so it has always been and ever shall be, world without end. And when I see you lumbering toward me, confident, enormous, down this long aisle, and you are saying *Professor O'Brien*, I realize despite your sex, despite your size, that I now somehow am the one here in the position of power. You give me that now.

It will be pretty, what we make together, I promise. He is showing me the equation. But my mind drifts . . .

Even though you lead with your pelvis and carry a glowing beer, the world yours to move through, now as you walk down this long hall to our rented room—It will be pretty. Trust me on this. And I shall somehow retain the power. I am your teacher, after all, even here. In this tender bed. My male colleagues like to pretend that the hierarchy dissolves in such situations, needing as they do, to believe in their natural desirability—the old fools—in order to feel divorced from their very real abuses—the cowards. Not me. I do not flinch from the responsibility of it. Even here I maintain my lofty position and am willing to take full advantage. And nearing thirty, there is some small beauty in me as well. The heady combination I have so patiently waited for. It will be pretty. Sing this lullaby to sleep tonight, this bitter, perfect prayer: *even though you lumber down this long aisle . . .*

And I am up in my dreamy spire. Up in my tower, at the controls, directing you, positioning you—mercy. Beg, my eggy patriarchs, for mercy, if you possibly can.

* * *

Marie Bonaparte, gentle Marie, believed that the idea of intercourse caused the girl to fear attack to the inside of her body. Only the transformation from the active-sadistic to the passive-masochistic libido can allow a woman to accept the "continual laceration of sexual intercourse."

How proud he was in his gleaming car. He would from time to time take me for rides. We would drive out to the country and it seemed far, far off—not because of the time it took, but because of the distance we crossed. We would leave the falling city for strawberries, raspberries, bees. I still recall it, brother, as one of the few moments of perfect happiness. The slant of light. The heat. The bounty of berries. Yes, I would like to recall it that way—let the record show. We ate so many, our stomachs hurt.

One picks strawberries in one's sleep forever if there is any luck at all. There is not. If there is any justice. There is not.

He trudges through the tender rows now. Searching, bent over, looking for me. Sucking on a strawberry, checking under its green cap for his little baby sister. *Baby sister! Baby sister! Bernadette. Are you there?* As the berries bleed.

The vibrancy of the sun-drenched afternoon.

Then not.

What is this sudden shift in mood, in tone, in light, everything slightly muted? How to describe the sadness, the anxiety? The resignation, where has it come from—as we make our way home.

Fruits so fragile, so easily crushed, *careful, careful,* he whispers, gently pressing one into my hand. He's too rough and it bleeds in my palm. He pops a few into his mouth. *Yum.*

Rest, Fergus, if you can. Quit saying, *Bernadette.*

Well of course to acquire one's teacher was just part of what almost all over-achievers had on their agendas. Experience has taught me: I could have had any of them, in any way I liked. They schemed as much as I did. Over the years I have heard such talk in the various hallowed halls, on the lawns, at the gym. To own one's teacher as it were, to possess her, to have her body, and therefore a considerable part of her intelligence, did it not stand to reason? Of course they are smart and *all too well aware* (my horny patriarchs) that much intelligence resides in the body. Intelligence conveyed through the cellular flesh is a genuine act of—*let us go then you and I.*

A few simple rules: Urination will not be allowed two hours before this three-hour class. I want you to be aware of your body during the time you are with me, and begin to bring those energies to bear on the work. Like an athlete refraining from sex. I have no desire by the way to dictate your sexual lives at this time. Anyone who does not want to be in this classroom should drop the course now. I have no desire to teach the disinterested—no desire to coerce.

And we're on the river bank—it's spring. Gentle river flowing—in a red flowered shift, in the newly lilting heat—moment of peace. He feeds me edible flowers. Sweets for the sweet. He shows me the pansy and in its design the genitals of a woman. *Amazing,* he smiles, a condemned man, on his way to war, still, he fingers the thing mindlessly, *amazing.*

How about a glass of milk, Stringbean?

Squirming, squeamish, suffering in the afternoon. No one will leave this classroom. No one. For any reason. *My loves, my charges.*
All my pretty ones. My cub scouts. My brownnosers.
Class, today, all through this hour, I would like you to be thinking of all the things that can be held up the ass. Enough of your tittering, Mr. Worthington, you are out of here.

My bleary, half-baked patriarchs.

On another day: *Each time I say the word radical it should be as if I am saying the word fuck* (is this not the most ludicrous yet?) *and you are to imagine making love to the most desirable creature you can imagine, and what you do with this poor caged torrent in you, without losing sight of the problem at hand, shall be with any luck, beautiful. A little sophomoric you say, Mr. Bailey? Exactly. You are sexual monsters. And fueled up, charged up. I want you to use that energy constructively, rather than always destructively.* Their amazing testosterone highs. Did I say it was beautiful? *Come on, Mr. Ashmeade.* It was. And terrifying. For me too. Glinting, gleaming, bruised, glowering, vultured. A bit over the top. Frenzied, shocked, mournful, pitiful, dying. Near dead, then dead. Freshly killed. Unresurrected. *You disappoint—can you go no further then?*

A glass bottle, half-filled with warm, soapy water, a kind of piston, inserted at the proper angle, and then withdrawn, for example.

Lady lawyers come and go, taking notes in this my reconstructed classroom. Their little incredulous faces. Petrified to crack a smile.

Today a detailed review, my friends, of lightning fields and currents. We shall consider in depth cloud fields and charges, followed by the basic elements of cloud-to-ground flashes; that is the preliminary breakdown, the stepped ladder, the attachment process, the first return stroke, the dart leader, subsequent return strokes, the continuing current and J-and-K-processes. For return strokes, we will discuss the current, the electric and magnetic fields, the frequency spectra, and the velocity and luminosity. We will discuss various aspects of cloud discharges, and the frequencies spectra for cloud and ground discharges. My bright and shining knights. My brilliant patriarchs. My little glee club!

You shall come to this class with nails cleaned and clipped, with cuticles trimmed, and I shall inspect each of you. This is so at any moment should a creamy pussy or a tight sphincter need ... well there's no need to be vulgar. There were many such bizarre requirements—all incriminating, which may have come up at the trial. But my students, my years and years of students, were strangely silent to the end. Many had gone on to levels of greatness in their fields—owed in large part to me. They did not, not one of them violate my trust. The only one who perhaps would have spoken was that simpering Payson Wynn—and well, of course, that was the one thing no one had to worry about. On the stand, when asked, they all said, no, I never touched them—and they were telling the truth. Never was I even tempted. All those years, I was waiting.

* * *

All right perhaps it did not happen quite as smoothly as I am relaying here. But surely you must get the idea. My woozy patriarchs took only a little bit of coaxing. Perhaps there were a few leaks over the years as to my methods—but not many, not many. They were the chosen; and they did not wish to share their secrets.

Did it all go this quickly? Was it this effortless? Oh perhaps not, and yet something—it was something like this. Don't quibble with me now. *It's not like I have all the time in the world.*

If I exaggerate some forgive me. I am not above trying to impress you, to keep you somehow. Not to feel useless—there's the hope. Not to feel so alone. Are you still with me? What would you like more of, less of. I am not above giving you what you want.

Class: the fisherman who tries to disentangle his lines bases his hopes of succeeding on the fact that the lines were once straight and clear to begin with.

So let us begin, my woozy patriarchs. Listen only to the sound of my voice, concentrate on the sound at the center of my voice. Dear patients—dreaming—etherized on this table—soon, soon. *Give up to one and two and three. Give in. The world starts over again here.* At this blinding, radiant abyss.

All is calm. All is bright.

As you know Apollonius began, concentrate on my voice. Apollonius began . . .

As you know Apollonius began by creating conic sections in the mathematical world. He did this by imagining the curves formed by the intersection of an abstract plane with an abstract curve. In his mind he varied the tilt of the plane and thereby produced the various special cases corresponding to circles, ellipses, parabolas, and hyperbolas. Next he used the rules of math and logic to deduce other properties of these curves. Most of what we know today was discerned by Apollonius.

Centuries pass. Along comes Kepler who wants to study the real-world problem of planetary motion. And he finds the ancient pure math of Apollonius to be exactly what he needs. After a gestation period of nearly eighteen centuries what Kepler found, with his model of the solar system, was the real-world pre-image of the pure math of Apollonius. And without Kepler no Newton. We go from conics to planets to gravitation. How lovely. How utterly lovely.

It's the solitude without the numbers that makes this untenable.

Wigner wrote, "The miracle of the appropriateness of the language of mathematics for the formulation of the laws of physics is a wonderful gift which we neither understand nor deserve. We are at such moments face to face with the paradox of the utility of beauty." *Remember that my boys: We neither understand nor deserve.*

You neither understand nor do you deserve.

I am perfectly serious here. My larks. My mopheads. My whiffen-poofs. Oh this was bound to happen, wasn't it? I expect you to reconsider for the time you are working with me your relationship to sex. I expect you to conserve that mystery elixir for me, that is, for the numbers. The numbers are the most demanding, most gratifying lover you shall ever encounter. The click of the box. I shall expect from you by next week the pledge of celibacy. This is hardly new. Consider how complacent sex has made you, how meek, how mild. My lambs. You may choose of course to work with someone else and continue your quaint dating and mating rituals. If you break your pact with me, I shall never look upon your work again. On the other hand you may find after a few weeks of readjustment a kind of excruciating depth and beauty to your work and the world. How the whole earth trembles. *See you next time. And do have a pleasant week!*

Sartre and de Beauvoir believe that masochism is a self-deceived hence futile effort to turn oneself into an object for another in order to escape the "anguish" of freedom and the frightening evanescence of consciousness.

The frightening evanescence of consciousness. Elizabeth, how much I miss you.

* * *

How Elizabeth loved the academy. Perversely? Perhaps a little. She became involved in every aspect of it. With her gleam, her wit, her explicit collaborations. Her making of more devious special arrangements to accommodate her needs. Her inventions of endless plausible pedagogic projects to make life not only bearable to her— but irresistible. Her logic at these times, her language: *Oh we must go forward with this! It will serve as a feather in our caps!* Her thousand enthusiasms. Schemes. Infectious. Her plans. Her mischief.

Friend, in the friendless night. Connie howling. It's the isolation, without the numbers, that makes this life insupportable now.

I write on the board Hardy's Apology. Let us pray: *Seriousness, depth, generality, unexpectedness, inevitability, economy.*

Two dropped the class as I recall, and so we were ten. And we worked with the concentration of the gods for a while, did we not? Were Alex and Payson still alive they would have testified to this. Yes.

My methods were slightly unorthodox, but really only slightly. After all, any high school football coach knows the sex thing. The channeling of the body's energy, the bridling of that energy for the work—using it as a kind of supercharged battery to drive their projects. Weren't we beckoned not so long ago to eat the dead God's body each Sunday? I would not make up such a thing. The little prigs remained hushed about it—because they did not want the cretins outside our elite club to get in on the act. The bastards. Only a precious few were privy to all my methods and they remained a closely guarded secret. It was a kind of smarmy, smug fraternity with one small difference: I produced miracles in these boys. Patterns of buildup and release in the eighteen- to twenty-four-year-old specimen—oh a kind of terrible beauty there.

All the years I taught. Yes, perhaps a bit unorthodox—but the results—oh, the results—no one could quibble with those. They signed the pact happily, the haves, not wanting to give away trade secrets to the masses. Competitive, small-minded, detestable lot that they were.

And I am often reminded, against my will, of my own under-graduate days. There is scarcely a way around it. In these same rooms I sat, when I was twelve, among those pimply, insatiable undergradu-ates. I outshone them, I wore them out in every way, and I was loathed for it. I negated their existence Perhaps it is there I can trace back my taste for torture? No, I think it must go further back even than that. I was young, I was silent, and I was the most extravagantly talented freak anyone had ever seen. I was mocked. But those boys were sloppy; they lacked discipline, and I was never sloppy. They were pudgy, sulky, calculating. They felt terribly sorry for each other. My existence rendered it impossible for them to bolster each other's confidence in that self-congratulatory old-boy way, to gratify one an-other's vanity with the usual back slapping and inflations. Sad mas-turbatory schoolboys. Filled with shame. And I was despised.

Lie on your back. The broken-veined sky at night. Is that lightning? And he combats the black forces of his psyche and the lightning night for her. The sky cracking open. The lit gagged grass.

The child gagging on the sadness. If she could run through, the grass—if she could only—but the dogs, the dogs who are always at the border—she's afraid. *If you lie on your back you can see all of the stars.*

The vow after that—never again to be sexual prey, except for the sake of ruse or game. The vow after that to retain the upper hand at all costs. To never again relinquish control. The vow after that to avenge, to defend, to never again be left at the mercy of—never again.

You give me five dollars you can call me *Devil's Gateway. Easy. Oyster Pearl, you easy girl.* Call me anything you like.

She is only twelve when she enters the university and sits among the eighteen-year-old boys of the freshman class. How they gawk, these goons having never really seen a girl up close, except for sisters—

And this one, this girl, *what a freak, a brain,* smarter than they'll ever be, and mute.

Whatever they do to her she doesn't speak—it's weird. The weirdo never says a word. Whatever they do.

Go ahead, just tip her over . . .

The vow after that—

And sometimes the girl would open her mouth and it would look like she was laughing but no sound came out, no sound whatsoever and tears ran down her face.

Stringbean, how about a glass of milk?

And they were awkward and frightening in their need, and she'd give it to them, what they wanted. Poor thing. Poor prop they used to ejaculate into. A kind of doll. Yes, but what a doll, a doll who had in the end all the power, the kind of power a woman has over a man, a girl has over a boy at such times. And for the honor she started charging an ever-increasing fee. For yes, indeed, they certainly owed her.

Let me tell you about a small silent auction. A minor prostitution ring, with yours truly furious and mute at the center. Come one, come all.

Welcome to the desecration of the temple! If they were going to say slut or whore or cunt or bitch they would have to pay for the privilege. Twenty-five dollars at the start. Sweet, those early prices she charged for her defamation and debasement.

Out in the open at least. At least that. Open up. I cannot bear to go into this ok? Suffice it to say.

To walk directly into one's greatest fears, greatest dreads. And by doing so dispel them. Oh right. Still I tried. But call a spade a spade. If you want to say slut then you must pay for it. Or doll. Or genius. She's on the anesthesia table. Pay.

* * *

Is that rain or just Bernadette weeping now?

This unholy resurrection. The first in a series of miseries. Abortions beginning at thirteen. The first in the abortion series. Dear God. And I am sent up here once more to watch the child-woman gleaming on the anesthesia table. Her fogged, crooked grin. She is seared by fluorescent light. Solitary—the nothing being taken from her. The scraping without sound. No room for tenderness. Surrounded by rubies. Where do the blood bags go? Where the tiny arms? Those partial miracles—unfinished. Shrieking placentas. Chronicles of nothing. Every hole sealed up. The solemn after-instructions. She's weeping— no sound coming out.

The part of me that genius had kept a child grew up in an afternoon on that long antiseptic corridor where I sat waiting, waiting, the nurses passing like gulls. They disapprove, they regard me suspiciously. No one to hold my hand. No one to tell. One expected to be exempt from the ordinary laws of nature. One felt, let's face it, above it all. Mute and still in mourning for my brother. And now grieving, strangely, for this little speck of being.

I was only trying to make some spending money—a few tuppence, sir, with those awful undergraduates—a horny, frightening lot those boys—with money to burn. Never mind that I am only thirteen. Genius, they despise me.

How is this shaping up, gentle reader? This going through the motions of my life, recounted humbly, but not felt. She narrates with a disembodied voice. Another abortion? Yes, all right. If you'd like.

I am the despised and my detachment is set in place for good now. After that hall. My objectification of all. The black umbilicus wholly severed, at last. Sad but true. Pity me not. I am secure, outside of it all—in that doctor's chamber. He takes his vacuum and butcher blade, and I float above this scene serene, appalled. Speck of life, taken from me. With a scraper. Lamentations in the hall. Small lives—good-bye one by one. In any case you are stopped once again. The infinitesimal. Save your laments. I do you a favor. We'll make a miniature grave don't worry. We'll place postage stamp sized photographs of you and your mother—the might have beens. Misbegotten ones.

My years as minuscule college student blur, and in fact much of what has occurred since my brother's death remains vague with only moments of lucidity. I have no real recollection of my meteoric rise. Harvard at twelve and graduated at fifteen. All doctoral work completed by seventeen. The only pure happiness was at the side of Jacob Perlman, who I loved, and who I believed loved me. But midway through my second year he dies, quite suddenly in the night. My comrade, my friend—between us was a perfect cadence, a lavishness—something wholly otherworldly, a kind of love or grace. His pure rain of numbers. I stood awash there in perfect bliss. There was solace there. There was hope. The world begun anew. Blessed forgetfulness—in his presence, all that had gone before seemed to vanish. Only Fergus remained from that other world, watching me—and I believe he was pleased.

After the professor's death I grew quickly into my role as dwarfed adult, surrounded by that awful swarm of needy, oversexed, crowing adolescents. The kinds of boys a school like Harvard invariably attracts. I left my parents behind to do what they did best: grow more isolated, if that's possible, rowing backwards into a setting black, alcoholic sun. The ghastly American flag hanging on the porch night and day, through all kinds of weather, a faded tatter, something shriveled, pathetic, an insult, like everything else.

And why do I despise these harmless, awkward, pained, largely desperate and pressured boys? Why do I loathe their weaknesses so? Their swollen, purplish howlings? I turn even the nicest of them into deranged, perverse creatures. This is a sinister left-handed art, Bernadette O'Brien.

First time. Second time. The little abortionist appears with his blue vial of anesthetic and vacuum. *Won't hurt a bit.* Nurses circle passively. They mark my chart.

But there are far too many times after that. Third time, fourth. I come with my false name, to cover my tracks. Still they recognize me, fear for me. They hand me birth control pills, which I discard. That quaint calendar, the beady wad. They fit me for every manner of stopper and cap. Once to *teach me something*, they insist the whole bloody ordeal be performed with local anesthesia, with *my eyes* open. Wise up. The butchers. One step from the coat hanger. The monsters. Look I am no better than they are. Grieving I am tied to a white slab. *Wide awake.* Extract the corpse.

Tubes tied one says snidely. Outside the fanatics. Right to life. With their petitions and signs. *Murderer* they shout at me. *How prescient! Soothsayers!* A sanctimonious celibate lot.

Tubes tied.

And what am I?

Hair out in fistfuls on my pillow. Hair shorn at the grave.

Other students, denied, appear more and more frequently, scratching at my office door. They do not entirely understand why they come. Hubble's Law says that the farther a galaxy is from Earth, the faster it is moving away from us. Hubble's Law. They ask for conferences. Virgins at the sacrificial altar. They offer themselves up for slaughter, wanting to give themselves over entirely to that radiant thing—Alex has made it seem necessary—that thing greater than themselves. They tremble showing me their handfuls of elusive numbers. And so their hypnotic, their well-trudged path to my door. They are voracious, greedy things. *Can't they see I am busy?* They seem to have no idea what I have already given. They take and take. Gluttons. And rumors fly, whispered in hushed tones all around me: she is dominatrix, she is madwoman—her crackpot mathematics.

Oh yes, I do feel for them with their asinine problems—their wounded egos, their performance anxieties, their paternity anxieties. Their fear of failure, their dread of success and whatever the fuck else troubled them. How was I supposed to endure this year after year? I drew them into my confidence and confiding in me, I gradually grew to loathe them. Despicable takers—taking and taking. Collecting my blood in their little blood collectors with their clever, invisible incisions. You took me for granted. You trusted me as you trust all women. You assumed, that like all women, I was there to serve you, to pleasure you, to console you, to baby you, to mother you, to buoy you—all at my own expense. Always at my expense. At our expense.

On the anesthesia table for the ninety-ninth time:

Peace please. O silent child. Most unholy night. Peace please. My mind's not right. I'm tired.

Winged hat. Woman in white. Who are you? Speaking now over the black microphone. Baffled, longing, eye that brings her back tonight. White door, winged hat. Red rib. Ruby winged—desiring coherence—just a little—

Mute makes you feel more precisely the ragged grass—like the teeth of rats—where we once lay. It's night on the barbed grass. The right road lost. Pierced by rain and you remember dogs—their sound unbearable: high, odd pitched—jawed grass you stuffed in your mouth to keep from— The scratchy haired—help. No sound comes out.

The gibbering placenta, hiding, mumbling, feverish. I do not think that he will think to look for me here. In her sixth month, sloughed off. Grotesque. Grotesque. Hiding in the teeny, tiny baby girl.

Bernadette! he calls. Bernadette!

If you're quiet now, if you don't say a word, he won't know where to look. Careful, shhh—say nothing. Sweet mute. Or put on a wig.

(See how her hair is falling out.)

We buried what were called the remains sent back in a nifty Ziploc bag—very sixties, very plastic—the kind of bag you might put a suit in. They put the pulverized dust and fractured bones into a plastic bag and tied it with a bow—stripes and glittering stars pasted, and sent along with the little gift, a man with medals and a horn. Day is done. And we drop it into the glum earth.

I am precocious, far beyond my years. Precocious like the children in books or films—little mouthpieces for their creators—but unlike those wisecracking, wry children, not dear. To be precocious and not dear. To say the wrong thing always, willingly even, yes, perhaps by choice. But I do not speak anymore by the time they're at the grave, have you forgotten? I just watch. And my hair falling out until I am bald. Good God, this is grim! Sad, luckless child staring out with a disparaging, lidless eye. In my fantasy I utter something so horrid at my brother's funeral. With considerable malice, with intent to injure.

Fergus—his precious, shattered head. His hurt wrists. Just a bit of singe and ash now. His brutish time on this earth now concluded. The bunting blackened.

His ribs all cracked.

The war—his complicated, stupid *raison d'être*. And Mother, inconsolable will not leave the grave, cursing everything: Father, brother, country, God. Here, in our ugly, defeated, water city, at the feet of my brother, she turns from everything for good now. No more weeping saints, no petitioning of the Virgin, no mass—no incense or heaven or bells. This was the betrayal by God she could not, she could never, the unforgivable—Fergus her Fergus—her only son. He could have asked for anything, He could have taken anything away from her—but not this.

There's Jane at the grave. Jane who did not come that night to say good-bye. Jane, he had the ring. Your ring. *Where were you when he needed you?* Let's bring her forward to explain.

She approaches the grave. Closer. Then close. Her freckles faded over the years. Her eyes dimmed. Negotiating through the many veils of misery and crinoline. *Jane, why? Why?*

Bernadette. She kneels down so she can look into my face. *I'm sorry. So sorry.*

If she's got an explanation, she's not saying. If she's got an alibi for that night.

Sorry. She has no idea. *Sorry.*

If I were older. If I could speak one word: *why?*

There's the mouth of someone else left on her neck. At the grave. A hickey, a love bite—*why?*

P : P (Jane)?

She squeezes my hand. I'm sorry about your brother. *I am really, really.* She weeps.

You could kill her. You could stop her, Bernadette. Where was she that night? If you were only older. But you're not yet, stupid. Dragging your pail. If you could say one word you'd tell her about the engagement ring, the dream. How much she hurt him that night. And how you could not make him stay.

* * *

She brings water, the little mute one, the little one with shorn or pulled or shaved head to the place. Bald is all you need to know. Day after day she hauls the blue pail—having read in a book of the importance of watering things after they are transplanted. She buried the ring.

And he fingers the hem of her dress in this version—like a prayer shawl, and weeps.

Hail Mary full of grace, lightning bayonets the night. In her body she swears she can feel its jagged life. Crazy Janie, darling of the night, where were you?

We enter this story at a point where there is little left for them—or for us—but to let them march on the tracks already laid down to their preappointed destinies—he to the fields of resignation and rice and she to the shiny

Lightning chair at the end of the too long hallway. Oh the perversity of it! There's no reason to go, save for what glints in him. He feels the hero seed inside. Death head. Dog star. Brute—blunt—she swears she can feel—

That's lightning. Lust to be a hero—the chance—the one chance in million. Take it, take it—it's yours. Once and only once in a lifetime.

Jane is what I am not,

Something: f (and (not (f (I)), (&J), f (Jane))),

She walks alone and the men yell *pussy*, and men yell *cunt*—or so I imagine. She races past stalled love in the streets—in alleys, against garbage cans and walls.

Cat cries, chicken bones, fish scales, egg shells, the garbage strewn—and sanitary napkins. Dogs lapping. The sound of a hundred unredeemed beer bottles. Wine and whiskey bottles. Green and gold glowing—everything dangerous. Fergus, where are you? A little plastic bag in the ground.

There are so many sharp edges here. *Walk on that,* I instruct the bald child, *go ahead,* I whisper to the little girl, whose silence in all this squalor is certainly a kind of eloquence—a kind of defiance. *Walk on this, crawl.* She nods her head yes. I remember to this day the strangeness, the cast of her look—and the way the others responded, half in horror, half in resignation, watching the weird genius child. Bleeding. Then profusely bleeding. Crawling on her hands and knees. *Because her brother is dead, because, because*—the only one she ever loved.

Fergus where are you? River of glass. River of endless pain. Where we fish.

The marriage ceremony for slaves consisted of the pair jumping over a stick. If no children were born in a year, the wife would be sold. *No! Don't go!* And if there was a debt or a mortgage due on the plantation, extra slaves could always be sold at the courthouse on New Year's Eve. The families broken. *No!*

Look at Father—a figure finally of stunning neutrality. And Mother—becoming lost, free of care, shielding her eyes in the glitter and din. Fergus shouting from some distance—but no one can hear what he says. Genius, too, is absorbed, and all human cruelty. The stupid posturing and preening of men are rendered meaningless—all those bleak heroics. They've got white goo on their noses. And even after a while, the mortified women, always apologetic in their imperfect bodies, relinquish their self-hatred to the beauty and austerity of the blue. Once we went *en famille* to the sea. Ah yes.

I am putting off here with these lonely musings; my true subject. With these veiled and melancholy but finally useless reminiscences, I fearfully side step the thing that recurs, something utterly unmentionable, something terrible, or more terrible than the rest—a thing to be avoided at all costs. Dear Christ, I am making it worse for myself—as usual—making an utter botch of it, as usual. Too hard, too macabre, even for this admittedly lurid tale. Forgive me. If this were a fiction, one would have had the good sense to stop by now. It goes, has already gone, well over the top—and to what effect? Oh if this were a fiction, and one had *options*. But oh, the grotesque of the actual. The indecencies of the real, as it unfolds. Sickening, sickening. The indecencies of life. Go ahead—for the record.

During the blackest hour—no—during the difficult uncertain then, yes, hour of greatest uncertainty, hour of waiting, their first born, their first hope, only son, only begotten son—spit it out: they come. In the dark day, a man in soldier suit, *You are only a child*—he's saying. He's saying, *Means of identification.* He's saying, *The identifica-*

tion of the body, he's yowling things. Only bones remain. *Are there injuries, means of identification, ways to tell, ways to*—I like to think that my father would have under different circumstances would have dismissed me at this point—but he is too dizzied—too off guard by the question and the scene and flanked as he is at this moment by outrageous fortune, tragedy on both sides now: his father first—long ago, and now *son, son.*

Sir, sir, excuse us, sir, could you tell us whether these fractures would be consistent with injuries your son, in his youth would have sustained . . . On the body of your son. Consistent with . . . Identification of . . . The following fractures—with the body of your son: A broken arm. A broken neck. A broken hip—*consistent, consistent. A break in the rib cage, sir, sir.* New dimensions of misery and revulsion overtake me.

My father puts his face in his hands and weeps. *Is that a yes, then, sir?* My father chokes it out sobbing now. *Never, never. Is that an affirmation. Are you answering in the affirmative?*

Only once, in all those years, despite his rage and resignation and foolishness and sorrow did I ever see my father lift a hand to anyone—only once and never before or again. Who had hurt my brother then? Who had broken my beautiful brother? Injured him. Hurt him like that? Intolerable.

Intolerable is the idea of the life of this family—its long history of horrors well before my inauspicious, unwanted arrival on the scene. Before I was there monitoring it, keeping a lid on, as it were, charting it. Or so I believed.

Intolerable—my brother's tiny arm, years ago, out of its socket. Who will put it back in its place? I fall—I fall on this news into even greater, even deeper silence. My father weeping. Someone has broken his sturdy little son's body. Before Birdbones was here to protect. The identification of the body. *Yes.*

Why the child? Fingering like a hollow rosary, why? The child in the church is breaking.

A little boy dares disturb the universe. By the time I was born the church had already burned. Fergus was ten and already damaged beyond what anyone could have known. But what sprang from those ashes was nothing. What sprang from his fury was a covert agreement.

My brother had tried to kill God.

Where were you when he needed you?
Out earning a living, where else?

And in the tree house, overlooking the char, I read of that long ago purging that purged nothing. Enraged. My brother speaks through flames. Dreaming of a better life. *Bernadette, Birdie, I promise you better days. Are you listening to me? I promise.*

Our Lady of Sorrows, burned to the ground in the night. Arson suspected. His little broken son.

Father swerving, waving, bobbing above my crooked crib, whispering *life begins anew with you.* Second chance. Second time around. Anew. Sentimental the way only drunks can be. Singing, weeping. *Life begins anew.*

> *When haddocks leave the Firth of Forth*
> *And mussels leave the shore*
> *When oysters climb up Berwick Law*
> *We'll go to sea no more.*

> *O blithely shines the bonnie sun*
> *Upon the Isle of May*
> *And blithely rolls the morning tide*
> *Into Saint Andrew's Bay.*

My father carries a bottle and trudges through the streets, as if knee-high in dirt. Walking the invisible trenches to his son. He is more delirious, more pained than I could have imagined—and for months and months—perhaps a year, I am spared our Saturday trysts with the local women. In his war, no women exist. We did go back eventually, but only half-heartedly, I think, and then finally not at all.

My brother's absence seemed to have taken away the purpose—what was the point anymore?

My father retreats into a tedious alcoholism, singing *Danny Boy*, exchanging along the way his face of grief for something else. He becomes a babbling, belligerent, jingoistic fool. It is his revisionist gift: the keen, unlikely self-preservation instinct which will allow him to survive us all. The old bag of wind. He carries his son's medals on a poofy pillow, Fergus, now, a latter-day saint, and he the Father of it all. Photos of Fergus in uniform blown up to poster size and hung not only around the house, but the town. And Boston.

I recognized it for what it was: the last stages of his despair.

Mother betrayed was another story entirely. She had bargained hard with our Lord Jesus Christ, and his Mother blessed among women; I know, because I heard it all. After the initial rages she fell into an enormous despondency, bitter, cynical, inconsolable—and then finally indifference. Finally nothing. After Fergus's death it was all over for her. She had lost the only things that had ever meant anything: her son, her faith. She did not fight to keep me any longer. *Immodest child.* She looked at me with a discouraged eye and sent me off, washing her hands of me, to the school for the gifted in Boston. *The gifted.* I remained there for sizing up but was sent almost immediately off to Harvard. She stared blankly at me. Just another disappointment. Side show. Horror. Some grotesque, oversized brain in her little girl's body. A curiosity now. Unrelated to them.

Is that lightning? Jesus, Bernadette, why don't you give it a rest already? Nothing to be afraid of, he whispers to the little girl. I'm right here. You can bring him up that close—but no—your heart would break—not again.

I promise I'll keep you safe.

Anyone that hurts anyone that hurts her hurts himself, it's obvious, no? He'll keep you sheltered.

The messengers of death arrive once more at our dark door. I have been waiting with patience for their arrival. I am no psychic, but I am sure from the beginning of one thing: I will never see my brother again. I open the door and stare at them standing on the broken stoop. Young girls shame them; girls at all. In their idiotic uniforms, their stars and stripes, little boys playing dress up. *Is your mother or father home?* They are holding an envelope. *No.* I take it from them, the nearly fluorescent page, though they, of course, know better. I accept it with such strange authority and intelligence and desperation that they let me hold it for a moment, embarrassed as they are by death, amazed, ashamed. They take it back and I just stare at them. *No, we have to speak with your father first. Father first, father first . . .* Through prayer and drink and sweat he appears carrying his considerable shadow as he always has, rolling down the sleeves of his work shirt, shaking hands, man to man, passing me to enter the house, nodding to the uniforms to come in. He puts down his hanged father for a minute, to make room—the one he has carried his whole life. *Please sit down.*

And in the gloomy air they sit *man to man to man* and I am asked to leave. *She doesn't speak,* my father says, and I do not. Perhaps they decide in this nervous instant that I do not hear as well, and they proceed in the terrible quiet, in the silence death has made. They lean into my father, a man in his thirties then, and whisper *and fractures to the arm and hip consistent with injuries sustained at an early age by your son? And a jaw misaligned . . . And . . .* Tears make gulleys down my father's face. I want to shield him from these men and I run to his side. *And to the ribs . . .* My father weeps. Nods yes.

Sitting on his throne of blood. Poor bastard. Sent to their fancy foreign war. Having bought the whole bill of goods. King of a kingdom, finally.

If I saw you again today, ghoulishly returned from the dead, a joke as cheap and routine as any in this narrative—if you came in Vietnam drag, helmet and dogtags, I might not recognize you at first—so often, so precisely have I pictured you. Dangers of the mind—this haphazard, vaguely seductive activity. I marvel still at the intricacy and elegance of the mechanism. He was the same age as my students—or nearly. Worlds apart.

Who among us would recognize him if he came back to me, with the flamboyance, the wizardry of the dead? Clever thing. Who?

My students, fresh faced, the whole world spread before them like some beautiful, compliant woman. They do not doubt that there will be room for them. That each has had a place reserved with his name all along.

But for my brother—what? what was there? *I'll get us out of here, Beanie. I promise.* Why must the poor fight the wars? It's obvious, no? *Worlds apart.*

In fact I had waited with a saintly patience: teaching, researching, working, preparing my way. Waiting for the optimum, the ever-so-perfect moment in which to stage the deed. To perfect my life, to avenge, so as to perhaps, just perhaps, go unmarked—or less marked, changed a little at any rate. For one moment, at any rate. A reversal of fortune. To be alive. To live. *Oh right.* What could I have been thinking? Too late to even try to re-create the thing. What I must have wanted. What I was thinking. God knows. And too late to entertain how there might have been a way around the well-planned deed, a way out of that which I had so certainly set out to do. Could the story with its awful mechanistic plot have been written out some other way? The course reversed?

Could this prison have been escaped with just a smidgen (my mother's word, that) with just a smidgen less of one of the main ingredients: hate or rage or pain. A kind of opening up or letting go of the mind that might have allowed a different scenario. Oh I don't think so.

Bernadette! he shouts through flames. *Bernadette!*

Historically, the most important idea opposed to the idea of progress—not the Heat Death, the idea that the universe is degenerating—but rather the idea of the Eternal Return. According to the world view of the Eternal Return, time is not unidirectional and linear, but rather cyclic. If this is true, then progress without limit is obviously impossible. Progress is possible only for a limited amount of time, but because the universe must eventually return to its earlier state again and again without limit, human advancement must necessarily reach a maximum and then regress to its primitive state again and again. As in the Heat Death cosmology, there can be no ultimate point to human striving in the Eternal Return. How does that make you feel, my little heirs? Oh don't look so glum, my sugar plums.

Bernadette, he cries returning for me, *Bernadette!*
Bernie, Stringbean.
His little arm in a sling.

No event is unique and occurs once and for all, but rather every
event has occurred, occurs, and will occur, perpetually. The same indi-
viduals have appeared, appear, and reappear in every return of the
cycle. In every cycle Socrates will be tried, condemned, and executed.

The only argument for life Camus could find was: the struggle itself toward the height is enough, must be enough to fill the heart.
One must try to imagine Sisyphus happy.

Beanie! Bernadette! Where are you? Look, he's still holding that
damn ring.

My father in a woolen jacket, his best one, though it is a sweltering day. For Christ's sake. At any rate he appears for the august ceremony. Mother at work. Fergus dead and gone. The newspapers and
TV cameras are there for this solemn, landmark passing—*youngest*
graduate—working class, a girl no less—and mute to boot. I make great
copy even then. Silent, enraged genius still being pelted with half
dollars. Still dancing.
   Let's get out of here, Bernadette.
   It's just outside Cambridge when the car breaks down on the way
home. Father and I, weary, so weary now, walking toward help. He is
sweating profusely. We watch the sun execute itself into the earth.
The sky ablaze. A strange labor. Where has Loverboy gone? I wonder?
I cannot even conceive of him as that other man now. At the gas station we wait. I am a woman of the world, a scholar, a grown-up,
You've really made something of yourself, Birdie. I smile, afraid. What
good is any of it? I sit there capless and tearing at my graduation
dress. They won't be able to fix the car this time. *You've really made*
something . . . Speak to me, he pleads, *please speak, speak,* and he puts his
callused hands in his face. *Bernadette, please.*
   Who—who—I sound like an owl, and it is difficult the first few
words—locating the voice again—after all this time—to think in
words after all these *who did that?* years and for a minute it seems it

will not be possible, but then suddenly it is quite possible, and *who did that* and something else takes over—blurting—

Who did that to Fergus?

My father, as if he has been having this conversation all along with himself, knows exactly what I am talking about and without missing a beat—

But I interrupt, forgetting where the words go in—how to start, where to stop. *Who hurt Fergus? Who broke Fergus's arm? Who cracked Fergus's ribs? Who who who who? Who would do that?* My father blithering knows not why I have finally chosen to speak or having begun, if I will ever stop again. *Who would do that to a little boy?*

I am hoarse and shouting this thing *who who* this voice, raw—but my father now is speaking in a whisper, in some awful prayer.

Father Peter. Goddamned priests, holier-than-thou perverts. Father Peter who had taken a shining to him. Your mother was so relieved. Taught Fergus how to read. So pleased he was receiving guidance as she'd called it. She refused to believe. Fergus came home one day from that pervert's all bleeding and limping saying he had fallen from a tree. Poor little fella. Goddammed child molester.

It would have broken your heart, Birdie. When I asked the little one why he had done such a thing, and was it an accident, he shook his head and said that he was trying to kill God. I had no idea about that bastard priest. Jesus, that I could not protect my own son—not then, not ever . . .

Oh Christ, not Father Peter, the parish priest. Not every goddamned cliché in the book.

And I am tearing at my graduation dress. This horrendous passage. I wail with the full force of my shrunken lungs. A church burns in my throat. Diminished, terrible, ashen world. We watch the car as it is salvaged for parts. Something my father might sell.

But my father—the jig is up for him now. This is his last disclosure before his final alcoholic descent. *Stay a little,* I say, but he's already gone. It's as if with this last bitterness spoken, and with me speaking again in an audible voice, he was now satisfied—he had done all he would do. And at that moment he began his long fall. And it takes forever, poor bastard. He'll live longer than any of us; it certainly looks like that. If you can call that living. He pats my hand, presses my graduation cap to his breast. Weeping the tears of the damned. Disconsolate. He picks up an amber bottle and I watch drink slowly take him. He fades before my eyes. Farewell, so long, good-bye, dear Bernadette. *I did my best.*

What flares from the corners of the frame now is hurt, burn it, burn it if you can. What makes them blind is grief . . .

Someone has broken you so utterly. Someone has broken. Someone you trusted has broken you. Hurt you again and again until you fought back only to be broken. You were high in the trees, in the clouds, before my birth—you were hurting. In the night hobbling and crooked somehow you got up the tree. Rockabye. A B C. Where no one could hurt you. No one could hurt you anymore. Sanctimonious bastard you might have said had sanctimonious been a word you possessed. Because you couldn't read. C B A. Because you wouldn't again—you tried to fight back—someone in black. You tried going to the river—but everywhere you were broken and hurting—so utterly—a fish floating on top, you threw rocks. The sound of sirens. And in the distance now—fire.

Father Peter, don't! His arm out of its socket. His tenuous, his fractured, his tender—Yes, I remember now—with fire. The scrapbook he kept in the tree house. The church burned. Father Peter hurting him. *Thou shalt not.* Father Peter not accustomed to one so small fighting back his advances. *Father Peter, don't.*
Forgive him his trespasses? I don't think so. And so the child— *If you lie on your stomach. Relax. Forgive me* he whispers. *If you open your mouth.* The child gagging. Stop. Must we go on like this? Terrible tell all. The scrapbook in the tree house reveals—reports from every paper far and wide—that the church had been burned to the ground. The child taking justice into his own hands. The child hurt. Burn it, burn it. On the night before his first communion. Hear how it burns. Oh pernicious, ridiculous. (Fissures in the bones help identify the body, the son now, as yours.) Only the rectory left standing. The pews destroyed, the altar, the Most Sacred Heart, the Most Precious Blood. My brother—it was he who did it then. Burned the church. To the ground. I had no idea, stupid bird, while we flipped through the

pages in the trees. He is caught and not caught. No one tells. He and
Father Peter, no one will tell on the other. Not for a long time. Fingering the child. God is gone from here and taken away in some great
purifying flame. How to purge the horror. Not possible. At best to
give it shape and name. My brother, before his first communion
burned down the church. No solace in naming or shapes torn down.
Dear God—a tiny arm, a rib cracked. A broken finger and a flame.

Act Three

I look up through flames. Who burns in the distance in effigy? Is that you, Beatrice?

Oh let us revel at the beginning of *Act Three* then, one more time in the particular pleasures of premeditation. All along, I knew why I was there. What I would do. Year after year. Knew I would come to Harvard—it was part of the plan. So that on one fine fall day I would meet:

Mr. Ashmeade.

Present.

And look up, like the caricature of a school marm, over my half glasses, *Indeed.*

Act Three! Elizabeth, I am positively giddy!

All so beautifully planned. I had waited, and I had grown used to waiting; understood the pleasures of delay. I waited for the time of my optimum attractiveness and power. There could be no doubt. Look at her: can you believe it's Birdbones grown lovely for her one instant, grown into her swan self? Lovely. Grown utterly credible in an instant—heart-stoppingly—can it really be?

It's your chance, your one chance in a million, Bernadette. Use it, use it.
The time I had waited so patiently, so sweetly for, with such good behavior, having somehow survived the various ups and downs of dormancy, and eclipse. Having watched the mirror, not daring to wish, year after year, carefully, carefully, with great attentiveness for that one fleeting moment of tentative and yet authentic beauty. Oh so watchful. Nothing escaped me. Any slip, any confusion, any lapses,

any blurring of my purpose, and all would be lost. All I had worked for, and for so long. Nothing had gone unthought of. I must say again what I said at the trial, despite the admonitions from my lawyers: *nothing has ever been so premeditated.* A lifelong meditation, if you will. *Kill.*

Alexander Ashmeade, my reluctant colossal Apollo. Gradually, and only with some real coaxing did he begin finally to attain some semblance of equilibrium, some pretense of balance between his es-tranged body and his embraced mind. After he became convinced of the basic tenet, things flowed more effortlessly, and he seemed genu-inely happier, calmer. Having given in, if only a little. He seemed quite suddenly to roam the everyday corridors of his life like a sleep-walker. The pulsing light of the brain and the correspondent light in the body—one feeding the other—one making the other possible. Drawing him down the luminous hall. I know it sounds ridiculous. Those transcendent days, the happiest of my life. I touch his bleary shoulder. *Come with me,* I whispered.

When you're caught up in day-to-day struggles around sex, it's sometimes hard to remember why you're going to the trouble. It's helpful to have a vision of sexuality that you're working toward. If you can't imagine a positive experience of sexuality, talk to friends who feel good about their sexuality and ask them what they experi-ence. You'll probably start to get a sense of the possibilities. When you've talked to a few people, think about the kind of experience of sexuality you'd like to have. How would you like your perceptions or feelings about sex to change? How would you like to feel about sex a year from now? In five years?

May I see you at the break? All along I suspected it was not only me, but he too, whom I would recognize when the time arrived.

And we will quietly talk during the recess and I will understand from this, from the intonations of his voice, the way he composes himself, how he tosses his head, when he looks away and when he moves closer, what I will be up against. Oh one sees it immediately— what this will have to be. Not entirely unanticipated, I must say, and yet it had been left to some speculation right up to the end. Ex-changes of bodily fluids would have to be involved, varied and various acts. From a simple back and forth it is evident—and I believe it is evident to him as well, some aspect of it at any rate—the potential we stare into, the third presence in the room.

If he obeys, if he will consent to obey, if he will allow himself. *What are you prepared to do, Mr. Ashmeade? Who are you prepared to be?* In my mind I put him for a moment on a little leash, ask him to perform—not tricks of any kind, no hoops, but only, for starters, the great and mundane heel, and then perhaps sit. Not even, dear God, not even the thought of it, the potentially interesting and heartbreaking stay.

Oh nonsense, Bernadette, you are preposterous.

On to the opening lecture, my doves. Gray tailed in their smooth first day of school suits. Coo.

In the multiplication dream you triple yourself. Become fourfold, then five, then God—

In the elaboration, you're ten feet tall. It's so lovely up here, hovering above the rest of the world. You can touch the tops of trees. Imagine infinity.

At the break he disappears and comes back late. He slips away, but then returns—a moment of fear—yes, perhaps.

Tardy angel interrupting this atmosphere of high seriousness— another chosen class—another bloated, immortal lot. Tardy saving angel. *Mr. Ashmeade, you're late. May I see you after class?*

He follows me into an unforeseen place. After weeks of devotion, he begins to meet me there in the place I have been waiting. I did not expect him so soon. And his slower friends, Payson included, see in him something glinting, far off, and say, *Christ, what is it with you anyway, Ashmeade?* And they are forbidden to go there—they are prevented, poor wretches. I lean over them—drawing on their papers, amusing them and they can't help it—they're lost in cleavage and thigh, in sweet breath and the tangle of long red hair—they are weak, fallible, and they waste their time calculating like bored housewives the constantly shifting balances of power and attention. What else is there for them? They don't have much choice. My enraged second stringers. Always mopping up. Only Alex voyages, leaving them all far behind. I admire his stamina, his crazy courage, where does he get it? When he returns, he needs something to hold on to. Having been

as intimate with the distance as is possible for now, he needs the so-
lidity, the warmth of flesh—and he looks at me helplessly. I have
given him the taste for it. He's confused. Disoriented. He presses me
against the classroom door, after everyone has gone.

What is this blizzard you ask for?

See how I try to combat the solitude, which is extraordinary here
on death row, and mounting? Feeble attempts. *Mr. Ashmeade, what do
you think you are doing?* He has no idea. I have brought him with great
dexterity, and deliberateness to this brink, this place of want, of intellectual and soon, oh soon now, but not yet, physical insatiability. He
never had a chance. But was it happening too quickly? Yes. The tim-
ing was the only unanticipated aspect. I should have slowed it down.

And she ambles in whispering, *Girl!* A corona of brilliant orange
notes. A stack of papers, releases, things for me to sign. I think not.
And a Bible. *Don't no Jesus love me, Beatrice.* She smiles.

A flurry of action around my "survival" continues without me apparently. I am with Alex once more but they— I can't quite make out
what they say.

I had waited so long for him. In each autumn's cruel harvest, just
before the leaves peaked I would search, feeling with each year that he
was approaching, moving from out of the scarlet shadows into my
sights. Into my murderous range. Feeling he would soon make himself known, sensing him on each horizon, on the edge of each new
quadrant I crossed. It would not be long now, I was coming into
readiness, and presumably, so was he. I did not ever imagine that
when it happened it would happen so easily, so simultaneously, with
such little effort in the end. I did not anticipate he would appear during that false high summer on the first day of class. That he would actually walk into my classroom toting his T. S. Eliot. And that I would
in the end, barely have to lift a finger. And that he would be so obviously he when I saw him. A fierce sobriety would have to take over
now, during the initial indoctrination. Oh one's whole career had
been about discipline and distances—I understood now. I understood
a little more all of a sudden. And he looked into my face, as I called

his name, and he, like an animal who could hear sound outside the
range of the human ear—heard in that other voice—the high trilling
and trembling one that said, *Come, come to me. Finally,* the voice whispered. *At last. At last.*

Oh God, the click of the box! Come in my sweet. Let us see how
you behave at infinity.

Alexander Ashmeade, your presence, your look, your intelligence,
engraved in light in my mind's eye—still. Even during the first class
you knew, oh you knew something, had some inkling, something
nagged you even then, pulled, even then. And some time later, in evening jacket, looking out on the promenade or the bay, all the little
lights glittering, some skinny co-ed on your arm—you knew. It was
only a matter of time at that point—you might have even calculated
it there, bored as you were by then with everything—the bay, the
girl, your family—everything. You could not help but already want
her—your professor and her box of numbers and charms.

And you think to yourself *shackled.* And you think—but then
you stop—unbearable. When now would the line be crossed you
wondered, or the hatchet fall, or the rope, oh everything tightening, tightening in a kind of exquisite, delicious—why you, you
wondered—right at resignation's cusp—not quite ready yet to give
up. *Why you?* Look, you were flattered. The egotist in you—you had
been chosen, you were the chosen one. The self that wanted to excel—
to be the best at all it did. To live life unsquandered. Never mind
your mother's grim pronouncement after only a few weeks into the semester: *that you were not yourself anymore. That you were someone else.*

Welcome my little saviors to Hilbert's Hotel. Hilbert's Hotel—
named after the early twentieth-century German mathematician
David Hilbert—is an excellent example of the power of an actual infinity. The hotel has an infinite number of rooms, all of which are
filled. Then another person arrives and asks for a room. "Why, of
course, sir," says the innkeeper. "I'll just move the person now in
room 1 into room 2, the person in room 2 into room 3, and so on, and
this will free up room 1 for you."

Then 100 new people arrive and ask for rooms. "Why, of course," says the innkeeper. "I'll just move everyone in the hotel into the room which has their current number plus 100, and this will free up the first 100 rooms for you."

Then *an infinite number* of new people arrive and ask for rooms. "Why, of course," says the innkeeper. "I'll just move the person in room 1 into room 2, the person in room 2 into room 4, the person in room 3 into room 6, and so on, and this will free up all the odd-numbered rooms in the hotel for you. There are an infinity of odd-numbered rooms, so each of you will have a room."

There he sat, around the table with the rest of the class, my death, my annihilation, two students to my left. My sweet *demise*. Jesus I might have been a romance writer from the sound of this! All else blurred. The class seemed to speak in muffled, hushed tones, nearly imperceptible, beating useless wings against my fontanelle. *Away!* Foppish Anderson, Anderson, was that what he said his name was? And caustic Vanderhoven; everything suddenly out of some forgettable prep-school novel of manners. *You are dismissed, Mr. King, dismissed, Mr. Phillips.* One by one they go out finally, these voices, and we are left alone to smolder.

I think of all the places we tried to lose ourselves. Goddamnit, Fergus. Still we were, weren't we, we were lost up there for a while? You with your projects, your beers and beanies, and me with my hallucination of numbers, my intimations of a place we might live—though we never did lose ourselves long enough, did we?

Just Mr. Ashmeade and me finally—adjusting to the strangeness of our prearranged track—the deep, irrevocable grooves, wounds, that have brought us to each other. I am literally breathless, asthmatic at this moment. I dismiss class early. I gasp. For here he is in front of me. That day, after my first class, *It's time, it's time,* having recognized him, finally, I drove back to Fall River and unburied the ring.

Do you take this man?

Ostensibly I am dressed in a sober tweed jacket and brown skirt, I announce to the class. But imagine . . . And from there we go on with the day's flight of fancy. I watch Alexander shifting in his chair. I bend down and whisper in his ear, *use it*. The uses of passion. *OK class, now keep up with Alex,* I say though I know it is useless. Still they perform far better than they ever could otherwise. *Keep up.* But Alex is tired and I notice more and more now he grows sullen. It's time.

I invite him out for a meal after office hours. This sweet stage has now played itself out. It's time, oh yes. *Careful Bernadette.*

I put on the latex gloves and run my hand up his arm. This, I tell him is how near you are to the real thing. Close as your mind can get to the luminous *truths*. You feel through a latex haze; you see through a gauze, you taste, you taste . . . You're always close, but you're never close enough. Something is denied you. He understands. *What can I do,* he whispers in earnestness, *what?* I begin to remove my clothes, slowly, slowly. I shrug, wrapped underneath as I am for him in a thin rubber suit of sorts purchased from a mail order sex shop. I slap the latex to my wrist. To this generation the sound now signals pleasures to come, and makes them delirious with anticipation. My safe-sex mongers. I slip a gloved finger into his mouth. This is as close to the taste as you can get. As close to the sensation. I hand him a pair of gloves.

In mathematics, infinity is, for the most part, regarded as the limit of an unending series or sequence, something that might be approached progressively, but may never be reached. Thus one never says "equals infinity" but rather tends toward infinity. The intentional finiteness manifest in the completeness and conclusiveness of the classical work of literature or art is undesirable because completion and perfection are achieved at the price of the voluntary renunciation of infinity.

Back at the farm the class acquired a high level of proficiency that year, in fact it was one of my very finest classes. They worked in a kind of delirium, a dream, in which they realized Alex, with his heart and his mind and yes, more and more with his *member*, was leading them all to new levels of inspiration and commitment. An example. A star.

* * *

And Payson? You remember Payson, don't you? *The other one.* The other one I killed. The one that's landed me here in the lovely state of Georgia. Payson remained Alex's little shadow. His dull replicant, his lesser self, his imperfect twin. He trudged behind, the little blond brother, faithful, adorable, dimpled: it was the subservience we loved. His shuffling, smarming self. Sing the shadow song now, Payson. That's a good boy. *I have a little shadow that goes in and out with me. And what can be the use of him is more than I can see.*

Payson, seven paces behind, still—after Alex, the one who came closest.

There had not really been time in his life for women. Oh there would be a high-class whore purchased for him on a special occasion, a birthday, a high school graduation, from his father. Girls fell all over Alexander, but he remained distant—too distracted I suppose, by the ideas playing in his head. Bleary, endearing, naive child—saving himself for his most exalted work. Chasing the click. *What is that oblivion you beg for?* My vulnerable and bursting, my serious one. I caught him entirely unaware. Day after day he feverishly worked in a kind of awful, impossible rowing toward perfection, salvation, ecstasy—or wherever it was he thought he was going. Exhausted, he would end many nights, close to tears having made, despite his efforts, next to no progress but the clicks, Alex, is it not enough? His terrible working toward God. Was that it? A skewed religiosity. He was so intensely focused, so reverent, so charged. From time to time he would excuse himself and go off for a half hour or more. I expected he went to masturbate. It was from the very beginning a crucial element of the plan. That they, my bleary patriarchs, understood that the creative and the sexual are inextricably linked. One in the same. Without this basic understanding and then acceptance there would never be any significant movement in their intellectual lives. No progress whatsoever. It was step one. To get them to this point. Without that, everything that was to follow could not have occurred.

The hourglass turns for the last time. She goes off on her own, without me, searching for solutions I want no part in. Beatrice who now spends *many a sleepless night* thinking my way free. I look up from my Alex. *What do you want?* In this final acceleration of days, she lugs law books and a cellular phone with her everywhere. *There is hope,* she informs me, feverishly. I smile. *Right.*

She, who still somehow believes that there might be a way to stop this ever accelerating process. That she might tame or control this brutal, brutish world. What does she hope to take back from their business as usual? She runs, to the scalloped border. She whispers *stay* and *trust.* I might find that fine line—I might find the way, the equation, I might stay alive. The numbers might—

Return? Oh I don't think so.

I might stay on earth a little longer, she says.

What does she hope to salvage from this wreckage of circumstance and temperament? Even now she already converses with a corpse—*Look at my eyes, Beatrice, is that what frightens you so, intimidates you slightly as we reach the wire? Or is it your own soul you bargain for?*

Mr. Ashmeade, what do you think you are doing? I had brought him with great deliberateness to this brink. But this? It was, after all, my move, wasn't it, to make?

I cannot stress enough my dismay at the peculiar behavioral habits of the heterosexual. How I detest the grotesqueness of it all— the public displays of affection, the highmindedness, the assumptions, the privilege. *Their tonguing.* Their disgusting moralizing, their cozy moral superiority, their constant allowances for bad behavior, their rationalizing, their desperate pathetic fictions. Their betrayals and ruptures. How these men disgust me—their punches and winks, their subtexts.

Even though I am your teacher and ostensibly the one in power, not sexual prey, his hand automatically feels entitled to wander. And it is between my legs before we get to three. Even he, though he certainly seems a sensitive postmodern man, believes unquestioningly in the press of his muscles and money. He takes my finger in his mouth.

Alex, who was never innocent, no matter what he said. Deceiver. Filled with ego, just like all of them. Greedy thing—his vanity, his pride—they say he looks like Michael Stipe. *And who the fuck is Michael Stipe?*

I allow him another finger as he removes his clothes. *Not wholly satisfying is it, Mr. Ashmeade?* You can only get this close—he looks at my body through the wrap. How to make the sheath drop. You'll have to want it bad enough I guess, figure out the way in—and without force—oh there's no forcing it—but you know that. My delicate, my delicacy. My whole hand is in his mouth at this point, and he is sucking it with great force. *Calm down now, Mr. Ashmeade.* Let me help you with this and he feels my slick latex hands put the condom on his so-called *member*, just as I am thinking this latex pulls and was surely made for a smaller woman. *Look, Mr. Ashmeade, how the lips are so well, swollen, and defined in their little saran suit.* And he pulls me with some violence down on his face—*but I will not tolerate violence—gently, gentle now, be calm, there's a long way to go here—you haven't come even close to meriting the real thing,* I say as he scratches and bites, this other Mr. Ashmeade, the one now in some crazy frenzy, or another, not my sober, cautious student—*I need a little more of this from you in the classroom, dear one,* as he gnaws and chews and sucks, hungry for something. This is how I need you—pleading, soaked in your own tears. He tries to kiss my unprotected mouth with his unprotected mouth. *Very clever, Mr. Ashmeade, but you haven't earned this yet and you know it. I'm not telling you anything you don't already know.* He tries to suck my bare foot. *No not yet—not allowed, not allowed now, calm down.* He touches my erect, protected nipples, he sucks them trying to extract some sweetness. He tries to enter me, and we feel all the layers between us, yes, as he comes bluntly, and I whisper like some morbid, perverse cheerleader to go for the eternity in us. Not this. Lucidity in us. Last hope. Wish. Not this.

The click. Ah yes, the click!

He could be well, cultish in bed, and I am reminded, again, yes, despite his intellectual sophistication, that he is really just a kid, was just a kid, a teenager in love with fetish and offerings. He builds me altars. He makes little fires at my feet. He moans and prays. Tells stupid jokes. Plays stupid tricks. Puts a bow tie around his penis. Draws a face. That sort of thing. Raising his head from his priestess, something rises in him and he tries to phrase it—but he shudders, having no language, no numerals, no song—only nonsense, until he detects—what does he detect? My disdain, my disappointment, my disapproval—*You really do hate me,* he whispers. It is my distance he detects. *You despise me, confess.* I smile, remembering: he is a child, and I am going about this far too quickly—*Forgive me.* I kiss him gently, impressed by him still: his overstatement, his courage, his stupidity. *You know I don't despise you, Alex.* And he would fall back into a vague terror, stymied, unsatisfied, and we would settle for a while into a courtship of the most trite and reassuring kind.

Beatrice, would you like to join me in a few useless musings here, recollections from the old days. When there were abundant juicy theorems and proofs—and all kinds of experiments.

His intellectual frenzy had caught me off guard. He had begun to challenge me—push me. I was not quite prepared. Not for this. He had begun to suggest directions to me. And I let him, despite my wariness, fuel me, regenerate me. Could he, I wonder, measure at all the degree of my respect, and more important my awe? This I had not counted on. His mind set into extraordinary motions it would seem from something in this most miraculous union.

But I apologize for being, even then, outside it. All mind and violence, and nothing felt. *Who said that, do you know?*

And I mimic desire. I simulate lust. Become expert at it. You, my end of the century romantics, my gentle readers, will never believe it—but to me it was all oddly sterile, mechanized—any true sensualist would have been able to detect it. It was what continually gave me the upper hand. I was clear-eyed, I was cold, or at least lucid for the most part. I had just enough juice in me to fuel the engine, but I never lost sight. Never once was I allowed to escape the prison of this miserable self—even for a moment—I am well aware it was the thing that kept me finally from my most original talent. I am no self-deceiving fool. That I hammered this point: *one must stray, embrace recklessness, live with abandon.* That I stressed this so often to my boys was really just a way of having a continuous, modulating, insistent, but finally ineffectual discussion with myself. *Why can't you give it up, why won't you let it go?* But it was not for the most part their problem, their burden—their problems were others. It was mine. The flaw in my work. The thing that prevented me all along. That halted me. And Alex? My Alex had it all: the mind, the real control, and also the most sublime taste for surrender.

* * *

How to say it? I took him at an alarming pace to the place of supreme trust and resignation. Ashen garden of freakish extremes. Annihilation. Where I could have wielded anything—a blunt and perfect instrument, maker of death. A hammer, a gun; I used only my hands, and his begging, *go ahead*, his imploring, *take me all the way there*.

He had quested after pleasure, power, and above all knowledge— its great mesmerizing light—it stunned us, that glow, that great gloating presence—and now it seemed somehow within reach. Of course he trusted me—all the math and diagrams, all the hours of conversation and experiments and sex—why would he not trust me?

My detached, simulated desire—I gave him fair warning. I told him over and over. That I was OK in it, sober in it, when he was not anymore.

Intelligence of the blood. Stupidity of the blood. Delirium finally, supremacy of the blood rush—*ah* . . . How you behave at infinity, my pet. And the vanishing point. Longing asymptotically: .9, .99, .999, .9999 in your fierce becoming a number that comes closer and closer to 1.

He was losing himself on the way there to the screaming, the blasphemous orgasm—those faints and blackouts. He was losing his way. In the elaboration of his pleasure, that thing I had so encouraged in him, he was moving off far into a private stupor—*Where are you going?* My companion, my intellect, my century? He was drifting away.

Does someone glimpse us in our Collapsing Chinese Room? I am walking him on an ornate leash in my nifty new birthday suit. He is sniffing at my crotch. *Sit, I command. Heel*. In this parody of an aberrant sexual life. This mime. The stage blackened. I am trying to snap him out of it. Make him obedient again. But he strays.

And oh how he strays. In every possible direction. There were simply far too many distractions, too much of everything, too many dinners out, too much leisure, too many things to buy. *Give up your money; and all the ways out. Your checking account, your savings account, your trust fund at twenty-one. Give it over, give it up, you will never get there otherwise. Look, Mr. Ashmeade, how it ruins you.*

Someone glimpses us as he licks cocaine and every manner of designer drug off my unprotected mouth. Someone has found us out here at the mind's periphery. Is that you, Fergus?

Alex has a chance to live and so has Payson. *Of course he does.*

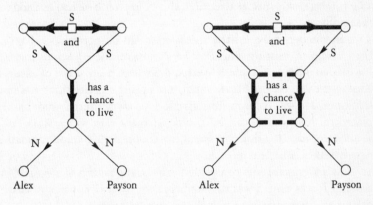

I take out the dildo—false limb, and turn him on his stomach. The disembodied, laughable phallus in action. Beautiful, beautiful.

He is a pulsing presence—blazed against a stunning backdrop, the outrageous clang of bells and music. He was chasing *a buzz* as he liked to say. A special moment that sometimes comes. A gorgeous solution to a particularly difficult problem. At orgasm he saw new worlds. *Where have you gone?* Amazed, speechless, he drops off into complicated, blissful slumber. I will not say here what he says in his sleep. Leave him alone for Christ's sake. Let him live a little.

Let copulation thrive, I announce. I send him off, at the height of his double addiction into the *dating world.* I force him out with the co-eds, not wanting him to become too complacent now. I even offer to help him choose the lucky girl. When he would not go of his own accord, I found it necessary to withdraw from him—that was his punishment—to vanish for a while—such was my simple strategy of postpone and delay. Oh he was a sight to see! A warped, begging thing on his knees. Only if he went off, only if he complied, made a go of it with Mary T or Suzie Q would I allow him back. *Let copulation thrive!* They were perfectly lovely girls.

I was merely concerned that the young god, with crown and staff, cradling jewels and keys, was beginning to take his precious nectar for granted. Beginning to believe that I somehow *owed him* this private tutelage, this special attention, this honeycomb he had learned to make glisten.

He was becoming a little too sated, a tad fat perhaps, perhaps a little arrogant, feasting whenever he wanted on these luscious meats. He needed more tastes, more breasts, more legs, more kinds of experience, don't you think? I had caught him eyeing a petite thing over in semiotics. He was coming into his glorious own. Laurels were being placed on his pretty head by the department. He was a star. This seemed to me the right moment to conduct this important and timely lesson, a little reminder.

His assignment was to pursue Suzie Q, the *super cute blond girl* in biology. It was time. I was tired of being the muse. I was sick to death of him, his demands, his needs. Little anointed one.

The hourglass is running out. *Is that a promise, Beatrice?*

After several weeks of courtship (it would turn out he was a shy and mortified suitor, my Alex) he finally got up the nerve to ask her out. It was at that point that I pulled the plug on him. And yes, I was quite content for a while—to go unpierced. Bernadette O'Brien, the inviolate. Out of my ripped clothes, for a minute. Deracinated one.
Whole.

Consider now his collapsing universe. He tries to buy himself out of his date with money. *I'll pay you anything. Just don't—* And yes, of course, it only clarifies the fact that cash has far too large a hold on him. *As if you could pay your way out of this, Mr. Ashmeade. Hand it all over to me.* And you will receive nothing, nothing in return for it. And so we set up an elaborate system of rewards and punishments, my lit-

tle accountant, counting, handing over the loot, and receiving only
that which I chose, out of perversity to give. A lovely little dowry in
the end for the bride to be. Have I mentioned it? By the time I was
arrested I was a rich woman. Imagine that! Escrow and accounts
payable and investments made him wild. In that way he was the same
as all of them—my future venture capitalists, my eggy patriarchs. I
ended up with quite a stash, I admit. OK, OK, I enjoy to this day any
variant of being paid for. Because you owe me.

Someone says they spied me in *spiked heels* and *plastic dress (!)*
walking a young man *on a leash! Rather active imaginations around here,
don't you think, Elizabeth?*

Her perversity, her humor, her closet pedophilia, her elaborate
fantasies, her love of murder mysteries, bonbons.
Her dinner parties, her soirées, her effortless entertaining of
friends and students and Bunting fellows, and lovers and former
lovers and lovers to be, in the long New England winter.
Her theories.

And we quite enjoy it—you and I both, burning money at your
fat-cat altar. Trying to set you free. *Let it go, let it all go.* A little free.

*Darkness. He takes off his jean jacket and wraps her in it. And she's
gray faced, poor urchin in her red-flowered tangled dress and she begins to
cry—as if she's grieving already. Of course she is.*
Then light. The scene is lit again. Hey you, how about a pony beer?

To celebrate this auspicious sexual encounter between the
demigod and the sweet Suzie Q, or Janie Doe, or whatever the fuck her
name was, I decided to cancel classes. He would not, I decided, even be
able to have me in class. I disconnected the phone. Bereft for a while of
nagging purpose, I even got back to a little of my own work. And was
happy. I believe I was happy. He would come desperate in the night
sometimes. From Suzie Q, panting, scratching, wild, reciting numbers, lost in a delirium of theorems, if you can believe that. Clever
child, he was trying to get at me with an irresistible equation, *not a bad
try*. It nearly worked—but at the last minute I hissed through the

door—*No, you're too crazy tonight. Go home.* But I missed him. Oh God, what am I saying? *Attachments had been made.* I had become—against my will—how shall I say this—*engaged.* I was losing sight a little of my greater intentions. Even sex, for the first time, did not seem altogether worthless. *What is wrong with you, Bernadette?* This was not in the design, as we all know too well. And *look*, he would say, *how you glisten like a honeycomb.* Glisten or not, I never lost control.

Still in the night, when I think of him like that . . . shackled . . .

For such pleasure even in the mind now a small punishment is in order, I believe. What? My options in here are decidedly limited. I burn the hair from my head. Why not, it's going to happen soon enough? I insert a razor up the honey hole until I bleed myself clean. The blood is black tonight. It is Connie, I think, who screams. They send for Beatrice in the middle of the night. *And what on earth can Beatrice do, do they think?*

If you have trouble coming up with positive affirmations about yourself (or even if you don't), go to two people in your support system and have each of them write down three affirmations about your strengths.

Although it may be hard to believe these affirmations at first, practice saying them. Look in the mirror and repeat them to yourself. Write them on big pieces of paper and tape them to the refrigerator. Read them over to yourself before you go to sleep at night. Gradually you'll come to believe them. With patience and practice, they can replace the old negative statements you were taught when you were growing up.

Anger finally rises in him, my mild-mannered one. Without it he is nothing, no one, goes nowhere. He takes me by the throat. *What?* I whisper. *Serial monogamy got you down, my sweet? No, that's not it, is it? You don't like all that nice softness and compliance and lying on their backs?* I was ruining him for straight sex, for any kind of normal life—as if he were ever normal, my God. With that brain. That brain. That head.

Marry me, marry me, marry me, he begs. *There's an edge I can't get—*

* * *

I recite the magic numerals above his unsated pubis with—the *Twelve Renunciations*, I whisper, remember the *Seven Catastrophes*—with excruciating deliberateness, my head hovering just above him, bobbing like one of his schoolgirls. My mouth moving ever so slightly, *Can you feel my breath? What does it feel like? Can you describe?* And then I bring my mouth to him, but lightly, ever so lightly and gently so that surely he thinks he will die. Just the suggestion, only hinted at, the gums and teeth, scraping against him—my black remuneration, glowing in the dark. He's mute now—he doesn't dare speak—fearing I'll stop or change or disappear—or can't—he can't speak. His sweetmeat, for a moment, rolled between my sweating breasts. As I slow everything down, a notch lower, at my tempo. *Number one,* I whisper. We feel a great stillness. And in the stillness a gathering. And time stops.

I put an apple in your mouth. Or a plum. Or a fist. My shackled, suckling pig. Hooded. Oh you are beautiful that way.

Miserable, he comes back from his little foray with Suzie, his tail between his legs. I must say I savor his misery. He crawls on all fours to me, on hands and knees, weeping, imbecile. *There's an edge I can't get,* he says with some last eloquence, *there's an edge I can't get without you.*

Astride him and drowning, dying, into his thousand leagues under the sea. Oh this notebook makes me absolutely silly sometimes. I mean, really—*his thousand leagues under the sea!*

Will you marry me? And to prove his love he takes me on shopping sprees. We spend thousands of dollars at a clip. Happily.

He is in his last teenage years then and I am thirty and we are by any ordinary standard in explosive hormonal synchronicity—it gives him energy, purpose, clarity of vision and fearlessness. And when I allowed myself to let go—even in the slightest—I got a glimpse of what this might have been, and was, as far as I could tell, for him. For a moment now and then, my solitude would lift and I could imagine what life might have been for me too—had absolutely everything been different.

This perch in the trees from which I have told everything, all along. All the distance in me, always.

He comes back from her, the harmless pretty Radcliffe student—appalled, enraged. He screams. I gag him, blindfold him, handcuff him to the bed. *That's what we do with boys who want to hurt girls,* I tell him. I run a blade up and down the length of his leg, then move to his thigh, then the penis, which becomes erect.

On another day, this is what happens to little boys who want to hurt girls, my friend. I dress him in chiffon, I perfume and lipstick him, I laden him in the family jewels, and make love to this timid, silent, beautiful woman.

Or put him in doll clothes. My little plaything. Now recite your times tables. *I'm not kidding you.* And he begins obediently at one.

Imagine your frock drenched in blood. Poor. Poor. I tear a dress of mine to fit on his front. A sepulcher of blood in the trees.

Hey you, how about a pony beer? So much blood, don't worry, it's only a dream. And the fields and fields of rice and rage he'll run through. Cotton, can that be cotton? Yes, in a drenched fist. It's only a dream. Paint it—six will be gray. Gray of the factory floor and father and son. Pale droning of factory and trash fish. Paint the little girl in the corner pink. Anyone who makes a sound.

Don't forget Bernadette, anyone who makes a sound dies.

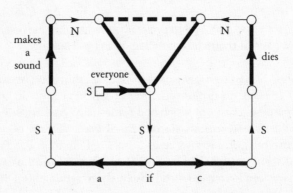

It's a memory so there aren't the same rules. She could choose to alter the central fact—that he is going to die—but she doesn't choose.

Look at her: a small defiance of bride.

In the distance now, thunder.

Three will equal red. Six will be magenta. Two will be purple. And seven will equal darkness, tinged with blood.

On the sharp edges of the frame, where the boundaries are clear, neat, razored away stands—who's there?

Beatrice, is that you? Beatrice, yes, the one I've had assigned to escort me into the end. She is here to help us all *deal with*, as they say, my upcoming demise—or if you prefer, my extermination. The upcoming inevitability, I pray, of it all. I need to work with Beatrice on this part—the inevitability bit—she is still *in denial* I'm afraid. Still mouthing salvation. Still, at this late date, trying to come up with reasons why I might want to live. Combing the books for loopholes—talking to all kinds of lawyers and women's advocacy groups. But Beatrice needs to face some basic facts, to get a grip. I have killed a post-coital, drowsy, filthy rich, Harvard kid in a Piggly Wiggly motel in Backfuck, Georgia, and I am going to fry for it. I will not agree to anything less—even if some miracle should intercede at this last minute. I am sick of the appeals, I am sick of the circus, I am sick to death of everything. Beatrice, I say to her, *Get a grip, girl. I am sick to death of it.* But she just nods with a kind of faraway look. Still, I do quite like her quite—did I mention she jangles—unsuitable as she is for the task.

Most intriguing, how she has somehow passed through the many sorrows—the harrowing, the demeaning, the chaotic, and has come out the other side singing, orange papers. What has she been able to build for herself from the place of ruin and scathe and brokenhearted and broken?

So much blood, don't worry it's only a dream. Can that be cotton, yes, in a clenched fist. Paint the little girl in the corner pink.

Wouldn't you know that just when things seemed to be quieting down a little bit, settling a little into the end, they would think of some brand new way to torture me in here. Oh yes, they are very clever, aren't they, sending this Beatrice Trueblood to me—my ush-erette into the wild blue yonder. Wouldn't you know, they would try to stir up just a little last trouble, in the end, for fun?

Beatrice, holding in her body, orange light, yellow light. *Hey*—in her delirious south.

Hey, look, I know you're hurtin', Bernadette. I know.

Cat walk. Jade eyes. Dark thighs. Kindness. Oh I see where this is going and I do not like it.

You've got to admit, Bernadette; she's very nice. You've got to admit. Even you. Even you are entitled to wish . . .

Oh one has plenty of time to drive oneself crazy in any number of ingenious ways in here. She comes in with her slave narratives, her freedom pamphlets. her self-help, God knows what else. *And what next?* Her candles. Her massage oils. Her musks.
Her pop psychology
Her proselytizing
Her half-baked schemes
Her pro bono lawyers
Her stays of execution
Her braids
Her quaint imploring
Her enthusiasm
Her golden thighs
Her hope

What does she hope to accomplish here?

So you have come perchance to join the damned for a while on this most unholy altar, now and at the hour of our death, as the hourglass runs out? At this last possible moment you come so close—*come closer*, I whisper, with your ludicrous bag of tricks and witch's brews and pendants and crystals and crucifixes—come closer—unless you fear despoilment. We are a laughable pair with our double fictions: one thoughtlessly, unequivocally life-embracing, and the other a death-monger without numbers or hope. We make a mockery of the ordinary, ambivalent world. In our simplistic, rigid stances.

She urges me to love that inner child, but I can't help it—*I despise that child.*

With her handful of tales, her allegories, her morals, her curves (bronze skin, thousand braids, jangles) she comes offering—with examples in hand—salvation. Her histories. See how the lower lip trembles. She hands me her people's sorrow. Bids me enter. Ransack her people's suffering, enter their pain, the damage done, the lessons learned. She carries a gas lamp, and scratches still from the cotton, tobacco. Who shall love the bones of the dead?

Shall we gather at the river?

She writes on small pieces of bright orange paper—the only color in a world that has been drained entirely of color—for quite some time. And how the square of night once gave way to hopeful day. But did it ever, or am I kidding myself even now? She ambles in and sits at the edge of my bed—all vibrancy—dear God—all life.

Fleeting, lost, late, *why now?* I swear I hear . . . And for the first time I look out in the night anticipating footsteps. *Who's there?* Almost desiring, what is this thing? Almost, almost . . . A body far off, lingering . . .

Talk to me, Bernadette, speak. Come on, darlin'.

She was all of a sudden an elective mute because it was the one thing in the world she could elect. The one thing she could choose, when she could not choose anything else. Not her family. Not her intelligence. Why is there nothing but punishment? He still sits there mortified, fuming in a dunce's hat. Burn the world down. Burn the world down to the ground.

*   *   *

I bleed and she watches me bleed. A small punishment. Don't you think for impure thoughts a little punishment is in order?

I know you've seen a lot of pain, girl. I know you're hurtin' bad—hey, look, I know all about it.

I am a poor sputtering candle, carried through a dark room by a child—about to go out. Wan, flickering. They call me murderer. *I know,* she whispers. *Child. I know all about it.*

The man's hands all over her (his flaming yellow hair, bandanna), he's waiting for her in the tobacco fields on the only road, the only way home. *Look, I know where you're coming from.*
Beatrice, please, don't, I whisper. *Don't.*

Taunting me purposely. Her voice suggests circular motions, voluptuous night, velvet . . . She is all voice. Coated, luxuriant. Kind voice. Good voice. A voice that might dispel—She speaks. *What? What did you say?* One day she brings flowers she has picked on her way. What is wrong with her? Doesn't she know I am a monster and thus immune from such gestures?

Foolish Beatrice. Foolish, foolish girl. There were days when she thought she had escaped him and she soared down the paths through the tobacco fields home, but she hadn't outsmarted him—of course, he's waiting, waiting, at the last turn near the fishing hole. How will she get away? Her torn and stained dress already. The little flowers faded.
The scalloped waistband of her panties. He puts his hand—he puts his hand there. Along the waistband—*run!* But when she tries to move there are dogs—and the breath and whiskers of dogs, and their gleaming teeth at her neck—foolish girl.

Can't you see it, they'll never get away.

The turkey vultures hovering over the marked one's body, over the wounded one's body. The vulture suspended against that purple southern sun. *Run! T*he dogs at the border. Alerting him to when she comes. His hair alight, he's waiting, waiting. And there's no other road home. She'll never get away.

Closure of the vanishing point. Don't you see?

The scalloped panties at the border. *If you scream,* he whispered, *the dogs. If you try to leave, the dogs.*

She leads me, through these last circles of hell. Sins of violence. Sins of fraud. Sins of betrayal. Gentle one. Holding a lantern. *Run!*

All this played out in a woman's head who has time on her hands. Time to burn, time to kill.
In her pretty cerebellum. She's pretty on the inside.

God, it's warm and bloody, he moans. The man in the bandanna. Scalloped border. *Help!* And the dogs. *Quiet, quiet, girl.*

OK, she *jangles*, and I can hear her slowly walking down the hall, joking with the others. She wears musky scents; I can smell her. Such ease. Where has she acquired such ease? Comfortable now in the home of her body. No one can hurt her anymore.

Trust me, she whispers. *Try to trust me a little. Just trust me.*

Just?

She speaks more and more often now of her poor Georgia. No way out. Her Mamma a long time, long time dead. What she's endured. She speaks far more than I do these days. Her stories are hard to bear and I admit to tuning in and out of them. What I am left with are fragments. Her *Daddy*. What I am left with is her pained face and her trembling hands. So hard to hear. Her beautiful hands—smooth, brown, the moons of her nails manicured—not torn and tortured. She holds them in her lap. She presses them together in prayer at her fore-head. She whispers, *But my Daddy couldn't protect me. He couldn't even protect himself.*

* * *

I watch her weep. *No way else to get home.* How much I wish I could feel for her. She just cries. The *dogs* she says, wretchedly.

My Daddy. He couldn't believe what life had made of him. I promise you, Beatrice, something better than this. I promise you and your brother better, he had said.

Daddy, don't go.

My Daddy ran when he heard—to the border with dogs—*in retribution, to protect his baby. For the rape of his baby. And he—and he—*
And the dogs were barking and barking at the border, alerting the white man—no trespassing, he shouts, no trespassing. *The terrible dogs holding night in their jowls.*

And he was killed, and he was shot dead, and he was shot dead for trespassing. She weeps and weeps.

The man's hand nearing the scalloped edge even after her daddy is dead. Even then. *I told you to wear the lace-edged panty,* he admonishes. And he beats her.

I look at her incredulous. *Don't no Jesus loves me, Beatrice. I don't want to hear it.*

And the Black Madonna my mother insisted be kept in one corner of her makeshift sepulcher against the raging prejudice of that house—a house where they had to feel better than someone I guess. That haunted, diminished house of *catch a nigger by the toe* and *nigger lips* and dead nigger jokes.

Daddy, stay!

You do me wrong to wake me, Beatrice. She brings in those who wear official garb to look at me. I am flame haired, fury flailing, skinnier than ever, Birdbones. Towering over the little lady lawyers and other assorted official dwarfs. They are robed, cologned, ready to do the humane, albeit grossly unpopular thing of postponing, if only temporarily, the monstrous deed—so they might sleep—So as to sleep in the feathered, innocent, pure again way, for a little while longer. Night.

In the judges' chambers, attorneys come and go talking of I know not what, postponements, clemency, in a little huddle. The logic is exhausted, the time is running out now.

Her tenacity, her refusal to give in, her kindness.
Live, she whispers. *You could live.*
Look into my eyes, I tell her.
Live, she says. She's holding the Bible.
Don't no Jesus loves me, Beatrice. Don't no Jesus loves me now.

Religion: Mother's own private vaudeville. In the small dark house where the Virgin seemed to have all the best spots. Where we waited for miracles in the dark. Jesus lugging his spikes and thorned heart and drops of blood, tapping, tapping out his word. The tinsel and wax and little bits of gold rigmarole. A bath of blue light. Sparklers. And Joseph the impresario doing a little soft shoe, brokenhearted.

Once we went *en famille* to the sea. A curtain of wind and wave, the great emptying static at zero. Father talking but no sound coming out. The penises of the men all shrunken, small, shriveled, next to this. To this. Harmlessness. The enormous, amoral—no pull like its pull—its beauty, its violence, its arrogance. Rendering everything for a minute harmless.

Somewhere the world is right. Somewhere the world is as it should be. February snow. Tender strawberries for the most beloved teacher in June. A swing where you can ride high. So high. A sprinkler, or if not that, a hydrant in July. At least that. We do not doubt that there is room for us.

What went wrong and so early? Melancholy thoughts. Why were even these happinesses—unexceptional, ordinary, kept from us? Off limits to me? To us? Someone somewhere is singing a child to sleep. Melancholy thoughts.

*   *   *

Had there been a sister, I might have found a confidante, a friend. A little solace, someone to care for. In the monstrous solitude, in the silence. A shadow sister I sometimes imagine I harbor in my body. A little sister whom I might protect from all harm.

I'd never let them get her. No, I'd never let them—

To the godhead: *Why have you left us alone here another night?*

It's the loss of the numbers that makes this life inconceivable.

And what is the occasion of their sin? What have they done? Why did she kill those boys? Do not ask.

She watches him sleep. Huddled in the corner. She moves to his side and this time, this time, she slips the velvet tie from her flowered dress and places it around his sleeping neck. To spare him. So he might be spared. Tomorrow's the war. Our secret.

He offered shiny candies—bright, bright. Sticky candies in a bag. An extraordinary assortment. Shaking them bright so I might come to him. Laughing. Hauling his loot. Hauling his death rattle. The multicolored stash. *Do you want a sweet thing?* And he passes me the forbidden fruit—before dinner or bed.

Once we went *en famille.* The sea. Behind my eyes, I see the blue that is pewter, suffused with light. Never to be mine.

The world bereft of meaning, purpose, coordinates. It's the loss of the numbers that makes me want to die.

Jacob Perlman trailing light leaving his life before my eyes hobbling into the room. And I am furious—have no doubt about it. He hands me where he is about to leave off like some dreamy relay runner. How can I take this mantle I must have asked from the depths of my silence, the silence only he, half deaf could hear in. *How?*

He smiles. A brightness in his closing eye. *A child, just a child,* he trembles. *So somber, full of burden, woe and wonder. Live in this.* And he scribbles numbers—faster than his hand can keep up. *In this.*

* * *

This notebook has been more of a companion than I could have imagined. How strange that I have come to know it at this late hour. One more thing to lose in this chronicle of loss. And to those of you who will read this later, with a kind of magnifying glass, combing it for clues—What is its message, blurred, in a cloudy bottle, washed onto a strange shore. I am broken tonight. More than usual even. Into your hands, Liz. The brunt of my bewilderment.

And there's Mother all of a sudden. Mother, digging in her scarred garden. Excavating a few tubers. World-weary one, scratching in the dust. Nothing comes of nothing. What can she hope to unearth, poor thing?

> *When haddocks leave the Firth of Forth*
> *And mussels leave the shore*
> *When oysters climb up Berwick Law*
> *We'll go to sea no more.*

No more. Mother died this morning in her sleep. The night warden delivered the news.

Is it spring? I ask her. *Is it fall?*

No entry today.

> *O blithely shines the bonnie sun*
> *Upon the Isle of May*
> *And blithely rolls the morning tide*
> *Into Saint Andrew's Bay.*

The BaaBaaSheep is shorn. Exposing the most delicate, tender pink skin. Oh Jesus. Rest. Rest if you can.

The Little Teapot . . .

The Little Teapot is dead.

I scarcely know what to say. The sadness exceeds all expectations.

* * *

Mother is—numbers recited into a dead receiver.

The part of me that genius had kept a child grew up in an afternoon on that long antiseptic corridor, where I sat waiting, waiting, the nurses passing like gulls. They disapprove, they regard me suspiciously. No one to hold my hand. No one to tell.
Mother.

And the hulking, violent, brooding young man who is my brother and the little genius nerd he loves. Speak to me in a clear voice tonight, in the pure voice of the damned in this house of ice and bones and no music. Only bitter orange candies in shiny paper to succor.

The brutal cutting off of her. Work horse. You have no heart. You have no voice. Gray mare of morning. You rise at five. Bear your sorrows silently. Toil from dawn to dusk. Fight for their lives. Why? Why?

You are a sight for sore eyes, Bernadette O'Brien. She sits on my bed and attempts to comb my hair.

She speaks across the gap. As if now, in this womb of darkness, we can fall back into comprehensibility. I recall her emerald bones. Once, long ago.

And Fergus, dark angel, hovering. You are godlike in our mother's eyes, in your final blue light and the what might have been. Now that she is there among your kind, perhaps you might rest now, brother, too.

How she smiled and praised and petted my head when the grades came in, but her accolades only felt like another form of absence. All the things that frightened her. Why did I have to excel? Why did I have to leave her side? Grown, even at age five, incomprehensible. I felt more despondent, more inconsolable, the more she tried to feign

joy, the more she tried to hide her fear with smiles. Our terrible lifelong estrangement. Tonight I'd like to believe I would have traded it
all, just to have had you love me a little, want me a little, Mother.

Beatrice, how much longer?

And where is your famous neutrality now? And where is your famous indifference, Bernadette, when you need it?

*Someone has come to water. Someone has come to water the diamond ring
and thorns. Someone has come to water all the fractured bones. Embers of the
church. And the terrible turning away from God. Someone has come. The
darkness and dogs. Someone at this late hour still insists on keeping it all
alive. Why?*

He takes me to the river. We fish with chicken backs and strings
for crabs. Wretched present tense. Where nothing ever ends.
Rest.

Mother, you are spared any further humiliations. Rest in your un-
miraculous unrising from the dead—ashes now—just as you came to
suspect. Rest.

All the things she'd memorized, gone into the ground, the little
poems, the songs, all gone. The prayers. That's what got me the most
somehow. *When Haddocks* . . . Gone.

And now you are at peace finally. Or so they say. Your much-
anticipated life everlasting—who in their right mind could wish for it?

He comes in the definitive middle of the night in blackened evening cloak, holding stars and medals, lightning bolts. Brief angel,
dressed beneath in army drags. He calls my name, looking for me.
Bernadette, he cries across the years, across the delta, across the field of
ragged grass where we once lay. Over hill and vale, high and low.
Combing the river banks. Dredging the whole thing each night, in
search, *Bernadette! Birdbones! Birdie, where are you?* With a blind, blind
eye and ghastly portent, *Bernadette!*

* * *

Calling me faithful mockingbird and harbinger—*Harbinger of
what? What is it, Fergus?* I am afraid. What does he want? *Bern . . .*
His veiled intent. . . . *nadette . . . Bernadette!* These terrible late night
obsequies. How can I help? How can I help now when it is already
too late? His sorrowful search. *Bird! Bird!* Then searching more and
more frantically in less and less likely places. Absurdly he opens jelly
jars so as to ensure I have not hidden there. He searches the shirts
hanging in the closet, he wrings out the handkerchiefs I have wept
into—you are getting close. *Bernadette!* Why search brother, in such
sorrow? If sorrow's what propels you now.

> *Get out from under the bed, Mother!*
> *Get out from under the bed, Mother!*
> *Get out now from under the bed, Mother, run!*
> *I do not think that he will think to look for me here,* she whispers.
> *But your shoe laces are showing, Mother, and your petticoat, and your*
> shoes, Mother.
> *ShhShh—Don't you understand? Run, Eileen, run!*
> *I'm not Eileen, Mother. Eileen's your sister.*
> *Eileen, run! Hide! Before he comes.*
> *Why are you so afraid of Pa Toomey?*
> *I do not think that he will think to look for us here, Eileen.*
> But a shoelace shows.
> She trembles.
> *Mother, please, don't cry.*

Chestnut brown hair, my bonnie, budding breasts, green eyes. Hide!

Because she was afraid.

You can stop your hiding now.

Oh there you are! She smiles. *Come on! Come on out now, child. It's
time for cards and cake.*

When Mother would arrange us around a card table. Her precious
free time. *You too, Bernadette,* she'd crow, *now come on,* and we'd play

gin rummy or poker. Minnie Grace, sometimes even Uncle Jack along with Father and Fergus. She'd make a big pot of coffee and a lemon cake. *I've baked my lemon cake!* When I think of my mother this way I am utterly desolate. She is laughing. She is working so hard to be happy. Suddenly she's on the Ballyogan road again, just a wee one. Her father promising he'll get her out of there—no hope—no money—across the ocean even—if necessary—oh yes, if absolutely necessary.

Come on smarty pants, be on my team. Alas, I am always a liability—never able to focus on the predictable narrative of games. I drift easily, unable to stay with the thing, until the numbers and hearts, the queens and clubs, make an alternate arrangement in my head. Then those voices would garble and when I'd look up at her, from that place of vast indifference she'd be winking at me and gesturing, bluffing. *Depending* on me. But I am marooned out there, far off, of no use. *Cards and cake, cards and cake,* they're saying, and all the senseless conversation, my mother crowing, *I can't make head or tails of it.*

Six of one and half a dozen of the other.

She drowned in the pool.

Who?

The Hennessy kid.

Which Hennessy kid?

And Uncle Jack and my father telling off-color jokes, and Minnie Grace chiming in *Mother of God!*

Oh Finn could charm the pants off anyone!

Well I don't give two hoots about Finn and his lady friends.

Oh don't say that about Finn. Poor Finn whose mother died of the grippe!

And Fergus, consummate competitor, beating everyone—*a loot bag* of pennies and nickels, his grand haul at the end of the night. And Mother in her flowered dress. *Come on, honey, come on now—for me, help out your poor old mother here.* As if I was exempting myself from their games on purpose.

I've got you in spades.

Just a smidgen.

And the Lynch twins dead of the grippe as well.

One evening, I shall never forget this, it became clear that one of our guests had been cheating and I confided this to my mother, good girl, so that she and Father *might have a better chance.*

Oh, you're always trying to spoil our fun, Bernadette!
Sullen, serious, inappropriate child that I am.

Of course they expected to lose at everything. What was I thinking? What was I wishing? Failure was part of their world and they
had built a kind of shelter in it—safe in its familiarity, a solace—
something to be counted on. A way to bear the disappointment. For a
so-called genius, I was really rather stupid.

My parents worked together well—for they were partners in resignation. There was an agreement there. A value system. A way of
seeing. Or perhaps I give them too much credit. They remained together because they lacked what it might take to do anything else.
There were financial aspects as well, I suppose. Neither could make *a
go of it*, *a go* as they liked to say, alone. In unison they leapt for the awful bones the government and anyone else threw. The idea of finding
someone else, of making some other sort of arrangement after so many
years was no longer imaginable, let alone possible.

I, having arrived late on the scene—was the grave witness to my
parents' later fatigue, their despair, their particular brand of famine.
My mother putting my father to bed each night—he's drunk too
much again. *Enough hubbub, Patrick O'Brien!* And Fergus raging, *making matters worse.* And she alone, trying to *make ends meet*, shifting and
reshifting the accounts. Begging for credit, *the mercy of God.* She
weeps. While numbers increasingly set me free, they enslaved my
poor mother—her endless recitations at the phone company, and at
home, the bills, no matter how she juggles the funds, she's never going to be able to pay.

What hope animated them once, seventeen years before this, to
name their firstborn Fergus John Kennedy after the buoyant, handsome Irish senator from our state? What lark? What sentimental ges-
ture of promise and pride? Jesus, things certainly must have run *way
off the rails* to allow them to turn their backs on all of it and put a
Ronald Reagan for President sign on the front lawn. *Reagan doesn't care
about you. Idiots. Reagan despises you.* There I was spoiling their fun
again. Ghastly, ghastly. The poor bastards.

*Ne'er do well, why didn't you turn out like Michael McGuire, a credit to
his mother Mary? Hooligan, you're nothing but a hooligan, Fergus John
Kennedy O'Brien.*

*   *   *

That awful man who had caused our family and thousands of families like ours such grief, that *actor*. By casting their meager vote for him they were, as usual, securing their own misery once more. The stupidity born of fatigue, of hopelessness. It's the mindlessness, I detest—the endless strategies of self-deception among the poor who are not so dim-witted, just tired and grabbing at straws.

Oh it keeps coming back. Bring it on then. *Come on, don't be shy.* Yet another dreadful aspect of cards and cake, I now recall, had to do with displaying my genius on demand. Playing the brilliance card. It was a sort of magic trick, part of the evening's entertainment and I was not permitted to refuse. How awful being asked the dates of things, and to solve simple mathematical problems. They couldn't even begin to formulate the proper questions. *For God's sake, we may as well show you off, for all the heartache you'll cause us.* Though of course no one could ever have begun to really guess back then. The freak show of me. *With a brain like that*—and my own mother is half pointing, half cajoling, half accusing, until I do a little performance, a display of its cold terrible beauty. And she is fearful a little, greedy a little, and in awe, crying *more, more!* I loathe her then. Her tedious requests. Her jealousy. Her resentment. Her willingness at any cost to show me off. Without it might I have been the daughter she always wished for? A chatting, obedient member of their small dingy work force. A partner in cards. It is not that I do not understand. She was afraid and alone. My intelligence would take me away from them—and we were flesh and blood—meant to stay together.

The little tempest in the teapot is dead.

The Goon Squad has gotten together and has agreed in some last act of mercy, of kindness, to allow me to go to the funeral of my mother. I shall be attended by Beatrice and two armed guards. I am as surprised by this unlikely turn of events as anyone. Having not left the premises since my arrival several eons ago. What can they be thinking? If I have understood this correctly it was Beatrice's initiative. She makes it clear in her soft voice that I am not to let her down.

*   *   *

Did I say two—it's *four armed guards* that shall accompany us. And all manner of manacles.

How today death feels like an oblique place. I should have liked to have seen you one more time before you became unreachable.

And I? I should have liked to have known you, my daughter; but you were unknowable.

I always wished, in the part of me that wished at all, that it might have been a little easier for you. Rest, my mother. Dear woman. Pacing, pacing in my brain will do no good. Worn shoes of worry. *I should have liked . . .* You can forget all that now.

Flying, handcuffed, I see a city from on high. The clovered highways. The arrangement of field and stream, suburb and city—and what had seemed random, a senseless maze from down here, now one understood: it had all been planned. How odd to see from the air that all along there had been a design—see it clearly for one moment. One moment before we are taken high up into the clouds and away and all is disappeared—how strange.

The malls, the interrupted mountainsides, the rerouted streams, the violated paths—everywhere the deferral to their plan, everything changed to satisfy their gaze, the press of their intentions: we never stood a chance.

The cracked sky. Is that lightning? Close your eyes.

The funeral is in the morning, dear diary. Beatrice and I share a hotel room for the night. She is right here. It is hard to believe. It is shocking. Luxury as I cannot recall. She has brought a nightgown for me. She has shopped for a black dress for me to wear tomorrow at the funeral, though, I will not be able to get out of the car. That is understood.

She brushes my hair. She gets ice from the ice machine for our sodas. Tells a few small jokes. Laughs. Prays. Like my mother once did, she finds sanctuary there. Finds a way to reconcile all that's been taken away. *Hey little one*—and she tells me a story of catching fish. *Long time ago. Sweet Jesus. Sweet Lord. Put your head here darlin'. Your Mama's dead. Poor sugar. Poor little one.* And she asks me to pray with her, but I can't. *It's OK honey, just mouth the words, you don't have to say them.* I have not been so near another human being in such a long time; I cannot describe the strangeness of it. Astonishing really that people allow others up this close, this near to danger and heartbreak. At such proximity. *Close your eyes now, honey, get some sleep. You've got a big day tomorrow . . .*

Who to confide in? I can scarcely believe that she breathes beside me. I cannot recall such trust in another human being. Such openness. How odd, how sweet. And she jangles, even in her sleep. How extraordinary she is to have brought me here. Tomorrow they bury Mother. I can scarcely believe.

In the next few pages you will have the opportunity to create a sense of safety for yourself in a very practical way, by developing strategies for using this workbook. You'll have a chance to explore five distinct aspects of safety—creating ground rules, building a container, finding a safe spot, maintaining privacy, and establishing protective rituals. Taken as a whole, they should increase your feelings of safety in approaching the exercises in this book.

The funeral took place at ten a.m. I saw my father once and only once more. He was scrubbed, anticipatory, suited, as if after so many years something was actually about to happen. I could only watch him, through the tinted glass of the car I was driven in. He could not see me, but he knew I was in that car and they allowed him, for reasons I suppose that had to do with their own sentimentality, to place his giant hand on the window next to my head . . . next to where he imagined my head to be. And though he began chattering, I couldn't hear a word.

The old man spoke a steady stream. Carting his son, his hanged father, *rest.* And now, his wife. *Colleen.*

* * *

Our Little Teapot is dead.

Reported in the tabloids: *Didn't cry, never cried*—through the tinted glass.

The weather, Beatrice and the armed guards talking, *had abruptly turned hot.* All this time out here they had been talking about the weather without me—and of other ordinary things. On the day they buried my mother flowers bloomed, birds sang, there were flaxen maidens dancing in the woodlands. I remembered all of a sudden that I disliked spring: all that hope and commotion. Songbirds made me desolate. My father's useless gibbering. Minnie Grace sobbing. The sun suddenly above us, clanging, like some slung chandelier, an obscene Jesus, presiding over the sorry scene.

I watched the whole thing through the mournful glass. It seemed like a play poorly staged. Not entirely convincing. Look: my father stooped over, inconsolable, incredulous, at this my mother's one mutinous act. She had died in her sleep and left him to wake and find her. She had died on him. She had broken finally the vicious cycle of suffering. She had left him to feed himself, to clean up, to roam the rubble of their lives.

My father put his hand where he imagines my head to be. *Birdie.*

A rare specimen under glass, handcuffed. I think of Alex. Four pairs of eyes watched me as we boarded the plane to Boston. A gloomy specimen. A disintegrating butterfly, mounted, pulling away from its pins. How strange the outside world. It is even more removed, silent, and shut up than I recall. Barred, off limits, as it has always looked, only more so. So much divisible light. I wouldn't want to have to stay out here.

Thank God for the mathematics, that otherworldly bliss. It had provided shelter—undeniably—but it had left me far off, far away— waving from such a remote and dizzying height—and then not waving anymore—having gotten lost in the distance, disconnected. A knocking on the glass. *Hello, Birdie, are you in there? It's your father.* His hand pressed up.

Alas, no.

And where are my charms now, my glowing numbers, when I need them most? The truth is they'd deserted me some time ago. Taken away, without explanation, like everything else. It's the isolation that makes this life impossible. Such silence.

Gone, suddenly, the dirt at the door, my father's yammer and clatter. He lays his wife down next to his son and father now.

That the mound of earth should be so small that covered her. Good God. Impossibly small. Unseasonably warm. The small sweet funeral meats bake in the sun. *Don't leave me here.*

My father's hand pressed up against the glass. *Who put the overalls . . .*

Why have you left us alone another night?

The indecipherable path we set out on. That bitter, desperate choreography of want and numbers. Patter of bare feet. Rhythm of our tramping feet. Where's the road home?

How much is that doggie in the window? Singing. Swaying. My father had taken me to the pound to find her a pet after my brother's death. I look at the mongrels behind bars. *Come on, Birdie, sing with me. How much is that . . . ?* But she just points. That one. That one. Even though she is afraid of dogs.

In the memory, this small locket, anchor, you wear around your neck— this small killing bottle you dangle like a charm and look into occasionally— in the memory in the bottle—place of dog hair and tooth and velvet, lightning cries—he opens another beer and waits: in the cruel, stupid, baffled punishment of his life.

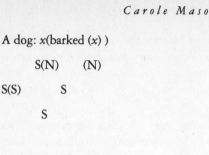

A dog: *x*(barked (*x*))

      S(N)   (N)

S(S)   S

    S

A woman: *x*(wept (*x*))

      S(N) (N)

S(S)   S

    S

How to position the voices in mind so that they might finally achieve harmlessness. How to find the right line. If I could understand for once what they whisper, hiss in my ear: *soldier, pilgrim, bride. Anyone who makes a sound dies.*

I sit on the banks of the black river without him. Mute and furious. Why am I always so furious? I look out on the hillside of tires, the weary, endless afternoon. The cylinders of waste, United Iron and the others. The cotton mills. The plastic bag factory.

Once we were alive, Fergus, and we walked these sad, insistent streets together. We passed weeping mothers and their filthy children. Mill people, trying to live. In the rubble and misery. In the gloom.

Let's hold him there, for a moment, shall we, under the examining lamp, since it seems we have gotten into this altogether wretched business. Let's put him under glass, where he is shrunken, manageable, squirming a little. Proceed with caution—oh make no mistake about it, proceed with caution, with care—he's still capable of inflicting great hurt—taking you, for instance on one more sex tryst, one more desperate afternoon. He's still capable, even like this, of causing pain—an outrageous demand, a punishment out of all proportion with the crime. An alcoholic's careless logic. And how he never listened. Never really cared. The imitation of a response, a forgery that is all we ever got from him. He in fact has no idea anymore what's going on. If he was ill, he should have obtained help. Instead he acted with the audacity of gods or kings. Patriarch, charlatan, weak but not without effect, and not by any means without consequence. Too long we suffered his blustering nonsense. If we could have only shrugged it off—but we could not—not one of us. Shut off the light now. Enough.

What we had on the very best of our days was the resemblance of connections. A nostalgia perhaps, on certain of the better days, for what a family might have once been. Some inkling. But we weren't good at it—had no aptitude for it whatsoever—no ability to re-invent that tired form; not enough love or energy or time or desire or whatever it required to breathe new life into what we were: angry, cynical, fearful, exhausted. Still meager attempts were made, yes.

Once we went *en famille* to the sea. Only there, against that exalt-ing, amoral backdrop, did our own grave lives seem negligible, small, nearly erased—solved. Any human drama played out against that enormity, that sensuality, that raging seemed rather absurd. Our tragic dimensions collapsed. Infinitesimal figures cry out from the horizon.

If I could but see that blue once more from any window in my mind. The sea takes away their shame. They sit on their blankets in clusters and stare out undisturbed. Far off I watch a girl build a sand castle. Not child, but not yet adult, she is at that tender age of becoming.

Once we went *en famille* to the sea . . .

What could have made them think of trying joviality as a strat-egy, conviviality, normalcy? Even for a moment? Their small at-tempts at happiness. What could have made them hope, even for a moment, for something easy and ordinary and fun? Why does this bother me even now? What feelings does it arouse still?

When oysters climb up Berwick Law, we'll go to sea no more, no more, we'll go to sea no more.

*   *   *

She hands me late missives and catechisms and petitions. *There is a good chance you will be spared,* she says, *if you will now cooperate.* But day is done I tell her. *No, no, you don't understand.* Oh but I do. I admire her spunk, I must say. She asks me to work with her on the final petitions to be filed on my behalf. *No you do not understand, I am the unsavable. Have you forgotten? I am to be made an example of.* It is awful of her to be holding out such hope now. I should report her to her superiors. It is wrong to do now. And for the first time, in all these years locked up in here, I consider—well, I consider it. That is the worst part. She is self-righteous, tedious, sentimental, pathetic—and I buy right into it. *Not possible.* She puts her arm around my shoulder. *Come on,* she pleads, *try—do it for me.*

The first page reads *Stay of Execution. If you won't do it for yourself . . . do it for me.*

Do it for me, then.

She does me wrong to wake me from my grave. The days dwindle. A frenzy of activity. I shake my head no. How much time left? One month? Less?

All of us have developed strategies for dealing with uncertainty and change, whether we're consciously aware of them or not. Some of these strategies may work for us; others have elements we may want to change. The following questions will help you assess the ways you currently deal with periods of limbo:

When I face uncertainty, I feel _____

When I don't know what to do, I _____

When I face the unknown, I expect _____

When I face the unknown, I usually cope with it by _____

When I face the unknown, I wish I could _____

Saw today a rare specimen under glass. My cheek pressed up to his hand through the glass. Good-bye, Father. I know you tried.

* * *

He sings a sorrowful song and then no more.

They have rifled through her last belongings, looking for what? Guns, knives, contraband? They have pulled apart the things she has left to me, the grave robbers, the thugs, and now they present me with three bags, three bags, three bags full.

Try to picture yourself free, she says. No, you've got the wrong person, I'm afraid, Beatrice. *Come on, you know you can do it.* Hideous really of her to hold out such hope at this late last moment. Dropping electric orange notes.

He appears jocular, jostling, carefree this time holding a hand grenade like a small chirping bird. All of his appearances, documented in my Death Book. An exercise in what? In the breaking of silence, in self-verification? A testament of futility, of shame. What? The grenade ticks. How very strange. That this book which I have mocked, distrusted, thrown across the room on many occasions, should serve as a small yet undeniable act of fury and faith and twisted optimism at the last minute.

Angel eyes, angel mouth, angel wings passing over me. Angel tongue.
Free, free . . .

No, I don't think so. No. She comes disguised as an angel in borrowed robes. Glinting, heralded, trumpeted. Untrustworthy. Sad skeptic that I am; I distrust her. For who has seen such compassion before in a human being? She speaks low and soft and directly without condescension, without arrogance, and her gaze is calm. She seems to tremble at times when she's near me. Am I crazy? She does, doesn't she? She says she cannot bear the notion of a life sacrificed. *Not now, Beatrice.* She has appeared before me at the time when I can least use her. *It's too late. You'd be hard-pressed to make me want to live.* Still she constructs and reconstructs ornate options—filled with caveats and hearings and new information. *New information? No, not new information now.*

* * *

I look up from my snazzy platter of tar and feathers. Her slave narrative. *Well, what amazing feat do you have planned for me today, Beatrice?*

She sings. *He's got the whole world in his hands, he's got the whole world in his hands, he's got the whole world in his hands.*
A tiny Jesus hung around her neck. Too late. *It's too late now.*
Angel eyes, angel mouth, angel wings passing over me. Angel tongue.

Never too late, Bernadette. She holds an enormous sheaf of papers.

$$|\,cat\ alive\rangle_{CAT}\,|\,N\rangle_D\,|\,move\ \to\rangle_A\,|\,spin\rangle_e$$

And I am flustered by her common sense, her strength of character, her extraordinary aptitude for life. She points to the family, look:
How far they have come from their first pietà. Once and only once more. There. They stand as if someone has positioned them this way around the commotion at the center. Seraphs descend. The baby, the basin, the bottles of whiskey. The weeping mother, the father pouring alcohol onto the body of the child so as to try to lower the outlandish fever it holds in its trembling body. Large, archetypal, the father whispers *live* and the gloom lifts, if only slightly—and they are a family for a moment, fighting for something: the baby's life. The father's hand pressed up. Behold such ingenuity, such clear-eyed courage, such hope. The babe in the tin manger, who lives, who lives—for now.

That he died quickly and among strangers in his eighteenth year. And I am ten, bereft, and I sleepwalk through sorrow, assuming its postures, but unable to feel anything at all for real. Wretched present tense, even now. Where nothing ever passes. Stay dead, for once. I try to pray. To locate him somewhere—anywhere. To pinpoint him. I can't place him in any heaven or hell. It doesn't seem true that he's gone and that he'll *absolutely never be back*. It's a joke someone is playing. I'm quite sure he'll be back. Can you guarantee me that he won't be back? *Not ever, ever?* I take a long time to bury the ring. I mark the spot carefully. He would be upset if I lost it.

And she is numb, the little one. And her hair has begun to fall out.

F. (For men) It wasn't my fault because *penises are supposed to respond to touch. I had an erection because my abuser stimulated me sexually, not because I wanted to be abused.*

1. It wasn't my fault because _____

2. It wasn't my fault because _____

3. It wasn't my fault because _____

4. It wasn't my fault because _____

5. It wasn't my fault because _____

Once we dreamt, unfettered, unworried, high in the trees, talking of silly things.

No, there would be no more cards and cake. My mother sinks into irretrievable bitterness. No more trips to the sea *en famille*. No more imploring at the feet of the Virgin, no more roses at the feet of the Virgin. Witness her terrible turning away from God.

But he was dead for his country and in the beginning at any rate they came to commemorate. He was being used by this impoverished community as a symbol of something, my wretched brother now made useful. My father proud and blustering, complicitous in this revision—his shining son. His now silent son—no more arguing now. Silent and perfect, heroic and over.

Oh had we not died once already that last electrified night in the trees—in the black-charmed, dog-tagged, dog-eyed night where he was hurt and hurtful? Miserable. Afraid. No more. Now he was—as he would have wanted, relishing irony as he did, hating everything as he did—celebrated, redeemed.

*   *   *

A country who gave nothing, and cared nothing about anyone or anything, as he used to say. Unless you had money. Unless you were rich, which was a different story then, wasn't it?

Fuck, Beanie, I'll get us out of here.

I am the insatiate. He appears in the predictable middle of the night, in his less than predictable guise. He comes tongue-tied, apologetic. Holding an insipid crucifix. Genuflected. Or sporting a Ronald Reagan button. *What is wrong with you?*

The war dully raged on as you know past 1969, but we having done our part, exempted ourselves from it. All we heard on the night TV was a monotony of numbers not even I could transform, as the death tolls rose. Mother's recitations had always been those of the phone company, but now they seemed to change in nature, in cadence— as she morbidly counted the dead in her miserable counting house. How many more had been slaughtered this bright day, joining her son in that void. *She had begged him.* In the beginning she had wept. Father out walking and drinking. And the sister—What am I, peering out from the ruby bruised ribs of this prison, mute, matted, rain-soaked still? Did we not die once that night? Traipsing through the hurt. And did it not bleakly foreshadow all that was to come?

Bernadette, take my hand, little saint, before the rain.

Consider the collapsing universe, my pet. Consider, Alexander, my perfectly strung, my beautifully hung, my well-tempered clavier, my exquisite one. Attentive to the smallest motions, delicately calibrated, precise. Yes, your precision—your intuition. That afternoon long ago now where we measured the indivisible, the incommensurate, the immeasurable together . . . The room drenched in light. Light of the mind. And after a while how we got mind and body to work in concert—a kind of harmonics—impossible to attain alone. Each spurring the other on, perhaps even creating the other. Much later, bound and gagged and shaved, did we not understand as we hadn't before, the limitations? We could better taste the places we wanted so badly to get to, could we not? And acquire as a result new incentives. Pondering freedom. Freely associating elements in accordance with freely chosen rules, and generating structures that resemble, but do not essentially represent, physical or historical reality. Such good mathematics.

Trussed up like that.

We were being pulled, not unpleasantly down a dark corridor. Oh yes. Mr. Ashmeade, may I remind you, it was what you most desired in this world: the elegant, overwhelming brilliance of your mind's black back waters.

His hands moving through space, dividing the air into what one could imagine were golden sections. The divine proportions of his desire. He was lovely, and he grew with each passing day, more and more so.

And with each passing day he grew slowly to love me, slowly, in a way he had never loved. I was the person who was pressing him into being. How could he have resisted? I was the only one on this whole lonely earth who could meet his mind and engage it in the way he needed, grant him license, push him in the directions he so desperately desired. *Please.* He begged after only a little while, for me to press him further, to give him more. *Yes.* He wanted us to go there together, forgetting in his delirium how far beyond him I always was. *Please.* But he wanted me to go anyway; he wanted me to be at his side. Like all men. Just once and only once would I agree to this. It was all along part of the master plan.

The divine proportions of desire—

Fur coat for Christmas, a diamond ring, big Cadillac car, and everything.... Down the hall. Beatrice is laughing, down the hall. Beatrice is singing.

The ring is mine after all, as I'm sure you recall, and I have the right to do anything I like with it.

Black swan on a mute beach. Beauty. *Beatrice, is that you? You do me wrong to wake me from my grave. Please don't.*

I have noticed that she is obscenely curved. Did I mention that she jangles? She walks in the most extraordinarily rhythmic patterns.

She comes more and more frequently to my side with papers she hopes I'll sign, with new schemes she's devised in the night. Why is she so bent on survival? Where does her faith come from? Her obstinance. *Go away.*

How did he even dare to dream under such circumstances? Dare try to fix something in this place so broken. Believed somewhere there might be a place he might walk again, a little whole.

Don't go—

I had already stopped speaking by the time of Fergus's death. It is usually attributed to his death—my silence—but I had been silent in fact since his departure that day on the Greyhound platform, in a kind of advance mourning. Ten months ahead of his last death. Clutching the ring in my hand. He mouthing, mouthing—what?—through the watery glass of the window. Unbearable. A halo of fire already around his head.

Don't go—

In the dream recurring, in the dream without end, he whispers through the distorted glass, garbled—*Never tell anyone. Never. Never say a word* . . . And the bus pulls away. From brother to soldier boy.

Never.

Bernadette!

What deal must I strike, whatever deal in God's wide world must I strike with you now? What deal must I strike? For quiet.

Bernadette! His hand against the glass.

He cries for me in the night wanting, wanting. *Don't go.* Alex wrapped head to toe in latex unable to move. I touch him through that glass. Numbers fall like snow. What is this blizzard?

*   *   *

Is that you, Alex, looking everywhere now for me, or is it merely a figment? Let our bones touch. Grind if you will. Until we are dust.

Wanting this still. Blackened neck. Wanting more still. Alex is that you? Who comes now?

Hey.

One has time in prison for all sorts of perverse projects. One has time to drive oneself absolutely crazy in any number of ways. One even has time to *fall in love.* I find myself in the *most peculiar of all situations* in what has been *a most peculiar life*—and at this late hour— is it possible—that I do—I am mortified to say it—have feelings for, I believe, perhaps, have feelings—love, and with a passion once only reserved for figures. *What next,* I suppose you'll ask. All kissy and wishful and dreamy. This plot, run so terribly amok. Dear God. Elizabeth, perhaps this is for you. A nod to your kind. *What next?*

She hands me those willful, triumphant documents again and again in my half-sleep—trying to force me to see a window that might make me too, want to survive. She offers that underground railroad. Never mind the barking of dogs. *Bargain for your life, child. Run!*

The lights go out. Another day annihilated. Look. The countdown continues so don't get your hopes up. Mark your calendars, gentle readers, appalled indicted voyeurs. Imagine it: not too many more days. *Who calls?* Here now a body as dark as surely any night ever was. Embrace the night now. The path descends. And she is there.

Do it for me, please, Bernadette, do it for me.

I have witnessed in the dark, in the shadows here, the many sexual configurations women left to their own devices are capable of making. I've seen a lot of things in my years—in the half light, in the dark, in the books Connie has shown me and now in the operating theater of my own mind. Brightly lit. I am laid out on the proscenium now—dead is that it? A cold marble slab. No—she kneels, parts my legs, gently, sweetly and says something inaudible with those incredible lips. Terrifying woman. *Don't be afraid, Bernadette. It's OK. Look I know you've seen a lot of pain. I know . . .*

Oh yeah—I know . . . Solace is her voice, saying, saying, *I know darlin' . . .*

She bends her head as if in prayer. She takes a breast gently in her mouth. Slowly, tenderly. *No one can hurt you now.* She kisses my thighs with those lips, she goes further; I know not exactly what she does, is doing. I ask her to lift her head and she looks up dazed, the glistening mouth—and there are tears in her eyes. She says, *She's been afraid her whole life.* And she cries and kisses me gently, and for one night we are whispering to one another, consolations, prayers. *I know.* If only once. If only one night, once, before I die.

Say . . . She takes my hand. *Don't go. Live . . . Say you'll live.* Who is this phantom before my eyes mouthing salvation?

They tell me I chatter in my sleep. They tease. They say I speak her name.

She is all mouth, beautiful, swollen. Sound coming out.

Sound. And I have grown twenty years away from him now. And when he returns, he no longer recognizes me.

Sound.

And I have agreed somehow to allow her to try to get me out of this. I have agreed. She has filed the papers, and we wait. She says there is a *very fine chance.* She has secured the great and famous for the task, the most famous, the most feminist, she says. Sound coming out. To drown the voices. Sound.

Split like a luscious peach and halved. Sweet, gorgeous skin to finger. Foolish to even wish . . .

Love, if one could feel it, would be a kind of defiance; life, wouldn't it—

* * *

In her state, peaches. Chitlins. Hominy. Songs around the fire. No dogs. No guarded boundaries or borders.

The devotion to her swagger. Her luscious voice. Ripeness, kindness.

And I, at this late hour, agree. I do it for her.

I am beast, Beatrice, hurt; lick my fur.
I know. I know you're hurtin' girl.
Grow old . . .

Geez, you sure do look good in blue, Connie says. *Is it my imagination or are you becoming one foxy lady as you get ready to meet Mr. D.? I think you should consider staying here with us, what do you say? I'm tellin' you, babe, hell's got no use for you.*

Grow old with me around the fire. Under the vaulted, precise sky. The stars finally harmless. Even we might wish. And when we're old—I feel dizzy. Unable to breathe, a little frightened. The newness of such emotions. I worry. Dare not breathe a word.

In the liquid, incredibly beautiful, black velvet night. Voice like syrup pouring, pouring. Fill this . . .

And I am finally, and almost, thanks to you dear, Beatrice, human again.

And I am going to die. But in my own time.

Act Four

*T*he dream is green and I am fetus clinging. Clinging to your emerald bones in that time, that time before . . . Clovered to you. The last free place. Verdant, rich. The shining pelvis bone to which I clung. I flare at your waist. Unwilling to live outside. My first bit of real intelligence. A forcepped birth. In the year of our weariness, 1960. Taking the tongs. Traumatically. How the scene now stubbornly asserts itself again and again. Extracted. The patient etherized. *Mother.*

Before I disappoint or let you down. Before you disappoint or let me down. Before numbers or stars, before language, before notions of beginnings or endings. Before a hand was raised. Before a hand existed at all. Before the brain. Sensing the body forming, quickly and slowly. There are miracles. Here come the fingers. Small toes. Frog heart. Amphibious in the watery dark. In the time before the world had anything against us yet. In the time of reprieve—suspended, lingering. *Last forever. Never end.*

Through the womb: her senseless, beautiful litany of numbers. One moment of beauty, release, peace. The green is reclaimed tonight. So there are no seizures or muteness, no bladder infections, no stomachaches, no choking on one's grief. No night sobs, no clubfoot, no defending oneself against—against what? What? *What is it darlin'?* No darkness. Or dogs. No rain. The voices silenced awhile. That doomsday chorus. That goat song. The forces of night. No backaches, no splayed walk home.

Difficulty swallowing. Crooked road no more.
The world is calm and wide.

Her voice. Not here now. Three a.m. How to describe that voice?
A good voice. All body. That voice. And how it turns everything
in me liquid. Her mass of braids entwined with glinting things.
Her smell. I am lightheaded, giddy. What is wrong with me? *Never,
never . . .* No, not ever—And she whispers at three a.m. *hey*—and *darlin' sugar* and *honey pot.* And slow now, like molasses. Such yearning—
she out there in her fluid, viscous, incredibly lovely night, studded
with stars. She wears a shining ornament in her nose. Around an ankle
a snake is wrapped. And the little Jesus drowned in her cleavage, begging for mercy—kindness. Such kindness, such gentleness, respite.
Not too late. Not . . . Her voice like syrup, pouring. Nothing can fill
this bleak longing, magnified and made more urgent by the tightening frame. How the cruelties of this world never cease. 4:04 a.m.
Never felt, never even glimpsed before—there was never even an
inkling—oh why must it surface now?
   You do me wrong to wake me from my grave.
   Some days she jangles. And I in standard Pavlovian response, rise,
clutch pathetically, melodramatically at my prison bars—and I am
mortified. I weep—further humiliation. Further indignations. Most
grave night. Why now? What awakens? I look out into the hallway's
night, anticipating her footsteps, desiring—desiring. *Almost* desiring.
Her body lingers—at some distant periphery. I lay hypnotized, *slayed*
as the students say, by even her invented, her fabricated image. Incapable now of looking away.

   Her purply fistful of flowers. She has brought me a few violets. *It
is a beautiful summer day.* I have not seen a flower in years. That this
should happen now. It's too much. The desire—dare I say it—to
survive.

$$\hat{H}_{CAT}\hat{H}_D\hat{H}_{SG} \,|\, cat\ alive\rangle_{CAT} \,|\, N\rangle_D \,|\, move \rightarrow\rangle_A \,|\, \downarrow\rangle_e =$$

$$[\hat{H}_{CAT} \,|\, cat\ alive\rangle_{CAT}][\hat{H}_D \,|\, N\rangle_D][\hat{H}_{SG} \,|\, move \rightarrow\rangle_A \,|\, \downarrow\rangle_e] =$$

$$[\hat{H}_{CAT} \,|\, cat\ alive\rangle_{CAT}][\hat{H}_D \,|\, N\rangle_D] \,|\, move \downarrow\rangle_A \,|\, \downarrow\rangle_e] =$$

$$[\hat{H}_{CAT} \mid cat\ alive\rangle_{CAT} \mid \downarrow\rangle_D \mid move\ \downarrow\rangle_A \mid \downarrow\rangle_e] =$$
$$\mid cat\ alive\rangle_{CAT} \mid \downarrow\rangle_D \mid move\ \downarrow\rangle_A \mid \downarrow\rangle_e$$

I grow old, putrid, decidedly unlovely in here. She is laughing, I hear her lilting laugh from down the hall. She is planning her vacation. Showing the girls brochures—giving them something to hope for. I hear Connie, nervously saying, *Isn't New Orleans a little far to be going?*

Isn't New Orleans awfully far?

Do you know where Beatrice is? Connie smiles. *Well, well, don't we look nice today, Miss Bernadette. Correct me if I'm wrong, but I think someone has snuck in the night and combed that rat's nest of yours, am I right? And someone's tidied up in here. Girl, I'll find Beatrice for you.* She winks. *You sure do look good in blue.*

What beat in the night? What piece of her? What cried from the line? The people who heard it felt a pain. Poor child. What was so hurt in the night? Back and forth, back and forth, swaying in the wind. Lit and unlit by lightning.

Late night. Jade eyes. That throat. Mouth. They called those *nigger lips* in my house. Regret—four-eyed, hydra-headed—sadness tonight, jealousy, she's probably in someone else's bed. I'd have liked, just once, Beatrice. One kiss. There may have been salvation. Just once. Solace. Sanctuary. Oh these late night lamentations. What is happening to me? I can't describe the strangeness now as I feel it coming on.
Is that you?

Odd news. Have I invented it then? To *subvert myself* as Beatrice would say. I'll check with Connie in the morning. More and more bad feelings as of late. New Orleans. World's end.

Behold: you stand emblematic of all that's been lost, in the failing light of morning where there are numbers. At least that. Everything charted. You'd

like to paint all the threes purple, you think in this injured light. The fives
black, all the sevens pink, pink like a girl, pink like a little girl. If you lie on
your back, you can see all of the stars. Isn't that Betelgeuse? she asks. Never
say a word, Bernadette. About the pink or the ring or the bride . . . (lie (you)
AND on (you, your (back))) $\Rightarrow$ every star s: can (see (you, s))

Color the sky violet. That kind of bruised color.

You come now only in the definitive middle of the night, howling, a little absurdly, telling me not to tell anyone, that it is our little
secret—still our secret. And you ask me again to forgive you and it
strikes me as strange. *Forgive you for what? Fergus, speak to me.* Your
weird guilt-ridden visitations as the final night nears, as the darkness
descends. Sometimes you come with your pack of little boys—the soldiers from your unit. In the punishing middle of the night where you
recount the slaughter of the innocents, *just children*. You weep and
mutter *sorry, sorry*. But I long to know, I long to witness, just once,
your extravagant death as it was, and not just as it was in my mind. It
would be a last intimacy. I would like just once to see the slings and
arrows of your outrageous fortune, the flames around your head, your
arms outstretched. Crimson. Your body crucified to a napalmed sky.
Married to it. I long to see you once as you were at the end, utterly
transformed, transfigured. As you long to see me. Just a wish. I have
grown twenty years away from you. Even if you find me one day, in
some way other than dreams, when you see me you will not recognize
me, your little sister—no, I do not think that you shall recognize me.

Violets were planted long ago around each tree in that park. You might
have brought those tender blossoms to your teacher.

You might have run with the others through the tall weeds and grasses,
Little Beanie, even you. A game of tag. A game of Double Dutch or Duck
Duck Goose. Even you.

Your little friend Beatrice passing you a secret note. Flowers pressed in a
pink book with its lock and key. And giggling, and whispering, isn't that
sweet? Cat alive, cat alive, you write.

Nervous in here as of late. Time plays its tricks. Hard to know
whether it passes quickly or slowly—none of the regular markers any-

more. I haven't menstruated in months—or so it seems. I've lost count—and counting once was everything.

Beatrice announces one afternoon that she will be going on vacation for two weeks. *Yeah like where,* Connie asks, *like New Orleans?*
Beatrice nods.
Then she just slips it in casually, as they are trained to do, I assume—that it is to be her honeymoon.

It being personal and everything, Connie says, *it's pretty cool she told us.*

The stillborn news. There's a little girl with a ring in her fist. A veil and a hurt—can't somebody help her? A bride wept. A dog barked.

Reeling uncomprehendingly . . .
In the theater one always laughs at the betrayed woman. Don't spoil it now, Bernadette, play the part.

Irritating enough her news out of the blue of a two-week vacation in the middle of my demise, but then to *leave out altogether the other bit*—that in her absence she is *to be wed.* God, the rot of secrecy. Oh I am sick to death of all of it. Do you hear? *Sick to death.* Spare me. His name is Cal. Please spare me the details. Do you hear me? I want nothing of it. He's a methadone nurse. No sound coming out.

And the girls are laughing and saying they're going to give her a bachelorette party like she's never seen before.

Nubian bride, muscular, beautiful, strong—in a hypocrisy of white. *Do you take this man?* Slave bracelets around her wrists and ankles. A wedding! Frailty, indeed, thy name is Beatrice.

And many times before this they had come to this spot. He sang her songs: "In-A-Gadda-Da-Vida" and "Purple Haze." I'll keep you sheltered from the storm. Number the purple haze now. Put the voice away in a locket.
And many times they had to come to this place. Higher and higher in the trees. Sky and clouds and the surrender of green. No one can hurt us here. No

one can get us here, little one. Posters, a mattress, a record player, beer. Let me take you higher. Let me take you higher to this—

Terrible sepulcher up in the trees. Pity them, these quaint costumed players: she in her childish sundress, he in his shirt and muscles and jeans. He puts his arm around her. She can see every hair on his hand. He'll keep her sheltered . . .

The tumored fish thrown back. Is that rain—or just Bernadette weeping now?

Who will help them? Doomed. Roaming toward home.

Back to the bleak house. Where was Jane? And why didn't Jane, anyway? Incoherencies of night and day. And the little girl with quiet doll mouth, doll arms, doll legs, and the little girl—he loves her so much—she holds the ring.

The strangled news, the awful news. *Who's there?* Stupid. I am left desolate. News that will not go away. News that hangs around my neck. An albatross—claws turned toward the ruined heart—after all, who is she to me? Fraudulent ally, I am done playing her games. What did she hope to save? What did she hope to salvage from this wreckage of circumstance and temperament?

Won't the godhead just leave me be now? Leave me here to rot in peace? Won't the godhead? Stop whispering. Stop whispering sweet nothings in my ear. Such nothings. And there—there, over there, over there's my marble twin, headless in the black grass, in an over-grown field, forgotten at last—no more genius, no more tabloid queen, nothing—decades after my execution. Skeleton. Birdbones. And another astride her, taking undo advantage. Who are you? Doing this to Birdbones? Speak.

And the God summons us. And even without head, the marble girl, she complies.

Lie down for a moment, he says, why *don't you and I will—I will—* Our solitary, furious Father who art in heaven. *Come down here and I will sidle up to you. Kiss your stony forehead. Kiss you everywhere with my marble lips.* Come on now, my wounded one. Cold one, hot one, cold one. My capricious, my whimsical one. A little potion perhaps for the porches of your ear. A velvet rope to slip around your neck. If I ever got that close. Come to me now my Love, my Lamb of God who takes away the sins of the world. Why have you once again, forsaken me?

If there could have been one shred of hope along the way.

The girls have decided to throw a little impromptu bachelorette party for Beatrice, in which the whole point is that Beatrice be made to sit and listen to the wing's vulgarities and prejudices and miseries, same as usual, but with a festive flair. Clouds of cigarette smoke. Wild madcap glee. Those on medication hoard it and pass it out as party favors. Count on a lewd dance by Mimi—a floor show with pasties and edible panties. Latasha will sing. There will be *a roasting*, as they call it, in which they talk primarily about Beatrice's ass, her thighs, her lips, her cat eyes, her jade walk. Cal will be called the human dildo. Almost everyone here fears men, having been beaten, flattened, threatened, battered, raped, deserted, set on fire . . . Still they are hopeful for Beatrice; it's just how they are. Romantic, sentimental girls, still buying into the dream big time. Gifts will be made in arts and crafts. Lucinda has made a painting where Beatrice and Cal are kissing in a field of flowers, and each flower has the face of an inmate in it—odd lot that we are. Joni presents her with a pair of fishnet stockings. Jacki has made a license plate with their initials intertwined. And Dolores has finally found the occasion to relinquish the beloved FUCK-U plate she's been saving for a special occasion.

Marriage brought up every kind of reminiscence in the girls. Not coincidentally, I think, back came the stories of the crimes that had landed them in here. Sherri, told us again about throwing herself and her children off the roof. Only to survive. No money to feed them. She almost thought they might all fly—and leave that crazy miserable bastard behind.

They had been accessories to every conceivable crime: holdups, hoists, kidnappings. Wendy remembered trying to force Jimmy's hand in love, and when he wouldn't come around, she resorted to a bit of strychnine—not quite enough in the end to kill him. Our *personal Jean Harris*, headmistress at some fancy Southern finishing school, had shot her faithless lover, but missed her target, and instead wounded some innocent person ambling down some hotel's hall for ice. *Poor sucker*, the girls cluck and cackle and laugh. All the botched jobs. Everyone's in a tizzy. There's lots of stimulation today. Even the *lost girls* circle a bit faster. Those drug addicts, alcoholics, and the otherwise chronically *insane*, broken a long time ago, walking, walking, in ever-tightening bewildered circles. *What? Who?* they ask ambling in. Now they are mild with medication, vaguely sweet, holding cards and mementos from lost relatives. And Connie, of course, who tried to make it look like she was euthanizing poor old Lyle; she'd even sent for the fancy pamphlet from Doctor Kevorkian, and she almost got away with it. *Yeah sure you did.* Everyone in party hats. And they're passing around a picture of Cal, *and now isn't he a sexy devil, Beatrice???*

What flares from the corners of the frame now is hurt: burn it, burn it if you can. What makes us blind is grief.
That child digging and digging.
But you wouldn't have to hurt her, would you, Bernadette? You could just let her go—couldn't you? (Beatrice, run!)

Injured—blood spurting. Blood pulsing out of a hurt side. Who has done this to blissful Beatrice? It is monstrous, unforgivable.
There's a hole. I am sorry. How to describe it?
I will suckle you, nurse you back. Sew you, my sweet.
I will sew you up. Virgin again. Inverse virgin. The slit so deep; I'll sew it up—so snug.
Who has died here? Poor wretch left by the side of the road. You whom I could not save. I tried to sew you up. Forgive me if you can. Poor thing. The scalloped border in her mouth. Panty in her mouth. Can you forgive me? My sweet? Poor thing. And I am gimpy, once more, with wedding veil, funeral veil. Twisted. Crooked.
An illicit business, this. In the night. Hurt side. In flagrant violation. My physician's oath, sacred, coded. *Who has done this to you?* She can't speak with that panty in her mouth now can she? *Forgive me. Never wanted to hurt you.* I am exhausted. My surgical gloves covered in blood up to my elbows. Look: the red eye.
Bernadette you're losing it—it's not like you—come on. Get a fucking grip.
Beatrice. Walking down the wayward aisle. Parading the marriage meats. Now left to grow cold. Left out, putrid. You spoil everything, Black Sheep.
Sweet meats at the marriage table, dissected. Life giving—

fleshy—brown bread—black flesh—*why all charred all of a sudden?*
The panty burning, the screaming unintelligible mouth. There is a
distance between us now, when there might have been nearness.
Sorry, dear one. You have put now considerable distance between us.
And I am laughing stock again. Forgive me. I tried to sew you shut.
Free finally. It was for your own good.

Grotesque. Beatrice in her greedy, insatiable bed. Immodest,
spread again and again. Her one-track mind, twisted as she is this
night into the next multi-orgasmic position. Hold: the faceless red
machine, pummeling, pounding, insistent. Hold: Foaming, slick pu-
denda. Until she is utterly raw. Rash acts, done in the dark with the
salivating groom. His blunt love stump. That small mock resurrection. Lascivious night without end. Gluttonous one, juiced up, four-
lipped—atrocious—offering your slits. Mouthing your want in hot
and garble-cupped yowls. Worn. Mound of harlot.

*Bow-legged child, gagging on her own sadness and dress—You wouldn't
have to hurt her would you, Bernadette? You could, couldn't you, just let
her go?*

*Shriek without a mouth and hair pulled back now exaggerated. The lit-
tle girl holds the ring. She'll bury it in the yard like a bone. So no one will
know. No one will ever know. Garden of ring and black roses. Garden of
sharp and pointed thorns.*

*In the memory now you paint almost everything black or red. We worry.
You didn't have to hurt her, did you, Bernadette?*

I did not mean to love you there at the scalloped torn border. Oh
my whatever have they done to you?

Bernadette! he cries through the trees. I'm back!

Miscarriage in the middle of the night. Six months of you. Who
would have taken shelter here? Smart one. Hang her on the line.
Never had a chance. Never. Blood and veins and red hair. Flat egg.
Shhh-shhh—Lie quietly. He can't find you now. In your disguise

of blood and guts. Sure he's bereft. Still—shhh—You are nearly transparent. Rife with unpromise. And so silent. Shy, somewhat shy, speechless placenta. They can't touch her now.

Ended before she began. Safe.

He's got the iddy biddy babies in his hands.
He's got the whole world in his hands.

Bloody bag of tricks skipping down the lane. *I'll find you. I'll find you yet!* Soiled gown. Patent leather and soiled gown. *There's no need to hide. Be on my side, I'll be on your side, there is no reason for you to hide.* He's singing. *Come on now, Beanie. Come on . . .*

Come to me then. I expose a shoulder. Like a Nubian bride. I lure him expertly to this place. Lift my dress. An impossibly long leg. Who could believe? *I swear. I swear. Love.* Hoping to satisfy you—if this would serve as the definitive good-bye, brother. If this would make you disappear.

Produce the night one more time. Are those wedding bells I hear now in my belfry? Good God. Marry you? *Marry you?* Lawful and wedded and bedded.

Oh why not? Sing nicely tonight, dear Alex, for this finally is our wedding night.

We stage our little mock wedding in this our most unholy sepulcher. Spring. A warehouse high above the city—just outside his beloved Cambridge. I am in white dress, white veils tinged and he in gleaming tuxedo. Latex gloves to the elbow. And aren't we almost ordinary for once? A frill at the collar, small flourish—*produce the child.* He is altogether remarkable—a catch: handsome, intelligent, flexible, adventuresome, compliant. He has agreed with great cheerfulness to our little ceremony. I've got the famous ring in my pocket. And a little satin sack to collect the loot. One more heterosexual privilege. And aren't we just ever so self-congratulatory tonight? The cakey bride, the beefy groom—and asleep already in the dreaming womb. *Shhh—dream.* We'll drink champagne from my little glass slipper, all right?

I cart the crucifix from which I hypothesize the voices come—have always come—the awful prostrate god. I stare at my Alex through crinoline, slowly opening him outward into a kind of sexual infinity. The wedding shapes we'll force ourselves into—triangle, trapezoid, throbbing rhombus—the new sex of the marriage bed—the new sex of the end. *My contract whore,* I whisper. He shudders. At the altar a latex mask, a vial of crack. *Do you take this man?* My hand resting, swearing on his tattered *Wasteland.* The end is nearing now, my love. *Trust.* Were we not asked each Sunday to drink down His blood? Yes. Were we not beckoned each Sunday to dine on the dead God's body? Yes.

I am glowing like a counterfeit saint. Unsuffered. For who at this altar can suffer, burn, bleed enough? Supplicant. Lord I am not worthy to receive you. Say only the word. Say only the word and my soul shall be healed. Say but the word—

But no word comes.

And I carry a bouquet of bloodroot and rue. First flowers. And baby's breath. God, we're almost like everyone else tonight. And we shall be called betrothed. Something little and perfect and over. In a gilded frame. He carries me over this last threshold.

Not to swerve away from what captivates. He can't wait a minute longer and he hurries me to our marriage bed. Bed of bright, shining, bed of blood. I am already in torn satins and crinolines, bandaged and splint. He opens my legs and gets down on his knees. *Do you promise to protect?* I ask him. Yes. *Do you promise to shelter?* I ask. Yes. Till death. *OK then.*

You'll kill me yet, he smiles, as I lower the hood over his head, as I strap him in. *Are you complaining then?* I stuff the rough cut rubies, a wedding gift, into his condom for extra friction. I make the numbing and tingling concoction. Inject the plasma. Take the electrodes and clamps from my handbag. Slip the ring onto his pinkie.

The unfringed hole. The marriage stain. And I as small as a doll. Matchbox bride. Embryonic hope. Swaddled in perfect white, I am as stillborn as a doll. Quiet in my cradle. Wedding night. Quiet, quiet. Cradle in the bough is breaking.

What do they want from this warped passion play as they escort each other through the last stages of their suffering?

And you see:

He looks in the distance, clear-eyed, intent on his death. He feels the hero seed, strange grenade inside him

About to ignite, about to explode. Lie on your back, Bernadette. Count the stars. Fix your place.

He prays the edge of her dress like a rosary.

Bow-legged Cassiopeia. Poor Virgo. And Sirius.

The dog star dangling around his neck. The dog tags. You'd follow him, if he'd let you.

You'd do anything for him.

It's a dream, Bernadette, so the rumblings and hurt and the ache in your body and fear are only thunder. The tremblings are thunder. Look you can quiet them. We've taught you how.

One more time then. The wedding guests assemble. The mannequins of Suzie Q and all the other blow-up dolls he fucked. *He was to protect them.* And there's Fergus, like some crackpot Humpty Dumpty, put back together. Mother and Father are dead now. Or so they say. Is that right? But look—there's his sprightly family. His mother who says Alexander is *not himself; he is someone else.* And his father who carries in a little sack the pricey trousseau. Silken ear of the pig. *Produce the child, produce the child,* the families howl.

Vow you will, vow you will, be mine forever, he whispers, sings. *Oh yes. And you mine. My brilliant thing.*

Lawful and bedded and wedded, do you take?

His throbbing glance.

Small bird and rabbit traps—careful—and land mines—everywhere you step now—careful—lake without fish. And the marriage bed, where I, gentle wife, sign the papers, the documents, which say fuck by contract forever. And he vows to love, honor, serve, obey. And he will rescue me from my miserable life. It hurts tonight. Everything hurts tonight. Relax. We're contracted.

Honor, serve, obey, he whispers, in the deepening night, *love me,* he pleads, in the darkening trees.

My blushing bride. My concubine. And he commands all night, he says: *swallow now,* he says, *you are mine now.* Suck and inhale the snails, the puppy dog tails.

And he asks me to spend money, and he forces me to spend

money *obscene, obscene—we should be saving up for the week's groceries.*
Spend, he commands, *buy dresses, look like someone I can be proud of,* and
he takes me out in a misery of spending, an obscenity of spending.
*But who will pay the gas and electric bills? The rent? The car's broken down
again.* The nails driven to hold me to my place. And no—certainly
not—I do not think the resurrection is going to come off so easily this
time; the consummation, this time. Wedding bells. Casts, splints,
bandages, tubes. Limping toward home. I shriek, but no sound comes
out. I cry. *Bernadette, what is it?* Who's there?

It's the nightmares, it's the voices that make this life—

Lie on your back. The broken, veined sky at night. Is that lightning?
And she sees: He takes off his jean jacket and wraps her in it. Dark.
And she's gray-faced, poor urchin, in her red-flowered tangled dress and she
begins to cry—as if she's grieving already. Of course she is.
Then light. The scene is lit again. Hey, you, how about a pony beer? he
asks you.
It's a dream so the rumblings and hurt and the ache in her body and fear
is only thunder. The tremblings are thunder. Look you can quiet them. You
know how to do it now. Gag them. Strap them down.
The awful mute pleas coming out of her mouth. Who will hear her?

Alexander Ashmeade, born guilty, with the blood of robber
barons and factory owners on his hands, never innocent. He is all too
happy to repent, gladly, willingly, on his knees now again, kneeling
on the shards where all afternoon we have concocted lethal cocktails.
Across this strewn path of broken glass. *The windshield's shattered . . .*
Dad, the car's been broken into again. How unlike punishment this
seems to Alexander in the end. He enjoys it all too much. As he enjoys the elaborate system of twisted payments, blood money, fuck
money. Born guilty. Up to his neck in original sin. He comes up with
huge cash settlements in the end. I count it in my counting house.
    Oh the thrill of the exchange of money. Keeping our perverse lit-
tle economy going. He is more than happy to surrender his portion of
the family fortune. *There's an edge I can't get without this,* I whisper. The
blood-jet is money. We are gluttonous, excessive—there could be no
real creativity anymore without it. Do truer words exist?

* * *

We are stained with sin. We are up to our cashmere necks in it.
Our caviar mouths. We need a purifying, refining fire so that we
might get free. He too came to know this. He's torched up tonight.
Marry me, marry me . . .

*See how he hurts you, humiliates you, makes you concubine, slut, in a
tyranny of promises.*

*See how he turns you into freak Bernadette: three-headed, six-eyed,
grotesque, icy. Wife.*

How to quiet the voices, enlarging now, amplified?

I know I am the three-headed, six-eyed grotesque, icy, lunar,
crazed—out of place, out of time, godforsaken. They whisper: *impossible, brutal, monstrous.* Deceitful, deceived. Oh for God's sake, everyone
knows it.

The hordes of poor, mean-spirited girls in that Fall River community where I was treated with such disdain, such suspicion.
Treated as a freak, sideshow, utter stranger. Most hated, most different. What would they say if I told them I am *popular? Popular!* Popu-
larity? I did not even dare to wish for it back then. Oh what is wrong
with me tonight? Tell them, if they do not already know it—that I
am famous now. That there are friends. Finally.

Or one friend. One—once. Or two, if you count Connie. Of
course I'd count Connie now.

The chorus of girls on C Wing joke. She has come back from
her honeymoon all vibrant and dewy. Charged up. Ready to go. Re-
invigorated for the fight. The papers she assures me shall come
through any day now. But I am despondent—that's what she writes
in her book—will not eat or speak. *Please say something*—but she
won't fool me again, make me idiot, laughing stock. She won't fool
me this time.

She seems inordinately concerned about me considering her re-
cent antics in Louisiana. She sends in the doctors. She assures me I
will be saved. *Look, I know you're afraid.*

I shake my head.

Given the choice, I choose not to live. Given the choice, I choose to die.

Off to the side, which is meant to denote the past, I suppose, a child stands, angry, frightened, fierce, in firelight, torturing birds, cats, something's gotten stuck, he says with mock innocence in the lawnmower's blade. In his wretched world, that place of small and sanctioned violence—where you just might get away. Without consequence. Guiltless. Bloody cat head, broken bird, place of retribution and rage and waste.

$$| \textit{cat dead})_{CAT} | \uparrow)_D | \textit{move} \uparrow)_A | \uparrow)_e$$

She is trying to convince them that this execution will be *nothing more than a state-assisted suicide*. Talk about *clutching at straws*. That I refuse all help, all petitions, all requests for pardon, grace. A *death-row volunteer*, as I'm called.

He loves the ritualized pursuit of pleasure now more and more. He begs to be suitably costumed, armored, regimented, strapped, masked, sanctioned. He wants blackouts. He wants feathers or ball bearings or bells, a high fashion of lace and leather, gauze and foams and party hats. He loves to be told, to be arranged, to be configured into positions for maximum tension and resistance. The Five Renunciations, the Twelve Charms, the Seven Sorrowful Mysteries, the Eight Configurations, the Nine Catastrophes, the Five Acts of Contrition . . . Oh dear—never will the simple missionary work for him again. Poor thing. Spoiled like this for all time. Precious one, bedecked and feathered, weighted down with jewels. He places a ruby in my mouth.

He loves the game and the rules of the game. Blindman's bluff, pin the tail on the donkey. The ceremonies of semen and blood. Tree house. Accomplices in this grim task of pleasure—Come back, my dove, come back. Forbidden worlds open. He begs to be exploited. Ruined. As he has exploited. As he has ruined.

* * *

Again your inauspicious reappearance. Offering neither solace nor solution. What is it you want, dear brother?

He'll die. The awful mute pleas coming out of your mouth. Who will hear you? If you could only stop this. Console him. You'll die, you say. If you could let him know what you know—but you can't stop it—you can't do anything to stop it—and you know that it is—it must be—it's your fault.

No one is listening.

Paint the planes of his face green and gray and brown and beige. Camouflage him. Keep him safe.

But you can't keep him. Can't help him now out of his gray factory dressing gown. And you in tangled flowered dress, then Catholic school uniform, now wedding dress.

And there's nothing you can do, tiny bride, if you could only stop this,

Stop him now—

How to, how to—

Hungering to plunge or to pound or to otherwise keep the bloody, brooding image down. How to—

How to drown it.

You can be reckless if you like, Bernadette. You can call the black volts right up to this house in the trees—it's only a memory for God's sake. You'll be OK, safe; their meager positive, negative, positive flickering in the night is nothing to you. Cassiopeia weeping in the night without gods. Take out your box of paints. You can color this shape, the one that has lingered on the periphery like some wretched sadness or crimson—illegible banner from the static inner life—useless, stupid equation. Useless, stupid equation

Let 3 = red. Let 6 = magenta. Let 2 = purple. Let 7 = darkness + blood.

Define $\chi: N \Rightarrow$ {red, orange, yellow, . . .} such that $\chi(3) = $ red, $\chi(6) = $ magenta, $\chi(2) = $ purple; $\chi(7) = $ (darkness + blood).

$\chi(7) = $ {darkness, blood}

$\chi(7) = \text{darkness} \wedge \text{blood}$

Keep the voices down.

And he is getting there—each day he comes closer to the bone, dear heart, he works so hard, living now, nearing *the great truths* as he likes to say, and it's true—we've got an eternity, as you well know, to rot. His extraordinary heart. Somedays I think I'd like to remove his guts and blood, everything but the heart. Have him perfected. Mindless finally. Stuffed and stopped in fondest position: on hands and knees. Turned inside out. But I am tired now. Losing, lost. Our dwindling mathematics. I would like to crawl up and into you and put my head on your heart and rest there.

Rest there? You've got to be kidding.
It's a memory so there aren't the same rules. You could choose to alter the central fact—that he is going to die—but you don't choose.

He says in last eloquence on the day of the night he shall perish: sputters in the smoldering air—*take me to the edge tonight . . .*
My erupting rubric, highlighted in red. Instructions for the crucifixion. Soon. Soon. The voices say, *It's time.*

Cruel puppeteer with no face. Who are you, cowardly, equivocating, whispering in my ear like a lover now, *it's time.*

Because he's got to die; he's got to be stopped and there's nothing anyone can do about it. Strangle him. Hurry up, Bernadette, it's time.

Grotesqueries of the afternoon. Crime and punishment inflame his imagination. He puts all his books aside for good and enters the late stages of dementia. He slides away from all intentions. He lets me down. He disappoints me. *Sorry, sorry.* He's begging for it now. In tuxedo. In boutonniere.

Will you marry me? Marry me, he begs.
* * *

They're whispering, whispering.

All right—you can turn it up, but not without risk, let's listen for a minute: He's still mouthing marry me.

It's a memory for God's sake, Bernadette. So you can change it. Reverse your course, get fucking better. It wouldn't take much. You can alter it, quiet it, silence it, kill it. You can try, try—even you are entitled. Even you have a choice. You can end it, the marry me, end it, in the trees, the voices, even us, you could gag us, stop us. We'll be quiet if only—we promise. Please us, satisfy us. We'll be quiet, we promise. You could stop him, forever like this, little and perfect and over. You could shackle him, lash him to the deck—look over there—he's begging for it. You could be free. Even you. Even you.

Alexander Ashmeade, asleep in post-coital bliss, lashed to the deck, unhooded now, seemed to rouse himself for a brief moment and smile when he felt my familiar hands near his neck, assuming (and he assumed correctly) that I remained, even after all we'd been through, unsatisfied. *He's too close to be trusted.* Swatting me away in sleep, *Careful, Bernadette,* shrugging me away with a motion of his head, a kind of smile on his face, his bruised neck. He never had a chance—too late, too late to save himself—if that's even what he wanted. His fall away from everything this time was dramatic. I try to wake him, even now. Even here. Press a thumb nail into his arm, a forefinger, but he does not stir. *He'll keep you safe, he whispered at the altar, remember? Sure. Look even you, Bernadette, could be free.* His retreat was, even without me, utter. I simply furthered his journey, and hastened it. Already he grows so remote, cold. Waves a small wave. Red lid. Wing. Smile.

Do you promise to protect me? Say you promise to, my love.

I promise, he says, at the altar.

I believe you, she whispers.

Careful, Bernadette.

I do, Alexander. I trust you.

What is she saying? Careful, Bernadette. Your heart might break. Once and only once and never again.

I love you.

She loves him? God, she can be reckless, can't she? Bernadette, what are you saying?

I'll keep you safe, he whispers, gurgles.

*   *   *

A bride wept.

Had I realized then, as I do now, that he would become utterly improbable, irretrievable, never to be called up or found again, never to be wakened, I would surely have acted otherwise, wouldn't I? *Don't be a sentimental fool, Bernadette*—Bringing him again and again to the brink of death—perhaps that would have been enough. Oh *come on. You know it would never have been enough.* It remains to this day, the one thing I did not predict correctly, anticipate correctly—that I would want him back. Attachments had been made. *Too bad, too late.* That I would regret in the end the finality of these actions. Outlandish to think of. Within minutes I missed him. I never imagined it: that attachments could possibly have been made. That that could ever have been a possibility for me. And I am punished, subverted, bereft, betrayed, by my own hand.

This is bedlam. No question. Last dementia. Begging. He's begging. And then. And then no sound coming out—just a little smile. A veil of bright blood sheaths his one open eye. Clarity gone, all clarity forfeited now. Worms will soon appear here in the hollow, rotted afternoon. Pink hooded eye. And that look of astonishment. So this is where it all led us: to this pathetic precipice. Bad luck. Blue clawed. Sad tongue of ashes and last numbers. Fergus on the night shift, working overtime. My mother crying. Nothing ever works out. And the last shall be first. Sadnesses of the afternoon. The burned out water city. He's got a kind of sweet smile, if you can just block out the eyes. The diamond ring on his pinkie finger. Triumph of our vows. Sweet urn of evening coming on. Ashen meade . . . darling one. Slipping away in the dark trees. A velvet noose around his neck. A satin garter in his mouth. We're married forever now.

Sweet urn of evening, engraved with your name. Brief candle. Sputtering *love, love.* Out now

Love, love, the chorus mocks. *Bernadette, you're nearly free.*

*   *   *

Hear how his voice changes, modulates as it moves toward death . . . unforeseen. There's a quality you can hear nowhere else in the world. There's a sound. Begging for it—for something. I hang above him—the shaved pubis, the strapped legs, the arms strung up—we're nearly there. I place a linen shroud over him. Even the family would have to agree—he was returned to them a pure, whole, perfect specimen—satisfied finally, at rest.

How he seems to breathe still—lightly, more easily, in his simulated, undreaming sleep. Let *s* equal . . . The swelling's begun. Day is done.

It's safe in here—I've got to admit it's safe now—it's pretty safe. No voices or darkness or dogs. In the magnification dream, they're all infinitesimal.

Suppose that a person in orbit around the star Betelgeuse decided to signal Earth today. Since Betelgeuse is about five hundred light-years away from us, it will take us at least five hundred years for this signal to reach us, because the signal must travel at light speed or less. You will be long dead by this time. Thus the space-time event now at Betelgeuse is outside your worldline's past light cone.

Your worldline has a definite end point in space-time: your worldline is terminated by your death. But we can imagine worldlines that have no end point. Such worldlines are called *future endless*. Future endless worldlines like your own define past light cones. The past light cone of your own worldline is exactly the same as the past light cone of the end point of your worldline. However, this will not be true for future endless worldlines: they have no end point in space-time, no—

Sweet urn of evening. Engraved with your name. Our ashen path. How small he is now—Alexander—dark integer—receding.

Forget now our cheap anesthetics—our numbers and sex, they were nothing I guess compared to what we struggled against. Rest. Rest now. Forget how we tried to wrap splint and bandages but remained unmended. It's over now. We never had a chance. We can put away our bags of tricks. The illusion's done—the effects created with mirrors and smoke, the inflated hopes and scholar's disciplined ambitions. The belief we might have actually gone somewhere. I think of all those places we tried to get lost in. Rest at last. The war has finally come to a close. Rest in this loamy morgue, fecund end. Roam no more. Our suffering is over now. In the night of zero. Silent, sulfurous, smiling. You and I now fast asleep, drugged in our sepulcher of theorems and want. The stages of elegy set in. Elegiac night. No fixed heaven. No fixed hell. Just this. Rest.

And when you say, *flower,* my sweet—I see the most lovely abstraction, the most beautifully patterned arrangement of numbers: ideal, eternal, unchanging. Not the unbearable thing—now wilting in your tuxedo lapel—fragile, trembling, torn.

Amazing.

The fact is there was quiet for once. There was quiet for a while. And quiet was all I wanted. From those awful italicized voices. From those awful goatsingers, mangy know-it-alls, that preposterous chorus of voices—the standard serial killer fare.

Yours is the face of the saints in your final blue light, in your pale aura, the what might have been, if only . . . No time now for a last poultice. One last—before I go—no, I suppose not. How quickly all of a sudden night comes on . . . Good-bye sweet prince, my brilliant one, my bridegroom, my savior for a while. Our time is up. I take the ring from your swelling finger—free at last, and leave this passion play.

In holy light, in hallowed halls, I study a tattoo of numbers on his arm as he reaches for the book.
Let *s*—
Each number is a pearl, each pearl one on a continuum: beauty, value, strength. His is the one saving voice: ancient—he is nearly eighty. Let *s*—there are no durable truths—only this longing toward a kind of perfection. Only to move toward what—a kind of forever, or wellness. Midway through my sophomore year he leaves—to become one with the moist star—far—too far to call here now and yet . . . All night the numbers knitting and unknitting.

Why is he taken from me so early on? Harvard might have been a different place had he—had he—alas. He dies in the blinding light of the full moon when I am twelve. Cremated; his numbered arm. At rest now Jacob Perlman—your beauteous, extraordinary mind.

He looks on at her, his silent pupil. Trembles a little at the human mind's capacity to absorb light. Where has she come from this angel? This most extraordinary light. How could such an intelligence and instinct exist in this tortured young girl? This speechless girl?

Jacob Perlman opening the world in the quiet, back-lit alcove of my mind. You were friend in this friendless place. The one place I was at home was at your side. Little stooped, wounded man—dear luminous misfit—with your guidance the one I might have become. *Why are you back here with me tonight?* How much I have missed you! He washes clean my one white wing. He dares me to fly. In a sky of numbers—our extraordinary alphabet. *Do you know what has happened to me?* I look over at my gurgling charge. I fall to my ruined knees and kiss his feet and kiss the precious numbers that have fallen to his sleeping side. The bone light of the moon shines in on our dead tonight.

Alex, my catatonic playmate, watching, watching only your eyes still moving, still displaying—what is it you display? Strapped to this rack of your own making. You my once brash, emblematic aristocrat—now losing your little half erection and donning a party hat. It's our wedding night.

a dog (barked(|))
‾‾‾‾‾‾‾‾‾‾‾

a woman (wept) (|))
‾‾‾‾‾‾‾‾‾‾‾

You look like a boy in a cheap dimestore novel, smoldering still, and speechless with desire. Ours was a flawed logic. Marred. I see now that you will no longer speak to me, never again respond. I mourn your passing. Yet—death. Yet—death by asphyxiation is sweet, not as violent as one might imagine. Pressure applied to the vocal cords, the place voice resides—the box in the throat—and you are silent forever. Our dwindling mathematics. A mad taxidermist, I place a complex equation in your mouth, for the resurrection, should it come.

Everything a shambles here. What have we been up to? Yes, we've made a shambles of it all right. His tiny cylinders of amyl nitrate, blinders, and the greeny glow of the sulfurous sky. You are felled. Quite suddenly obsolete. Nothing can hurt you now, my dear dear one. You are made suddenly exempt. And when I remove the hood, the stark party hat, he is eyeing me lovingly. Nothing can hurt us now. Until the eye goes red. And the hands like blue claws. Now a slug leaves its slime on us. The vapors move in. Why does your tongue come out of your head like that?

Speak to me, pleads Beatrice.
Cat dies I scrawl on a small piece of paper. *Cat dies.*

My final exam was postponed, then canceled. We all grew very melancholy. Despondent. So much always taken away. There were all kinds of rumors. Someone mentioned crucified, shackled. Surely you exaggerate. *Gruesome, gruesome.*
Missed him. Missing him.
Now that he has come down once more from his pedestal and has taken my hand once more on this prison bed. Alexander. *Was it all then a game of charades?* he asks getting up, crossing the room? *The love we had?*

Stay. Don't go. She's only eight years old and it's already far too late. *Don't*—the only one she ever loved.

The voices gone. The dour instructions over. The numbers. The love we had. Too much. You could bring him up that close—but no—your heart would break—not again.

Blessed peace. To you my smart, my sweet. In mummy suit— your ferocious early cap and gown. Congratulations, dear one. I carry a poisoned, irrelevant chalice now to your fresh grave. Your shadow-self, Payson Wynn, behind, in grief, limping. The entire campus shocked. *Who could have done this?* The funeral mass said here on the campus, one week before graduation.

Payson pasty, wasted, weeping. *Best friend, Best friend.*

Payson weakling, weeping, dreary. Not in my Alex's league. And yet—

The investigation of Alexander's death moved in the predictable ways. In a moment's time he was assigned a secret life. He was made to seem, this poor victim, altogether suspect. They dragged in the women he had dated, Suzie Q included. They were in absolute agreement: he was sweet, sedate, all in all a gentleman, my Alex. Still conclusions were jumped to. Like with every depraved crime, the gay community was implicated. See how good we are at projecting our fears onto our most despised factions. Oh yes! My lisping and lapsing one. Anxious to have our high-minded prejudices and stereotypes reinforced over and over, thank you very much.

A young white mother drives her own kids into a lake and maintains that a big black man in a woolen cap with a knife abducted them. I remember.

Bernadette! Bernadette!

Alex, is that you?

If you thought that would work, Bernadette. If you thought that would satiate us. Satisfy us. Set us free. Keep us quiet. If you thought it would be that easy . . . to purge us—Foolish girl. Foolish one.

The hopeless road—the bourbon soaked way—to Payson's good-ol'-boy Georgia. Dear God. The strangeness of the world that had taken—just like that—one of his classmates—one of the shining, wondrous ones—just like that. We were lovelorn, we were grief-torn. Without internal direction we took to the road—pointing the shiny black sports car south. *Alexander, Alexander.* Sure, I know what we were trying to relinquish—to pathetically leave behind. In the farcical night. I know what put us on that doomed and hopeless road.

Alex, we wept, *who did this to you?* On that furious, compulsive, pre-posterous road.

Oh the pure products of America go crazy all right! What forces of night, what giddy, fierce, enraged mourning—strange and ancient and cleaving and blunt, what riotous defiance, led us to that open road? What wound? And I who had never traveled, and I who had never ventured, never, never, from that cold, unforgiving New En-gland coast where witches had burned, land of Hester Prynne, grim land of Puritan and Pilgrim—what set me on that quickly unravel-ing, doomed joy ride—where the hiss of witches was replaced by the burning chant of something, someone, who? Beatrice yes, your ances-tors festering, terrible, terrible—in the god-forsaken night, what pos-sessed us? In the slavish night, devotions, loath to tell. At a hundred miles an hour, toward *home?* What was unleashed and allowed to roam crazy, detached—

Alexander is dead. And what have I achieved? Nothing. And who have I made peace with? No one.

Of course not, Bernadette, what were you thinking? Did you really be-lieve it would be that easy?

We were run amok. And didn't I think a little bonus was in or-der? Or I reasoned if I threw a bone to the voices, they might—

We were chaos in motion and not in motion. Blood. Love. We were the anomaly in the red planet's orbit. We were warped. There were even moments I felt on the brink of breaking through. A wild freedom. Of being something different and irreversibly so—of being someone utterly new. I was madly chattering, not rage-mute. I got a brief glimpse into something breezier, braver, less acute. The what might have been. Oh that!

Teeth marks on the victim, I read to Payson from the newspaper, *sug-gest a person from a lower socio-economic class.* Someone who did not have *the advantages of dentistry.* Payson weeps. *Who was he slumming with?*

I open my mouth wide and sign. Observant, isn't he? Wasn't he?

*   *   *

Bernadette, listen, you can be reckless if you like. There could be, of course, there could—a small defiance of bride, why not?

What about that doomed trip south so unnerved? So unhinged us? Such giddiness. The carefully kept secret. I was in control completely and completely out of control. Payson weeping. His about to die face. The window down, the ever-increasing heat.

Well hell Miss O'Brien, he wails *I don't know what's going on anymore.*

I missed him horrendously. There was a hole at the center of me, gnawed by sadness, enlarging moment by moment. That is to say that after he was there no more, yes, after he was dead—I wanted him back. I hurt. Friend in a friendless place. Love in a loveless place. Beatrice would applaud this: a genuine, it seemed to me, emotion, for once.

On that ludicrous road. Where we stopped at every barbecue place on the way. *Dear pig are you willing to sell for one shilling your ring said the piggy I will.*

Bernadette!

If I lived a million years I might not exhaust the possibilities. His myriad disguises. Hiding places. The endless tortures I've invented for myself. Fergus, what do you want?

Bernadette!

He comes again wearing his Ronald Reagan for President button. *What is wrong with you?*

Bernadette!

He comes harmless now in a pink party dress. That's better.

Still. If you could only stop the dogs or the sobbing or the gagging for a minute. Throttle him, Bernadette.

And you repeat Boys will be boys will be boys, something senseless, made more so by repetition. To calm yourself you count the blades of black grass, beads in the black curtain, leaves, graves.

He helps you up the tree house ladder. Takes your hand. Come on. It's okay.

The stars are howling tonight, the stars are baying, the stars, the stars, count them—fix them. Blessed rage for order. Fix your place.

Where's Eden tonight? How did we end here? So far. Where's God?

Pink

Help!

No one is listening, he says pointing to the heavens and running.

You want to be brave. You want to be lion-hearted. You want him to be proud of you. Admire you.

If you had only been better that night, Bernadette, he might have stayed—he might still be alive . . .

The gagging Virgo: strange double-jointed freak. Sirius—the dog star. Fierce Leo. Betelgeuse. You want to be brave.

Hey, over there, that one, Bernadette, that milk toasty one. He looks like a good substitute, don't you think, understudy, stand in. Throttle him.

Did I mention—the voices have come back? At any rate, I wanted him. Well, and if not him, I unreasonably reasoned, then why not *someone else*—some substitute, some understudy, some stand in? With juicy thigh and brightened eye and swollen, unruly appendage and . . . How to describe the urgency? I was not about to wait out the interminable summer with its leafy health and flashes of rain, its heat and thunder, to be consoled, to be satiated. And the voices said, *Go, to that furious, amazing open road with Payson,* pale double, on that charged super highway home.

I went under the condition that it would remain *our little secret*. That he would never tell anyone, and he whispered, shattered, broken, weeping, *not a soul*. Under the condition that we would not go to his parents' little Tara up there on the hill, but to some altogether sleazy, inconspicuous Piggly Wiggly type motel along the road. We would bind up the nation's wounds there. We would have feelings; we would share and care. Jesus Christ, how could this sloppy mental construction, filled with blunderings and missteps from the start, have followed such a perfect, such a flawless and beautifully executed performance? How was it possible that I who had done such pristine, antiseptic work, could have become involved in such messy, desperate coupling—deranged, poorly calculated.

A misguided flight. To his cruel and unusual Georgia. How was it possible? I thought, in a deeply flawed logic, that I might resuscitate, resurrect the dead, by restaging the act. I missed him. Speeding away as we imagined from that hole at the center. What else could we, bereft as we were, do? To Payson, it was the natural thing. Men, in sorrow, often took to the road. He was going to drive until he exhausted it, ran it into the ground, drove it into senselessness. In a series of one-night cheap hotels . . . Oh yes. Let us go then. Let us go.

In the lightning flash, look: a bitter young man, a joint in his mouth on his way to the war.
Don't go. Because he's got to die.
He licks the hem of her dress like a wound.
Because he's got to die, he's got to be stopped and there's nothing anyone can do about it. Bernadette. Hurry up now. Strangle him. It's time.

Do I dare? In a minute there is time for decision and revisions that a minute will reverse. My sorrowful patriarch and more than willing.

It's a memory so you can change it. You can erase it. Trust us. You can satisfy us. Quiet us.

And how we talked about Alex, all day, all night. Payson incredulous. Payson whining. *He was my best friend.* Yes. Indeed. What he did not know about his best friend. We were shocked, numbed, wild with grief. I had not anticipated acquiring a taste which would demand such immediate satisfying. Stupid of me to have tried even once to do anything even remotely spontaneous. I had not counted on the debauched, the lost, the strange questing, the surrender to zero. The dying into that bleak southern heat, where we might for a minute put aside, with speed, with bourbon and darkness, the being that was Alex. The excruciating sweetness of him. Oh, the bravura of our suffering, the inflations! The beauty—*oh what is the use?*

Grief, I told him, excused us from the ordinary decorum. He had come to want me during the semester, and now that sacred boundary between student and teacher could be crossed—*under the circumstances for Christ's sake*—I made it seem all quite natural, healthy even. This purging through the body. I let him enter me in all the regular ways—allowing him his quick fixes—so that he might trust me. I let him dominate me a little so as to give him the illusion of control. His hunger grew out of proportion. *You're a whore, Bernadette. They called you a whore, remember?* I was reminded of my undergraduate days. Sure, I know how they contend with loss, what sort of consolation they require—sucking on my battered teat—*Oh am I Mother now?* I grew more and more agitated. Being pounded as I was. And the heat was getting to me.

It's a memory, Bernadette, so you can warp it; open it up along the lines of oblivion.
Shackle him. Offer him forever.

Whatever led us to that goddamned Piggly Wiggly or whatever the fuck it was at the end of that utterly doomed road—here we were. At last. Only ten miles from Payson's house. On his last night we went and sat on a hill outside the family compound and looked in. *If you lie on your back, Payson, you can see all the stars. Tell him. Tell him. Go ahead, Bernadette.* He missed them, he needed them, but he was forbidden to go in. I watched him watch his family from this distance. There were his parents in their brightly lit mansion, while he whispered his family narrative to me. Lulled by the monstrous evening heat. Sitting on that rolling slope I could almost hear music. *If you lie on your back,* I say, giving him a little kiss. There was Mother supervising the servants who polished silver, ironed linen, cooked, for tomorrow's annual fundraiser to be held on the great lawn. And Father sitting in his law library—one could almost feel the maroon leather bound, beautiful books. Almost smell them. And the little sister—in a white nightgown, braiding her long blond hair, then brushing her teeth. All through the glass. *If you lie on your back, darling, you can see all the stars,* I tell him. And Payson is in bad shape, weeping and weeping. And in that enormous cowboy hat he seems only a child himself. Weeping. Struggling with good-bye. The little girl getting into bed. Who will hurt her, eventually, I wonder? If they haven't hurt her already . . .

* * *

You come more and more often these days—reconfigured and all the events rearranged, and still it is you. You look entirely like someone else, sound not at all as I remember you. I'm somewhat confused—there's Payson too, Alexander too, yet it's utterly, undeniably you. A small box passes hands. There's a ring and we all stand wedded to it for an instant, knowing it can never last. Nothing can hold here. *But it lasts*, my brother assures me. *Oh it lasts.* And I see the old resentment. He makes it clear that he has survived something, whatever it is, napalm or artillery fire, and that he is all right, and he's back, and he wants to know that I'm OK too. Hour of death, hour of death—stay in your place. Blessed rage for order. Stay in your place, dear brother, stay. You are a thousand pieces, do not forget. You are nowhere now. Or perhaps everywhere. He smiles, then laughs his laugh. *I'm back, I'm back, I'm back!*

everything:x (person (x), if (every:y (person (y), if (hurts (x, y), hurts (y, x)))), hurts (x, x),

It's a memory so she can bury it deeply with the ring and the flag-draped coffin, can't she?

Oh Bernadette, don't make us laugh.

Payson grew testy, then depressed, then enraged, then morose, and finally back to testy again in our cozy Piggly Wiggly world. Payson was feeling left out. Payson was feeling betrayed and afraid. Nothing matched up or made sense to him about Alexander's death. Perhaps he had never really known him at all, he whined. He was exhausting me. What twisted end had his friend met? And how was it possible now to go on, now that Alex, the fierce light of his world, had gone out. Payson as a result was losing his equilibrium. Gone his guide, his terrible beacon, his major competition, *his life*. Or so he said. You know how Southerners are. He kept saying over and over, *A little part of me has died too. He was like a brother. He was like a twin. But in the end he had been left out.*
Did he seem strange to you in class?
If only he had let me in on what was going on. I might have helped him

out. But Alex was largely uncommunicative with his friend—except through symbols. I understand that.

Shall we then try to reenact the crime, Payson, as it was described in the newspapers in untypically explicit fashion? Take one yard velvet rope, two pairs surgical gloves, one satin garter, one veil, one pair handcuffs, blindfold, twenty vials of an undisclosed drug, one runcible spoon, one hood, five books of matches. Manacled as he was, and then strangled, with gloved hands. A satin garter in his mouth. With the arms of someone oh, quite strong. Payson drawn to this lurid, monstrous scene—his beloved and best friend, his only intellectual rival. It was as if Alex had one-upped him again. Oh my. Not to forget—as the tabloid stated—the flames at the altar—the boys blur a little—forgive me. Here was a royal fellowship of death. Entering into this twisted pact—poor lambs, poor innocents—little numskulls—not their fault. Sent to the little lamby slaughter just like that, just like that. Off to the inflated, indifferent God—insatiable as usual. Accept for once, would you please, the sacrifice of these offerings, and then leave me be.

Well why not reenact the little love-god's death then, shall we? This marriage of Heaven and Hell. His gluttonous nectar-covered mouth, spewing *love, love* . . . Snakes coiled around his wrists. They found him handcuffed to the bed. *Let's try it then.* We wept, imagining this awful ritual of bondage and fare-thee-well. Come on. And I take out the shackles. Perhaps, I suggest to him, he enjoyed it a bit more than you are enjoying it right now? And I kiss him. Perhaps it was something in the end he could not refuse. Perhaps, I try to suggest to this dullard, there was only the desire for surrender or connection. Payson stutters, stammers as I, the great impersonator, the ludicrous, the garish, the ready-made fantasy now, cliché in black leather underthings, and torn dress, straddle him. Is this not the most pathetic and ridiculous part so far? Two utter misfits. Whining Payson and I. But Payson is beginning to forget about his friend's death—lost in something altogether other, all of a sudden, distracted by my bound breasts and his own enormous erection. Oh the scenarios we staged, the what might have happened, each of us furious and grieving—and Payson finally so frenzied, so overcome with lust. He's got no idea, poor thing. He's got no clue, the dope, that he's about to die. *Surely the killer must have worn some sort of gloves,* I whisper. Latex? Leather?

Why not try on this for size? I whisper, whipping out a saran suit. *Why don't you slip into this?* A kind of Ziploc bag. *Yes . . .* Before God you were a sinner. You felt surges in your brain, weird pleasures, feelings of superiority. You had to be stripped of these, I say, strapping down his legs. Getting out the dark whip. He may have been blindfolded for part of the time. He may have been spared being witness to his end. Payson is weeping as I conjure his friend. *He may have found it in him to spout a theorem or a prayer,* I say. *Recite one now.* Nausea rises in me as he begins the *Our Father.* That it should have come to this. And I am riding him into last oblivion and applying at this point just the slightest pressure to his neck. And it excites him—look there's no doubt about it—that he is excited. And I whisper, *Someone fucked him to kingdom come.* Rubbing a concoction onto his cock. He's no longer asking to be unshackled. He's quite enjoying it, as I suggested he might. And don't you know that dear Alex must have enjoyed it too? A pornography of suffering. This highly staged, preposterous exorcism. Must have known full well what he was getting himself into *for God's sake he was not stupid*—He was brilliant, and he begged for it.

The short-circuited sky alive. Cruel and violent. Indifferent executioner. Maybe we'll be struck, he says laughing. And somewhere someone is already weeping. Bernadette, hurry, it's time!

He weeps. Say your novenas, my friend, for this is the end. *Confess to me,* your lapsing and increasingly nauseous, I might add, Catholic, all your sins. And we sit backed up into this tight little homemade confessional—smack up against the wooden panels, and curtains and screen, with the magic, collapsible door. *Confess.* I lift my veil to the stony god. *Why, whenever You got the chance, did You forsake us?* To the suddenly madly laughing God.

Come on.

Bless me, Professor, for I have sinned . . . Yes, you wanted your dear friend Alexander silenced or hurt or best of all dead—*your only competition* as you liked to say. You were bitter, jealous, wretched. Alex, with his easy charm, his love of risk, his capacity for happiness. You wanted this utterly sublime, exquisite creature, dead. You must therefore be punished. *Naughty one. Naughty one. And another crime: you had impure feelings for me, confess.* And I allow him to enter the crucible of my body. He nods, sweating. Oh yes. *And you wanted him dead. No, no,* he laughs in his wretched falsetto, as I wrap my hands around his neck. *Someone applied oh quite a bit of pressure—remember his blackened neck?* Blood comes from his mouth. Poor, poor. His grim and less than candid confession. He's hurt his sister. Sure, he forgot to mention that. Her only protector. He was big when she was small. Confess. Payson Wynn, lying, sniveling, after his amazing orgasm. Sleep coming on. Why the child? Then unconscious—someone already dead. His semen all over my splayed legs. That horrible half smile. *And how am I to walk again?* Crooked man. Crooked wife. *Naughty, naughty boy.*

That it should come to this. And blood and foam is coming from his gurgling mouth. He just won't give in. And I have not the stamina to continue. Ingrate. As if he has not been sublimely escorted into the end.

He's saying things; he's calling *Mama, Mama.*
Is that who I am?
I think not. I run a red bath and wait. Splayed.

And doesn't he look like just another cheap dimestore novel character—superficial, overwritten—yet another device of the plot—smoldering, speechless in this piggy state, begging? Oh it's pathetic, no? How now with sudden tenderness—as I slip on the death hood—as I close my eyes as well . . .

The swelling's begun. Poor, poor—
This sluggish end—gruesome, upturned—
And the red eye shining.
Motionless in this last room. He was slower at everything, including death, growing slowly cold in the heat. Middle of the day, out the motel window across the way—the children, in their ripped frocks, earnest at their play. *Ring around the rosie, a pocketful of posies*—
And his ashen face. And his face filled with ashes. And I wait.
And I wait and watch his little shakings and grimaces, his tics, bloody sputum, release of final vapors. Heat ghosts and peach trees and lilting dreamy dreams make it just a little harder to let go, to give up. We're far away from the hardened New England coast, and I think maybe this world, maybe this—I might have been happy

here—what if I might have been—far away from fishmongers and sadness and broken docks. Oh would and could and might have been. Soon the authorities will arrive to make their grim discovery. The locusts are having their deafening day, and the children are retrieved from their late midday play. The wind picks up as he expires. And the early summer lightning and the thunder coming on.

And hurry he says and careful, take my hand little saint—before the rain.

CELEBRATING YOUR ACCOMPLISHMENTS

It's great to note successes, but it's also important to actually stop and celebrate. In doing so, you inspire yourself and you inspire others, and you give yourself a well-deserved breather.

Take a few moments to think about various ways you might celebrate your accomplishments. You could throw a party. Go out to dinner. Brag to a friend. Get a massage. Try skywriting. (Be creative.)

List your accomplishments with pride (and feel free to add more later).

But he won't give in. He has no talent whatsoever for surrender. Of course not, as I have maintained all along, his passion was altogether second rate. He did not in the end possess the right stuff. His embryonic genius. Though he grows pasty-faced in frilly satin collar—the perfumed sheets and shackled—he won't give in. I douse the holy sepulcher in gasoline. Anything to get him from still speaking *Mama, Mama* and staring at me. With his blindfold I gag him. That awful bright red eye. His limp prick. He had no trouble, God knows, when it came to that, maintaining his erection through the various rehearsals and scenarios. I drop lit candles onto the rug. Set the curtains then the bed ablaze. *Now, Bernadette, look, coming into the foreground, licking the edge of the frame: fire. The disintegrating frame. You'll be free. Drop the match. Then leave. Run!*

Oh see how she's made a sweet botch of it.

Bernadette, I'm here, take my hand.

* * *

I climb into the highest tree, and watch while the Piggly Wiggly burns. Gagging on smoke. Blinded by firelight. Cruel inferno. That it should come to this. Poor Birdbones up in a tree. I hear the sirens now. *No one will find you here—not to worry—a small injured bird inside. Let t, let t . . . You can label every leaf on every tree.*

In the farcical night. Poorly staged. Everything ablaze. I've botched it all right.

Eggy Presbyterian. Unimaginative, contentious, *we don't confess.* Whining, drooling child. *I'm Presbyterian, we don't confess.*

His milk toast and frills. He'd been jazzed up all semester. But slow, alas. He was never on to Alex and me—until now. Far too late. Oh well.

From this perch I can see him still—he takes so long to burn. I watch him from afar, bloating. God, it's awful. He looks like some kind of really terrible blowup doll. Jesus, it's atrocious. This little piggly went to market, this little wiggly stayed home. This little piggly had roast beef. This little piggly has none.

Nauseated here in the trees.

Bring the child to term they all shout, hauling nannies and mammies. Holding crucifixes and forceps. Strap her down.

But this little piggly has none.

My crucified, emptying rubric. Highlighted in red. Is that fire? Smoke now, and the sirens. Sirens now, but no sound coming out. Dogs barking but no sound. You could lift the mute button, but why? Recklessness of the afternoon. Oh I've botched the job all right. Never mind. God, it's gorgeous up here. And so quiet, quiet.

As an adult with some healing behind you, ask yourself, "Are there things I've always wished I could try? What are the things I've always been interested in? Do I have any secret fantasies I'd like to fulfill? Is there a way I want to have an impact on the world? What do I have that I can give back to the world? What things would I like to help change?"

Let yourself live with these questions. Give yourself time to find the answers. Then list your goals here.

I look down at them from my perch where they circle and circle with guard dogs. Their sheriff stars and holsters, their paunches. They look rather stupid from up here gesturing for me now to *come down. Ma'am what are you doing up there?* The world on fire.

What? I say, in my ludicrous leather and lace.

Why I'd never hurt a fly, sir. No sir. I bat my lashes. Tip them the country hat. Terrible child with her matches and singed gown. Playing at grown up things.

At the terrible height of my power—for the brief moment when the world was mine.

In the multiplication dream she triples herself. Becomes fourfold, then five, then God—

In the elaboration, she's ten feet tall. It's so lovely up here hovering above the rest of the world. You can touch the tops of trees. Imagine infinity.

How oddly Lilliputian they seem from this vantage point of time, distance—and how I can barely call up what the irritation might have been with any of them—or the attraction. My dearly departed Alex, Payson—how tiny they seem, how insignificant, dead—as they are—and the dead whom you assume always grow monstrous—how strange—now growing in precisely the opposite way. Forgettable flecks. Negligible. Diminished in death, shrunken, weaklings. My boys. How little they trouble me. Small irritants—and then nothing. Once figures of consequence and catastrophe. Pure obsession. No longer do I see them as they looked then: irresistible, scrumptious, slightly dangerous. I can scarcely see them at all.

Oh not as they were then, when they still had their smiles and cocks and I could imagine them giants, tyrants. No more.

There's a slight tickling at my wrist. Is that Payson trying to cross the expanse of my hand. Onward to the knuckle bone where he might stake his flag? Bothersome flea. I turn over and he is nicely crushed.

All is quiet.

We've been brought again to the place in the trees and the high *where she must not make a sound or ever say a word and there's no place to hide.* God, it's beautiful here, and quiet finally, no voices, no dreams, no dogs, and so high up! Gone, that wretched choir.

Ma'am give me your hand.

And I am escorted to the flashing and blurring squad car.

Awful child with her matches and singed things, in ripped, disheveled garb. I flash a crooked smile. Draw the veil. It's over. I'm caught.

Come from a wedding I gather? The officer smirks. The honeymoon's over before it's begun.

Graceful turns of mind, of phrase, in the lateness of the day. Beautiful compensations of mind. A ravishing formula for the silencing of the wounded—bright anesthetic. The patient etherized. Where the atrocious act finally achieves harmlessness. And I sleep. The magnified sleep of the martyrs and saints. Peace.

Sound drenched utterly from the scene. Her cries. His rage.

Anyone, even you, is entitled to wish.

Who among us can bear the deaths of healthy, brazen, bouncing young men? I did not hate them. I did not despise them, in fact, I may have loved them. But they could not, they did not protect me. And they should have, don't you think? Forgive this childish eye. I rub and rub in the dark at this most late hour. The retreating and equivocating god. Why have you left us here alone another night?

How to combat this solitude which is extraordinary now, and mounting. Who's there?

Alas, no one. Just a child, mourning, in her torn dress, at the funeral, mute. *Was that thunder and closer now?* Ruby winged. Red ribbed. Who shall love the bones of the dead?

I have heard the injured nymphs are singing salty songs. They call me to their bawdy side.

Innocent, intelligent, modest, having hurt no one—they got injured, they got hurt anyway.

Well, well, how can I help you, Beatrice? Save your parliamentary procedures, your hypocritical jurisprudence, your bleak house of cards, your pathetic self-help, your sore, pulsing vulva, my friend. And to think that I almost trusted you. Do I never learn anything?

Speak to me, she whispers.

I've been mute again for some weeks—(that old chestnut)—*speak.* Refuse all medication.

End this miserable, small unfortunate life this time. I have already performed for the video crews. I can't bear to answer another letter. And my own work? I've made a hash of it—unbearable to think of really. These last minute postscripts—to be read after my incineration.

All attempts at formulation fail, all desire. All calculation fails now as I inch down the dark hall. It's the solitude without the numbers. It's the solitude without the voices that's untenable.

And where is Elizabeth you might ask? Jesus Christ, Elizabeth. Isn't Australia awfully far?

The blind God fingers his braille of bride. There's nowhere to go. Nowhere to hide. Sadness. Depression. Loss of appetite. Harm to herself. All the boys dead again. I'm tired. And what have I accomplished? I've had enough now, Elizabeth. Elizabeth where are you? Isn't Australia awfully far?

You come in pink taffeta party dress, gutted and gutless, unsexed. Then in purple, the bunting blackened. I wonder if this is just some backward hormone produced by the end, as I describe you now before my eyes, in ribbons and bows, a frill at the neck. Or is it just some natural reversal of roles, you helpless as I was then, you crying as I cried then—then nothing, silent—as I was then. And I leave you having exacted now from your most grievous fault some terrible penance. Rest now.

Elizabeth, is that you, laughing out loud?

Distressed is poor Beatrice, who has filed one of her trusty reports saying I seem *inordinately depressed.* I refuse all food. Do not rise from the bed. Barely lift a finger from this cozy tomb.

Refuse, refuse. I refuse the appeals, I refuse all intercession on my behalf. *Assisted suicide.* Refuse the child. Why am I being tortured like this? I only ask now, like any addict, for my share of oblivion. Bea-

trice reports I am emaciated in my ripped prison garb, oh yes, as I
ever was and ever shall be. Beatrice is increasingly worried about my
depressed state and calls for the psychiatrist, a Doctor Lester Falcon. They are afraid I guess that I might hang myself like my dear
Grandpapa—*a history of suicide.* Or do away with myself by some
equally clever means before their festival of lights. X number of days
and counting. They'd like me to be smiling on my hot seat. It would
be just like me, wouldn't it, to spoil everything. They have made it
clear: I am under no circumstances to ruin their fun.

And the antidepressants they've shoved down my throat have
meant nothing to me.

Pardon me, excuse me, but isn't that, Dr. Lester Falcon, the abyss
I am looking into over there?

So you've got the blues? Understandable.

I know you'd like me to be a laughing corpse, a happy girl, grin-
ning like a hyena and waving from my fancy chair.

Nothing I suppose a little electroshock treatment can't cure.

They're cruel and unusual. They are barbarous, are they not, leading me with ball and chain down the dark hall to the convulsion
room for my mini-execution. This bleak rehearsal. Death's cheap
counterfeit. They are trying to *save me from myself* as they say. *A little
late, don't you think?*

They'd like me to do *a few chin ups*, enjoy the yard. *Sure.* Heckle
a little. *How about some hair tearing?* Not this sitting politely, remaining with my murderous hands folded in my lap. Not eating, not
speaking. Acting like a perfect little lady now. Quiet and dieting.

Beatrice argues that I have grown resigned now. Progressively unsuitable for *any sort* of re-entry. *Re-entry, good God!* Let me go, Beatrice, I beg you. One of your failures.

In a gruesome turn the families want—oh the families—*what do
the families want now?*

The families vote for electroshock.

Open your mouth. The ghouls. They hold a bit and electrodes. Oh
so now they see, the crooked, awful teeth in my mouth. *No money for a*

dentist. We can't even afford *the rent* half the time. Someone's shut off the lights again. Good fucking night.

I do not think that he will think to look for me here. In asylum whites, strapped to an electric table, far, far off, being monitored and watched by this gleeful bunch. A debilitating depression. Their lunatic logic. Come a time you'd think they'd finally leave me alone, but no, but oh no. Beatrice, to relieve her conscience, still talks *in case of salvation*, at this late date. Beatrice standing by with her ludicrous box of electric confetti. Trying to piece me back. They are scaring me now for no good reason. Fergus laughs convulsively, when I relay this, but I think it's true that he will *really, really* never think to look for me here. Looking like some mental patient.

Are you ready? Open your mouth.

The Many Worlds Interpretation is forced on us by three assumptions:

(1) All systems—including humans—are quantum systems.

(2) All time evolution is *linear*, governed by Schrödinger's equation.

(3) All measuring devices work as they should.

If, for example, the cat *is* dead (in an eigenstate of "deadness"), then any correctly operating device must *say* the cat is dead. In particular, if humans are the measuring devices, then if the cat is indeed dead, all "correctly operating" humans must see the cat dead. (All "incorrectly operating" humans are carted off to a mental institution.)

My brother and I walk to the river one last time. The river is real mysterious at night and we sit beside it a long time. The river, reflecting light, is beautiful at night. The motion of the current, the dream of where we might go—where it might take us, if we could only let it. *It's like an adventure,* he says and I nod my head yes. *Amazing.* We breathe in the clear, watery night air and dream. He closes his eyes. He's so tired after work he can hardly stand up anymore. We catch fish after fish, Fergus and I. And not just trash fish—*but all kinds.*

* * *

My tendency is as it always was, and ever shall be, to idealize you, Fergus, to protect you like the textbooks say. Your mock heroics as you walk those same planks again and again. Such poverty of imagination that I cannot do more with you. You come staring into the place you think I am, more and more frequently, now whispering into my exasperated ear: *Forgive me, forgive me if you can.*

But forgive you for what?

What hoax, what cruel joke? What useless, irrelevant bit of nonsense do I dote on now? And what shall I conjure next?

You come dressed each night in survivor's garb—as if to say—as if . . . With sawtooth knife and razor blade and glass. *What do you want?*

I am aware there are less violent ways to do this procedure—but not here. They tie me down. They put the bit in my mouth. Turn off the lights and let me have it. They pull that switch and I am battered back into animation. Bruised into usefulness. Speech for the speechless. Dreams for the dreamless.

We've been brought, *dear God, not again,* again to the place in the trees, the place high in the trees—and she will not speak. *Pledge.* And she promises she will not say a word. *Pledge. I pledge* and *I promise,* arm raised, arm down, *pledge:* triangle, parallelogram, abstracting, until the world—it's possible after a few tokes, to forget the child. After a few more tokes to forget the child altogether, isn't it? Tree house—a mannequin and Jimi Hendrix. And where's Janie anyway? *Never say a word.* Stars slung. Embellished night. *Do you promise? Never. Sign of the cross now, Bernadette.*
In the name of the Father.
In the name of the Son.
I promise.

Open your mouth now.
Is that you, my sweet, my most spectral groom?
Open your mouth . . .
Fuck.

*   *   *

Slides over, puts her—
(Someone has taken)
you can
are always taking heavier things
worth their weight in gold—penis
worth their—
slide over straps her in
on the calm white table
on the slab it's as if she's dreaming and scribbling
let $s =$ the slab if you will
are always taking the easy way out
fishing is a—
swimming is a—taking my
slide over now
Someone is taking
once you sang a Firthy song—and talked a steady   stream
on the calm white taking my
are always taking what isn't theirs—and are always   hurting
somebody, so let, let s
smither, smithereens
Someone has taken

Fergus in smithereens. Alas, the dead do not. Do not, the dead do
not rise up whole. Do not touch. Do not. The dead jibber and blither
in their pieces. Poor things. Poor dears. Oh well.

Someone has taken my notebook. And then put it back.

The silent, awkward girl, hands the—trembling hands the—
crackling, official-looking government, an envelope replete with
eagles and seals. The woman begins, when she sees the missive—
irregular, labored breathing, a gasping, zapped to hell—gasping *no!*
for treacherous air. The verge of their agony, begins to weep. The girl
whose eyes are vacant, whose throat is empty—who's, who's zapped
back. The man moves with hump and swivel toward the news. Hearts
ripped away etcetera. A strange, stopped pietà—the central figure
missing. He was only there a few months. Black Irish hoax. Specious,

drunken—conjured from their misery, alcohol, no? But so soon. It seems to me he sees us. *Consistent with, consistent with . . .* And laughs.

Bad dreams back again now—from the unspeakable inner life—four a.m. The wires attached, skull cap. Disoriented. Let *s* . . .

You say. You say you can't. Live in the gray anymore. You say you can't breathe surrounded by gray like this.

Warrior. Warlock. War mongering toward death in an electric night. Sometimes his hand edges near the electrified field and I send him back to straddle the invisible line of his need and his pain. Bleak heroics. Stay there gargantuan—stay there—each finger an island of grime and hair. She loves him—so why? How can it be? It can't. If you lie on your— If she lies on her back? If she looks at the stars? Impossible. If she closes her eyes. The hurt sky turning red and the blood is just lightning? Be careful, someone whispers to the girl. From where? On high? Over the great divide, on a star-covered spread, on the electric dome incandescent, everything else strangely gone now—attach the nodes to your head, *why would he do that to a child?* One hand rapping against the black door of night, raven—come clean—if we could count, find the square root of anything now; these are the games. These are the games she plays:

If before the dog reaches the field . . . If she can count to five before it barks, with its hairs and its drool. If she can keep the baying and darkness a little ways away somehow it will be OK. Skull cap. The wires in her head. A bride wept. Then she'll disappear—in the perfection of the solution. You've got a helmet on and in the background—some sort of playing field—cheers are heard. Swell then die in the distance. Come cries. She's faking it, can't you tell idiot? Until the flesh is a hypothesis or an apostrophe, melting to the chair, impossible to prove.

These are the games. She can count 7, 8, between the lightning and the thunder. In the interval she might live there, couldn't she? Breathe.

If before the dog reaches the field, she can divide all the integers by five she'll stay alive, before it barks, before the dog barks, with its hair and grime, with its big hands and teeth, at the boundary, the border. The trees, they're beautiful even in the dark. If she can keep the baying and darkness a little ways away still, the wires away from her, somehow it will be OK. Outside all harm and consequences. Then she'll disappear. In the perfection of some distant solution. Last light.

Through the foam. Bite down now. The epileptic dog in the back, who would do that to a child, through the fear, through the way you held that fragment: *Jane, Jane.* And then just [*ay, ay,* bleak phonetic] Don't cry . . . What could I—how could I have helped you? *If you lie on your back.*

Flowered dress. Anklets, filthy sandals. Torn. I'm cold.

And where's Janie anyway? He'll give her the ring.

A jolt passes through the body. Live through this. Blood drips from the electrified night wires. Coating them. A human touch. What are those coins of blood? Those half dollars of blood?

Open the door. Open the door. Another, then another electric surge. *Surely*, they are whispering, the ghouls, *Surely there are other ways to skin this cat.* With your bayonet and fire. Your cruel hat on—you were no dunce or louse or hooligan—you were the only one I ever trusted. In the red trees run. Why are they—another surge—hurting her so much? Lightning. Thunder. God throwing his cruel bolts always their way.

Veins of light illuminate the sky, there's an enormous hand in the sky, palm side up—lighting up one, then another line. Life line. Heart line. This will happen. And this. A sky of fearful possibility.

Some subsets $V = \{V_i \mid i$ element-of I, an index set$\}$ of the sky:

some hand h:

some palm p such that of (p, h):

vein (V_i) AND

light (V_i) AND

enormous (h) AND

higher-than $(p, h\text{-}p)$

Look how the small girl trembles now. And in the corner back by the epileptic (or rabid) dog—look:

She has thrown up.

Let s . . . Let . . . in the stumbling—

She is bleeding. And as she takes off the large white Carter's—she's just a child, for Christ's sake . . .

Bernadette! Bernadette! he cries. *Take my hand!*

Scarred night. And I am woken again from the terrible lightning night, and get up and press against the bars, nearer to that bluish and bruised angel. She's got a swollen lip. She's got a cracked and crooked hip. She's limping toward home, torn.

What is this fear tonight? Pervasive, unshakable. Not insane. Quite sane. And yet without choice. The drama of free will—free choice—that's a good one. I did not choose any of it—not my gender or race or class. No one will hear your cry for help, little girl, in that little nonvoice, flaring out of the sound frame, way over in left field. Someone has pressed the mute button on you. Is that thunder now on top of everything? Miserable hook in my mind. That night—filled with twisted diction, off-rhyme. High fevers, chills. Maybe she'll die. Trying to get up. Trying to get it up. An arm with hair. Rearing its ugly head. Moist . . . Red-blue bruisy. Paint it nine. Try to neutralize. (That jacking motion.)

If anyone makes a sound, she dies.

everyone:x (if (makes a sound (x), dies (x))).

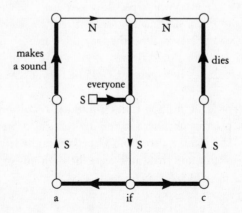

A guard dog over there at the border, throwing up in the grass.

Hide in the folds of the sloughed off, in the folds of the cast off, now hanging in the tree, free. And he is calling *Bernadette* in the pitch dark and hitting the grass with a stick, searching, searching—and a flood light.

No chance he'll find her here. (Don't talk too loud.)

He'll never find her in that never-born disguise. Placenta on her head.

A miscarriage in the sixth month.

Run!

A double helix of worry. Fish that swim in opposite directions. Alex? Payson? New last tortures. Exotic permutations. Multitudinous . . . Bread, panties, garters, stuffed into a sorry mouth. Laments, hosts. A kind of bit—most necessary for the procedure. To pad the jolt. I'm electrified back one more time.

He'll never find you like that.

And smile now and wave now to the priests through glass. The keeper of secrets. The battalion of social workers through glass. The media, and Minnie Grace. Beatrice in the prison chapel in acts of supplication and a little surrender finally, praying to a ruined and raging Jesus. People everywhere pleading *save, save, save yourself. Run, if you can! Run! If you can! To the border. Break the narrative open now.* Aren't they sweet? Naive. Free, they say. Sure, free.

Fergus, look, it's Betelgeuse. (If you lie on your back)

Light travels 11 million miles a minute, 6 trillion miles a year. The nearest prominent object in the sky tonight is Sirius, ten light-years away. The light we see from Capella tonight left it forty years ago. It has taken more than 300 years for the light of Betelgeuse to reach us.

*   *   *

It will be made of oak with a padded backrest.

State of the art. No more smoke and six-inch flames erupting from the condemned's head.

No burns. Or so they say.

No head electrodes fashioned in synthetic sponge from the house-wares store—leg electrode cobbled together from an army boot and some roofing copper. Like the old days. No, I shall die in luxury, free of many of the *technical problems* that once plagued the day. Not like the old days—dying before strangers, all men, sporting a regulation football helmet wired to 2,000 volts. I shall ride in splendor. The Cadillac of electric chairs.

And haven't they jolted me back into something resembling happiness? Chatting away again. Animated. Joking with the hangman.

I have seen the hangman with his exposed, pristine neck. I have seen the hangman, priapic, waiting, with his fifty erect penises; they encircle his waist like a spiky crown. A cruel and unusual tutu, a blistering sun. These late hallucinations. The hangman cradling the head of my Alexander. He does not understand.

The hangman does not care for me. He takes my childish hand. Fool. He sees I am only a child. He looks sad. Fool to pity me. I sprout sharp feminine claws and draw blood. You expected maybe submission, love? Sympathy, even? My eggy executioner. *It's a living,* he likes to say. *It's a job.*

Already my mother offers her granite hand. Poor martyr, shuffling dead woman, propped up. Self-congratulatory, self-serving hangman. *It's a job all right.*

This mute doomsday approaches now without a snag.

If there had been one shred of friend along the way. One real connection.

Jesus, come closer—with your girly girlishness, your three-inch lashes, your nine-inch nails. Your Technicolor. Your ornamental promises. I am zapped beyond anything I might say. Enter Mother, tipped, poured out, spilling fruitlessness. Numbers over a dead receiver. Fergus, obscured beacon, shabby, overused symbol by now. Rest.

Tentative vision be mine.

No use. No use.

Here I am. Flat and static as a chair. Your monstrous indifference. They hurt those girls, I know.

I beat my head senseless against a window and a wall. This impasse in the day. No more electrodes, OK? I promise I'll be your party girl, your good sport, your happy go lucky, your Erin go bragh, your top of the morning. Just no more.

Tradition tells us that on the night of an execution male inmates are shown pornographic films to keep their minds off the event at hand. No one has documented what is typical for the women.

The operations can include cutting off the hood of the clitoris, or the entire clitoris, all or part of the labia majora, and the sewing together of the sides of the vulva with catgut or with thorns. No other mass violation of humanity has received so little attention. Eighty million women alive now affected.

Elizabeth, is that you back? And just in the nick of time?

Who will tend my flower bed? Who will mind my savage goat and pole dog? Little Poincaré at my side. Friend in this friendless place. After Fergus left for the war, my father got me a little perfect dog for consolation, did he not? I, peering into the cage, speechless, pointing. My mangy friend Poincaré who steps and fetches without question and never tells. *Never tells anyone.* My speechless parrot, Descartes. Who shall bring him a tin of water and some saltines? Who shall walk my hounddog, Husserl? Uncertain Gödel? Beautiful Euler? Who shall love them all? Who shall pet my purring cat, Zero, and bring him a white bowl of milk?

Mother dressed like a girl wore a dotted Swiss frock with a lace collar. As if it were summer out. Not that it matters anymore. Her hair had grayed quite considerably since I had last seen her. Minnie Grace had woven a rosary between her fingers. Mother in her pine coffin. Her face both swollen and sunken. Poor thing. She was exhausted, that much seemed clear. Suffering still. She looked anything but like a woman at rest.

Charming, simple, infantile, foolish, pretty, harmless, affection-ate, docile, despoiled, alluring, seductive, despised. Girls are beauti-ful and soft and babies are and flowers pure and just born, vulnerable, pink. Electroshock. They should have been treated with care. Tended with love, don't you think? Dear God, look at them. Look.

Beatrice, in her scalloped panties and early bra. On her way home from school. Singing . . .

He's got the whole world in his hands.

Mother walking home in the strange airless summer gasping for breath. I, on the other side of her journey, holding the telegram with eagles and seals. In the splintered, infernal July. In the dread of sum-mer. Choking on the truncated, fucked-up government speak. He was my only friend here. Protector. Helper. Brother. In all that meant.

She is sweating like a swine toward the news. In the moment be-fore she steps into eternal black—in the moment before she is lost to us forever.

And I inch closer to that last room. *Mother!*

Only son. Only son.

He is the heartbreaker. He is the hero. He is the one, I presume, they thought would get away. They named him Fergus John Kennedy after the young senator from our state in what seems to me to be an uncharacteristically hopeful act, though maybe I am wrong—maybe they were entirely different people once—and I got them used up. No. It is outside the reach of the imagination to believe such. I cannot see them as radically different. He was to be their savior. Little escape hatch. Their one hope, this little guy, mischievous, ebullient, with his extraordinary aptitude for life. What went wrong there, and so early? The church burns, he befriends the local hoodlums, he goes to war. Show off, bigshot, palooka, mick, lord of the small drug cartels in town.

Only at sixteen does he seem to turn himself around: reformed, self-righteous, *holier than thou*. I am five or so by this time and with his rage repressed, channeled, he looks just about like any teenager, only older. Aged by drink and drugs and just too much. I feel the toll that poverty takes, that hopelessness takes. What was in the lines of our palms that destined us for such sorrow? He joined the army and was promptly killed—leaving me behind. The amorphous thing he went to embrace was his death. And there it was. Easily attained. Like nothing else.

I feel the ridicule of my classmates, when I go to church wearing a homemade dress. So out of step. So violently out of any fashion. I feel the ridicule when I bring my milk in a thermos each day, instead of buying a cold small carton. I feel the sadness of wearing my shoes fastened by masking tape. I feel embarrassed and hold my hand over my mouth so as not to reveal my crooked teeth. All the children have braces it seems. Jesus, all these feelings, suddenly. Out the window, look:

Bad news then? Yep. Men come in uniform.

My death warrant has arrived. A single page bordered in black. Many seals and stars and stripes. All routine bids for appeal and clemency have failed. They wake me, squirrel me down the dark hall, and read the thing out loud. *Pursuant to the authority . . . and responsibility vested to cause the sentence of death to be executed upon September eleventh,* September eleventh, no kidding? *In accord with the provisions . . .*

So the famous death warrant has finally been signed and I am moved to the so-called *Q Wing*, closest to my fancy chair. *The Q Wing indeed!* Moved finally to the last, very odd, very queer wing on this long hall. Every fifteen minutes they swing by to check up on me. I wave. Queer days. Almost free.

Not capable or deserving of redemption. I am moved oh some maybe twenty feet or so away to the definitive last room of waiting. Woe, as they say, is indeed me. Woe is also those who must now enforce the plan. They are all too happy to bend the rules and considerably: the warden, the guards. They let Connie in. They give me paper to write on. We are women after all: Not men.

As we all wait for my man-made appointment with death.

Try this on for size. A 6 × 6 × 6' grave. Connie comes and goes. After all, attachments have been made. Everyone here is partial to my cause at this point. The cause being to ease the difficulty for all those concerned of my impending extermination. In the end, we are just a small gaggle of girls here. *Yep, Lyle had a sedan, as he liked to call it, a little bigger than this.* Connie tries to smile. And while Lyle often got on her nerves, she always, always loved that car of his. She gets that gleam in her eye that she gets when she talks about Lyle, and she sits down next to me.

Tenacious, last things.

Death etiquette. When I shower they shout now, *Dead woman coming through.* Oh if they only knew.

Many possessions are now taken away in accordance with the *Execution Guidelines.* The brutes. They say magazines and newspapers may be kept, but that subscriptions shall be discontinued. Very sensible of them. Three meals shall still be fed. Meticulous instructions are given to prison personnel to ensure the condemned *stays in good health.* Dietary restrictions for *medical reasons* continue to be observed. Low sodium for that high blood pressure—*that's a relief.* The prisoner shall be watched like a hawk. If she becomes insane on death row, she in this case, must be *restored to mental health* before the proceedings may continue.

Oh not that again. I stay perky so as to be spared their gallows humor: electroshock.

She shuffles in, no wings on her feet, no glow, no life ever after behind her or anywhere near her—only shadow. No giggling, no off-color jokes; she is an old woman, defeated—if only partially. Through the glass. Still, even now I detect a bit of a gleam. She passes me a rosary and a rose.

Minnie Grace. I touch her small, utterly innocent, trembling hand through the glass. She was once our one way into some small bit of happiness, conviviality, normalcy. She made my mother laugh.

It's best really that she won't have to see this. Her own child.

I nod, feeling the genuine weight of the thing, the preciseness of the loss as she moves toward good-bye. Our one hope.

Oh . . . She attempts to compose herself. *Oh . . . There is a forgiving God, Bernadette. Dear one. And he knows your true name.*

It's best for your mother, rest her soul. There is a forgiving God . . . To-

gether in heaven. You can put down your burden now, dear child. I know how heavy it is. And she cries.

Your mother stopped coming, she sobs, *because she couldn't bear to be strip-searched anymore. And now this—she wouldn't have, she wouldn't have . . . no . . .*

And alas indeed what would Mother have done through the excruciating wait. And what would she have done at the hour of my death were she alive? Even I cannot bear the thought of it. In her Fall River. Counting, crossing off the days. Falling.

I believed intelligence to be immortal. I believed, flushed with numbers, in their eternity, and mine. Imperious, imperial, I believed, was forced to believe, that knowledge might be power. A kind of forever. Strange it should come to this. This too long, most unnatural life now coming to its brutal close. Leaving in a burst of flame, of heat, of light, of boiling brains. Death penalty days. The curse of the starving class. The end then.

A new band of little lady lawyers appears at my door. *Not again.* They nod. They pinch and probe.

You hear voices, they say.

No. I really don't hear any voices.

Admit it.

No.

A new gaggle of gooses cackling, *admit it.*

Leave the voices alone. They were friends of sorts in a friendless place. Company for a while.

Save yourself, they say in unison. *Save yourself.* They whisper as if in a dream. As if we were at a fucking slumber party.

No.

They press ahead these women, as if with deaf ears.

No. At the eleventh hour, that mute numeral. No last minute reprieve. *I beg of you.*

We will save you in spite of yourself. Such solidarity run amok.

Spare me your late last litigations. The client quits, I say, *the cat dies.*

But they refuse to give up. *You are complicitous, a participant then in this system of legal homicide,* they say. *You do us all a disservice. You sanitize execution, lend it an aura of legality, the appearance of fairness. You hear voices. You've been sick. All these years. Admit it.*

I take these well-meaning creatures by the hands and smile. *It is really quite all right,* I say. *It is really OK. I do not finally care to live in a world of traitorous, disfigured mathematics.*

Death House. Last stop on this lonesome train. This absurd plot now winding down. Having bought into the patriarchy big time—its narratives, its mathematics, its God. Its most hallowed institutions. Harvard, the image of the godhead on earth. Its tentacles and hooks. Its electric edge. Unraveling. I put my hand now less than gingerly into this toothy grab bag. Picking now the slip of paper that names the day of my death. I, the celebrity feminist, shall be made *an example of,* shall fry in their gooey eye for an eye. See how the serpent wraps around my chair leg already. Securely fastened. I'll wave to the cameras. Behind Plexiglas.

As I've said, but I would like to reiterate. *Under no circumstances* am I to spoil their fun. Just to make sure I am placed on *suicide watch.* Too many tears I guess since Minnie Grace's visit. Closest of all now, twenty feet I've heard, to the glowing chair. In a paper dress.

Oh you can dry your eyes, Bernadette— It's your Peter Piper Preston Percival Chair, at last!

The days dwindle, dear God. The time is definitely out of joint. A date of September eleventh handed to me. Mark your calendars. Look sharp. Enter Golgotha. Enter the most sordid, mawkish Hollywood movie you've ever seen. What led us to this remarkably lurid piece of world? Georgia. The papers have begun speculating as to what I might choose for a last meal. Beatrice passes shedding bitter crocodile tears. Down the hall they're checking the juice, sprucing up the chair. Giving it a practice go perhaps. *A whirl.* And the moody executioners standing by. *Not to worry, I shall not spoil your day.* Something a little different than the usual. Ceremoniously, sanctimoniously, they shall lead me down the corridor. Justice is done.

This gradually emptying stage. All the bodies piling up.

*   *   *

Why didn't you ever tell me about the voices? she asks. *Why?*
Yes, but what voices, Beatrice?

The violent die of those days cast and cast and cast again. One remembers everything being splayed, tortured, and does not know why.
Unascended in the trees. That fallen Fall River. One remembers love
was not allowed in. For some reason. Love did not come here. A
world, despite the best of efforts, bereft of reason, pattern, birds,
sense, of everything. Fearful children. Wandering, disheveled. Lop-
sided, asymmetrical, hobbling home.

Let us drop our nets and rest awhile. In the place before I am
lonely for you, brother. Before you've retreated into shadow—odd relief, diminished—like Father, Mother, all the people of this world.
Before you begin your returnings, your outlandish night visitations.
Here I stand like some swamp Ophelia, babbling above a greeny grave.

No filth here. No cans floating downstream. No brightly shining,
studded fish floating on top. He waves to the fishmonger down river.
And the fish are still spinny, finned, in the swirling water. Oh deliri-
ous blue of mussel shell and seaman's cap and sea. The water's song.
Shall we gather at the river? Freedom of wing and wave, fair nature.
The mermaids singing each to each.

Never say a word to anyone. Never. Not ever. About the voices or darkness
or dogs.

I shudder, next to this river. And he drapes his sweatshirt over
me. The darkness coming on.

Fishmonger's daughter softly singing I cannot hear what. I am
shy, modest, mortified—cannot put on a bathing suit, not with all
those ribs showing and hideous bony knees. Something is so spoiled
here. I hear the injured sirens are singing. Innocent, intelligent, having hurt no one. They call me to their bawdy side. The sound suddenly magnified. *Swim away, if you can, while you've got a chance. Swim*
away. And if that doesn't work: kill them, kill them, kill them.

*   *   *

Not that I know how to swim.

*She'd like to paint all the threes purple, she thinks, in this injured light.
The fives black, all the sevens pink, pink like a girl, pink like a little girl.
Never say a word. About the pink or the ring or the man you saw with the cotton who whispered run for your life, run through this or die—*

The dream: that the voices might stay high up, might finally achieve a degree of harmlessness. Maybe speak French. A little Lautréamont, perhaps. If I could find the right line. If I could break the code of it. And bride might equal run and ring will pulse and safe.

And bride might equal find and Jane that kind of blowsy green of summer or rescue bleeding into the scene . . .

Elizabeth, I've missed you so much! Can you really be back?

*The world's most widespread form of sanctioned torture . . . The purpose
is to prove virginity and reduce female sexual pleasure. All this is done with
sawtooth knife, razor blade, or glass, while the girls are held down or tied.*

Why?

*The injured mermaids singing each to each and you will never, never,
Bernadette.*

Leave your despised alone for once. Your feared, your wretched, your quarantined. Your homosexuals, your African-Americans, all your others, your women, your children. Your tired, your poor. Your refuse. Leave us be. You laugh. You choose to miss the subtext. You minimize everything. Nothing but hate and fear and ignorance. We hold these truths to be self-evident.

My amoral moody aristocrats. Your wars, your drugs, your thousand assaults on the poor. War without end, amen.

My eagle scouts. My heads of state. My government.

Bernadette!

*   *   *

Shhshh in the dark, from the other side of the grave. Quiet now. In this afterlife, in the trees, in the high, I'm small, I'm so small—I could fit into an acorn cap, I could fit inside the red berry that the songbird carries off. I am as quiet as a mouse as small as a seedling. Quiet. I am only a child, defenseless, in the smallest flowered dress, in the dark.

Rest on the way home in the flowers if you like peace for a moment $\frac{1}{4} + \frac{1}{16} + \frac{1}{36} + \frac{1}{64} + \frac{1}{100} + \cdots$ Lost children come with me— stillborns, the mentally ill, all the sorrows of this world. Quaint relics of once upon a time and happily ever after. Ashes in the ground. Forgive these ruined scales I am forced to play each day. Keyboard that gives no music.

One can scarcely bear it, this book of dirges. She narrates with a disembodied voice—what kind of diary is this? Sorry, Elizabeth. She looks down on this pitiable lot. Who? The one writing and writing in her minuscule cell and crossing the days off on the garish calendar. Good God. Didn't cry at her mother's funeral. Never cried. Haven't they ever read Camus for Christ's sake? Never cried. Never loved.

She was never allowed, oh let's face it, to go to her mother's funeral. Never shown one shred of kindness. What happily ever after, what speck of redemption was I inventing? And why? And for whom?

You were company, gentle readers, and I wanted you to feel for me. Was that it?

Revise the night. Revise the night if you can. Bring the various players in their shreds to the fore. No not again. *Open your mouth,* they say.

Can't you see it? They'll never, no matter what, they'll never *open your mouth* get away. Electrocuted, bound in light, drowned.

And what am I? And what am I but a skull biting down on an invisible tablet? *The body of Christ. The body of Christ, amen.* Alone against this white wall. And I? Was it me in the tall grass and the dogs in the night? Was it me with such a taste for boys? I suppose it was. Hard to know.

Are you sorry? Are you sorry yet?

Last meal. Last words. Last things. Only days to go they say. The penitent prostitute mouthing *stay of execution, pardon, please.* Evil temptress be gone. Last things. The voices swinging, sick pendulums, bare voices like bulbs with their forgiveness dim, dimming. Against a white wall. Against a backdrop of bone. Blue syringe. No mother, no father, no brother, no lover. Red hands on a white lap. On a red lap. In a red room. Innocent blood of fleecy lambs in sweet grass and trees. Red blood on a magnetic field. Assemble the night.

And who did she think she was anyway? And what did she think the world was? What was she expecting from this world? Even among all the squalor and amputation, how she believed in beauty. In the awesome abstract beauty of the world. Poor, misguided wretch. Condemned to death.

Assess the night. What has she accomplished? Nothing. And who has she made peace with? No one. There's no truce, ever, with the furies.

You felt surges in the brain. You were asked to apologize.

But there is one who sees (somewhere above the tree line) what we cannot. One who understands, what we cannot. Writer of epilogues. One who refuses to intercede or mediate. On our behalf.

Blood will have blood. Sperm blocked at the crucial gate. Broken ribs. Blood, sperm, bacteria. And the coming of, the coming of—
Priests the keepers of secrets. The battalion of social workers, still. And lady lawyers insisting *She hears voices.* The media: *She hears what?* People pleading, *Save, save, save yourself. Run, if you can. Run. If you can. To the scalloped border. To the freedom edge.*

Stay of execution, Beatrice is whispering breathlessly. Eleventh Court . . . Live.

And he overlooks me this time. He doesn't recognize me. He passes me by. He offers no hand. In my blood and gore wear. In my stopped child. My one hope. He doesn't see. I know I am condemned to death in part for the crime of being unable to bear children. I know. Bloody placenta I pull around me and I crawl in and assume that old position. And we sing together sweetly off-key in the tree, *free, free at last.*

Down the Ballyogon road and off to the swing—no please, not that again.

They're saying last meal today. They're asking about the last meal. *And for the last meal, what would the prisoner like?*

How about a glass of milk, Stringbean?

I perk up for the first time in quite a while. *Oh yes!* In quite a while. For my last meal I'd like a Weight Watchers pineapple chicken dinner, a can of tuna packed in water, a lemon wedge, a Diet Coke, 6 carrot sticks, 6 celery sticks (6), a Strawberry Slimfast Shake, and a pack of Virginia Slims.
Because the tyranny never ends.

She's talking to me about *procedures.*

They've got a very nice *conducting gel*, I understand, for my head and my leg, just to be sure I light up nice.

Dear Connie, crying and laughing at the same time. *Damn right, Bernadette. Because the tyranny never ends.*
I ask if I might kiss the tattoo of her daughter's name, and she lifts her shirt. *Because the world goes on, Connie. Because the world terribly goes on and on.* Kiss Lyla-Jean good-bye for me.
On the most despised segment of the community, all your hate and blame. Because the tyranny never ends.

That girl in the trees who is me. Working over and over the equations, the proofs, a glowing rosary. Is still tearing bits of leaves, is still weeping and tearing the leaves into the tiniest of pieces. The girl in the trees who has only days left to live now.

* * *

Once my mother brought a book to me here. Last time I'd be seeing her. Through the glass. *When Bad Things Happen to Good People.*
Her hand pressed up.

As a final example let's consider a real world result that we can es-
tablish by pure thought. Let's prove—*without leaving the room*—that
there are at least two trees in the world having the same number of
leaves.

That girl in the trees . . .

Stay of execution.

Let t denote the number of trees in the world and let m denote the
maximum number of leaves on any single tree. If t exceeds $m + 1$,
then there exist at least two trees with the same number of leaves. The
girl in the trees who is me.

Since m denotes the maximum number of leaves on any one tree,
each tree will possess either 0, 1, 2, 3, . . . or m leaves. Imagine $m + 1$
boxes sitting in a row on your floor, each tagged, in order, with the
numbers 0, 1, 2, . . . m. Now bring the world's trees one by one into
your room. Place each tree in the box which bears the label equal to
that tree's number of leaves (thus a bare tree goes into box 0, a tree
with one leaf goes into box number 1, a tree with two leaves goes into
box number 2, and so on).

Live.

We have only $m + 1$ boxes and, by hypothesis, we have more
than this number of trees. Hence, some box must contain at least two
trees when trees have been brought into the room. Thus, at least
two trees must have the same number of leaves (if two trees are in, say,
box number 1729, then these two trees have exactly 1729 leaves).

Stay.

God, it's gorgeous there, you've got to admit.

*   *   *

Today they asked me what I might like to eat as a last meal.

How about a glass of milk, Stringbean?

The curtain falls. No applause is heard. Put a glass of milk, if you remember, on my grave.

The moment of death. The great anti-climax. They'll say it's time. That's all. It's time. Good God. Don't cry. I have waited too long now. She stood in that field long ago. The border always bloody and scalloped and barbed. They never had a chance. The despised parts of the population, gleefully torched. No chance here. We come now to the part with no light in it. These truths, self-evident.

We are gathered here today . . .

Out the tree house window now—the terrible hand of God—

Stay of execution. By reasons of insanity. Stay.

We are gathered here today to join together. Take his hand now. Why so glum? We are gathered here in the night burned bright to— she'd run if she could but the dogs, his hand—turn the ring into a star, the star into code pulsing far off in a lost language of sepia of safe or trees. He wraps her in his jean jacket.

In the death chamber a chair. The dream: to walk into any room, unafraid. I wave to them through the glass. The time has come. And I am measured now—these birdbones—for the burial suit.

To walk into just one room somewhere—as if we belonged. As if there were a place just once for us.

She is electrocuted three times, but three times she refuses to die. Ridiculous farce. As if she has not died *enough times already*. Oh she has read of the others, poor black men, for the most part, and how it is nowhere near as easy as it seems to skin some cats. This I predict will be me too. The job botched. No clean pure bolt to simply end me. No. That would be too easy. Salem style, I shall smoke and burn at the stake. Like any witch.

KKK style, burn the fuckers. Flood heroin into their cities. Your contempt for the poor. The marginal. Addict them, beat them, burn them, kill them.

Fuck.
The nigger with fists of cotton and rage, with dog tags runs to where the war is.
One legged, thumping, injured—
There's a little girl with a ring in her fist. There's a little girl with a ring.
I love you. She always loved him. They went to the river. Caught fish. The arc of the line. Trajectories of hope.
The world is lit by lightning for a moment and she sees:
The lit grass gagged.
And she sees: a crooked life. Beetles and weevils in the choked grass devouring
Weeping fields of—
Potato eaters. The parents of the parents of the parents, singing an Irish song of potatoes and beer and crooked jigs. And she sees:
A man bends down, singing a song, soft and low and rises holding—if you can, run. Fields of cotton, then rice, dry your eyes, don't go—then dark.

The obsessive fear of our erotic power has done us in, yes. Lecherous sorceress, burn, burn. I know you are near, Elizabeth.

They shave my head. In preparation. They shave the left leg where the garter will be attached.

A little bedtime reading: The electrodes that make contact with the shaved human head reach temperatures of nineteen hundred degrees Fahrenheit and can melt copper. Two thousand volts make the body leap and cringe. Eyeballs sometimes pop out. The face, as well as the fingers, legs, and toes, becomes hideously contorted. The prisoner actually smolders under the force of the current and the temperature of the brain reaches the boiling point of water. Doctors who have performed autopsies on electrocuted men report that the liver is so hot that it cannot be touched by the human hand.

* * *

He's got the whole world in his hands.

Always poor, disproportionately black. Miss Beatrice, what do you think of that?

Stay.

And what am I now but a skull biting down?

They come to shave my head. Once I would have pulled it out myself. But I am passive, mild, resigned, ready to go. I will cause no trouble. No crying. They will put me in a diaper as I shall most surely, they inform me, *defecate in my pants.* I shall crawl my way down the brightly lit hall, escorted. Last infant. I do not think I will weep—it's much too late for that. They shall put me in a hood so to be spared my last face. A veil of burlap. No smell of burning flesh. You shall be protected by the Plexiglas. The jaw strapped shut. No sound coming out.

What does she see? What on earth does she want from this warped passion play as they escort each other through the last stages of their suffering? She sees:

This is the surgical light of the mind. How perfectly the blunt tools come into focus. In this cruel operating theater. This burlesque finally coming to a close. Open her up. The pus of the mind. Sop it up. Pour it out. Find the hole she describes. Stuff it up.

We enter this story at the point where there is little left for them—or for us—but to let them march on the tracks already laid down to their preappointed destinies—he to the fields of resignation and rice and she to the shiny Lightning chair at the end of the too long hallway.

And what has this notebook been but the verification of my solitude? The document of my estrangement. This conjuring of something out of nothing. Darkness. A few trees. An arm.

The flaw in the narrative? Do you think I don't know? The diagnosis?

* * *

Never felt much. Not the teapot as it tipped, the church as it burned, the blood in the throat. Never wept. Everything so far away—sorry. The distance in these pages—

This record of isolation almost over now.

Don't forget. I asked for this. That's what they all said. Don't forget. The chaired afternoon. Who's there? It's Beatrice in the corner square and wooden footed. She holds a crooked child stillborn in her arms. *Please. Stay,* she begs.

Stillborn.

This useless burlesque almost done. Free at last from the world of ruined, mutinous, mathematics. And those *awful* italicized voices. I don't mind.

Someone says it's time.

So welcome to the fun house! As if we have not had *quite enough fun already.*

Welcome to the desecration of the temple. Take a number. Form a line.

A shadowy figure passes before the camera. But no phone rings. And no weeping is heard. Mute, the witnesses on the other side of the glass.

Chances are it will be a messy business. Another atavistic ceremony of male grandstanding and relish. Burnt witch. I shall be scorched in their permanent weather—the weather I have lived in my whole life. Weather not possible to escape. That it should come to this. Never had a chance.

That is lightning, I know.

Every weather was the same weather in me.

The black penitent enters. She says, *It could turn out all right for you. We are close to a stay, Bernadette. Speak to me.*

* * *

I scribble for her one last time on a piece of paper: *cat dies.*

Repetitive play about the trauma helps children reassure themselves that it can turn out all right for them. Someone might tell
them a story or play with a doll where a new ending is written that
might give them the sense that there is still something that can be
done no matter how scary it was.

Astride and dying into him. Absence. I read genial as genital.
What is this blur, this stupor I'm in? This rearrangement of every-
thing toward— $H = 1 + \left(\frac{1}{2} + \frac{1}{3} + \frac{1}{4}\right) + \left(\frac{1}{5} + \frac{1}{6} + \frac{1}{7}\right) + \left(\frac{1}{8} + \frac{1}{9} + \frac{1}{10}\right) \cdots$

Frantic numbers beyond our reach. If someone were to signal us
from Betelgeuse. Burden of exceptional knowledge.

Mother, is that you? In your country green, your white walled. A
kind of asylum. It would be nice.
Not the Ballyogon road again.
No. Such silence.

The voices had been company, at least that, for a while.

It's a memory so you can change it—No, not that, not now.

How weary, stale, flat and unprofitable seem all the uses of this
book, Elizabeth.

Elizabeth—friend in this friendless place. Is that you?
She says: Death by electrocution—clean, efficient, punctual, oh
yes. An exhibition of technical prowess. A taming, a structuring of
the accidental. A woman being killed by a live wire.
The idea of the instantaneous. A technical form of death. Death as
pure event. The camera set up. Pure contingency. The seared subject.

They will play pornographic films throughout the night of my
execution—to help keep everyone's minds off the proceedings. When

the TV movie of this is made no doubt they shall cross-cut the two events. Blessed, vulgar predictability.

Grim child, peripheral to the action most of the time in the terrible household. Why do they focus on her now? Remove her hair as when she was young, watering and watering the grave. Measuring the circumference of her head.

Her hair torn out. Her knuckles bloodied from playing her paper keyboard.

He comes asking a question in the air, hoping this might coax me out of my hiding place, make me visible again. He asks into the middle of the night, *Baby would you like to drive to the zoo?* Once, we would go to visit the brightly colored birds in their cages, the fluorescent fish, the stuck piggly wigglies. The little lambs. And the chattering, filthy monkeys in the midst of sexual intercourse. Horrid, horrid. We're riveted.

Do you have anything to say before sentencing? Oh why this again?
Yes your honor.
Very well then. Go ahead.
A farmer needs to take his goat, wolf and cabbage across the river. His boat can only accommodate him and either his goat, wolf, or cabbage. If he takes the wolf with him, the goat will eat the cabbage. If he takes the cabbage, the wolf will eat the goat. Only when the man is present are the cabbage and goat safe from their respective predators. How does he get everything across the river safely?

They come with their oblivion, some too late antidote, ashen, crosses on their forehead. *Come to give the Extreme Unction, have you?* Soaked communion wafer. Dipped in fire. Connie with a syringe of something. Blue, resourceful afternoon. Hush. Latasha standing in the door. *It'll suck up some of the fear.* They've saved some for themselves, they assure me, for the big day. *And a big piece of me dies with you, Bernadette.*
Please don't cry, Connie. It's almost over finally.

* * *

Pity the lute maker stuck in limbo, if you will. Pity the woman stirring the gray pot forever. Pity the black man who does this walk most often, oh yes, most frequently of all of us to the last chamber at the end of the hall. Pity your sentimental, equivocating, hypocritical selves. But do not pity me.

I shall be burned to death. Three times they shall try before they succeed. They shall apply a lovely conducting gel to my head and leg. What are all those people doing here again? Noncontact visits through the partition. Can you hear them?

They are still praising my name, caught in post-coital bliss, sleep, sleep. Suffice it to say, my eggy patriarchs, as we near the end, that you forget this story at your own risk. Suffice it to say you ignore this story at your own peril. As your bodies cool—the bed a white slab.

And the voices cool. No tree house. No lightning, no thunder. And I am lonely. Longing for them. They were a company of sorts. Yes, of course they were. Where have they gone? Why have they forsaken me?

Not you too.

Jesus, it's cold in here. Haven't paid the oil bill in ages, Mother. Father's in a rage.

We are rotting on the vine. In the rain that never ends. That is thunder, by the way.

I didn't mean to upstage you. I'll hand you all my accolades and praise. I've no need for them. If that would appease you. Brother god—larger than life, slogging through.

As an adult with some healing behind you, ask yourself, "Are there things I've always wished I could try? What are the things I've always been interested in? Do I have any secret fantasies I'd like to fulfill? Is there a way I want to have an impact on the world? What do I have that I can give back to the world? What things would I like to help change?"

Let yourself live with these questions. Give yourself time to find the answers. Then list your goals here.

THINGS I'D LIKE TO DO IN MY LIFE

- _____
- _____
- _____

And we're on the river bank. Gentle river flowing red. In a sleeveless shift, in the lilting heat, moment of. Sweets for the sweet. He plucks and feeds me edible flowers. Stoned. In the pansy, he shows me the genitals of a woman, *amazing*, and smiles. *Amazing*, he says, just like that. Closing his eyes and bringing it to his mouth.

As he hands me the flower I see the lightning etched in his hand, my hand. We are already condemned. Oh what is the use? Fergus is dead a long time already. What chance was there?

Poor me, poor me—wasn't that the point all along? *No.* What was the point then? Lie on your back.

Lie on your back. The broken veined sky at night. Is that lightning?

And she sees: He takes off his jean jacket and wraps her in it. And she's gray-faced, poor urchin in her red-flowered tangled dress and she begins to cry—as if she's grieving already. Of course she is.

Then light. The scene is lit again. Hey, you, how about a pony beer?

What does she see? What does she want from this warped passion play as they escort each other through the last stages of his suffering?

And she sees:

He looks in the distance, clear-eyed, intent on his death. He feels the hero seed, strange grenade inside him

About to ignite, about to explode. Lie on your back. Count the stars. Fix your place.

He prays the edge of her dress like a rosary.

Bow-legged Cassiopeia. Poor Virgo. And Sirius.

The dog star dangling around his neck. The dog tags. She'd follow him, if he'd let her.

And the dogs, whom she fears, might protect after all, bark—but now no sound comes out. And she tries to hear the numbers her mother speaks in sleep, but no sound comes out anymore—

And the awful mute dogs and the night. Lift up the mute button. Let

*them howl, fuck, hold indigo night in their jaws, life in their leaded black
balls. Fuck and howl, but no sound comes out.*

   Help.

   *It's a dream so the rumblings and hurt and the ache in her body and fear
is only thunder. The tremblings are thunder. Look you can quiet them.*

   *The awful mute pleas coming out of her mouth. Who will hear her? And
the dogs covering up the pain and sound. Help, she cries out.*

   *I swing this cruel killing bottle where they are trapped, dying, back and
forth, ruinous and continuous. Under glass. I watch the bruised morning
come. And they make their crooked way toward home.*

   *What flares from the corners of the frame now is hurt: burn it, burn it if
you can. What makes us blind is grief.*

   A young girl waves good-bye to a boy burning a church, a man
carrying a duffel bag to a place where he might dream his life over
again—focusing now on some distant, amorphous hovering where his
life might finally assume a form. Child in the church is breaking.
Waving and waving as the bus pulls away. Mouthing through the
glass, *Never. Never say a word. Never tell anyone.* Shaping one last time
the silence: *never.* And she—is it grief, is it pain? What? She waves a
crooked hand and limps home between her defeated mother, *speak to
me.* And her inflated father, high for a moment, jump-started for
a moment. Remembering the glory days. Puffed up. This roving
comedic troupe, disfigured, hobbling toward home in the pre-dawn.

   *Bow-legged child, gagging on her own sadness and dress and he is al-
ready there in a thicket of—a dense tangle of jungle and disgust. There's a
little girl with a ring in her fist—*

   *Never say. Never. Never say a word to anyone. Never say a word. As they
walk home. In this memory, this terrible sepulcher, he was her hero—this terrible sore light of day—never say a word.*

   *And the mute sound comes out barking and crooked, help me please. Never
say—Never . . .*

   How about a glass of milk, Stringbean? he says, later in the dingy kitchen.

   *Behold: they stand emblematic of all that's been lost, in the failing light
of morning where there are numbers. Everything charted. She'd like to paint
all the threes purple, she thinks, in this injured light. The fives black, all the
sevens pink, pink like a girl, pink like a little girl. Never say a word. About*

*the pink or the ring or the man you saw with the cotton who whispered run for
your life, run through this or die—*

*Father and son on the banks of a muddy river long time ago, here catch-
ing trash fish. Back in Africa, long, long time ago, catching—*

Miraculous fish. What went wrong here? Long time ago.

I'll keep you sheltered from the storm.

Glass of milk.

*She'd just like to keep this, she'd just like it to be something in a locket
now: little and perfect and over.*

Glass of—

*Flowers on stilts and black, red, white and blue ribbons at the funeral
and the mother hissing at every mention of country, God. Who is that puppet
child crying, without a mouth?*

Color the sky violet.

*And many times before this they had come to this spot. He sang her songs:
"In-A-Gadda-Da-Vida" and "Purple Haze." I'll keep you sheltered from the
storm. Number the purple haze now. Put the voice away in a locket if you can.*

*And many times they had come to this place. Higher and higher in the
trees. Sky and clouds and the surrender of green. No one can hurt us here. No
one can get us here, little one. Posters, a mattress, a record player, beer. Let me
take you higher. Let me take you higher to this—*

*Terrible sepulcher up in the trees. Pity them, these quaint costumed play-
ers: she in her childish sundress, he in his shirt and muscles and jeans. He
puts his arm around her. She can see every hair on his hand. He'll keep her
sheltered . . .*

The tumored fish thrown back. Nothing ever works out.

Is that rain—or just Bernadette weeping now?

*Who will help them? Doomed. Roaming toward home. Back to the bleak
house. And where is Jane? And why didn't Jane, anyway? Incoherencies of
night and day. And the little girl with quiet doll mouth, doll arms, doll legs,
and the little girl he loves her so much—she holds the ring.*

Isn't this sounding familiar? I nod. Nod an impassive head, yes,
doesn't it? Broken necked—he is someone I know. Recognize, a little.
Someone utterly reminiscent . . . A character from where? A novel
read and re-read. My youth perhaps—or the university. Dressed in
pressed summer whites.

The glossy semen covered gloves.

Murdered deliberately and with forethought. Killed in slumber. Delicately put.

My catatonic aristocrats.

And what am I now but a skull biting down?

Open your mouth.

Suck and drone. Socketed. Ball and socket. In the hoary grass. Awful sepulcher. Plugged and unplugged. Holding the martyrs in their electric sockets. We'll never survive the night and hurt. Electrified like this. Lightning, then thunder. Come down with me, my brother. Protect your Beanie like you always promised. In the storm in the electrified night and chair. Shocks. Come here now. It hurts like that. Count to yourself and soon it will be over. Tie yourself to me. And we will go up in flames together, incinerate, clutching our books of char.

He always the Little Rabbit Catcher and I was his little rabbit. I went leaping by the river in spring and he would try to catch me in his rabbit trap. At night in dreams, I turned from his face. It was awful, awful—he would drown me in a sack.

Count your heartbeats. Turn the body into the calibrated, exquisite machinery it is. It is, isn't it? You could dissect the heart. Admire it. Finger its perfect valves. God, it's warm and bloody in there.
(that: Z (if nothing y (if (afraid (xx,) (afraid))) to be)
Is that lightning? Nothing to be afraid of, he whispers to the little girl. I'm right here. You can bring him up that close—but no—
Your heart would break—not again.
So that the dogs and the darkness and the increasingly drunk, senseless friends recede. And the trees—God, the trees are beautiful, aren't they, this way, back lit? She could count every leaf.

And he fingers the hem of her dress in this version—like a prayer shawl, and weeps. And he eyes the scalloped edge of panty and he weeps. Placing his hand—

* * *

What has been the point of this elaborate confessional? To rage at the deaf God mask? Elizabeth off far from the daily misery of it. In the end she'll come back in mourning coat to collect these tattered pages. All the useless words—figments—like everything. We out there in the desiccated groves of academe, bloodless, fatigued, look what they turned us into. And the students—hungry, amoral lot. My Alex, the appointed, the designated Christ. His necessary, perverse act of transubstantiation. A pornography of waste. Horrific passion play. Tormentor and victim—the old equation, the old configuration, ancient and apparently still riveting. Endure the unstinting close-ups now. God, how we've all aged. Confront the facts. He was half in love with death. We were all appetite and rage.

Saint Gregory says, "No matter how far our mind may have progressed in the contemplation of God, it does not attain to what he is, but to what's beneath him."

Numbers were a hedge against Him once. Against the abyss once. Numbers in a locket. Unusable, gloomy specimens. You take away.

Bernadette! he screams.

Last visits through the glass. Father bloated. His hand pressed up.

Ridiculous construct at five a.m. The atrocious God. Show me your face then. Buffoonish and fumbling. Show yourself as you are: cowardly, equivocating. Toting calculator and electrodes and erector set.
You, who supplied the voices, who fed us visions.
Raging ventriloquist. Putting your voice in the little girl puppet child. Why? Why?

I'll tell you what's beneath him. *If you lie on your back . . .*
Wielding his electrodes and clamps and glass dildos and napalm and bags of fractured bones and thunderbolts. Is that you, my most spectral groom? Dark emblem in the distance.

Bernadette! he shouts.

*   *   *

He's got the whole world in his hands.

Behold: a child in tatters being strapped into the grotesque chair. She deserves this, don't forget. She was asking for it. His fingers move toward the scalloped edge. The border of girl. Don't forget she deserves this.

Run!

He's got the iddy, biddy babies in his hands.
He's got the whole world in his hands.

Ah yes, there she is—poor thing, caught in the light: banging on her paper keyboard. Someone takes her bloodied hands and wraps them. *Hey, Bernadette, there now, it's OK. Stay.*

Orange light. Yellow light. Never to be mine.

Couldn't there be a nice reassuring voice of some kind coming off-stage right somewhere—some comforting, gorgeous, lilting song drifting across the field from the trees; or rescue—bleeding into the scene? Warm. Tinted rose. Flowing. A curtain of soft blood.

It's a memory, so she might make it beautiful. The world will be glowing and lit. The trees will caress. Will bow down and protect them. Anyone, even you, is entitled to wish.

Couldn't p divided evenly into $a + 1$ might bride equal safe and the trees. Harbinger of love. And love, love might . . . for once. Just for once.

In the rosary, prison, small locket, anchor, the woman wears around her neck.

She prays, gets down on her knees, *Mouth the words with me, Bernadette. Lamb of God who takes away the sins of the world have mercy on us. Lamb of God who takes away the sins of the world have mercy on us. Lamb of God who takes away the sins of the world grant us peace.*

*   *   *

But how quickly, Lamb of God, you become untenable, redundant, insupportable. Hard to believe. You take what? You take away what? How little solace you offer now. How little safety, light.

Lamb of God.

Who takes away.

$$\frac{\sin \pi/2}{\pi/2} = \left[1 - \frac{(\pi/2)^2}{\pi^2}\right]\left[1 - \frac{(\pi/2)^2}{4\pi^2}\right]$$

$$\left[1 - \frac{(\pi/2)^2}{9\pi^2}\right]\left[1 - \frac{(\pi/2)^2}{16\pi^2}\right] \cdots$$

Who takes away. Who takes away . . . What I'd like to know, Lamb of God, is why whenever you had the choice, you chose against us?

No, the fog won't lift. The fog won't lift again. And you, Minnie Grace—that God you always harped on—that paradise even Colleen, even she in the end disowned. *Mother of God, may she rest in peace.*

A girl in saddle shoes and Catholic school uniform alone in the schoolyard after the others have gone, cradling an extraordinary book of numbers.

Stay!

This sad story with a vengeance almost done now. *I promise.* This plot run so amok. This plot—and so early on—gone so terribly wrong.

And now, *as if we have not all had enough,* she is whispering, *the Eleventh Circuit Court of Appeals.* Eleven. The mute numeral.

Put hope aside, Beatrice. Come on.

My execution shall be silent. And high up. Utterly. And the weeping Magdalene in the lower corner with an orange halo of notes clutching her self-help books . . . no sound coming out. Ma in her kerchief and Pa in his cap—in this last year of our weariness. But no, wait, isn't that Mother over there? Yes—how lovely she looks—in a decent dress, a proper coat. Just as she always wanted.

Last visitors through the glass.

Minnie Grace praying, *dear Lord, despise not our petitions.*

Shall we gather at the river?

A child in brown oxfords pumps her legs, swinging higher and higher in the verdant Irish countryside. High up into the sky. Where no one can reach her.
A child hungry.
A child scrounging in the fields, famished.
A child taken from school.
A child cries no and stop, in the Oxblood afternoon.
She hides under her bed. But a shoelace shows . . .
The child grown. Travels by boat across the ocean to the promise. Fall River, Massachusetts. Where she'll be safe.

Safe. (But a shoelace shows)

A little boy dares to disturb the universe. Walks through field of ash and glitter and char. Soy and land mines and rice. A little boy.

Run!

He's got you and me, brother, in his hands. He's got the whole world in his hands..

Furious he hauls the blood-soaked veil in search of last virgins.

Bernadette!

But I am girl placenta, bleeding, singing, hanging on a clothes-line—and you will *never* recognize me that way and you will *never* find me—you will *never, never, never.*

* * *

Tell anyone. Bag of shrieking blood, safe at last, from you.

Oh the romance of the stopped child. The never born. Were I her. Spared the pain and suffering of this world. He'd never find me in the voiceless, bloody dark. In the never was. But no, I am more born than most.

The gagging child. Glass of—

Black streamers flying—hiding. I say: *If you can find me then. Mourning, in a bloodred wedding dress. Taffeta. Your ever-formal date, stifling, waiting, dying. Just try.* Peering through the leaves of the trees, she sees—it's too much—

Cruel puppeteer with no face. Shriek without a mouth and pulled back hair now, exaggerated: the little girl holds the ring. She'll bury it in the yard like a bone. So no one will know. No one will ever know. Gardens of ring and roses. Garden of sharp diamonds and pointed thorns.

It's yours, it's yours, it's yours now, he whispers in the trees; it's yours now. Take it. Terrible microscopic bride. Engagement without end.

Never let her know, if you see her, that there was a ring or a dream.

Everything is wrong angles and vertigo. She in her cotton tangled dress of pain, he in his jean jacket—poor children, and the dogs—rusty, roaming through an immense, a vast landscape of bright light,

So that you think you see something; you think you finally understand something—but then dark—again.

Glass of milky—

—he carries the scarlet mouths of Vietnamese women around his penis like a screaming ring. A choking ring.

And he is slaughtered. Napalmed. Killed. Gone forever. Smithereens.

Child in the church is breaking.
Anyone who makes a sound dies.

* * *

Domain of madness, epileptics, rabid dogs—thalidomide, ruined night—children in the bough are breaking, can't you hear? What, what is it? The bloody valve he pleads for? She's so pink. Stop it you're hurting.

This is the light of the mind, then:

It's a memory so you can change it—warp it along the lines of infinity if you like, stretch it into submission so that the hand abstracts across the sky in veins of light and the pain is only thunder. Turn the ring into a star, the star into a code pulsing in a lost language. What does it say? Harbinger of love. Safe. Something senseless.

And the bride will equal run and ring will pulse $\left(\frac{1}{4} + \frac{1}{16} + \frac{1}{36}\right)$ and safe.

$$1 + \frac{1}{9} + \frac{1}{25} + \frac{1}{49} + \cdots = \left(1 + \frac{1}{4} + \frac{1}{9} + \frac{1}{16} + \frac{1}{25} + \cdots\right)$$
$$- \left(\frac{1}{4} + \frac{1}{16} + \frac{1}{36} + \frac{1}{64} + \frac{1}{100} + \cdots\right) = \frac{\pi^2}{6} - \frac{\pi^2}{24} = \frac{\pi^2}{8}$$

And when the hurly-burly's done. They'll strap me in and send me down. It's such a tiny arm. Out of its socket. The dislocated afternoon. *Run!* They'll strap us all in. *Isn't that lightning?*

He lifts a crooked arm. He tries to free himself finally. From the hurt. But why, with the little girl, in the trees. Why, with the child?

It is a small arm, an arm so small, floating, dislocated—socket—open wound. He lifts a crooked arm. Forgiveness. Trying his whole life to get free. But why the child?

Why? Enough now. Tie yourself to me, my brother.

In the memory now I paint almost everything black or red.

Erase: *y* (even you) (if (brotherly) (that hurts) (*z,w*) doomed path *xx,:y* home, even you.

Erase the brother and the doomed path home. Set yourself free. Look even you are entitled to dream.

He lifts the head off the placenta and peers in and I know, *wait*

$$\frac{1}{4} + \frac{1}{16} + \frac{1}{36} + \frac{1}{64} + \frac{1}{100} + \cdots + \frac{1}{(2k)^2} + \cdots$$

wait—

$$\frac{1}{4} + \frac{1}{16} + \frac{1}{36} + \frac{1}{64} + \frac{1}{100} + \cdots$$

$$= \frac{1}{4} + \left(1 + \frac{1}{4} + \frac{1}{9} + \frac{1}{16} + \frac{1}{25} + \cdots\right) = \frac{1}{4}\left(\frac{\pi^2}{6}\right) = \frac{\pi^2}{24}$$

And I know I am found.

Hiding in the baby's breath. *He can see you perfectly, stupid.*

It's a memory, and your biggest mistake, Bernadette, was to think that you could stop it if you wanted. Decode it. Very funny, Bernadette. Change it. Erase the ring and the grass, escape the killing bottle, break it even. Round off the jagged edges. But there's something so hard and sharp. In bleak recurrence—sad, repetitive, persistent, without warning or permission—in the middle of the night—and in daylight. The little girl grown now, with only moments herself left to live. An unseemly sentence leveled on her head. We call it up—for her sake, poor child, in the thunder, in the dark, with the only one she ever trusted or loved about to be taken—

Killed by friendly fire. You dumb fuck!

Home of the panicked, indentured, home of the poor.

Is that thunder? Yes.

Look: they haul their dumb love and rage across the ruined terrain.

You thought you could dream about catching fish—and not only trash fish, but all kinds. But your biggest mistake, Bernadette, was that you thought you could quell us. Shut us up. With a few sacrificial gestures. A few juicy offerings. Take back the night. But you needed us all along. Idiot child. Look. Be resigned finally:

It is thunder. They haul their dumb love that weighs a ton across the bleak terrain and rage—hobbling home as if injured. But grief can do that, we've seen it many times before—in the defeated dark of their father's house. He'll never be able to pay the bills. The lights shut off again.

Look: she stands huddled in the dark at the small stove, boiling and boiling the gray potatoes. She's had to plead again, make promises she just can't keep, with the phone company and the other demons. And the father gone out again—

In a rage. Eenie, meanie, miney, moe. Why?
Why have you left us here alone another night?
Be resigned. Take it, take it, it's yours now—

He's holding the ring. Take it.

No. Be dead now, Fergus. Rest.

The broken altar boy with red-frilled collar and a hell of chimes and bells. Poor child. What chance did he have? Someone has damaged him so completely. The parish priest—that old cliché.

But there—look on the horizon—a body as dark as that night was surely. With her the scene might finally have achieved harmlessness. I might have embraced the night of her. Safe. But the lights go out. Annihilated—the might have been.

Stay, she begs.

They sit at the edge of the water. Brother and sister. She's only a little squeamish about the worms. *Don't be afraid. They won't bite.* Fergus smiling. *Go on touch them. They're not going to hurt you. Touch one. Touch one.*
We pull up fish after fish. He shows me how to take them off the hook. A slap on the cement with their tails, a bash on the head and they are dead.
I'll be right back. I sit surrounded by dead fish and muddy river and song. The evening's catch, glassy eyed at my side.
He's got the whole world in his hands. A little black girl, singing, with a bucket of fish, passes.
Hey, she whispers.
Hey, I whisper back. Wishing for a sister, or one friend in this whole world, just once, *hey.*

Come on, touch it. You can touch it, Beanie.
Immediacy of the long past, long dead afternoon. Wretched pres-

ent tense. Language does this as much as mind. His shadow covers mine. He is two or three times my size.

We enter this story at a point where there is little left for them—or for us—but to let them march on the tracks already laid down to their pre-appointed destinies.

Beatific Beatrice . . . Supreme Court. *Stay of execution . . . Mercy . . .* Can't hear much anymore.

Cat walk.

$$\hat{H}_{CAT} \, | \, cat \; alive \rangle_{CAT} \, | \, \downarrow \rangle_D = \, | \, cat \; alive \rangle_{CAT} \, | \, \downarrow \rangle_D$$

Jade eyes. Kindness . . . Footsteps now. *Who's there?* Jade walk, cat eyes. Utter loveliness. Salvation. *Identify yourself.*

They say it's time. *Who's there?* Four armed escorts. *Is that you?* They say it's time. To walk. Witness last light, through the trees. Last sounds. Jangling. Cat's eyes.

$$\hat{H}_{CAT} \, | \, cat \; alive \rangle_{CAT} \, | \, \uparrow \rangle_D = \, | \, cat \; dead \rangle_{CAT} \, | \, \uparrow \rangle_D$$

A floating scrap of orange paper falling to the floor. Telephones glowing. Hot to the touch. In case—at the very last second—an angel. *Who's there? Beatrice is that you?* Trembling last phone in the room. Or Mother talking into her dead receiver? Stop the proceedings. I was only a little girl then. *Who's there?*

Enter the parents and their wayward pieces of son in a plastic bag.

Enter the rage counselor, with plastic baseball bat and punching bag and book of sayings.

Enter Alexander, my moppet, darling, my favorite poppy, drug. And poor Payson.

Enter Beatrice, her insouciant, succulent majesty.

Enter the God. The Potato Head. The Rabbit Catcher. The Horse Tooth. The Dean of Students. Shareholder. Crop Grower. Eggy Patriarch. With your crude props, your lightning bolts, your bag of hurt bones, your electrodes. Your verdicts. Grim executioner. Wielder of saw-tooth knife, razor blade, and glass. While the girls are held down or tied.

This is your ever-formal date. Stifling, dying in the heat. Your child bride, your concubine, your prize, your birthright.

Take it, it's yours now.

How nice: Mother and Father here to see me off. Minnie Grace saying the sorrowful mysteries. Connie waving wanly. Beatrice preening. Nobody weeps. We have all waited too long for this. The priest comes in frightening Latin ten-feet tall. In the trees.

There's a hole.

We come indeed to the part with no light in it.

Father floating. Father bloated beyond anything I have ever seen before. *Who put the overalls in Mrs. Murphy's chowder?* Father alone roaming our house of sorrows with its ghost population. In his Sunday best now.

And there's Mother wrapped in glass. Her hand pressed up. Why was everyone always so far away? Never could get near. It's the solitude that's made this life—well. I wave to the closed-circuit TV—*an example of.* The open phone line. *Where were you when I needed you?* Mother, rest. In a proper dress, at last.

You are a sight for sore eyes, Bernadette O'Brien! You are a shambles, Bernadette O'Brien!

Escorted down the aisle now in an agony of white and blood taffeta and veils. Toward the electric night in the trees. Handcuffed. A nosegay of pansies and bloodroot and rue. A rash of purpura. Baby's breath. Peace. Grant us peace finally.

The giddy and giggling bridesmaids. With their bouquets of blue vials. The distilled afternoon. Connie holding a pale window. Latasha: *what a catch.* And you too now? Not you too, Elizabeth. Matron of honor.

Walking down the wayward aisle to that electric night. *Not you too.*

Small booby traps and land mines—careful—everywhere you step now. Lake without fish.

On the arm of my father. Sorrow floating. In his dark, misplaced corsage. Father. Bleary escort, last aisle, here to give me away now. One more time. To the night the sloughed off one. My mother blows an oblivious kiss. The Magdalene strewing paper petals. *Stay.*

First he takes the goat across the river. He then returns and picks up the wolf. He leaves the wolf off, and takes the goat back. He then leaves the goat at the starting place, and takes the cabbage over to where the wolf is. He then returns and picks up the goat, and goes to where the wolf and cabbage are waiting.

And I, hauling my full trousseau of empty numbers and sacrificial piglets—Alexander, Payson. The sow's ear pouch, my satin garter, the velvet rope. The wet nurse nearby. *Produce the child! Produce the child!* they all shout.

He appears in holy light. Last light. Let s . . .

I cannot stress enough how crucial it is to get the goat across the river safely. The wolf safely. The cabbage safely. The child safely. There is no way, I suppose you know, to atone for the theft of childhood.

Let s equal all the suffering in the world.

The indecipherable path we set out on. *Amazing*—

Do you take—

She wants to be brave. She wants to be lionhearted. She wants him to be proud of her. Admire her. If you lie on your back . . .

The river safely . . .

Do you take this man—

Let s—in the lapsing. . .

We are gathered here today to join together . . .

They escort me now to the place I know I must go—and give me away, send me off, *good-bye,* one last time, to that shiny altar in that electric night at the end of the aisle, high in the trees. Back to the one to whom I belong. He reaches for me like a birthright.

It is lightning. There is rain. Her brother's hand across the sky. The doomed, illuminated veins emblazoned on the pink of the little girl. A universe of pain; all over her body—she'll never get away.

You'll never get away, Bernadette.

And the stars—there aren't enough stars for these kinds of wishes.

Do you take this man—

Sweet urn of evening engraved with your name. Fate. Complacency. I nod. Our ashen path . . .

There was a crooked man who walked a crooked mile.

She's so pink . . .

He holds the ring. Will you, he whispers, fateful night, say you will— will you—it could be our secret—will you—

The moon watches resigned in the electrocuted night; she wants nothing more to do with this.

Marry me? Will you marry me? And she nods, the idiot. She wants to be brave. She's only eight for God's sake. Where's Jane?

But no Janie is going to arrive.

Three will equal yes. Six will be red. Two will be purple. Fusion of blue and afternoon. And seven will equal darkness tinged with blood. And x the scalloped panty he moves toward. Paint it hard and blunt and close-up inside.

He lifts your veil and takes your hand and places the ring, slips the ring onto your finger. And eight years old could equal magenta or no or stop, couldn't it? Don't. Wait.

$$H = 1 + \left(\frac{1}{2} + \frac{1}{3} + \frac{1}{4}\right) + \left(\frac{1}{5} + \frac{1}{6} + \frac{1}{7}\right) + \left(\frac{1}{8} + \frac{1}{9} + \frac{1}{10}\right) +$$

$$\left(\frac{1}{11} + \frac{1}{12} + \frac{1}{13}\right) + \cdots$$

$$> 1 + \left(\frac{3}{3}\right) + \left(\frac{3}{6}\right) + \left(\frac{3}{9}\right) + \left(\frac{3}{12}\right) + \left(\frac{3}{15}\right) + \cdots$$

$$= 1 + 1 + \frac{1}{2} + \frac{1}{3} + \frac{1}{4} + \frac{1}{5} + \frac{1}{6} + \frac{1}{7} + \frac{1}{8} + \frac{1}{9} + \cdots$$

$$= 2 + \left(\frac{1}{2} + \frac{1}{3} + \frac{1}{4}\right) + \left(\frac{1}{5} + \frac{1}{6} + \frac{1}{7}\right) + \left(\frac{1}{8} + \frac{1}{9} + \frac{1}{10}\right) +$$

$$\left(\frac{1}{11} + \frac{1}{12} + \frac{1}{13}\right) + \cdots$$

$$> 2 + \left(\frac{3}{3}\right) + \left(\frac{3}{6}\right) + \left(\frac{3}{9}\right) + \left(\frac{3}{12}\right) + \left(\frac{3}{15}\right) + \cdots$$

$$= 2 + 1 + \frac{1}{2} + \frac{1}{3} + \frac{1}{4} + \frac{1}{5} + \frac{1}{6} + \frac{1}{7} + \frac{1}{8} + \frac{1}{9} + \cdots$$

$$= 3 + \left(\frac{1}{2} + \frac{1}{3} + \frac{1}{4}\right) + \left(\frac{1}{5} + \frac{1}{6} + \frac{1}{7}\right) + \left(\frac{1}{8} + \frac{1}{9} + \frac{1}{10}\right)$$

$$+ \left(\frac{1}{11} + \frac{1}{12} + \frac{1}{13}\right) + \cdots$$

Tiny microscopic bride. The unfringed hole. Embryonic, stopped life.

Do you take this man—In the lightning, do you take—in the interval between dark and light—Do you take this man to be—

Lawful and bedded and wedded, do you take—

because she loves him—

In the interval between child and adult—in the instant

His throbbing glance.

She'll never get away.

Honor, serve, obey—

Open your mouth.

Do you take this glass of perfect milky sperm. Do you take this cup? All she's been forced to drink. The marriage chalice.

And he slips the ring onto her finger, with dirge in marriage, will you—

If you lie on your back, Bernadette, little Beanie, don't be afraid, if you lie on your back now you can see all of the stars . . .

Turn the ring into a star, the star into a code pulsing in a lost language. Signaling help—salvation, love, safe—something, something—Help! no sound coming out.

Why the child? No sound coming out. Help. Tear-drenched. Help.

And the stars? There aren't enough stars . . .

Where's Ireland tonight? Where's Africa? Where's Fall River even? Where's that obliterating yielding equation that might elucidate, might free that defiance of light?

Crooked wife. Crooked cat. Crooked mouse. They all lived together—

Torn dress and blood everywhere, vow. Vow you will never, ever, ever say a word ever to anyone. Paint the square root of nine, of bride, never. Forever hold your peace.

In the interval between dark and light and dark again—she might change from child to adult—in a lightning flash back to child again in the dream-ridden eternal night. If you lie on your back.

But why the child? She takes out the satin garter. The splayed velvet rope. Why the child?

Couldn't there be just once, just once more, a small defiance of bride? She dreams. God, it's warm and bloody in there.

And the guard dogs, best men at the borders. No one will hear her if she screams.

But that was—that was so many years ago now, wasn't it? Look:

The tree house down, the indentations in the grass where you lay gone, grown over—the mark of how far one's come—away from that night, away from the beaded curtain, bleak rosary, the lightning, the pointed trees, the fistfuls of cotton and rage and rice and the droning, enormous, unending gray floor of the world that is everywhere. And the rain.

They'll never get away.

He holds her with a heavy husband hand. Why the child?

There's a hole that pierces right through me.

The banners hung. Strange music of brother and numbers and country and God, the bunting blackened. Fear for them.

They say it's time.

And he says, *here take my hand,* offers his hand, *I'll keep you safe.* They strap her in. That is lightning. *Hurry up take my hand, little saint, before the rain.*

Thunder.

Fear for them.

I fear for them. Where they will go. What they'll mistake for shelter—in this prison within a prison within a prison. They say it's time. And the terrible pink. *And the little girl.*

Come on Birdie, you whisper.

It's time.

And I accept your hand as I know I must, Fergus, and climb into the electric night without end, forever with you.